THE GR

R. W. Jones lived i
working as an edu
two years in Anguilla, he is back in his native
Wales. He lives with his wife and three children in Caerphilly, Mid-Glamorgan.

SAVING GRACE

'Clever, original and quite painful'
                Marghanita Laski in *The Listener*

'This is one of the best read-at-a-sitting crime
novels I have come across'   *Punch*

'A powerful talent and a grand ear for
dialogue'   *The Scotsman*

COP OUT

'R. W. Jones' gripping second novel is tough
stuff, lightened by humanity as well as wry
humour'   *Mail on Sunday*

'The relationship between the characters, the
sensitivity and compassion beneath the apparently callous behaviour, and the ability to
handle the development of a story, are of a
quality very rare in crime fiction'
                Birmingham Evening Post

Also by R. W. Jones

SAVING GRACE
COP OUT

R. W. JONES

The Green Reapers

FONTANA/Collins

First published in Great Britain by
Michael Joseph Ltd 1988

First issued in Fontana Paperbacks 1989

Copyright © R. W. Jones 1988

Printed and bound in Great Britain by
William Collins Sons & Co. Ltd, Glasgow

CONDITIONS OF SALE

This book is sold subject to the condition
that it shall not, by way of trade or otherwise,
be lent, re-sold, hired out or otherwise circulated
without the publisher's prior consent in any form of
binding or cover other than that in which it is
published and without a similar condition
including this condition being imposed
on the subsequent purchaser

For Zak, Kirsty and Huw

PROLOGUE

Summer 1965

He woke dry-eyed yet heavy at heart. It was ghostly out, he knew by the hush and the pallor. Dawn, grey and slim, and songbirds struck dumb; mist down the mountain had silvered the pasture and shrouded the glen. A grand day brewing, all right; and no use whatever to a boy condemned.

No use to be blaming a mother, either, who would profit naught but the darning of britches and the salvage of shoes. But his daddy's treason had cut to the bone.

'Not yet, Sean,' he'd argued. ''Tis a desperate place, and the task beyond you awhile. Rest easy now. Your time will come.' A strange look to him as he said it; sorrow and pride and a kind of longing. Betrayal, just the same, for hadn't they fished together since Sean was big enough only for the drowning of worms?

The rooster sounded, late and forlorn. A tearful, miserable beast, no doubt; which makes two of us. Get a hold of yourself, Sean Daly. It's twelve you are, too old for childish sniffles. 'Tis guile that's required, not a tantrum.

He sat up, hatching a scheme of rare boldness. Suppose a body were to follow, unseen in the friendly mist; and meet, by chance, at the river? A powerful anger had Kevin Daly, and a tongue to match the fire of his hair. A lecture there'd be, for sure, and maybe a cuff on the ear. After which he'd forgive the prodigal; for a fairer, gentler man had never lived. Nothing to lose, anyhow, and better than skulking in here.

Sean stole from his bed and sidled the dusky passage.

His tiptoes light on smooth cold stone, he made not a sound. At the slant of their bedroom he paused, held by a bond of trust. This was their private place, and not to be entered unasked. But the need to know was urgent – had himself already left? Softly, Sean eased the door ajar and peeked in.

The village beauty, his mother, yet demure and simple of dress and speech. No matter how lean the harvest, she kept her room and herself as fresh as a spring posy. The soul of purity, too, smelling of soap and faithful to Mass of a Sunday. So who in the Dear's name was this stranger, naked amongst such unholy disorder?

She lay as though crucified in the wreck of a bed. The midnight hair, usually pinned and pleated, had streamed out over the pillows, and her nightgown furled like an abandoned glove on the floor. Sleeping, she smiled through lips bruised and tender; a pearly glow shone from her neck and cheeks. Ashamed yet helpless, he stood and gawped. His eyes lingered on wondrous pink-tipped roundness and dwelt in the secret shadow between her thighs. She stirred and shifted, and the scent overwhelmed him. Salt sweat underlain by something heavier, something which caused a thickness of throat and loin and a terrible heat in his blood. He turned and fled, his legs aquiver, his face aflame with remorse and guilt.

Alone in the narrow dimness, he laid his brow against the rough whitewash while grief took him like fever. They did it, just as the beasts of the field. The worst word he knew, to be whispered with a smirk amid older boys; a word not even to be thought, much less uttered, in their presence. And for this, their door stood barred. Yet even in the depths of anguish, he sensed an approaching threshold; once across, he would not be the same, ever.

The sickness passed, leaving him sorely puzzled. Was not the act a celebration between man and wife performed in joy for to bring forth issue? Didn't Father O'Neill himself wax strong on the righteousness of wedlock? They did it often, sure they did; so why wasn't the cottage abrim with little Dalys? And why the onset of faintness and nausea, this feeling of being a spy? Questions for another day, Sean. One fact is certain: Daddy's away to the river, you'd best be at his heels.

Downstairs, he wolfed bread and dripping and swigged from the tap; the taste of copper and his teeth humming from the cold. The kettle still murmured, a mug and a platter sat draining in the rack. Not far behind, then. Poised and prepared and itching to go, he came upon the deepest mystery yet. There in a corner, gleaming gold, his daddy's one indulgence – the split-cane fly rod. Could the man be after salmon, having borrowed a two-handed caber from butcher O'Byrne? Aye, and ducks might calve. He grinned like a fox, seeing the chance. 'Ah, Daddy, 'tis a blessing I found you, for you went without the rod!'

Out, then, in the fragrance of morning; of kine and peatsmoke and fresh dew on the turf. There was sport to be had after all, and the reason sweetly balanced in his hand. The mist was no hardship; he could find the way blindfold. Besides, there were tracks on the meadow, broader and darker than his own. Kevin's for sure. And what did his grandmother say? 'In the border lands, me darlin', 'tis only fishers and Fenians abroad of a summer's dawn.' A curious word, this 'Fenian', a thing for the adults alone. It had to do with night meetings and soft-spoken men from the town, and steering wide of the Garda.

A noise alarmed him, a sudden roil in the smoky blankness. But it was only the O'Byrne's nag, an old daft creature starved of love. Relieved, Sean thrust clover under his velvet nose and thumped his flank and sent him about his business; and forgot the politics altogether, for the river was near.

He reached the ford, the murmur of rapids in his ears and the crunch of shingle underfoot. Too damp for insects

9

yet, though a boy might wreak havoc with a worm. Sacrilege, that, and a danger to the precious split cane; which he was permitted to use only under Kevin's watchful eye. He waited, uncertain, while the sun climbed over the mountain and the mist thinned and the colours came slowly to life. Again, he sensed a hinge in time; as if, in some mysterious fashion, he was about to step into his daddy's shoes. Despite the prohibition, it seemed as natural as breathing to wield the rod and test the silent current.

For no good reason, he turned northwards, upstream. Within minutes the guilt had left him, bled away on the last of the mist. There was only warmth at his back and the rhythmic hiss of line on the wakening air. He cast but twice in each pool. Even when he touched something livid and heavy, he calmed himself and moved on, not to disturb the prey. It was a morning rich with promise; the promise of a killing to come.

Thus he arrived at the Border, where O'Byrne's fence ran down on either bank. Just a few strands of wire, by no means new; but a divide between North and South he must never cross. Here, he took heed of the growing day: meadowsweet perfume, a flight of doves, the lowing of cattle and the ever-present lilt of the stream. The rod was a part of him now, a magic wand to deliver a fly at the place of his choice, and set it like thistledown on the shifting surface. So it should be, for wasn't he the son of the champion fisher, Daly? He would go back and take a full basket, and hear no more of being too young.

He glanced upstream. At the next bend, a tumbled oak had created a pool and a slow, deep glide. The finest water he'd seen; and, as he gazed, the rise began. He ignored the flurry of fingerlings in the shallow, his eye fixed on a spot where the current faltered and spun. And there, at last, it showed – the steady quiet dimple of a well-grown trout.

Not a soul in sight, no hint of trouble, and temptation crooning in his ear. 'Tis just another strip of land, Sean, no different from where you stand. Your time is upon you; and time to become a man. And so did the last and the strongest barrier yield before him.

Ah, and *what* an hour he had there, with his blood up and the spice of forbidden fruit on his tongue, and the trout berserk for his fly! Several were lost through being too eager; but thrice the hook struck true and the reel clattered, and the split cane arched and kicked at his palm. Possessed, were these fish, now running deep with the peat-stained stream, now cutting the surface to rainbowed spray. His heart in his mouth, he contained their thrusts and conquered their leaps and drew them, gasping, to the mossy bank. He killed them clean and laid them out, feasting his eyes on the breadth and the mottled beauty. By which time he was a half a mile into Ulster, near to bursting with joy and pride. His daddy should see him now!

Well, perhaps not. Poaching, was this, and using the rod without asking; and altogether too far from home. Then, borne on the breeze, lending force to his doubts, he heard a hue and cry; raised voices and the bay of dogs. At this range, the volley rang no more deadly than a babe's rattle, but border folk were weaned to the sound of guns.

'Hark!' his grandma would cry. 'Some poor brave divil afoul of the Patrol. Raise the shutters lively, and bless the Dear for your own patch of sod!' Aye, away with you Sean, where the foreign soldiers can't go. Better to be prudent than proud.

He jinked downstream through dappled shade, quicker by far than the current, heedless of fish in river or creel. In this suddenly harsh and hostile place, all claims to manhood vanished; he was only a boy, running.

He swarmed the fence and burrowed like a hare to a favourite lie – dense briars under a strand of rowan. Here, snug and secure, he recovered breath and courage. A fearsome venture, this; desperate, surely, as any of his

11

daddy's. And still he had time to fish his way home! As body and mind steadied, one mystery was solved. Kevin had gone *downstream*, of course, for wasn't that where the waters ran icy and strong? Well, so he might. We'll see who has the heavier bag. He smiled drowsily, savouring the triumph ahead. Beneath him, the turf smelt cool and fresh. High above through a network of thorn, a lark rose, singing. Stealthily, peace and sunshine and an early start overpowered him; he dozed.

And woke once more, to danger and a wholly alien noise.

'Wot did I tell yer? 'E's long gone, if 'e came 'ere at all.'

'Balls! Hurt bad, see, taking the shortest route. Be 'ere any minute, mark my words.'

'Hurt bad, runnin' like that? Do us a favour!'

''E's *Irish*, for Chrissake. They *always* run.'

'Shouldn't of shot 'im anyhow. Papers is all 'e 'ad.'

''Ow was I to know? Reached in 'is coat, didn't 'e, could've been goin' for a gun.'

Harsh cold accents, at odds with the land and each other. Curled in his hideout, pressed to the sod, Sean Daly shrank from the bag at his side. Even if they didn't see him, they'd surely *smell* his ripening catch. None the less, he wormed around and stole a quick peep.

They stood at the border, men in brown, their weapons held as casual as farmers at the hunt. From here, they looked monstrous; cropped heads, moon faces and heavy boots. Two of them argued, loud and sullen. The third, having stripes at his shoulder, eyed them in weary disgust.

'Knock it off, you've had your fun. We're due for relief at ten hundred. Let's go.'

'Aw, come on, Sarge, 'ang around. I 'it 'im square, honest.' The one they called Sergeant stiffened and spoke like the cut of a lash.

'He's right, Mills; you shouldn't've fired and you

12

shouldn't've missed. Now get fell in, you cross-eyed, trigger-happy little git!'

Briefly, Mills tarried, his bitter gaze scouring the South.

'One less of the bastids to worry about,' he muttered; and hawked a slimy gobbet across the fence, '*Fuck Ireland!*'

He trembled for minutes when they'd gone, cowed by foul language and the rank breath of hatred. And what did we ever do to *them*? Thanks be that Daddy's down-river, who'd never abide the insult. He crawled out, trailing the bag and the rod. Just dead trout and a sliver of wood, he'd *felt* the magic wither. For the first time, he would fish as a chore, not a pleasure: and never go northward again.

At the fringe of the water he halted, head high, ears cocked, his entire being taut and high-strung. Holy Mary, they're coming back! Up on the bank in a twinkling, and a headlong plunge at the only safety he knew. The rod was fouled and he wrenched it through, careless of damage in his haste. He lay there in dread, the grass to his chin and his chest throbbing.

For this was not the Army's measured tread. A wild weird blundering, the thrashing of trees and moans to freeze the soul. Briefly, despite the sunlit hush, he was away to his grandma's knee at nightfall and ancient tales of banshees in the glen.

Then, slowly, reality and a soldier's curse came back. A poor brave devil stumbling home, hit square, hurt bad, and keening. And only a frightened boy to help. He screwed up his face and fought his fear and drove his fingers into the earth. Ah, Sean, why did you stray from your daddy, and meet with the Troubles too soon?

He heard the creak of the fence and a rasp of breath. One fierce lost cry, and the sound of a man, falling. A terrible, final fall, and tremors that ran the length of his own coiled frame.

13

Even so, as he sighed and straightened, there came a moment of choice. Be off with you, Sean, don't meddle, it's no place for a half-grown boy. He was leaning away like a runner, wanting nothing but the skirts of his mother. And, once again, a sense of the future stayed him. However bad it is, you'll see worse. You can't be leaving; *your time is come.*

He swallowed the bile in his throat and went forward, shaking, to the huddled form just a yard inside the fence.

He knew, almost at once; maybe he'd known from the start. Something about the tone of the flesh and the cut of the coat; but mainly the play of light on red hair. He had no memory of the walk; only that his blood had turned to ice, and it was an enormous effort to put one foot before the other. He knelt. For the second time, he gazed on a stranger's body with the face of one he adored; the ashen, ruined face of Kevin Daly.

And so it was, in the bloom of a green and gold morning, under a flawless summer sky, that he cradled his daddy's dying head by the river they both loved so well. Perhaps they spoke; if so, he never told a living soul. But in the few moments left them, Sean Daly learned of truth and injustice, and unquenchable fire in the veins, and the need to cherish his mother and die in the land of his birth. He sat there long after the blue eyes clouded and the strong weathered fist fell limp; watching his tears fuse with blood and seep into rich dark soil. And knew, even then, that the mingling would nourish a seed in this same soil and his own cleft heart: the seed of war.

CHAPTER ONE

The Present Day

On Sundays, the tramp preferred curry.

He paused in the darkened alley, drooling at the spicy scent. Saliva flooded his tongue. His shrunken belly growled in anticipation. Had there been a sound in there, a stealthy rustle, the clank of a bin being moved? A haze covered the quarter moon. He craned into dimness and made out the shape of the foe. Lean, sway-backed and hot-eyed, the dog lowered its head and snarled a warning. He reacted without thought, baring his own teeth, reaching out taloned fingers and growling deep in his throat. Briefly, man and beast circled; the mongrel cringed and fled.

'Ar, away with you, you filthy cur,' he muttered, and did a triumphant little war dance. The hunger was upon him now, fierce and consuming. He rummaged among the reeking containers, scraping out handfuls of cold grey rice and cramming it in as fast as he could swallow.

They appeared suddenly, as if they were part of the night itself; two large shadows, still and soundless, blocking his way out. He stopped in mid-gulp, his courage fading, one greasy hand rising automatically to his forelock.

'It's only Old Jim, mister, he'll do you no harm. Spare us a penny, could you, or a drop of something warming?' The grains were gritty in his mouth, his appetite had shrivelled away. He could make nothing of their faces; they seemed in some way hooded or muffled.

'Jaysus,' said a cold voice, 'and isn't he a ripe one.' Something in the manner of speech struck home, a vague crippled stirring in the murk of Old Jim's brain.

'Quiet!' hissed the other, 'I'll be dealing with him now.'

'Ah, leave him be. 'Tis nothing but a witless ould tramp.'

'Aye, but he's *here*!'

There was menace abroad, sharp and sour as vinegar. But when the bigger man spoke again, you could hear the smile in his tone. 'I have something for you, Grandpa. It will ease your troubles entirely.'

Old Jim came forward eagerly, his hands cupped in supplication. Briefly, the moon played on silver; he couldn't believe his luck.

Movement too fast to follow, and a terrible pain in his chest. The legs seemed to slide from under him; he lay shocked and slack on the dusty, stinking cobbles and heard them walk unhurriedly away.

Overhead, the stars wheeled and the moon grew brighter. He could feel the moisture oozing out of himself. In that dying instant, the earth beneath him shuddered. The night blazed gold and scarlet in his face. Noise battered his eardrums and smashed the breath from his lungs. It seemed to Old Jim that hot winds seared his flesh and wrenched his soul adrift: and sucked him, screaming, downwards through an endless, deep-blue void . . .

'I'm wondering, Huw. When are you going to make an honest woman of me?'

Megan Powell, launching a sneak attack from the bath; Evans could tell by the swash and the echo. Her classroom voice, this, the one she saved for the awkward questions.

16

'I'm the tame cop, remember? How honest can you get?'

'You know what I mean.'

A rare summer Sunday, long and hot and lazy: drinks at the pub, roast and three veg, and a friendly grapple on her mattress for afters. He knew what she meant, all right.

Routine.

Propped against the pillows, he surveyed the floral duvet and his own incipient paunch. Going soft, he was. Past forty, divorced, in a career doldrum, and having it away with an art teacher. Steady, bach. Too much excitement could kill you.

'Carry on, girl,' he called. 'I'll make tea.'

'*Tea*, there's romantic!'

He clambered into his Y-fronts and returned fire from the bedroom door. 'Sorry about that. The shampers is corked and the beluga's got mould. Do you a fishpaste butty, shall I?'

He padded downstairs past Welsh brasses and the photo of Caerphilly Castle. The kitchen was full of sunshine and cooking smells. Nice place, fair play; a legacy from a husband who'd died of leukaemia at thirty. Evans filled the kettle, lit the gas, and opened the door for a breath of air. Domesticity smothered him, raising the ghost of his own doomed marriage . . .

Eirwen from next door, slim and dark and gentle as rain in the valleys. He would have abandoned everything for her; his home, his work, even rugby football if she'd asked. The love of his life, and it lasted five years. She wasn't to blame, mind. Exile and duty's demands had worn her down. In the end, their failure to make babies had driven her back to Wales . . .

The kettle was singing. He could hear Megan moving about upstairs. She'd be down soon, perfumed and pink and ready for Round Two. He didn't want to fight, hadn't expected it to turn out this way.

Working late, he had been, closing the file on a grisly suicide. Saturday, winter, and rain coming down in buckets. Not at his best, then.

She barged in, hatless and bedraggled, swamped by a paint-flecked mackintosh.

'Posters,' she gasped, dumping a sodden package on his desk. 'Beat the deadline, just. Take the prize now, will I?'

'Lady,' he grunted, 'one of us is in the wrong office.'

'The road safety competition, man! The school porter should have brought them yesterday. Head like a sieve, he has.'

'Crime, it says on the door. Don't expect you noticed, in the rush.'

'*You're* on duty,' the sergeant said. 'Evans the Basement, right?'

She was quite pretty, despite the awful gear, but reference to his lowly status hardly helped her cause.

'It's Marchant you want, in Traffic. Off till Monday, he is.'

'Monday's too late!'

'It's a hard life, teaching.'

'You mean I braved the monsoon for nothing?' Above the angry blush, her eyes pleaded. Nice eyes, sort of smoky brown.

He avoided them, glaring at the puddle on his blotter.

'Oh *bugger*!' she snapped, snatching the parcel and whirling around. From the doorway, she shot him a venomous over-the-shoulder glance. 'I think you British policemen are *wonderful*!'

Her footfalls and the rustle of her daft coat faded. The basement seemed shabbier for her absence. Echoes of her Valleys cadence shamed him. He shoved the files aside and went in pursuit.

She was waiting in the porch, high-collared and grim-faced, while the downpour clattered on to waterlogged black asphalt. 'Give us the stuff, then,' he muttered. 'I'll see it gets to Marchant.' In the brilliance of her smile, he weakened further. 'It's a pig of a night. Run you home, if you like.'

'Oh, *would* you?'

She talked music all the way there, above the rhythmic ticking of the wipers. Something else they had in common. He wasn't asked in, not that time.

She was right about the posters. A month later, while Marchant was otherwise engaged, he found himself on the school stage dispensing prize book-tokens. After-wards in the staffroom, Megan brought him coffee and the biggest doughnut, told him she was widowed, and consented to the first weekend meeting.

For quite some time, it remained a casual friendship. She blossomed in his company, but modestly. Then, one evening in her flat, after a bottle of plonk and a mild argument, she went very quiet. Respecting the mood, he prepared to leave. She stood up, kicked off her shoes and led him by the hand to her bedroom. There, she offered a well-rounded body and a hunger every bit as urgent as his own.

And breakfast, Sunday mornings.

She came in, flushed and fresh and no old make-up. The pale yellow shift set off her dark colouring and showed a hint of rounded cleavage. Despite earlier exertions, he felt old Adam stir.

'Down, boy,' she ordered briskly, 'there's things to discuss.'

'It's me you're talking to, mind, not the Lower Third.'

'Sorry. Do take a seat, Inspector. Please?' She poured tea and studied him through upward-curling wisps of steam. 'There was someone in the village, before I met Ivor. Said I was making a mistake, he'd wait for ever if need be.' She caught his expression and grimaced. 'I know. Sounds like one of those sloppy romances. Anyhow, he's done well. Deputy at the old grammar school, a detached bungalow and the mortgage paid off.'

'Local boy makes good,' growled Evans. 'There's lovely.'

'They have a vacancy,' she continued. 'Head of Art, Scale Four. He wants me to apply.' She sat straighter, her eyes flashing tawny. 'They'd be getting a bargain!'

'After the posters, you mean. Go on. I'm listening.'

'You're a hard bastard, Huw: do I have to spell it out?'

He waited, while the sun slid lower and a neighbour called kids in to supper.

'Oh, all right!' she snapped. 'He's promising comfort, security and a kind of love. I'm thirty-four, mind, a widow. Where will I get a better offer?' She took a plain blue envelope from her bag. 'Forms, filled and ready. Post them, shall I?'

He stood and paced, scratching the stubble on his chin. He felt cornered, deprived of dignity – an overweight cop in underpants and bad books, and no easy answer to give. Tell her the truth, bach, it's the only way. 'No contest, Megan. Your man home at nights on his chin-strap, smelling of vomit and death. No peace and no prospects. I've *been* there once. A good Valleys girl like you, and we finished up strangers. Grab him while you can. You'd be a fool to stay.' Gently, trying to ease the pain, he added, 'Name the first one for me, if you like. I'll miss you, girl.'

She faced him at last, bright with unshed tears. Then,

quite suddenly, her eyes cleared and hardened. He saw the pain and disillusion gather, as though she was reading him right for the very first time.

'I don't think so,' she said. 'I wouldn't like a son called Thomas.'

'Thomas?'

'He who is too full of doubt.'

She sat like a statue before her untouched tea, and her expression held only pity. After *that* there was nothing to do but collect his toothbrush and razor, get dressed, and take his leave. A last ceremonial and emotionless kiss, and mind how you go. They parted as they had met – coldly.

Driving homeward, beset by traffic and the lowering sun, he felt old and bereft and weary to his bones. Aye, he thought, next time you're looking for love on a Sunday, go to the professionals.

'Oh Roy,' murmured WPC Parrot. 'Oh *Sarge*!'

Yeah, Beddoes thought, nibbling her naked shoulder, personal investigations are best. They'd met on a recent case and had offered, in their separate ways, comfort and support to a rape victim. The shared experience had brought them close; very close indeed. Now, as the bed began to creak and his own pleasure built, he drove her towards the most intimate moment of all: and the phone rang.

'Don't stop,' she pleaded. 'Please don't stop!'

'Wouldn't dare,' he grunted; but the clamour persisted, his rhythm faltered, and the professional in him woke. Must be important. Coppers don't get social calls at dead of night, even those as tasty as Pol Parrot.

'Better answer it,' he advised, making a gentle and reluctant withdrawal.

'Damn!' she whispered. 'Damn, damn, *damn*!'

21

He lay in the heated darkness and brushed the sweat from his face. Her musk eddied about him; hold hard, my son, we could be headed for extra time.

She was back in a jiffy, glistening pale and lovely but sounding none too chuffed.

'It's Evans, for you. Bet you told the whole bleedin' nick!'

'Give over, Pol, business is business. 'E's my oppo, right?' He was already scrambling out, hunched and painful, towards the hallway. Her snigger didn't help.

'The three-legged race,' she said; all right for *her* to talk.

Evans was brief and brutal. As most of his body stiffened, the best of Beddoes faded away. Back in the bedroom, he screwed up his eyes, flicked on the light and gathered his scattered clothing.

'Sorry Pol, panic stations. There's bin a bombing, up West.' He paused, trousers at half-mast, struck by a sudden thought. 'Could be casualties, a chance to get your pitcher in the papers. Coming?' Silly question, he realized. She hadn't taken it in, she was lying there rosy and purring, her mind on other things.

'Not quite. Wouldn't take much, though. Hurry home.'

'Too right!' he agreed, and legged it before she changed his mind. A good big girl was Pol, enthusiastic and uncomplicated. In the past couple of months she'd done wonders for the old id and ego; both of which had taken a battering from that self-same rape victim. Keep it warm for me, lovely; shouldn't be difficult, this weather.

At first he drove fast with the window down, enjoying the coolness on his face and the bore of the beams through the empty streets. Then quite suddenly, he was carving past a convoy of press cars and TV vans, and the implications sunk home. Where there's a bomb there's a

22

nutter, he thought, changing down and blasting through an amber light; 'ere we go again. Terror in the wind, blood on the sidewalk and the media goin' spare. Don't knock it, sunshine; better than missing persons and petty theft.

The 'accident ahead' sign flared orange. Beyond it, he caught the red wink and flicker of a lengthy tailback. Time to ditch the motor and take to Shanks's pony. As he locked the door and straightened up, the wail of a klaxon reached him; the familiar knot of tension coiled in his gut.

He was making for the High Street through an ever-thickening throng. Like Guy Fawkes, really, only milder. He elbowed past briskly, apologizing to no one. At the cordon, he showed his warrant card and received a harassed-looking salute.

'The Inspector's waiting, sir. He's in there, some-where.'

'Ta very much.'

Funny thing, first impressions, he mused; a lot of fuss about nothing. Three silver fire engines straddled the pavement, an ambulance and a gaggle of squad cars crowded the kerb. Half the Force seemed to be hanging around, and men in yellow oilskins hurried to and fro. The hiss of hoses, a stench of burning, a babble of confused orders and blue lights spinning steadily. As he watched, the first big TV lamp blazed, muting all the colours and bringing an air of artificiality to the whole scene. And at the focus, a blackened frontage, a scatter of smouldering furniture and the glint of broken glass. Anti-climax, then. Geared for carnage and an inferno, he'd stumbled on the remnants of a kid's bonfire.

As he watched, a familiar blocky figure emerged from the drifting smoke. Evans, his broad face flecked with

23

soot and sweat like pebbles at the fringe of his receding sandy hair. Knackered and grim he might be, but he couldn't resist an opening dig.

'Glad you could make it, boyo. Manage, will they, back at the harem?'

'Do me a favour, uncle. Next time *ask* if I'm there. The girl has her pride, see.'

'Oh sure. And the way you two carry on, down the nick? Bloody obscene, it is.'

'Obscenity's in the eye of the beholder mate.'

'Aye, well, you do it your way, and I'll do it mine.'

Beddoes was edgy, thinking about bits of charred flesh he might yet have to collect. He hit back absently, out of habit, more or less.

''Ark oo's talkin'! 'Ow *is* Mrs Powell, anyway?' And, seeing Evans' look of pained and almost comic dismay, added, 'When you're screwin' a married bird, you didn't oughta park outside.' It hit him hard, anyone could see.

In the pitiless glare, his pale blue eyes turned stony and a muscle bunched at the hinge of his jaw. 'First, she's widowed, not married. Second, I was in my own bed when the phone rang. And third . . .

At this point, luckily, a uniform intervened. 'Inspector Evans? Fire's out, guv, and the owner's come. They're askin' for you.'

Evans controlled his temper, the effort plainly visible.

'Right. Keep everyone else away, mind, till the boffins arrive. Sarn't Beddoes'll talk to 'Is Nibs.'

''Ere, 'ang about, you'll 'ave to brief me. I'm in the dark, see.'

'So what else is new? *Late*, weren't you? All right, I'll say it once. A fancy curry house, Punjabi Sikhs, no warning and no claims so far. Suss him out, then, you know the form.' Evans waved wearily at the chaos around them. 'Could've been worse. A small bomb, a confined space and the fire boys were bloody quick. Closes at midnight, see; a lock up job, no one about. No casualties and limited damage. With some elbow grease and the insurance, he could be at it again in a month.' He swung on his heel and marched clean through a gather of waiting reporters. 'No comment,' he snapped. 'When I want to talk to you, I'll ask!'

The owner was slim and immaculate in grey sharkskin and a brilliant purple turban. He gave his name as Kuldip Singh; as he spoke, his silver-streaked beard quivered with emotion and tears brimmed in his wounded brown eyes.

'Father Mindee won allied medals, you know. After, he is taking wife and young ones to good life in Africa. Many years he is working tooth and nail for fine house and Mercedes car. Then mad Amin chucks brown men out.' He waited, dabbing his cheeks with a snowy handkerchief while the first of the fire engines thundered past. 'Okay, he come to Leicester, start all over. Eighteen hours a day we are keeping shop open, paying fines, no problem. Two years back, I come here and start special place, exquisite oriental cuisine, I'm telling you.' He paused again, pointing an unsteady hand at the gaping, ruined façade. 'What do I get? More maniacs. Oh my God!'

Beddoes wrote stoically, the ink smudging in the blobs of sweat on the page. For all he knew, there could be a pile of compensation to be collected. 'Any enemies, Mr Singh? Any jealous business rivals?'

'Pah! Kuldip cooks best Parsee dish in town, maybe in the whole country. Mughal, palak, tandoori, ask anyone. Already famous people eat here, two, three times a week. Before was only Bengali takeaways; you know a Bengali who can cook?'

25

'That's what I mean.' Beddoes glanced pointedly at the smart threads. 'You're a well-set-up man, Mr Singh.'

'You don't understand. All Indians here have suffered. When one makes success, all celebrate.' He saw the scepticism Beddoes couldn't conceal, and added, 'Tomorrow, you see. They come from all over, to help clean mess. For friendship, mind you, not money.'

'That's nice. Okay, 'ow about extremists? Don't look like that mate, you've had your share; lootin' the temples, knockin' off Gandhis like there's no tomorrow, and playing Old Harry about skid-lids.'

The Sikh had gone rigid, and his eyes were all at once hard and dangerous. No telling how nasty it might have got, then; but a second dishevelled beat man broke it up. A raw lad, this one, and looking a bit green around the gills.

''Scuse me, Sarge, the Inspector's out the back. Urgent, he says.' He edged nearer, lowering his voice. 'Found a stiff, we did.'

'All right, Mr Singh,' Beddoes said tiredly, 'We'll be in touch. Don't blow town, will you.' And left him there, an erect, angry figure silhouetted against the floodlit wreck of his dream.

Beddoes followed the boy, blinking at the sudden, acrid gloom inside. Hard to blame the Turban; a right bleedin' shambles. In the wavering glow of the beat man's torch, he grimaced at the scorched paintwork and overturned chairs. Underfoot, Persian carpets swashed around in several inches of oily sludge; the water seeped clammily through his shoes. Jesus, he thought, catching a still-appetizing whiff of curry, I'm starving. Remembering the message, he changed his mind.

Outside, there was thin moonlight and a ripe stench of garbage. The boy waved him forward and he picked his way fastidiously among overturned dustbins and empty wine bottles. He caught sight of Evans, hunkered down near the head of the alley. Beside him, a shapeless sprawl blotted out the gleam of the cobbles. Beddoes' palms went moist and his stomach writhed uneasily. Death in the darkness: it never got any easier.

Evans glanced up, hollow and haggard in the dimness.

'Spoke too soon,' he muttered. 'About casualties, I mean.' He straightened, and his knees cricked loudly. Beddoes swallowed hard and glanced down.

At first sight, it could've been a bundle of rags. He leaned closer, taking in the details and wincing at the unclean smell. A gaping mouth, a snaggle of rotting teeth, and the waning moon reflected from glassy eyes. The blood was amazing; a thick ribbon coiling through the matted, rice-spattered beard and creeping like pitch between the rounded stones. Not much doubt about the cause, either – a ragged chunk of masonry trapped in the bow of the chest.

'The kitchen wall, that is,' Evans was saying. 'You should see the hole inside. Scavenging, I expect, and took the full force. Doubt if he even felt it.' He held up a medicine bottle half-full of cloudy liquid. 'Meths and milk; dulls the senses lovely.'

Beddoes said nothing, staring in quite unanticipated sorrow on the strangely peaceful and wholly familiar face.

'Know him, do you?' Evans asked; and he nodded.

'A vagabond. Well, it's obvious, innit. Used to be a regular client.'

The boy shouldered between them, recovering and determined to prove it. 'Got off light, didn't we? I mean, the only victim, and '*e's* better out of it.'

'Go away, son,' Evans advised him, and you could hear the disgust in his voice. 'Come back when you're feeling human.'

27

Pottering homeward through pre-dawn stillness, Beddoes fell prey to nagging doubt. Too much blood altogether, and the brickwork hadn't looked right, somehow; which meant another unwelcome chore, come morning. A visit to the morgue.

CHAPTER TWO

'Wotcha, Huw,' called the deskman, through a press of lounging uniforms already late on shift. ''Eavy night, was it? You look like something the cat dragged in.' Out of character, this. Sergeant Warner was old school, nicknamed Jack after a TV folk hero of the sixties; your archetypal British bobby. Understandable, mind. Another blazing morning, the media shrieking bomb outrage, and him due for retirement any day. New-fangled regulations didn't help, either – beards and shirtsleeves and too much licence altogether. Heavy with fatigue and unanswered questions, conscious of smirks in the gallery, Evans played it frosty and official.

'Working, I was. How about you lot?' Sheepish glances, the clearing of throats and a shuffle of boots; the foyer emptied fast.

'Marvellous gift, authority,' sighed Warner. 'Used mine up, I reckon.' Sunlight from a high window burnished his thinning hair and brought out the liver patches on his hands. 'Coupla messages,' he continued, more formally. 'Ready?'

'Oh, sure.'

'Beddoes rang. Gone to an autopsy, back soon.' He showed his dentures slyly. 'Some blokes have all the luck.'

Evans waited, raw-eyed and unamused.

'Had a Turban in,' Warner confided, 'slagging off

young Roy. Bleedin' sauce! It's duty, I told 'im, protecting *all* our interests. You don't like it, shove off back to the Ganges.'

'There's diplomatic,' murmured Evans. 'Race relations'll have you, mind.'

'No way, mate, I'll be long gone.'

Not before time, Evans thought; the Empire's dead and Commonwealth cousins rule.

He leaned on the desk, watching dust motes dance in the brightness. 'Bombs in a curry house,' he grumbled. 'Where's the sense?' Warner nodded like an ancient, rheumy tortoise.

'Wanna know what I think?' He didn't, particularly. But ten months back, while a sex-killer ran amok and CID chased shadows, Warner had done some unscheduled homework and more or less cracked the case. A throwback, maybe; but you couldn't afford to ignore him.

He sat, head cocked to the clatter of a nearby typewriter. His gaze rested on a pair of gossiping WPCs along the passage and well out of earshot. Even so, he huddled conspiratorially and kept his voice low.

'Paddy's feeling flush, see, pops in for a touch of the extra-hot gubbins. Costs an arm and a leg, and what does he get? Nehru's revenge, the howlin' squitters. Soon as he's fit, it's out in the dark, blood in his eye and gelignite under the dirty raincoat. Blim-blam, gotcha, man; quality control, they call it.'

It would've been funny, only you could see he meant every word. Walk on, bach, humour him in the twilight of his life. Casually, Evans asked, 'Why d'you say he's Irish?'

'Took the call, didn't I? You could *smell* the Guinness on his voice.'

Seeing Evans' anger, Warner added hastily, 'No need to get shirty. Soon as he spoke, I started the tape. Even had copies made. *This* message comes from the horse's mouth.' He lolled in his chair, hands folded on the blue of his tunic and a comfortable sunlit smile on his face. The procedure as laid down, and by no means as simple as it sounded; so much for senility.

'Darro, Jack, what'll we do without you?'

'You'll get by. No more crazies for me; dahlias from now on. Lovely blooms, the missus fancies 'em no end.'

'Don't bank on it,' Evans cautioned. 'Indiscriminate lot, bombers.'

'Give over, a little allotment down the embankment? They wouldn't dare!' Brave words, but he spoke them like a querulous old spinster.

Soothingly, Evans said, 'Only joking, mun. Give us the tape and we'll have 'em inside before you can say fertilizer.' And bore the evidence away with more confidence than he felt.

Heading for the basement, he was, through a building stunned by summer and neglect. Pitiless golden light revealed every crack and cobweb; in this heat, the pungent whiff of toilets hung like invisible fog. He trudged on past the posters in traffic section, his footfalls ringing hollow, his mind dwelling on memories of Megan and the prospect of atrocities to come. The laughing policeman, duw, duw.

He paused at a grimy window overlooking a corner of the sunlit city. Mid-morning, and the pedestrians were mostly women. From here, they might have been so many moths, wheeling and drifting on wings of lemon and green and pink. A bus passed, ponderous and scarlet, and the chug of the diesel reached him clearly. Situation normal; but ten hidden pounds of TNT could turn it to gruesome chaos in the wink of a deranged eye. The thought sent a prickle along his spine; shuddering briefly, he started downstairs.

The office climate was continental; the Tropics in August, Antarctica in January. He barely noticed the peeling grey paintwork, rickety furniture and greasy lino. Instead, he watched the spin of small black wheels and listened in growing puzzlement to a loud but wordless crackle. Wake up, stupid: rewind!

The sudden blare almost lifted him from his seat. Lunging forward, he twisted the volume knob and recognized Warner's homely dialect.

'Belt up, you lot! Beg pardon, sir, it's Bedlam round 'ere. Could you repeat that, please?' Nice touch, buying time to activate the tape and start the trace. Didn't fool his caller, though: a humourless chuckle and a voice as rough as emery.

'Be sure the wee gadget's working now, Sergeant. 'Tis the whole world I'm addressing and not just yourself.' There was a loaded, insolent pause; then, 'We'll not be so careless again, for wasn't the timing your good luck?' A note of suppressed rage, Evans reckoned. 'Ye've murdered our fellas and looted our riches too long. 'Tis justice we seek, for the sins of the past. Stay clear of the busy places: beware the fiery sword of the Green Reapers!' As the line buzzed, faint and unmanned, Evans shivered again. The threadbare rhetoric of terror, but the passion sounded dangerously real. Then Warner spoke, calm and sane. 'Turn it off, Willsy, the bastard's 'ung up.' Aye, and so he should be.

Alone and uneasy in the clammy gloom, Evans played it through once more. Old Jack had it right, no question, the accent thick and scratchy as Irish tweed. Not much else to go on, though. Check the statements, bach, what else is there?

Reams, there were, and agreements on only two points. The moment – one thirty, near enough – and it had been a *small* explosion. 'Seemed like a backfire,' one witness had declared. 'Didn't take no notice till the missus saw the flames.' As the morning advanced and sweat gathered at the small of his back, a single question taunted him. Why would the Irish hit an empty Indian restaurant in the middle of the night?

Movement took his eye: Roy Beddoes, bright as ninepence, his sharp nose raised and wrinkled in disdain.

'Bit niffy, innit?'

'Honest toil. You should try it some time.' Beddoes crossed the room and draped his lightweight jacket carefully over the chair. Sporting a cream shirt and snug tan slacks, he looked like a toff in a coal hole.

'Take my tip,' he advised. 'Snuff it *natural*, like. It's diabolical, down that morgue.'

'Don't fret, boyo. Die in bed, you will.'

'Me life's ambition. It's not easy, though. Look what 'appened *last* night.'

'Ought to be grateful. For the rest, I mean.'

Prowling, his dark eyes hooded, Beddoes abandoned the skirmish much earlier than usual. 'Old Jim,' he breathed. 'Part of the scenery, know what I mean?'

'Aye. Nasty way to go.'

'Nastier than you think.' Cocking his index finger, tapping the brown embroidered logo on his breast pocket, Beddoes explained, 'Straight in, it went, a dirty great stiletto. The fireworks came later, the path. man says.'

Evans' brain reeled at the sheer wantonness. 'Jesi Mawr, bombs and butchery all in one night!'

Still pacing, neat and immaculate despite the fug, Beddoes nodded at the machine.

'Becomin' a pop fan, are yer?'

'Martial music,' Evans told him. 'You'd better listen.' He juggled buttons and winced at the now-familiar, ominous rasp.

33

'Jesus,' snarled Beddoes, standing bolt upright and cutting across Warner's postscript. 'Bleedin' Paddies!'

'A bombing, see; what d'you expect?'

The younger man might not have heard.

'Jim wasn't his real name. Lost a wife and kiddy, they say, long ago and far away.' He snapped his fingers, splintering the hush. 'In *Ireland*, uncle!'

A smart lad, Roy Beddoes; streetwise and versed in certain deadly arts, he had the makings of a first-rate cop. Impetuous, mind, and a pushover for a pretty face; a combination which had caused them a fair bit of aggro in the past. The excitement fairly gushed out of him, flooding the confined space like cheap scent.

'Going somewhere, are you?'

'Upstairs, mate. A confab with the Laird.'

'Oh aye? About what?'

'It's a long story; why tell it twice?'

'Guessing, you are,' Evans warned him, 'and none too popular up there.'

Framed in the doorway, pale and hard-eyed, Beddoes retorted, 'There's meat on this one, believe me, and I'm a hungry boy. You coming, or what?' He had a point; better go and see fair play.

The Super's office was the highest, biggest and best; and quite right, too. These days, Evans entered rarely and cautiously. Beddoes, less inhibited, knocked once and marched straight in.

'Ye're uninvited,' growled the occupant, dwarfed by a massive, battered desk. 'Sit down and keep quiet.'

To the sound of Beddoes' fidgets and the scrape of the Super's gleaming bronze pen, Evans took note of the surroundings.

Spartan, you'd have to call it, reflecting the nature of the man. The ice-grey carpet, straight-backed chairs and matt white walls said it plain; this is a workplace, abuse

34

it if ye dare. There was only one picture – winter on Ben Nevis, craggy and unyielding; and only one book – a well-thumbed King James Bible bound in red leather. Above and behind the desk, an illuminated text shone gold and purple. 'He that is not with me is against me: and he that gathereth not with me scattereth abroad. *Matthew 12:30*.' Very apt, really.

Presently, McKay holstered his pen and deigned to notice their existence. The sun darkened his freckles and struck flame from his short-cropped thatch. Squinting against it, his eyes were a narrow, pale blue challenge.

'To what do I owe this dubious honour?'

'Old Jim,' said Beddoes at once. 'Gettin' the chop like that. It's bleedin' wicked!'

'*None* the less, Sergeant, the accidental death of a derelict is no passport to yon seat. And I'll thank ye to mind your language.'

Not a muscle had moved in Beddoes' lean face, but his tone oozed satisfaction. 'Beggin' your pardon, but I'm just back from the morgue. He was stabbed.' He allowed a nicely weighted pause. 'A Paddy himself, see. Heard the tape, have you, sir?'

McKay's habitual glower deepened. 'Heard it? Ye Gods, I know the blessed thing by heart! *Here*abouts, we've been at it since dawn, whilst *you* were away in the land o' Nod.' His upper lip curled sourly. 'Or the arms o' some doxy, more likely.'

Wisely ignoring the jibe, Beddoes stuck to his guns.

'It makes no sense,' he admitted, 'the timing and the victims. Till you listen to that nutter and do a few sums. They're a new bunch, right?' He waited, eyebrows raised.

'Green Reapers!' muttered McKay in disgust. The Scottish burr was very strong and his fingers drummed on the polished wood. Tarantulas, they are, thought Evans; red and furry and itching to pounce.

''Eadlines, they're after,' Beddoes continued. 'Maximum exposure and no such thing as bad publicity. Upmarket, then, smack in the middle of the 'Igh Street. Favoured by the famous, too, according to Gunga Din.'

A shadow had crept across the desk. Within it, McKay sat perfectly still, his gaze abstracted and colourless. Faintly, from the distant river, came the mourn of a pleasure-boat siren.

'Come on, boyo,' Evans objected, 'the place was *shut*.' Beddoes turned on him, alight with triumph.

'What if it went off at one thirty *in the afternoon*? Carnage, mate, that's what. 'E's livid, on the tape, anyone can tell. I mean, a twelve-hour hiccup between Paddies? Par for the course, innit?' He shifted, adjusting the crease in his trousers and homing in on the silent Superintendent. 'They plant the goodies and toddle off – slap into Old Jim. It's dark and they're jumpy, course they are. A witness, mind you; they're not to know 'e's boozed to the eyeballs. So they do 'im over. Straight murder, that is, never mind the politics.' Beddoes leaned forward, his eyes glittering with fury. 'Let us at 'em, sir!'

A persuasive theory, fair play, tying all the facts together neatly. Too neatly for Evans' liking.

A compact silhouette against the cloudless blue, McKay spoke coldly to the emptiness outside. 'And what does our resident Welsh genius have to say, I wonder?'

Cunning, mind, setting one against the other; divide and rule, okay? Choosing words carefully, Evans voiced his doubts. 'A small bomb, an outfit no one's ever heard of, and shoving knives in one of their own. Doesn't sound like the Irish to me.'

McKay turned, erect and bristling. 'Wrong, as usual! Bombers have handwriting, y'know. The experts can tell by patterns o' wiring and preference for primers.' He advanced on Evans across the sunlit pile, baring his teeth

36

wolfishly. 'This laddie's trademark was familiar, it seems. A muckle of outrages to his credit, and under maximum security at the Maze till the break-out of '83. Name of Cavanaugh, Nial: present *where*abouts unknown.' Retreating into the shadow, he ladled salt on to the wound. '*Irish*, wouldn't ye say, Inspector?'

Back at his station, his satisfaction plain, McKay continued: 'The Sergeant's reasoning concurs very nicely with my own. You're a fortunate wee man, Evans. Thanks to your subordinate, you've a real case on your hands – for now.'

Later, chewing corned beef in the sun-stifled canteen while Beddoes was off mending fences with Pol, Evans mused uneasily on Irish connections. Something about the Reapers' furious wording bothered him, something which struck a faintly discordant note. Try as he might, he couldn't place it. He sighed and shoved his plate aside, wincing at a sudden waft of fried fish. Leave it there, bach, give the subconscious a dabble.

Making for the salt mine through a lunchtime bustle of uniformed human traffic, he felt curiously isolated and remote. It would be nice to sit down somewhere cool and quiet with a bottle of Scotch at hand and a Beethoven symphony playing; and someone sympathetic to share his woes. Someone like Megan.

'Keep your hands to yourself,' hissed Polly Parrot, waylaid in a shady corridor. 'The blooming *nerve*!'

'Ah, give over,' Beddoes pleaded. 'Unfinished business, this is.'

'That's what I mean. You had me bubbling like a kettle till dawn, you should've belled me.' But her indignation was fading fast. There was a becoming pink flush on her cheeks and a glow of languor deep in her soft brown eyes.

'Call of duty, girl. I'll make it up to you.'

'My, you don't half fancy yourself!'

'I fancy *you*. C'mere.'

She melted against him; then stiffened and shoved him away. 'Cool it Roy; company.' She scrubbed the lipstick off his mouth, buttoned her tunic and leaned against the wall, her face fresh and innocent. Amazing creatures, women. *He* was still panting.

A bevy of WPCs turned the corner, their heels clacking sharply. As they approached, the chatter died away; nudge and wink and knowing silence.

'Hi, gang,' said Polly, much too airily. 'Mind if I join you?'

A chorus of assent, a flashing, vengeful smile and she was off, wagging her rump saucily. Her parting shot rang above the swelling laughter. 'Give us a call some time, Sarge.'

Games people play, he thought ruefully; makes it one-all, and the decider to be arranged. Could've been worse, my son; matches have been abandoned for less.

Dawdling the quiet passage between yellow patches of light, he pondered the business at hand. Slow down, Paddies crossing. At the head of the basement staircase he checked, watching Evans climb towards him; steady and square and slightly shabby in faded fawn sports coat with leather patches at the elbows.

'How do, uncle; taking a breather?'

'Fat chance. There's more important things than courting.'

'All work and no play,' warned Beddoes, tongue in cheek; and saw that inexplicable anger flare once more.

'Listen, boyo, it's your theory and your patch, *you* can go chasing Reapers. Cautious, I am; I'll play hunt the victim.' His pale eyes narrowed and he jerked a blunt thumb upwards. 'You heard the man; no time to lose.'

38

He was on his way, coppery strands trailing across his tanned and thinning crown.

'If it's all the same to you,' Beddoes retorted, 'I'll take five, down the dungeon. Thinking about it, right?' And again forfeited the last word.

'Oh sure. Don't strain yourself, mind.'

As it happened, he didn't get the chance: the basement was occupied. Your actual city gent, complete with bowler and a rolled umbrella dangling from the crook of his charcoal-grey pinstripe.

'Sergeant Beddoes?' he enquired, low and cultured. 'The name's Slade. Do forgive the intrusion – it wasn't locked.'

'No problem,' Beddoes consoled him. 'We never close. Take a pew, Mr Slade, there's no extra charge.' The mild humour missed its mark. He hovered, portly, bespectacled and apologetic, eyeing Evans' chair distrustfully. Privileged, anyone could tell; bespoke threads and the high complexion of one who fed often and well. The glow of embarrassment seemed apt; in the financial pink, don't you know.

He sat gingerly, the bowler perched on his knees, his pudgy fists gripping the curve of the brolly. 'Oh dear, this is most distressing. It's Harriet, d'you see; my daughter. You *will* be discreet, I trust?'

'Flown the coop, has she?'

'Yes.' The expression and the implication caused him obvious grief. 'We have some idea where she is, of course.' Momentarily, his fleshy features hardened. 'And we know well enough who she's with. Unfortunately.'

'Harriet would be how old, sir?'

'Just sixteen.' He fumbled in a monogrammed wallet and offered a studio print.

'Pretty girl,' murmured Beddoes, preserving the amenities. In fact, she looked like any other teenaged schoolkid: blue-eyed, dark-haired and wholesome in a fancy braided blazer.

Slade smiled dismally. 'When that was taken, yes. She was responsible and loving, too, and quite a promising classics scholar. You wouldn't believe the change. Freakish hair, lurid cosmetics, and her clothes scarcely decent.' He shuddered, and the colour flooded his cheeks. 'She's very mature, physically.'·

The old, old story; might as well shorten the agony. Laying out his notebook, Beddoes adopted a brisk tone. 'The boy'll be older, no doubt. Name and address, please. We'll send a uniform round and have her home in a jiffy.

Slade recoiled, his white cuffs flashing in the gloom. The brolly clattered, unheeded, to the floor.

'For heaven's sake, no! The last time was total disaster; the squalour and the language, you've no idea!'

'Don't you fret, sir. Hard cases, some of our lads, not easily put off.'

'You don't understand. I'm talking about *her* language.' He produced a sky-blue hanky and mopped his shamed and shining face. Behind the glasses, his weak brown eyes looked hunted, and guilt covered him like a shroud.

Under Beddoes' persistent probing the story emerged reluctantly. There had been a messy divorce. Slade had married his secretary. Harriet's mother had taken to gin and Mediterranean cruises. The girl, they all agreed, would be better off in boarding school. She was; until she met a boy called Gerald. Slade pronounced the name like some dread disease. 'A performer of sorts. Calls himself Gerry Jewell and makes hideous noises on an electrical keyboard. They are *squatters*, apparently, in some ghastly musical commune which shifts from one derelict property to the next. My wife is prostrate, the girl's mother is at her wits' end, and my own business is faltering. I'm a stockbroker,' he confided, causing Beddoes no great surprise. 'I used to be one of the best.' And picked up his umbrella as if he needed the reassurance of full dress uniform.

'And I'm a copper, Mr Slade.' Beddoes told him, not unkindly. 'We can't interfere, if you won't press charges.'

'Out of the question, the publicity would be ruinous. Couldn't you talk to her, Sergeant? As a man of the world, someone closer to her own generation?'

Jesus, thought Beddoes, that's all I need right now; hide and seek with a foul-mouthed little scrubber while her dad stands pat and counts pennies. As he paused, framing a tactful brush-off, Slade removed his glasses. The portly face was suddenly naked and vulnerable, and wholly unexpected tears dripped steadily from his chin.

'*Please*, Sergeant. I'm so afraid she'll be hurt.'

Wrong again, my son. He really *does* care. 'Give us the last known contact,' Beddoes muttered gruffly. Seeing the pitiful flare of hope, he added quickly, 'No promises. Even if I find her, there's no way I can make her come home.'

'Bless you,' said Slade simply, redeeming a little dignity. 'It's more than I deserve.' He gave the address, gathered his paraphernalia and went, leaving a whiff of expensive cologne and one more cross to bear. But as his heavy footfalls faded, Beddoes found himself grinning slyly. What *you* need, young Harry, is a warm, understanding WPC; just like the one I'm due to call.

'Wake up,' she whispered, wide-eyed and urgent in the pattering night. 'Come on, Gerry, *please*!'

The sounds drew nearer, mean and stealthy and menacing. The boy beside her shifted, and her frantic fingers skittered over heated, greasy flesh.

41

'Gerroff,' he mumbled. 'Gotta sleep.' He was stoned again, no use to man or beast – or woman. The words and the movement unleashed a familiar nosegay of body odour, marijuana and stale booze. After all these weeks, it still brought bile to her throat.

She recoiled in disgust, squeezing a whiff of mildew from the mattress and a warning creak from the floorboards beneath. Her fearful gaze darted from one shadowy, inert form to the next, drawn like a doomed moth to a faint pink glow in the furthest corner. Murder in the dark, she thought wildly; but this was rancid and real, a far cry from the girlish pranks in the virginal and antiseptic dorms of St Catherine's.

''Tis only rats, Miss Harriet.' A chill, mocking voice – so unexpected and shocking that she actually jumped, pressing herself back against the damp and mouldering wall. 'If it's a *man* you're in need of, sure he's ready and waiting.' The glow brightened. A cigarette, she realized, held in a cupped hand. Smoky red light played on a cruel nose and hollow cheeks, and glittered hotly from hard black eyes. 'Tell us, Your Holiness, is it Joe or meself you're wanting?'

She'd placed them now, two so-called violinists whom Gerry had welcomed 'to smarm up the sound, like'. So far, they'd shown neither instruments nor the smallest interest in music.

'Thank you,' she snapped, in best Sloane Street and much more hauteur than she felt. 'I'm suited at present.'

A flaring intake of breath and the red dot arched swiftly across the room. 'Be off, ye scummy creatures!' There were squeaks and scuffles and an icy chuckle. 'You see? Gutless vermin!' A measured pause; then, 'Aye, and the rats as well.'

She waited, tense and foetal, clutching the rough blanket to her naked skin.

42

'No hurry, Harry,' mocked the Voice, 'for we're power-ful patient men.'

Maybe, but she charted the sounds of undressing anxiously, flinching at the murmur of sly male laughter. At last there was silence; even rats must sleep.

Joe, she remembered, had tried it on the very first night, while Gerry strutted and vamped Marillion numbers in a crumbling, nicotine-stained cellar. He was nervous but quite nice in a stage-Irish way, and she'd squashed him almost kindly. 'Come back when you've grown up, kid.' In spite of herself, she smiled at the memory; he reminded her of Eric.

Poor Eric, the gangling fifth-former who looked like George Michael and spoke like George Cole. He'd done such dreamy things to her growing breasts, then exploded like Polaris as soon as her untutored hand brushed his bulging fly. Still, he'd shown her the awe-some power of her own body – which was more than she'd every learned from Mummy.

'You're almost a lady, dahling, there are things you must know.' She delivered a fastidious account of the curse, and the painful mechanics of mating. 'Men adore it, don't ask me why. Personally, I smile and think of something nice, like supper at the Curzon or Chanel No. Five.'

Harriet had adored her mother; the assured, beautiful presence who controlled their three lives so completely. As a little girl, she had yearned for the breathless, perfumed embrace at the end of every day. 'Sleep tight, dahling, Mummy loves you *so* much.' Mummy, who after the divorce had developed migraine and miserliness and a passion for cruising the Greek Islands with flaccid, florid estate agents. Actions speak louder than words.

Daddy was good with words, too. 'We've decided, your

stepmother and I, that a boarding school would be best; and I mean the *best*, my dear, that money can buy.' At first, she *had* enjoyed it. Then their visits became shorter and less frequent, and she tired of riding and Girl Guides. She hated the uniform, the discipline, and the deputy-head. 'Harriet Slade, is that *nail* varnish I see? St Catherine's girls are *ladies*, not strumpets!'

In the nick of time, Harriet discovered sex and Eric; and Eric introduced her to Gerry.

Gerry was alive and real. He had talent, a dream and a place of his own. He loved her, too: he said so even *after* they'd been to bed. He'd come to town for the Big Time, and it had gone sour right from the start. They drifted from one seedy gig to the next, dirt poor and never more than a week ahead of the demolition men. ''Ang in there, 'Arry,' he would mumble, when he wasn't out of his mind. 'Somethin's comin'. I can feel it in me water.' About all he *did* feel down there, these days. At his best he'd given only a little more than Eric; now he gave nothing at all. He on longer cared for himself, let alone for her.

Meanwhile, the hopheads and hangers-on gathered; eating, drinking, smoking and shooting up. Taking everything and giving nothing but trouble, just like Joe and the Voice.

She didn't even know his name. Until tonight, he'd been simply a bearded, scornful presence who did little and said less. But she'd sensed his cold, hungry eyes on her body and noticed the curious, watchful way in which he sat. There's something secret and dangerous about him, she decided; something attractive. At least he's a *man*. Whereas Gerry . . . her nose wrinkled, and she kicked his smelly, snoring form viciously. He didn't even stir.

All right, Voice, she thought, let's see how patient you are. Tomorrow we'll wear the see-through top and no bra – it needs a wash anyway. Deep in her mind, she carried a bitter picture; her stepmother, plump and pretty in a pink nightdress open almost to the navel, and her father's eyes out on stalks as he chewed his breakfast croissant. She pushed the sweat-soaked blanket off and ran her hands over her own slick and fevered breasts. Mine are at least as big as hers, and that's what men like, even Daddy.

Daddy had thrown her out for that fat, simpering cow from the office. Though he begged and pleaded over the phone, he sent the money to keep his daughter absent. He'd only come looking once. All the time she was swearing at him, calling him everything she knew, her eyes and her heart were begging – please take me home! And he'd stared at his handmade shoes and gone away.

I'll *never* go back, she vowed; back to the big bright house and nice clothes and bathsalts and cool clean sheets. Never, never, ever. In the stinking, shifting darkness, she hugged her mature, woman's body and cried herself to sleep like a child.

CHAPTER THREE

Honour among thieves, Beddoes had learned, cut no ice with their women. Given a trusty mouthpiece and the promise of riches to come, a small-time hood might shield the Godfather and take the fall; his spouse, legal or otherwise, was left to nurse the toddlers, the mortgage, and a man-sized sense of outrage. 'Blimey, Roy, it's 'ard enough when 'e's inside for *doing* something!' They knew where the bodies were buried, too. Villains need to impress their bedmates; who else would they tell?

Guarding his sources jealously, Beddoes had built a unique network of feminine snouts from whom, in exchange for certain not unpleasant labours, he tapped a steady stream of underworld gossip and a curious brand of loyalty. 'If it wasn't for you,' he was once breathlessly assured, 'I'd've bin on the game long ago.'

Enacting Evans' orders, he began with one of his regulars. She was bold and bleached and thirty; not for the first time, her man had drawn a stretch for GBH. Greeting him like the long-lost, she led him into a sunless bedsit smelling of bacon and nappies, planted the sprogs at the telly and plied him with lukewarm tea and ready answers.

He kept it simple to start, the tale of a teenage toff.

'Slade?' she repeated blankly. 'Never 'eard of her.' Then the rather lovely violet eyes widened. ''Ang about, just remembered. Arnie was out at some disco, celebrating 'is last job. After, he went on about some little tart 'anging around the band.' Frowning in concentration, she muttered, 'Acts like a scrubber, dresses like a tramp and talks like the Queen. 'Ow does that sound?'

'Promising,' said Beddoes, and took down the details over action music and a rising, childish howl.

'Leave it out, Sidney,' she snapped. 'Belt up and watch the box!' Astonishingly, the noise ceased; but his next question wiped her complacency clean away.

'*Irish!*' She snorted, in utter contempt. 'Wouldn't give 'em the time of day. Vicious they are.' She glanced at the kids and lowered her voice. She needn't have bothered; two tiny, goggle-eyed statues totally absorbed in Transformerland. 'Gawd knows, my Arnie's no angel, I've felt the weight of his hand a few times. But *bombs*? I'd shoot 'im myself.' She stretched voluptuously, and the housecoat parted in several strategic places. Well made, was Doris, and tanned all over; not your natural blonde, though.

'I'm *hot*, Roy,' she breathed. 'Bin a long time, know what I mean?'

'Yeah, hellish,' he agreed, staring pointedly at his empty cup; but she wasn't taking hints, either. 'Cavanaugh's in town, no question,' he insisted. 'If the hard men don't want to know, 'oo's hidin' him?'

'Amateurs,' she snapped, her eyes turning narrow and almost mauve in disgust. 'Amateurs and weirdos. All you need is readies to flash and the busies feelin' your collar. A bloke could kip for weeks in that lot, and no one any the wiser. Oh Christ!' There was a violent gurgle and a hot whiff of milky vomit. 'Sidney,' she wailed, 'you '*orrid* brat!' She was off, in a flurry of green and pink. Somehow, she had a napkin in one hand and a bottle of Dettol in the other. As she knelt and scrubbed, the housecoat

47

puckered in the cleft of her rump and inched slowly up her thighs. It'd be the easiest thing in the world, he thought, teach old Pol a lesson.

The moment passed. She was in and out of the kitchen in seconds, and nothing to show but Sidney's smug red face and an aura of disinfectant.

'I was thinkin',' she said, resuming her seat as if nothing had happened, 'your little duchess'll be in there, too. Communes, they call 'em; bleedin' addicts, they are. Didn't oughta be allowed, if you ask me, in a respectable neighbourhood!' She grinned at him, recognizing the absurdity. 'I know, look 'oo's talkin'.'

An artist, Doris, nudging him ever-so-gently away from that dodgy and still unanswered question.

'The Slade bird can wait,' he admitted; 'the Paddies won't. Come on, girl. I'm almost family.' He nodded at the 'A-Team' set he'd bought for the boys and she puckered her inviting lips.

'Whaddaya mean, *almost*? Kissin' cousins, aren't we?'

'Business before pleasure, right?'

'You're a hard man, Roy – thank Gawd! Oh, all right! They're maniacs, the Irish; long memories, short fuses, and a permanent cure for them as talks too much. Nobody squeals on those lads; *nobody*.' She took his hands and brought him to his feet, standing very close. 'Wanna slip into something comfortable?'

He was going down for the third time, drowning in the heat of her need. Lifting his head, scenting the air and pulling a sickly grin, he murmured 'Methinks ole Sid just did number two.'

'I'll kill 'im,' she promised. 'I'll murder the little sod!' And while she descended on her son like the gentle wrath of ages Beddoes made his escape.

She was right, though. As the heatwave dragged on and the media stoked public fear and fury over the blast;

with Evans riding him hard and McKay's implied warning echoing in his mind; Roy Beddoes encountered for the very first time, the total and unanimous absence of tell-tale female voices.

Evans' quest for the victim's past took him on a three-day traipse through the dosshouses of Dockland in blistering heat. The reek of Lysol, stew and unwashed bodies would haunt him for weeks; three good reasons for staying on the wagon. Everyone knew Old Jim, but his true identity remained stubbornly buried. Until, at the hind-end of the third afternoon, a Sally Army major rummaged in the archives and came up with a result. Old Jim's full name was Eamon Cavanaugh.

The news caused a stir at the nick, and a round of increasingly fanciful conjecture. A Celtic blood feud, someone suggested, played out on foreign streets, and a bomb thrown in for good measure.

'Cain and Eamon, is it?' Evans enquired sarcastically; and, having dispatched a lengthy telex to Dublin, he resumed the hunt.

Next morning, to general astonishment, Evans received a concise, pithy response:

1. Only recent picture, Cavanaugh, N. useless. Subject comatose, thirty pounds underweight and unrecognizable, viz. lengthy hunger strike.

2. Eamon from Kerry. Nial born and raised Sligo. No known connection.

3. For your information, Cavanaugh common Irish surname.

O'Brien, Garda.

And don't be wasting our precious time, he meant.

'Cheeky berk!' Beddoes protested, and Evans put him straight.

'Don't knock it, boyo, at least he's on the ball. It's more than you can say.'

'Charming!' said Beddoes, and sat to attention as the door swung back and McKay marched in.

He hunched like a terrier at the hub of the room, his small head thrust forward, his rufous hackles quivering.

'Ye'll be intrigued to know,' he announced, 'ye quarry has been active this day. An explosive charge placed in main-branch Tesco.'

Evans winced. Only the biggest supermarket around, and a Friday morning, too.

'That's Central turf,' he pointed out, and the Super snapped, 'All the same to me, laddy. Babel, d'ye ken, and the highways and byways brought to a standstill.' He smacked a knobby fist into his palm, and his eyes blazed icy blue. 'Then, if ye please, we receive a *second* recording. Lunatic chuckles, it's all a hoax, wait till we plant a *big* bomb.'

'Same geezer?' asked Beddoes, and shipped a withering glance.

'Who d'ye expect, faeries? We're granted a period of grace to broadcast agreement to a *political* reform.'

'Let my people go,' Evans grunted, and McKay nodded in grudging appreciation.

'No doubt. Failing such agreement, a campaign of "random reprisals" will begin without further warning.' His scowl deepened, his bristly eyebrows almost meeting above his nose. 'According to informed sources, the IRA has disclaimed responsibility. Dinna smirk at me, Inspector, they're not precisely devoted to the truth, and yon wee bomber's a founding brother!'

Aye, happy families, mused Evans; aloud, he launched a summary of progress to date. McKay cut him off with a contemptuous Caledonian sucking of the teeth. 'In short, laddie, ye havenae advanced an inch!'

50

Unjust, mind, and Evans wasn't having it. 'If it's miracles you're after, I'll need higher powers and eleven more apostles.'

McKay towered over him, white with righteous fury. 'Ye're a blasphemous oaf, Huw Evans! Ye've a week, no more. If a single device explodes, ye'll be held *personally* culpable!' He whirled and stamped out, slamming the door savagely.

'Buck up, uncle,' Beddoes advised, 'it's only the bun-fight tonight.'

'Bunfight?'

'You know, auld acquaintance, forgive and forget, one of our number is departin'. Warner's party, mate!'

'Forty-two years,' boasted Warner to a packed and rowdy audience. 'Forty-two years of service, man and boy.' It was after ten in the plush dining-hall, and the ritual nearing its climax. 'It's been my privilege,' he continued, swaying stiffly in his best uniform and dabbing his eyes with a wine-soiled napkin, ''cos there's no finer bunch of people anywhere on earth!' He brandished the glittering memento like a grizzled sporting lion. 'Me 'n' Elsie thank you from the bottom of our 'earts; there'll always be a brew-up for weary beatmen, down at yer old Uncle Jack's!'

The wave of approval rumbled and burst; continental whistles and the pounding of heavy fists on white-clad tables. Inevitably, some idiot struck up 'For he's a jolly good fellow'.

Alone and aloof at the heart of the crowd, Evans held back and watched the proceedings sardonically. Maudlin, mind, and a good way over the top; chandeliers and singing, like the eve of Waterloo. It *was* like that, fair play. With McKay hunting scapegoats and a bomber on the prowl, each dawn could be your last. Drink deep, lads, it's back to the trenches tomorrow.

Movement near the door took his eye — Beddoes breaking parole, closely followed by WPC Parrot. Bound for less public celebrations, no doubt; and why not? No better way to round things off, as Megan used to say. Back in the Valleys, she was, a long way to go for tea and sympathy.

The party had fragmented and the surge bore him steadily towards the bar. Could've been the Arms Park, except for the uniforms and the red carpet. The brass were there already, hogging seats and the barman, and plenty of space for their women. Among them, he could hardly help noticing, a real knockout.

She stood there, creamy and slender, in a black dress cut very low at the back; her auburn hair swayed and glinted as she spoke. Bees round the honeypot, see: even Friar McKay was hanging on her every word. Aye, and so he should. In public, at least, police wives tended to be demure — had to, really — and she stood out like a pin-up in a nunnery.

Briefly, over a sea of talking heads, Evans caught her flashing, green-eyed glance. In utter astonishment, he received a cool smile, a delicate shrug and a faint but engaging wink. Mistaken identity, he thought, feeling the flush on his face and wishing he could be so lucky; by which time she was otherwise occupied, accepting a pale golden glass from the Assistant Commissioner himself.

An elbow jarred his spine, and heavy shoes trampled his instep. He was still several ranks away from the counter, he'd had easier moments in the loose mauls. To hell with it, he thought, shouldering clear and following Beddoes' example, no one'll miss me for a while.

In two minutes flat he'd threaded the palm-lined

corridors and spotted an empty bar. Basking in the cool and quietness, he ordered a pint, took a navvy's pull and eased into neutral. Idly watching the bubbles trickle upwards, he asked himself the obvious question: 'What's a girl like you doing in a place like this?'

'Hey, marn, you the fuzz. Inspector Evans, right?' He'd come from nowhere, it seemed, a tall black man resplendent in skin-tight jeans, a yellow T-shirt and purple shades.

'Off-duty I am, mind.'

'Ah got word, baby, you better believe. Not here, though. Ah'm burstin'.' He strolled to the door, fluid and rhythmic, one pink-palmed hand beckoning urgently. 'Pee-break,' he commanded hoarsely, and disappeared.

It's the TV that does it, Evans reflected bitterly, these days every snout's a performer. You had to humour them, though. Once in a while, they delivered. Wearily, he forsook his half-filled glass and went in search of the Gents.

Palatial, it was, with umpteen mirrors, a Durex machine and hot-air hand-driers. Ancient and modern, automation and mothballs, and painted hospital white. A solitary, exotic figure, the negro had taken a classic stance halfway down the row of gleaming urinals: legs straddled, curly head tilted back as if reading the secrets of life from a lavatory wall.

'If you're havin' me on,' Evans cautioned, 'I'll do you for importuning.'

'Just wait,' he snapped, with quite unexpected authority. His backside twitched and a zip buzzed softly. Unhurried and graceful, he glided to the washbasin. When both taps were gushing nicely, he murmured, 'Sorry 'bout the hassle – he said you'd be here.' The rasta sing-song was gone, replaced by a faintly transatlantic drawl.

'Oh aye? Who's *he*?'

53

'Your once and future boss. Mine too. Smythe.' A former mentor, Smythe, who'd moved onward and upward two years since. Public knowledge, though, that was.

'Show us your card, boyo.'

The shades lifted, revealing level brown eyes, and the sullen mouth split in a broad white smile. 'My pleasure. I bet him a fiver you'd ask.' 'Sergeant Errol Harrigan', it said; and in small print, 'Special Duties'.

'Fair enough,' Evans conceded, nodding at the swirling water. 'So what's all the mystery? Knows where to find me, Smythe does.'

The door flew inwards. A pop-eyed, whey-faced young uniform from Traffic staggered to the nearest cubicle, bracing his belly with one hand and clutching his mouth with the other. The sounds of retching rattled from the tiles.

'Boy,' breathed Harrigan admiringly, 'that's what I *call* a honky.'

'Drop too much to eat, more like. Carry on, you, he's in no state to eavesdrop.'

The Sergeant's mobile features sobered. 'No mystery, man, just a straight message. Pretty soon now, you'll need some help. You'll know when it happens, he said. So call him, on this number.' He passed a slip of paper, screwed down the taps, and straightened up. 'Nice meetin' yuh, marn.' The shades dropped into place and he sauntered away, his camouflage restored.

As Evans tucked the paper into his wallet, a fearsome noise erupted – a long, violent breaking of wind. From the doorway, Harrigan's grin glistened like snow on a coaltip. 'Oh man,' he whispered. 'I waited *years* for this!' In a rich, Louis Armstrong baritone, he bellowed, '*Blow* dat thing, baby!'

* * *

When Evans returned, Warner's party had left – having an after-hours knees-up in some pub down East, probably. The babble and the crush had dwindled, there was room at the inn for a thirsty and puzzled traveller. The brass lingered; on to the stickies by now, he reckoned, and still in thrall to their star attraction. Even with his back turned, he could feel the warmth and animation seeping from their corner of the bar. All right for some.

He ordered one for the road and settled without pleasure on a blue velveteen stool. He didn't much care for hotels, chromium and formica, or drinking alone. On the other hand, Harrigan's message wanted a quiet brood, and a good stiff Scotch would oil the wheels. Swirling the tumbler, enjoying the muted jangle of ice, he tried to see some sense.

Once, he and Smythe had seemed booked for the upper levels in tandem. Personally and socially poles apart, they had worked together remarkably well. Aye, but things had changed a bit since then; what would a Chief Super want with the Basement Bungler?

'Mind if I join you?' A waft of perfume, a warm contralto carrying the faintest of rural echoes; this time, he knew, the intrusion would be more than welcome. In close-up, she was truly stunning – a sensual mouth, a delicate nose, high cheekbones and jade-green eyes he'd gladly drown in. He came to his feet, making no attempt to hide his admiration.

'You mean someone refused you?'

She smiled, dazzling but rueful. 'You'd be surprised.'

'Damn right I would!'

She waved casually at the now subdued group behind them. 'Take your pick, they said: so I did.'

'I bet you say that to all your leading men. What'll you have, girl?' He wasn't usually this free; she brought out the best in him. And every other male she met, no doubt.

She sat, poised and graceful, a thin-heeled gilt sandle swinging from her toes. The pearls at her throat were real. So, clearly, was everything under the dress; and the gold bracelet she wore. Darro, breathed a mean Welsh voice in his mind, this'll cost a gin and tonic at least.

'Half of lager, please,' she said. 'Harp, if they've got it.'

Seeing his astonishment, she added, 'Too many liqueurs – I need something clean and cold.'

The drink came and she swallowed gratefully.

'Ah, that's good.' Watching him steadily, she confessed, 'I'm a freelance journalist. Don't panic, I won't bite.' A sudden, impish grin. 'Not till I know you better, anyway. I'm doing a piece on policework; human interest stuff.' She made quotation marks with her fingers. Strong hands, he noticed, ringless and well-shaped and no nail-varnish. Striking an attitude, mocking herself, she intoned, 'Beneath this bold and rugged exterior, there beats a heart of . . . *you* know.' Evans knew, well enough. The bird of paradise turns out to be a lady ferret; bloody typical.

'I'm a rugby man,' he grunted. 'Tippin' Neath for the Welsh cup.'

A touch of frost had crept into her smile. 'Ask someone else, is that it, Inspector?'

'It isn't easy, believe me.'

She was twisting her glass on the polished surface, watching the froth sway forward and back. The huge room had gone very quiet; it might have been just the two of them. 'I meant what I said,' she assured him, intent and lovely with it. She inclined her head towards the officers' mess, and the deep red highlights glinted. 'The high priests gave me carte blanche; I've set my sights on you.' She took another sip of lager, her long white throat rippling gently. Then, leaning forward, her face close and concerned, she asked, 'Does the shoulder still hurt?'

He reached for the spot instinctively. 'Only when I laugh.'

'Perfect,' she said. 'That's exactly what I want. The scars you carry, the prices you pay, the things you don't talk about.'

For the moment, at least, she had placed him at the centre of her universe – and very nice too. The media, mind; walk soft, boyo.

'No tape-recorders,' she coaxed him, 'no loaded questions, and you can read everything before I submit.'

Now, *there's* a promise, he thought; the submission, not the reading. He didn't say it, though.

She shook her head reproachfully. 'My, Inspector, you *are* hard to get!'

'Not me lovely; *you'd* be surprised.'

Their eyes met. Briefly, there was something electric between them, something which went way beyond mutual professional curiosity. Steady, bach, keep your fantasies under control. It warmed him, all the same, and his resolve wavered.

'There's a code, see,' he told her gently. 'It comes with the badge. Beware of face values, get things on paper and *never* talk to the press.'

Her green eyes sparkled with genuine humour. 'That's really funny – it's *our* code, too!' She set her glass down. Gravely and deliberately, she reached out and laid her hand over his. '*Please!* This is very important to me.' Her skin was cool, but the contact burned him. She showed the naked, vulnerable appeal against which he'd always felt powerful. 'I'll think about it,' he mumbled huskily; and basked in the brilliance of her smile.

Though she'd released his hand, the air of intimacy lingered, curling around them like incense. She spoke of deadlines and deviousness and the problem of lecherous editors as to a close and trusted friend; more than once, her caressing sidelong glance sent a surge of pleasure through his veins.

She managed her withdrawal beautifully, too. Coming to her feet in a single, flowing movement, looking and sounding as if she meant it, she said, 'Sorry, I must dash; and you've hardly touched your drink.' The glass stood abandoned, three-quarters full and beaded with condensation. He shrugged sheepishly and she offered an embossed card. 'Call me, please, when you're ready to talk.'

Again, the subtle tingle as their fingers touched; then she was gone, moving like royalty across the hushed hall, clearly conscious of greedy male eyes and not giving a damn. Jane Neale, he read, Investigative Reporter: and grinned at the irony. Plain Jane, duw duw. Flat and tepid as it was, whisky and soda had seldom tasted better.

CHAPTER FOUR

Saturday, the morning after, sweltering but subdued. The nick was funereal; grievous glances, stricken tones, and the sweet morbid whiff of pickling. What d'you expect, thought Evans smugly, from chateau pis de chat?

Beddoes was already seated, wearing faded denims and a conspirator's grin. 'Look who's 'ere, then; behold a dark 'orse!'

'Book learning, is it? Dunno what you're on about.'

'Oh yeah? Only ended up with the tastiest dish on the menu, I hear. And it shows, uncle, no question.'

'Business, it was, mind.'

'Professional, is she? Must've cost a mint.'

'Fat chance, boyo. All for free love, I am. And where were *you* off to, straight after the Queen?'

'After a queen, *me*?' Beddoes spread his hands, the picture of innocence. 'She fancied the early night, okay?'

'And early to rise, no doubt.'

'I do me best, mate.'

'And it shows,' retorted Evans, tilting his chin at the strew of papers on the desk.

Beddoes sighed. 'Join the Old Bill,' he suggested. 'Fight crime with a biro.'

All at once, it was just the basement; hot, dingy and devoid of inspiration.

'I'm snookered,' Evans confessed. 'Old Jim was Irish and he was there – end of story.'

'Theory's holdin' up, then?'

'Aye. By default.'

Beddoes lounged in the chair, hands behind his head and dark damp patches under his arms. 'Ever see *Psycho*?' he asked. 'Eyewhites gleaming in the dark, waiting for the next bit of madness; fear in the air like sour milk and not a whisper to be 'eard?' He waved at the open doorway, his sharp features shadowed and bitter. 'That's 'ow it is, out there. They're petrified, uncle, wise monkeys'll tell you more. On *our* turf, right? Bastards!'

'Easy, Roy. When the highroad's blocked, you go the pretty way.'

'Huh?'

'Weirdos, you say. Don't know who told you and I won't ask. So we pull 'em and sweat 'em. Druggies and drop-outs, see, no need to invent charges. Call it a clean-up, shall we?' As a rueful afterthought, Evans added, 'Time we can't afford, though.'

He actually saw Beddoes ignite; the stiffening of resolve and sinew, and a predatory glow in the dark eyes.

''Ang about, I've had a thought. Somethin' else you weren't in on.' He brought out his notebook, riffling pages briskly and loudly. 'There's this toff. You know – we're worried sick about young 'Arry.' He was bubbling now, into overdrive again. 'The pretty way,' he repeated happily. '*Nice* one.' And blinked at the sudden squall of the telephone. 'Sod it,' he snapped, lifting the receiver. 'Sorry, not you.' He listened; nodding; then, 'Be right there.'

Cradling the handset and coming swiftly to his feet, he explained, 'The new deskman, Wassaname. The Laird requests our presence, immediately or before.' His enthusiasm was catching; Evans found himself hurrying to keep up.

'This time,' Beddoes promised, 'He'll get something to chew on.'

Chewed out, they were, and the door scarcely closed behind them; not even invited to take it sitting down. Padding the sun-striped carpet like a caged ginger bear, McKay launched a swinging assault. 'Boobies,' he growled, 'Armageddon looming, and I'm stuck wi' a pair o' boobies!'

He drew himself up, aiming a stubby finger somewhere between them. 'Call yerselves detectives? Och, ye couldnae detect farts in a florist's! An entire week, and what do I get?' He stormed to the desk and thumped the slender casefile with his hairy paw. 'Trivia, that's whut! No sightings, no patterns, nothing to report.'

'Give over, guv,' Beddoes pleaded. 'We just came up with a handy little lead.'

McKay's diamond-blue fury was awesome. 'A *lead*? Ye puir dumb fool, no but a *pinch* can save us!'

Though he stood like a guardsman, fingers down the seams of his jeans, Beddoes was struggling to hide a smile. Getting used to Jock's little tantrums, no doubt; too soon. Beneath the thickening Scottish rasp, Evans caught a rare note of genuine distress – and felt the first chill breath of premonition.

'Funnies,' snarled the Super, in utter contempt. 'Pale wee men in bowler hats, watering the whusky and pansying around in *my* manor. Affairs of state, d'ye ken, not to be entrusted to mere working bobbies.' He rounded on Beddoes, and twin red spots blazed on his craggy cheeks. 'Hands off, ye'll kindly observe; let's see ye smirk about *that*!'

'They *can't*!' breathed Beddoes, haggard and chalky. ''Armless, Old Jim was, and cut down in the streets. That's *our* business; for Chrissake tell 'em, sir!'

It won't wash, thought Evans grimly, you can't fight the Funnies. A short ruddy figure in the lambent glare, McKay made it official. Holding the corner of a single typewritten sheet disdainfully between thumb and finger, he raised his eyebrows and invited them to read.

'Don't bother, boyo,' Evans murmured. 'It's only the white flag.'

'Aye,' said McKay, dangerously soft, 'and signed by the Commissioner himself.' Slowly, almost unconsciously, his left hand came up and he shifted his grip on the document. Evans could've sworn he saw the tendons flicker and the tearing motion begin. 'Weak-kneed, overbred, puling, *Sassenach* as he is!' A nasty bugger, McKay, but you couldn't doubt his instincts.

The fair eyelashes flickered and his gaze cleared. 'These are *orders*,' he warned. 'Mind them well. Ye'll repeat what ye've seen and heard this day to no one. Ye'll forget yon Cavanaugh and all his heathen disciples, and ye'll repair to the basement *forth*with. Do I make meself perfectly clear?'

Evans turned, conscious of heat on his neck and acid despair in his belly.

At the doorway, Beddoes halted, casting a taut and curiously defiant glance behind. 'Chief? Permission to continue a missing person investigation?'

'Investigate? So far as I'm con*cerned*, laddie, ye've just *become* a missing person!'

They trudged, side by side and downwards, through pools of filtered yellow sunlight.

'Summer hols,' said Evans. 'There's lovely. What's this about a missing person?'

Beddoes laid a warning finger beside his nose. 'You 'eard the man; don't ask.' He had that look, the one he wore for judo and shooting practice; mean and inward and steely.

'Watch your step, then. It's dodgy, just now, private enterprise.'

They had reached the staircase, and Beddoes eyed it resentfully. 'I'll take my chances, mate. I'm going out.' And he strode off, his thick-soled trainers squeaking on the dusty floor.

Back in solitary, Evans sank onto his chair, ran a finger round his clinging collar and surveyed his meagre crop of files dismally. Shysters and shoplifting, exciting. Amazing how quickly things changed — from cloud nine to ground zero in two hours flat. What *you* want, bach, is a pick-me-up; small but nicely packed, with green eyes and auburn hair.

As he scoured his battered wallet for her card, a scrap of lined paper fluttered tiredly to the desk. A blurred blue-figured scrawl; and Harrigan's rich brown voice echoed in his mind. *'You'll be needing help — you'll know it when it happens.'* Too late now. Smythe might have made a few steps up the ladder, and he's always fancied a crack at the IRA; but even he would be impotent in 'affairs of state'. The 'help' would doubtless involve a roasting — be a good boy or else.

Evans hunched forward, studying the slip more closely. Home and office listings, mind; Smythe was leaving nothing to chance. Forget it, boyo. It's lunchtime, Saturday; put pleasure before business for once. He lifted the receiver, fully intending to call Jane; and found himself dialling Smythe's number.

The ringing burr ended abruptly; two beeps and just the single word 'Yes?'

Typical, this. Clipped and concise and inquisitorial, a voice which took command for granted. Evans sighed and gave his name.

'About time, too. I'm at home, remember, speaking *en clair*.'

'Come again?'

'Guard your tongue, man, we're not scrambled.'

'Could've fooled me.'

The faint hiss of irritation carried clearly. Smythe didn't care for humour, especially from subordinates. He wasn't above a sarky retort, though. 'Not a great distinction, these days.' His tone mellowed, sounding almost nostalgic. 'You remember my obsession?'

A preoccupation with Paddies, he meant. Evans remembered all right.

'Does 12 October 1984 ring any bells?'

Duw duw, guessing games, thought Evans, trapping the mouthpiece under his chin and wiping a greasy palm on his trousers. 'Not specially. Should it?'

'A watershed,' Smythe declared, with the deign of a man vindicated. 'Our demented Irish brethren came within an ace of wiping out the entire Cabinet.'

Aye, of course; the Brighton bombing. The eve of the Tory Conference, and their seaside hotel blasted apart.

'I am no longer a voice in the wilderness,' Smythe proclaimed, 'but the one true prophet of salvation. My reward is charge of a special unit committed to the prevention of such outrages in the future.'

'Power to your elbow,' Evans muttered, staring blankly at a flaky patch on the wall.

'I've been checking up,' Smythe went on blithely. 'Still in the basement, I hear, and no silver lining in sight. Unattached, too, formally or otherwise.'

Evans sat up, stung. 'Here, steady on!'

'I have to be *very* careful in that direction. You're available, then; and you have the prerequisite qualities.'

Evans was aware of sweat and stillness and the pound of blood in his temples. A glimmer of hope, after all;

64

tread soft, bach. Cautiously, he asked, 'And what qualities might they be, sir?'

'Dedication, courage, resourcefulness and discretion.' Smythe was quoting, obviously. 'And the greatest of these is discretion. Incidentally, the scenario calls for two people. Sound out Beddoes, would you?'

'Oh sure. What do I offer, a one-way ticket to Dublin?'

The humming silence turned positively glacial. 'I warned you once; an open line! For God's sake, use a bit of common!'

You could actually hear him swallow the rage and try for a more reasoned approach. 'We've said too much already; I wouldn't have thought either of you needed much persuasion. Neither should you fear "random reprisals". The parties concerned are under constant surveillance.'

Harrigan, thought Evans suddenly, in his extravagant gear, out there tracking the hitmen through hippieland.

'Oh aye?' he murmured. 'The messenger, I presume.'

Another silence; then a note of grudging respect. 'Hmm, you *do* still function. Good. I'll expect you on Tuesday at ten.' He rattled off a totally unfamiliar address and hung up, just like that.

Evans replaced the slippery receiver, very thoughtful indeed. Ought to feel flattered, really. Smythe had demonstrated influence over the top brass, a firm grip on the anti-Paddy mob and an uncanny fund of information. Apparently he even knew of Megan's defection. What was it she'd said – *Where will I get a better offer?* Good question.

On the other hand, Evans didn't care for the implications of being 'courageous, available and unattached'. Sounded like a want ad for kamikaze pilots. Secondment would be dodgy, too, winning precious few housemarks from McKay. Hard to imagine being any lower in *his* estimation, mind. Evans shook his head, conscious as never before of the drabness of his office and the futility of his work. When you live in the basement, *any* way out is up . . .

Sandwiched between TV Test Match coverage and a welcome lunchtime pint, Beddoes made two short but productive phone calls. From the proprietor of the disco favoured by Dot's neolithic husband, he bullied the name of Gerry Jewell's manager. Astonishingly, the number appeared in the Yellow Pages under 'Impresarios'. To the background rumble of a busy pub, Beddoes made his pitch.

'Who wants to know?' asked an oily suspicious voice.

'Barney Ringwood, BBC,' said Beddoes promptly, naming a minor showbiz acquaintance. 'Checking the talent for a new off-peak slot.'

The manager's manner shifted to instant deference. 'You made the right choice, Mr Ringwood, sir. Star quality, that boy.' After which it was easy as pie to extract forthcoming engagements. 'He's at the Sombrero tonight, up East. Why don't I meet you there?'

'No hurry, squire,' Beddoes told him. 'I'll call *you*, okay?' And hung up, smiling.

Back at the nick, Evans looked about as chirpy as a damp dishrag.

''Eard the latest score?' Beddoes enquired. ''Alf a dozen specks in the Caribbean and they're set to black-wash us again.'

'Cricket!' Evans snorted. 'An ordeal, not a game. Dead slow.'

'You oughta try facin' Big Bird.'

'That's what I mean, see. Daft names, it's like the Black and White Minstrels.'

66

''Ow about Wimbledon, then?'

'Tie-breaks, tantrums and tartan bloomers; bloody showbiz, mun!'

'So what do *you* do in summer, uncle, while the miners are 'ibernating and Rugby's just a village in the Midlands?'

'Bit of fishing, when I get the chance.'

'Stroll on, 'ark at it! Cricket's too slow, 'e says, *I* go fishin'. How does yer 'eart stand the strain?'

Evans eased back in his chair, his broad forehead creased and glistening. 'You're a troglodyte, Roy; set foot outside the city and you'll die of ozone poisoning. Can't beat peace and quiet and a nice stretch of river.' He grimaced ruefully. 'At least, I think so; been a long time.' He pushed a file aside and clipped the pen into his breast pocket. 'Darro, it's warm. Roll on the football season.'

'Civilized blokes call it soccer.'

'Never. Mutually exclusive, mind, civilization and soccer.' Evans was watching his partner, calm and composed, and a foxy gleam in the pale blue eyes. Not nearly as glum as he ought to be, then. 'Chief Superintendent Smythe was asking after you,' he said.

'Terrific. Told 'im I'm in the pink, did yer, lapping up the low life?'

'Tell him yourself if you want. We're due for a visit, Tuesday. He's after recruits, it seems; for Cavanaugh's war.'

The first good news for a week, a chance to nail Old Jim's killer. But though he stalked the stuffy cell and hurled questions like grenades, Beddoes could make no impression. Stolid and unyielding in his grey shirtsleeves, Evans sat firm and kept mum. 'Leave it there, boyo, you know as much as I do.'

Which was enough to save the weekend, Beddoes reckoned, leaving early and seeking WPC Parrot. A touch of the dancing shoes tonight, and maybe a second string to the bow.

But Pol, looking worn and flustered as she crossed the long shadows of the car park, was having none of it.

'Sorry, Sarge. Gotta wash my hair.'

'It'll dry in a jiff,' he coaxed, nodding at the lowering sun. 'A disco, mind you, the late late show. Say about ten?'

'No way,' she snapped. Remember the *last* late show?' And flounced off without a backward glance. All right, girl, he thought, if that's the way you want it; I'll go anyhow . . .

Jailbait, thought Beddoes, watching Harriet Slade's antics from the bar. An awful lot of sixteen-year-old jiggling beneath the blouse, and the skintight leather jeans were an open invitation to child abuse. Despite the disguise of the day – spiky black cockscomb and green mascara – he'd picked her out at once. Flushed with excitement, her painted face alive in the intermittent rainbow glare, she *was* prettier than your average Sombrero scrubber.

Sipping flat and exorbitant beer, he cowered under the next assault on his eardrums. Gerry Jewell suited the joint to a tee; overloud, overdecorated and utterly devoid of tone. Didn't seem to bother the punters. So long as the groupies squealed and the strobes wobbled and the beat played on, they'd be up there, prancing. It's down to the drummer, he realized; a spaced-out black in purple shades and a golden gown who looked like Baron Samedi and riffled the skins like an angel. Somehow, he nursed them through their set and got them to finish at more or less the same time. The lights came up, revealing the place in all its tawdriness, and a tinny voice announced 'your very own topflight DJ'.

The groupies checked in mid-spasm, milled around

uncertainly, then gathered and charged the bar as solid and frenzied as the Light Brigade. Beddoes nipped smartly aside, fading into a dim corner and keeping the target in sight.

Isolated, she gazed forlornly at the darkened stage. Presently the superstar himself appeared, tasselled and tousled and moving with the tell-tale spastic twitch of the heavy user. Her face lit up; and he lurched straight past, grinning vacantly. He slumped on a wallside bench, legs thrust forward, sweat-soaked hair hanging back. His eyes flickered and closed and his upturned face had the colour and sheen of putty. The idol at rest, and his fan beside him soft and still as intensive care. Poor little Harry.

At least the DJ had taste – Diana Ross, no less. High noon, Roy my son, time to make a move. He *looked* the part, no question – black leather jacket, ruched white shirt, silver buckled belt and Cuban heels – your East End cowboy to the life.

'Hi, gorgeous,' he said, jerking his thumb at the half-empty floor. ''Ow about it?'

She started and turned, her cherry-red lips curled for the instant brush-off.

He spread his hands and gave her his most affecting grin. 'No guns, honest. Go on, 'e won't even miss yer.'

The Jewell was snoring wetly, and she couldn't hide her bitterness.

'I'm sure you're right. Why not?'

Close to, the illusion of maturity vanished. She was anxious and gawky, off beat and out of step. Keeping it deadpan, hoping she'd seen the right movies, he asked, 'Come 'ere often, do you?'

'I'm with the band,' she admitted, and there might have been the ghost of a smile. 'If you can call it that.'

'Yeah. More my style, this is.' He manoeuvred a little

nearer. Under the filmy blouse, her body felt cold and tense. 'Yer not local, are yer? I mean, talkin' like that?' He was coming the heavy cockney, trying her out; and she reacted like the spoilt child she'd been.

'Is there anything *wrong* with speaking correctly?'

'Course not. Like a touch of class, I do.' Bad timing. Diana faded, and Harriet looked set to follow. Lionel Ritchie saved the day, smooth and creamy and 'Stuck on You'.

'Oh,' she breathed wistfully, 'I *love* this one!'

'Relax, girl,' he advised her, 'let the music take you. With this guy, *nobody* can go wrong.' He brought her to him gently, gazing deep into her suddenly trusting blue eyes as if she were the only girl on earth. Which, in a curious way, she was. He sensed her growing confidence and added an occasional flourish. By the time it ended, she had nestled into his shoulder, eyes closed; and followed his lead as to the manner born. 'Thank you,' she murmured, 'it was *super*.' Her voice trembled, and he saw bright tears in her eyes.

''Ere, what's wrong?'

'Nothing. My da . . . my father and I used to do that, sometimes.' She blinked and straightened. 'He's dead now.'

'I'm sorry.'

'I'm not.'

The DJ was in a groove – 'Endless Love', yet.

'Again?' he asked; and realized he'd lost her. She stood rigid and pale beneath the make-up, staring across the now-crowded floor.

Following her narrow gaze, he made out a tall bearded figure lounging near the exit and eyeing her greedily. She drew herself up, thrust out her breasts and wove between the dancers with a sexuality way beyond her years. When Beddoes looked again, the shadow had gone. A minder, maybe, hired to see off the lechers? A lot of 'em about, lately.

From his post at the bar, Beddoes watched her chivvy the singer into some kind of wakefulness. The second set started no better than the first, but she was straight in there, chucking herself about like a Dervish. A loyal kid, Harry, and closer to her old man than she let on; but a fair way out of her depth. Alive and well, all the same, and living in Weirdoland. Speaking of which, he'd had a gutful of glitter and heavy metal. Contact established, time to go home.

Not quite a write-off, he mused, outside in blessed peace and darkness. If worst comes to worst, we've got a bit of insurance, Tuesday.

She wore a simple pale green shift which set off the bronze of her hair and the tawny highlights in her eyes. A breathless summer eve, a modish restaurant overlooking the river, but her entry provoked one of those hungry silences which have nothing to do with food. Go ahead lads, suffer, Evans thought. Just for tonight, she's mine.

He'd phoned her on impulse, immediately after Smythe. Intuition told him it was now or never. Intrigue on the wind, no telling where he'd be next week, she might not pass this way again. There had been a short, pleasant haggle about the when and where. In the end he'd settled for Sunday at Mario's and bugger the expense.

'Oh *good*,' she'd purred. 'I'm crazy for Italian food.'

Rightly, as it turned out. Visibly blooming under her attentions, the soulful latinate waiter had served them promptly; her expert choice of dishes did the rest. Just as well he'd dressed for the occasion – dark slacks, navy blazer, pale blue shirt and his police rugby tie. Hardly Savile Row, mind, but passable. When you took the likes

71

of Jane Neale to dinner, you'd better be ready for public scrutiny.

Overwhelmed by her presence, trotting out smalltalk he never knew he owned, Evans let the fantasy take hold; a night on the town with his woman. Something in her manner, the glow in her eyes and the way she leaned towards him, suggested she was prepared to share the illusion.

It had to end, of course. She pushed her dish aside and smiled, rueful and appealing. 'Thank you, that was delicious; and I'm afraid the bell has tolled.'

He watched her muster concentration, saw the professional stir behind the mask.

'You're a career policeman, forty-two and divorced. I've been doing my homework; sorry.'

'No need, it's history. Something that didn't work out. Wedded to the Force, I am.'

A smooth operator, our Jane, backing off at once and hunting safer ground. 'They told me that, too. A good man, they said, destined for higher things. Suddenly, you were in the news; twice in so many years.'

He sipped his coffee, conscious of that special continental tang and the unlikely tenderness of her gaze. She'd done it again. The lap of the river and the buzz of conversation faded; it was just the two of them, and the flicker of candles.

'We handle trouble every day. Bound to get your name in the papers if you're at it long enough. Meat and drink to *your* lot, I know.'

'My lot,' she echoed wryly. 'How can I convince you I'm on your side?'

'You could tell me a bit about yourself, for openers.' Her discomfort looked wholly spontaneous.

'Gosh, how silly! You've no idea, have you?'

The waiter was hovering and Evans beckoned him.

'We'll be a while yet, boyo. I'll call you, all right?' He bowed and left, his spaniel eyes at once pained and resentful.

'Poor little man,' she said. 'He has a gentle face.'

'And big ears.'

She gave him an appreciative glance and a graceful, open-handed gesture. 'I am what you see. Spoilt and single, and cursed with money, talent and good looks.'

'And modest with it.'

An urchin's grin, a deliberately affected mien. 'A country girl, but *very* genteel. I was born to the hunt, raised in the farmyard, convent-educated and finished in the *most* exalted places.' It rang true. Just listening, you could smell the fertile acres, see the discreet gleam of crystal and fine silver and imagine the queue of Hooray Henries panting in her wake.

'No rings,' he said flatly. 'No encumbrances. Hard to believe, considering.'

'Wow,' she breathed. 'You don't fool around, do you?'

'I like to start even, see.'

She toyed with her wine glass, twisting the stem and watching candlelight turn in the ruby liquid. 'All right, Inspector, I confess. There were droves of boys and one or two men. But they only wanted a pretty face to grace their tables, a clear mind to run their households and a healthy body to bear their young.'

He leaned forward, offering his open admiration. 'Hard to blame 'em, I'd say.' But for once, he won no answering warmth.

'For me, it's not enough. I found out late, but in time. I'm wedded too, you see; to the cause.'

'Oh aye? What cause is that?'

'Justice and truth.'

Just for a moment, her loveliness set harsh and pure;

a totally unexpected fervour. Go careful, bach, it's the crusaders you need to watch.

'Well,' he grunted, 'something else we have in common.'

It brought her back, soft and attentive once more.

'Yes, and it's your turn. Tell me about Grace Yardley.'

It *was* his turn; to waggle the spoon in his coffee, to observe the burnished sunset on the river outside, to buy time and measure words.

'*Bereaved*, she was,' he explained, 'alone and desperate. The meaning for living ripped away and no one to pay the price. I only looked out for her. Anyone would.'

'Not anyone. Especially not any policeman.'

He shrugged, slipping back under her spell. 'It wasn't professional, no one had to tell me. Sometimes, you do what's right, whatever. Understand that, do you?'

'Oh *yes*!' The improbable urgency again; he believed her.

A pause while she poured more coffee. Briefly, the world beyond intruded; a braying laugh, the glint of cutlery, a rich whiff of cigars. Then she set her cup down and asked an odd question.

'Do you know what became of her?'

'Oh sure. Married Mr Right and went off to the wily orient. Singapore, was it?'

'Hong Kong.' For the first time, she wouldn't meet his eye. 'It didn't take. There's divorce and scandal in the air, it seems. She's very attractive; I've seen the clips.' Glancing up, seeing his expression, she added, 'My colleagues can be insufferable; I'm sorry.'

Me too, girl, he thought, shaken to the core. He cleared his throat, getting over it by sheer force of will.

'They can be mistaken, too, often as not. She wouldn't do it, not Grace. No way.' Astonished, he felt her hand on his arm and looked into green eyes swimming with sympathy.

74

'You're very loyal. I envy her.' An admission to savour, really, even in his misery. As if reading the thought, she released him and resumed the delicate inquisition.

'You made headlines again, last year: cut down in the line of duty.' She only had to say it for the shoulder to ache.

'Routine,' he mumbled. 'Just bad luck.'

'That's not what I heard.' She was pleading, and the soft light worked its magic. Irresistible, really.

'Basically,' he conceded, 'we got our sums wrong. The guy should never've been loose. One chance we had, see, to put things right.'

'So you went, unarmed, into a darkened building after a psychopath with a meat-axe?'

'Aye, we all have our moments. Not too clever, was it?'

'Clever?' she repeated wonderingly. 'What a strange man you are! Didn't it touch you at all, the talk of dedication and heroism? Didn't you read the papers?'

'*Papers!*'

'Oh dear,' she said, in a mischievous and mock dismay, 'we seem to be back at square one.'

But they weren't, not by a very long chalk. In fifteen years, not even Megan had watched him like this; the plain declaration of a very pretty intent.

'It's been lovely, Huw. Can we walk for a while?'

'There's a danger, mind, on the streets at night.'

'With you, I'll risk it.'

He paid the horrendous bill without a flinch, and tipped the reproachful waiter lavishly. It's only money, cheap at double the price. Outside it was mild and balmy, and the river lay like frosted glass under a quarter moon.

'Interrogation over?' he enquired, and her teeth flashed in the dimness.

'Just beginning, I'd say.' But she wouldn't let him take her home.

Quite right, he thought, and quite clever too. If she meant what her eyes suggested, it would keep. If she was merely chasing a story, she'd get nothing from him in bed. Nothing you'd write about, anyway.

CHAPTER FIVE

She lay in expectant shadow awaiting the Voice. Throughout the sultry weekend, she'd flaunted near-nakedness and her last dab of perfume under his hot dark stare. Now, while the commune sank into drugged slumber, her skin tingled and her juices stirred at the very thought of his touch. She was as ready as she'd ever been.

Even so, he took her unawares; big as he was, he made less noise than the rats. Suddenly, he was there, a shaggy outline etched on the ribbon of moonlight between the sleeping ranks. He crouched, and she caught her breath; the heady whiff of tobacco and aroused male. Awed, she watched him cradle Gerry's inert form effortlessly and pad away into the darkness. A muffled thump, an audible grunt of disgust; then bony knees were prising her apart, and his beard scraped the soft flesh beneath her ear. He entered her, every bit as fierce and quick as Eric or Gerry, only heavier and stronger. His body arched and quivered, and his smooth buttocks clenched under her eager hands. Looking upward, trying to match his rhythm, she watched the tendons in his neck fill and writhe like ivory snakes. Inside her, there was a fiery eruption. His mouth stretched in a wide but soundless cry; pale light gleamed on exposed teeth and single silvered thread of saliva. Slowly, the rigour left him. His head hung, and a fat droplet of perspiration splattered on her cheek.

'Bless you, girlie,' he gasped. 'There was a terrible need for that.'

The floorboards groaned as he twisted free and collapsed at her side. He left one limp arm draped across her belly; gradually, his breathing steadied.

Captive but alone, drowning in the essence of stale hash and loveless sex, she faced darkness and a stark, pervasive fear. This was a man, not a boy, yet he'd left her aching and unfulfilled. Perhaps, after all, Gerry had been right to call her a 'frigid little lessie'.

She wasn't quite sure how it happened; somehow, the Voice's hand found its way to her face.

'Here now,' he rumbled, the brogue thick and sleepy, 'and why would Her Holiness weep, I wonder?' There was no concern in the question, only curiosity; she didn't bother to answer. 'If the Dear had meant ye for the convent, he'd never've built ye like that. And is it a virgin ye were, then?'

'Certainly not,' she snapped, and his laughter fell soft and mocking.

'Indeed. It'll not be gratitude either, I'm thinking.'

'Hardly!'

A creak and a rustle, and a bare shoulder gleaming as he heaved himself up on one elbow. 'How old are ye, Harry?'

'I'm sixt . . . old enough!'

'*Big* enough, to be sure. Ah me, sweet sixteen and never been rightly screwed.' He was edging closer, and she didn't want to know.

'Leave me alone. I'm tired.'

'And how can I, when one good turn deserves another?'

She was wise enough not to resist as his long body moulded to her again. Beneath his scalding flesh, she sensed the coldness of him. He was crude and ruthless

78

and dangerous, and she'd challenged his macho pride; otherwise he'd've been asleep already. Yet even knowledge held a germ of excitement. There was a strength and a certainty about him, an air of absolute self-confidence which had drawn her to him in the first place. He's the sort of man, she thought light-headedly, who would thumb his nose at death – and live to tell the tale. In spite of everything, he was bringing *her* to life once more.

Don't respond, she warned herself, it's just technique. But under his hard and accomplished hands, her body had taken a will of its own. Her limbs felt weak and languid; she sighed and surrendered as he drew the resistance out of her. Arching her back, she pressed her nipples against his palms; through half-closed eyes, she saw the cruel enjoyment in his bearded, shadowed face. The mean and sordid room retreated. Soon, she was lost in the play of light on sculpted muscle, the overpowering scent of his want and the mounting urgency of her own pleasure.

This time, his entry was slow and smooth and lingering and the silky friction made her gasp in delight. His beard caressed her throat and the raw power in his voice destroyed the last of her restraint. 'Spread yourself out, little girl, for there's more where that came from!'

She obeyed him joyfully, bucking and moaning and urging him deeper within.

Suddenly it was happening, a slow ripple of ecstasy which began at the secret centre and flowed like molten lava along every nerve in her body. She was vaguely aware of her own astonished cry and his sinewy hand covering her mouth. Then she was floating weightless and delirious while spasms surged at his beautiful pulsing hardness; and he reached a second explosive release.

'My God,' she whispered in grateful wonder, 'I didn't know!'

'You're not bad, girlie; for a beginner.'

'For Chrissake,' whined a male voice from the shadows, 'there's people trying to kip!'

'Is that so,' he retorted, rolling off her and coming to his feet in a single cat-like movement. 'Perhaps ye'd care to make it permanent?'

'Oh, it's you. No offence, man.' He stood above her, pale and taut and proud by moonlight, and her stomach turned over. If she never saw him again, she'd carry this image to the grave. He glanced coolly on her sprawled and quivering nakedness and his hand rose in a casual, American-style salute.

'I thank ye, Miss Slade. I'll be holding the advanced course whenever you've a mind.' Then he was gone, as swiftly and silently as he'd appeared.

She pulled the rumpled sheet around her. The world may have changed, but this was still the commune, where nudity might be taken for invitation. Weariness smothered her, but her mind dwelt on the discovery of the moment and the key to past mysteries. Mummy didn't know the secret, or she would never speak of sex like that. Poor Father, no wonder he'd gone ga-ga over his tarty secretary.

She smiled in the dark, remembering what the Voice had done and said.

The quest is ended, she realized, the hidden has been made clear. The accusing glares of older girls, the deputy-head's fury, and Gerry's petulant cry; all was envy, the impotent longing of those less favoured than herself. The knowledge freed her; she could leave tomorrow if she chose.

Yet in spite of the misery and squalor, his presence

lingered around and inside her. There'd never be anything tender between them; soon, she knew, he'd go away. Until then, perhaps she'd stay. Balanced at the very edge of sleep, she smiled again; wryly. She still didn't know his name . . .

'You're late,' Smythe greeted them, tapping his wristwatch. 'Four minutes late, to be precise.' There's sociable; two years since they'd met, mind.

'Aye. Had a bit of trouble finding you.'

'Well, that's *one* excuse you'll not be able to use again.' A stickler, the Chief Superintendent, of sinewy build and military caste. He shoved papers across the rosewood desk, eyeing Beddoes' casual clothing distastefully. 'Sign, would you.' He hadn't changed, then; the same economy of word and gesture, the same inborn arrogance. Best read the small print, bach.

Mumbo-jumbo, it was, of the secret variety. 'I Huw Dafyd Evans do hereby pledge not to reveal any information regarding casefile 84/MD/65 to unauthorized personnel. I understand that breach of this agreement may render me subject to disciplinary action and/or criminal proceedings. Given under my hand . . .' Not quite watertight, but it made Evans uneasy.

Beddoes, too, it seemed. 'Beg pardon, Chief: *what* information?'

Sitting severely in a crisp white shirt and a yellow cravat, Smythe looked younger and fitter than ever. A touch more silver at the temples, maybe, but a good high colour and an alert grey gaze. Comes with promotion, see, a new lease of life. Which made nonsense of his opening declaration.

'I'm tired, Sergeant; tired of swabbing English blood off the walls and turning the other cheek. We're taking

81

the offensive, courtesy of the Reapers. The start of a mainland campaign, obviously, the ideal moment for a pre-emptive strike.' He nodded at the documents. 'We have the will, the strategy and a green light. It only lacks for troops.'

Stirring stuff. The trouble with bugles, Evans reflected, is they always end up playing the Last Post.

Beddoes looked positively hawklike, his sharp nose lifting to the whiff of combat; but even he knew when to stall. 'I dunno, sir. A man's got to think of his career.'

Smythe leaned back, hefting a purple chunk of onyx in one neat hand. His former talisman had been butterflies in perspex; must've worn that one out. 'Your present prospects are bleak, I'd say.' He fingered the paperweight absently, watching the play of sunlight. 'I won't deny the hazards. Success, however, could open numerous doors.'

'Maybe,' Beddoes conceded, 'but only mugs sign blind.'

Well done, Evans thought, someone had to say it.

Briefly, Smythe's prim mouth set tight; then, surprisingly, curved into a conciliatory smile. 'In the circumstances, we can afford to lift a few more veils. Follow me.' And he was up, ramrod straight and marching to the door.

They trailed his spruce figure along spotless air-conditioned passages overlooking a shaded green quadrangle. Through a series of half-open doors, Evans glimpsed pale blue carpeting and executive chairs, and caught the hum of electronic gadgetry. The air smelled of lavender and quiet industry. Smythe *had* come up in the world; a tidy little empire. 'Gordon Bennet,' Beddoes muttered, 'a designer cop-shop already.' And that was *before* he saw the cinema.

Smythe called it the 'private screening facility' and

operated the projector himself 'in the interests of security'.

'Probably sells ices, too,' breathed Beddoes, dropping into a beige tip-up seat. But Evans had seen the slides pre-loaded and ready to roll; which meant they were expected, like it or not.

The lights dimmed. At first there was just the whir of the fan, a shimmer of dust in the beam and shapeless brown blobs on the screen. A press-button, remote-control job, you could tell by the finite little leaps into focus. Gradually, figures and features and a background emerged: a school photo from long ago. Basin haircuts, jug ears, shorts to the knees and baggy socks, and all embalmed in sepia under the loom of a misted hill.

'Somewhere in Eire,' Smythe told them; revealing, in three words, his contempt for an entire nation. 'The class of '65.' The picture blurred as he zoomed in on the right foreground and a dozen fixed stares only faintly more mature than the rest. 'Gentlemen,' he added softly, 'the target.' This time the change came quick and dizzying. The grainy close-up filled the screen.

It was just another boyish face, bloated by magnification. Craning backward from the sheer size of it, Evans glimpsed something which sent a prickle of anticipation down his spine. Some trick of the light put depth and passion into the eyes; a sense of tragic, brooding intelligence far beyond the compass of a child. The father of the man, he thought, grasping the cliché's meaning for the very first time. As he gazed, a second uneasy sentence took shape. One day, boyo, our paths will cross. There was no *reason*; yet he knew it, sure as eggs.

Beddoes broke the spell. 'It's a bleedin' awful mugshot. Did they get his dabs, too?'

'Many a true word,' said Smythe, very dry. 'The picture is twenty years old, the only known likeness. It would have saved much bloodshed, not to mention lives, if they *had* taken fingerprints. For a decade he has masterminded Provo terrorism.' In cool and flickering dimness, he allowed a showman's pause. 'His name is Sean Daly.' The image died and the lights blazed. Smythe stood before the blank screen, the loathing etched deep into his drawn and livid flesh. 'Upstairs,' he snapped, and they were off again. Darro, Evans thought, it's going to be an ugly little war. What price a contract that spells your name wrong?

'The Grand Old Duke of York,' hummed Beddoes to himself, following his leader up through the palace again. Any day now he'll march clean over the top. It isn't *natural*, wanting Chummy that bad; could endanger your health.

Back in control and his own territory, the Chief bade them sit and stalked to the bay window. Evans sighed like someone who'd seen the act before, and Beddoes took stock of the office.

Though smaller than McKay's gaff, it was a good bit further upmarket. Plain gold Axminster, wall-to-wall and shin deep, and the kind of dark wood furniture they don't make any more. The prints were classy, too. If they aren't Constables, Beddoes mused whimsically, they bleedin' well should be. Olde Worlde, then, glowing rich in the morning sun. Today intruded, all the same. From outside and below came the putter of a two-stroke engine and glimpses of a bare-chested boy on a motor-mower; whom it seemed, the Chief preferred to address.

'Daly has no official *rank*,' he murmured, as though the interruption hadn't happened. 'He's never mentioned in dispatches.' His tone hardened. 'A man who deals death from a distance and grants others the convictions of his courage.'

'Others like Cavanaugh, you mean?' Evans asked, and Smythe inclined his head.

'There are two of them. Cavanaugh and a bomber's apprentice called Joseph Duffy. Standard practice, we've found; on-the-job training. They are butchers – Daly's blunt instruments.'

'Sure of that, are you?' Evans sounded deceptively mild. 'Green Reapers, mind, and officially disowned.'

'Rubbish! It's the classic Irish approach, the hell difference does it make what they call themselves? They're on round-the-clock watch; I could pull them in tomorrow.'

'Aye,' agreed Evans, 'and frighten the game.' And received another appreciative nod.

'Exactly. This time, we'll follow them all the way home.'

A royal we, Beddoes observed, without pleasure.

Smythe's trim outline tilted towards the glass. 'Dear God,' he wondered plaintively, 'where do they find them these days?'

The mower had stopped and the scent of cut grass filtered in. Tarzan down there would be taking five, Beddoes reckoned, guzzling tea and ogling the birds. 'Breaktime, Chief,' he explained. 'It's down to the unions, okay?'

And Smythe finally turned. 'You demanded this lecture, Sergeant. I'll thank you to pay attention and take the cretinous smirk off your face!'

Beddoes recoiled; even Evans blinked and sat straighter.

'Good,' said Smythe, 'I'll begin.'

Parading the lush carpet, he sketched a portrait of perverse genius. Daly, he claimed, had planned every major outrage in the past ten years. Operating from an unknown Southern lair, he'd assembled a network of well-placed informers, a reputation of near-infallibility and the unswerving loyalty of the rank and file. His capture or elimination would reduce the organization to chaos.

'Elimination?' Evans queried; but the Chief was in full cry. Light at his back gave him added stature and a strange, almost holy radiance.

'His followers invest him with magic. He is fey, apparently, a leprechaun able to alter his form at will, the better to confound his enemies.' He spread his arms in a scornful arc. 'In truth, he is a psychopath whose monstrous exploits inflame a backward people.'

'Wanted, dead or alive,' Evans prompted, sandy and sarcastic in the sun. 'For murder and better morale.'

Smythe rounded on him, passing sentence in a single, chilling syllable. '*Yes!*'

He's a head-hunter, Beddoes realized, awed by the glittering, implacable stare; like that Jewish bloke, Simon Wassaname, who winkles Nazis out of Sambaland. Obsessed, they say. Glad 'e's on *our* side, someone's gotta do it. Jesus, he thought, in a flash of rare insight, maybe it takes one to catch one.

''Ang about, sir,' he blurted, 'you can't put a collar on your actual Paddy. Foreign country, innit?'

Smythe's crafty grin was no better than his fervour. 'If he could be – persuaded – into the border zone, I'm sure we can count on reinforcements. Don't look so shocked, it's been done before!'

'Smash and grab,' mourned Beddoes, 'and me an upholder of the law. You're not serious?'

But Smythe was. Back at the desk, he hitched up his cavalry twills, settled and collected that bleeding rock again.

'Cover,' he announced calmly, 'should be kept simple. Particularly for those unversed in deception.'

'Ta very much,' said Evans, flat and cold as Welsh slate; and was once more ignored.

Like a crystal-gazer in the reflected purple glow, Smythe outlined their fortunes. 'You will be suspended pending internal investigations. The charges range from perjury to manslaughter. You are alienated, desperate men with information and talents of inestimable value to would-be terrorists. Our Dublin people will feed you into the pipeline. Within three weeks, we should have him in the bag. Going somewhere, Inspector?'

Evans was on his feet, square and formidable. Suddenly, the room seemed smaller and darker. He didn't look angry, exactly; more an air of humouring the feeble-minded. His broad forefinger stabbed at the papers. 'Sign in blood, I will,' he promised, 'and swear blind it was three other blokes. It's not on, see. Sorry.'

'Indeed?' Smythe murmured, still intent on his touchstone. 'Allowed to know why, are we?'

'Come *on*, mun! Contacts behind the lines, scuffles at the borders and no prisoners taken? Commandos you want, not coppers!'

'Dear me, *scruples*; and from one whose suspects have been known to meet premature ends.'

Below the belt, this, but Evans braced and bore it, sticking to Queensberry Rules and common sense. 'The man's a genius, you say: and pack us off with a licence to kill and a fairy tale. Hired guns, duw duw!'

'You'd better sit down.' The Chief's tone was murderous; Evans dismissed it with a flick of fingers.

'Lend us your pen.'

Smythe set the paperweight aside, just so, watching the outstretched hand coldly. 'I had hoped for volunteers, but I'll settle for conscripts if I must.' He drew himself up, facing Evans squarely for the first time. '*You* perjured yourself during a murder trial.' His gunmetal stare settled on Beddoes. '*Your* derelictions on the Holroyd case have never been satisfactorily explained. Cover, gentlemen, could very easily become fact.'

87

'You've no right!' Evans protested. 'You wouldn't dare!'

'Don't tempt me. A word in the right quarter would launch the enquiry. I daresay you'd be cleared, but mud always sticks. There are worse places than the basement, believe it or not.'

Bloody stroll on, thought Beddoes, medals if you do and Traffic if you won't. A fair old carrot, but *what* a stick! Evans stood like an upright corpse, his big fists bunched at his sides. Even McKay had never reduced him to such abject rage.

Outside, the motor crackled into life and a small blue cloud eddied past the window. That's where *we're* going, my son, thought Beddoes. One way or another, up in smoke. Well, if burning's inevitable, lie back and enjoy it.

'When do we start, Chief?' he asked, and won a thinly disguised sign of relief.

'Yesterday.'

'Two against one, is it?' snarled Evans. Uninvited, he seized Smythe's fancy biro and scribbled savagely. His hand shook, and the back of his neck was brick red. '*If* we get back,' he vowed, 'I'll be making some enquiries myself.'

In victory, the Chief turned mellow. 'Perhaps. Though you may yet have cause to thank me. *And* the date, please, Sergeant; *that's* right.' He gathered the papers, pushing them into line. 'Don't fret too much about cover. A meeting is arranged; you'll be briefed by an expert.' His watch glinted gold above a snowy cuff. 'Two thirty, by the lake in the park. He's tall and grey-haired, wearing civil service blues, and he'll be feeding the ducks.'

'*Funnies!*' Evans said, in utter disgust.

'He's first-class,' Smythe insisted. 'To disregard his

advice could be fatal. Literally.' And showed them the door, bold as a white-fronted bantam.

Curious; at close quarters his skin looked waxy. Despite the ritzy air-conditioning, bubbles of sweat twinkled along his hairline. Not quite as chipper as he pretended, then. Still, fighting Evans was always a struggle: even when you won . . .

'You mean you've never *been* there? Either of you?' He was tall, all right; a pukka English beanpole. He had gold-rimmed half-moon specs, an OHMS briefcase and a supercilious air that made you feel like an advanced case of herpes. 'Good grief,' he muttered, 'whatever next?' And broke into a cautious stork-like strut along the lake shore. His coal-black eyes tightened against the glare and the narrow nose wrinkled fastidiously. It *was* a bit niffy, but what with exposed mudbanks and half a ton of duckshit dotted about. They had it to themselves, though, and no wonder.

He'd chosen well. The far end of the lake, screened by weeping willows: too damp for courting couples and twenty blistering minutes from the nearest car park. 'You will call me *Snow*,' he ordered, 'and answer only to your formal titles.' Then he'd listened calmly while Evans preached the word according to Smythe and revealed their total ignorance of Paddyland. At which point he'd opened the briefcase, produced a hunk of Hovis and cast brown bread upon the slimy green waters.

'The mission is vital,' he said. 'I was promised dependable, case-hardened men.'

'You've got 'em,' growled Evans. 'Press-ganged, mind; but still.'

'Spare me the sackcloth, Inspector. Your record is scarcely the model of propriety.' He cocked his head and

89

held up a long pale hand, forestalling Evans' anger. 'Be quiet! Watch!'

There was a whoosh and a clatter above the trees. The big bird wheeled and splashed down in a glisten of gaudy droplets. Bobbing brightly above its own splintered reflection, it came honking and paddling to the water-logged feast.

'Remarkable!' whispered Snow, rapt and human with it. 'Full plumage, at this time of the year! A mallard drake, d'you see; he should be in eclipse. Isn't he superb?'

'He might be,' Beddoes drawled, 'with orange and green peas.'

Snow stiffened, and a pink flush of humiliation warmed his parchment cheeks. 'Forgive me, Sergeant; a lapse. *Your* enthusiasms, I recall, incline to *destruction* of living things.'

Evans had smouldered all lunchtime, supping his ale glumly, breasting the rush-hour traffic like a madman and saying not a civil word. Now, quiet but cutting, he erupted. 'Come off it, mun, that's why we're here. Priming the hit squad, you are, and wringing your lily-white paws over some bloody *bird*!'

A lank scarecrow in fancy threads, Snow took a stand at the water's edge. Behind him, the mallard dipped and chuntered; sunlight through the railing branches flickered on his glasses. His silvered head swung slowly and his icy glare covered them with equal and total contempt.

'I do not propose to suffer one of your notorious interrogations! The idea was to avert bloodshed – principally yours! We shall proceed on that basis. Otherwise, I bid you God-speed, and the unlikely good fortune you will certainly require.'

Evans was watching a pied feather flutter across the

mud. For two pins, you could see, he'd be off and after it.

'What you're saying, Mr Snow,' Beddoes suggested diffidently, 'is no shooters, right?'

'Of course! Absolutely *no* unnecessary violence. My God, you're British policemen aren't you?'

'Darro,' sighed Evans. 'Thought you'd never ask.'

They eyed each other warily in dappled shade, the immaculate Funny and the drab Inspector. Then, awkward and tentative, Snow offered a mouldy crust.

'Here. *You* feed him.'

Amazingly, Evans obeyed.

It was hilarious, really, the long and short of it vying for a drake's favour. Somehow, they'd fashioned an uneasy truce, Beddoes reckoned; like a couple of dogs who'd bristled and snarled and decided to rub along after all. But he was given no time to observe. 'You, too, Sergeant. Soothes the most savage of breasts, I find.'

A squadron of smaller, dowdier ducks came arrowing towards the willows.

'Females,' Snow stated, needlessly.

Soon they were surrounded: quack and shimmer and the lap of small waves, and even the stench seemed tolerable. A smart customer, Mister Snow, to have them eating out of his hand.

'Gerald Smythe is ex-Army,' he informed them casually. 'He prefers the frontal approach.'

'Smash and grab?' murmured Beddoes, and Snow nodded agreement.

'He saw service in Kenya and Cyprus; rather harrowing experiences. He's very militant on terrorism.'

Evans turned, a blue and bitter stare; and Snow headed him off. 'Wait. He has not yet made his mark, and time is short.'

Odd; the Chief didn't look *that* old.

Snow moved on, still tossing out crumbs. 'It's a *major* initiative, d'you see. Smythe has only partial responsibility. Oh, *look!*'

The drake was airborne, purple wing feathers aglow and an out-thrust neck flashing emerald. Quite a sight, no question. Snow's thin body craned higher and his upturned face looked lost and luminous. Talk about obsessions . . . The instant passed. When he glanced down, the black eyes were shrewd and steady.

'Daly is an elusive creature; therein lies much of his charisma. We need to place him, know where he goes and who he trusts. Which is where *you* come in, Sergeant; starting from the periphery and burrowing inward. You're a marksman and a karate expert, correct?'

'Judo, actually.'

'In which case, Smythe's scenario will serve – with minor adjustments.' They were strolling like old friends, and the navy of ducks for an escort. 'Use your own name, be yourself only more so. Tell the truth inasmuch as you can; people don't expect an autobiography. *If* anyone asks, the Inspector here is on your trail. That is the only difference.'

'You're splitting us, then?' Evans had halted, poised and suspicious.

'It's a question of safeguards. Two men operating independently are more alert and less vulnerable than a team.'

''Old on,' Beddoes demanded. 'You're sending me against hardcore Paddies without a gun?'

'For your own protection, man. Don't worry, the back-up team will be on constant alert. It's only *information*, remember.'

Snow brushed the last of the bread from his fingers, causing a flurry of buff-coloured bodies in the shallows.

Spreading his arms, he advised, 'Fix the moment in memory; mistrust and the smell of stagnant water. Hold on to your present feelings of hostility and isolation. *This* is how you must always speak of your erstwhile colleagues.'

'Yeah,' breathed Beddoes. 'That'll be *no* problem.'

'Quite. The Chief Superintendent will complete your briefing – travel arrangements, contacts and so on. You will be leaving very shortly; I needn't detain you further.'

Beddoes jerked a thumb at Evans hovering nearby.

'What are you cookin' up with him, then?'

Finally, Snow reverted to type. Peering down his nose from a great height, he snapped, 'From now on, we observe the golden rule, Sergeant; need to know.'

Even so, Beddoes reflected, skimming pebbles and counting the hops, you had to hand it to him. Positive, precise and pointed; what more could you ask of a Funny? And he checked in mid-swing, appalled. The official briefcase sat abandoned on the mud.

The strange, quacking procession had passed on. Snow and Evans were deep in conversation. Now's your chance, sunshine, always fancied a dekko into the 'most secret'. He bent, slipped the catch and peeked inside; and shook his head in sheer disbelief. More bleeding duckfood!

'Do you *trust* that young man, Inspector?' Briefly, heat and brilliance faded. Evans was back in rat-strewn darkness, fending off a phobia and a maniac's knife.

'Put it this way,' he said. 'He's handy in a tight corner.'

'Perhaps. But also headstrong and rather *lightweight*, wouldn't you say?' Snow was fiddling with his spectacles. 'At this very moment, for example, he is spying on the contents of my briefcase.' He tapped the gold rims lightly. 'Useful as rearview mirrors, these.'

'Course he is, that's why you left it. Which is it, then, plain or sliced?'

Snow managed a shamefaced smile. 'Well, at least *you* passed the test.'

Flattery will get you nowhere, boyo, Evans thought grimly. 'Listen, I hope you're not thinking he's expendable; sending him in as a sacrifice, like?'

'You missed your vocation, Inspector. Such deviousness is much prized by *my* masters.'

Snow had paused between the twisted roots of a willow and was watching like the good shepherd over his plaintive, feathery flock.

'Shoo,' he said gently. 'You've had your ration.' He removed his spectacles, pinching the bridge of his nose and exhaling wearily. 'Once, it was a game for gentlemen. No holds barred, naturally, but there *were* conventions and a general embargo on thuggery.' He produced a paisley handkerchief and wiped the lenses absently. 'Then the Cold War came along; Al Capone in one corner and Stalin in the other. Here endeth gentility. Nowadays, we trade with fanatics and innocent blood is the common currency. Lord save us.' In greening afternoon shade, his voice held the greyness of utter despair. Evans listened, numbed.

'Every agent needs a legend,' Snow continued remorselessly. 'Not to be *believed*, of course; merely to protect his contacts, and to buy time for whatever sordid barter may become expedient. In this case, separation provides one more layer of protection; a second deception which has to be checked and exposed. Which brings us to *your* cover.' He seemed to wake visibly from his private nightmare, blinking bemusedly and nakedly at the vacant sparkle before him. Replacing his spectacles briskly, he set out along the bank once more. 'Do *you* have any enthusiasms, Inspector?'

'Rugby,' Evans said, at once. 'A fanatic myself, and no apologies.' He hesitated, stretching to match the taller man's stride. 'I used to fish a bit; trout mainly.'

Snow stopped in his tracks, and his horsey face creased in unaffected delight. 'Serendipity at last! How *nice*!' And he was away at the double, hands behind his back, head bowed and shoulders hunched. Only needs the nappy in his beak, thought Evans, and he could be delivering babies.

'Even in this business,' Snow confided, glancing down and back in a flicker of gold, 'spontaneous plans are often the best.'

They walked in silence to a spot where the willows thickened and the reek was truly awful. Swinging about like guardsmen, they began the long hike back. In the bright distance, Beddoes stood lonely watch over the decoy briefcase.

'It is current protocol to notify the Garda,' Snow began. We have unofficial links with a man called O'Brien in Dublin.'

'We had words, once,' said Evans. 'By telex. He won.'

'He's a sound man. You're going on a fishing holiday, Inspector. First, though, you must make a courtesy call. O'Brien's local knowledge will be a considerable bonus.' He was taking it slower, frowning in concentration and picking words carefully. 'Do the tourist bit, would you? The Kerry lakes, Galway Bay for sharks and some of the rivers in Cork. That's your first line of defence. Pressed, you can reveal the O'Brien connection; it's an open secret, anyway. If you're really in trouble, play the hunter's card – you're tracking down a deserter. Cover, d'you see; a series of fall-backs.'

A breeze stirred the hanging fronds. Faintly, the chimes of an ice-cream van filtered through. And Beddoes waited, still.

'Daly grew up near the border,' Snow continued. 'There is a trout stream which has special significance for him; a crucial part of *his* legend. Don't glower Inspector, it's one of the few things we *do* know. You will be given the precise location by O'Brien. Once there, you will establish a routine – fish the morning and evening rises and make yourself known at the village hostelry.'

'Oh aye,' said Evans. 'Find him in the bar, will I?'

Snow's smile was thin and frigid. 'I doubt it, Inspector. I rather expect that *he'll* find *you*.'

He marched up to Beddoes and retrieved his briefcase.

'Thank you Sergeant. I trust you found everything to your satisfaction?' He shouldn't have said it; Beddoes was clearly itching for revenge.

'No way. Prefer a bit of crumpet, I do.'

But Snow had the last laugh – Funnies always do. 'Indeed? Then I trust you will exercise restraint during your forthcoming excursion. In Eire, *that* commodity is strictly for home consumption.'

Watching Snow's lean figure stalk away, Beddoes grinned admiringly. ''Ere, you wouldn't think he'd know about things like that.'

'Don't underestimate him, boyo. Been about a bit in his time, I'd say.'

They trudged over burnt-out grass in the low but still-scorching sun.

'Jesus,' Beddoes muttered. 'An hour to opening time and me tongue's on fire. Fancy a couple down your local, later?'

Evans hesitated. The very best part of the day to come, mind; but he could hardly refuse. 'Just a quickie, then. I'm meeting someone. And don't ask, okay?'

'Stone me,' Beddoes exclaimed, setting two amber pints down reverently, 'You never said it was fancy dress!'

It wasn't, not really. Casual, she'd insisted over the blower last night, a cop's-eye view of Dockland for the article. He'd broken out a new blue shirt anyhow, and the bottle green cords he kept for special occasions. Jane Neale rated better than working gear, even for saying goodbye.

'Business,' he grunted. 'Cheers.' The first swallow went down lovely, cold and clean and bitter; a bitter evening, fair play. But Beddoes was sniffing the air sceptically.

'Oh yeah? Since when did you wear pouf mixture to the nick? Smells like *my* kind of business, know what I mean?'

'Walk soft, Roy. Near the knuckle, you are; like this afternoon.'

Beddoes slumped into his chair, sank a dredger's mouthful and grinned bleakly. 'Leave it out, uncle. We're stuffed, no question, but it cuts both ways. They're stuck with us, too; no need to kiss arses.'

He had a point. Evans mulled it over, taking the pulse of the pub.

Late sun through frosted glass glowed on the polished wood of the bar and the chromium handles of the pumps. It was early and slack; the usual darts and cribbage, a couple of sad-eyed pensioners and a regular from the council estate talking horses with the landlord. The smell of pipesmoke and real ale, and traffic rumbling gently outside. Tidy, it was. Enjoy it, bach, it could be your last chance.

Beddoes was leaning back, nursing his beer and watching the dartboard. 'Bin thinkin'.' He murmured, hardly moving his lips. 'Smythe wants a scalp, that's why we got drafted. Butch and Sundance, right?'

'You heard the man. Information only, and no gunplay.'

'See what I mean? Left hand, right hand, and a coupla mugs in between. Meanwhile, oo's mindin' the store? What about the likes of Old Jim? Dodgy, innit?'

There was a whoop and a patter of applause; a pimply youth in a bilious T-shirt celebrating a three-dart finish.

Still looking elsewhere, Beddoes added, 'You'll be on your own, mate. Watch your back, okay?'

'You, too,' said Evans gruffly, unexpectedly touched.

Beddoes faced him, and this time the smile came bright and easy. 'Paddies, see; no sweat.'

Daft young bugger was actually looking forward to it.

'Drink up, uncle, it's your round.' He paused, glass half-cocked, eyes and mouth agape.

In the sudden awed hush, Evans knew she'd arrived. 'Put it on the slate, boyo. This is for me.' He stood up and went towards her, conscious of Beddoes' heartfelt tribute.

'Gordon Bennet, I'll do business with *that* anytime!'

She wore plain white trousers, a sea-green silk blouse and the gold high heels. Her auburn hair was tied at the nape and her smile was for him alone.

'Hello,' she said, in a tone of mock-reproach, 'what happened to the spit and sawdust? This is highly civilized.'

It would've been very easy, just then, to walk away; to settle for Traffic and whatever time she might offer. But he fancied he could see the outline of a notebook in her soft leather handbag; and a single word tolled insistently in his mind. A word which had ruled him for most of his adult life, and would doubtless hound him to the grave: duty.

'I'll get you a drink,' he said.

He leaned on the bar and watched her cross the room, revelling in the taut sway of her hips and the coppery fire in her hair. She sat gracefully, her green eyes alight with amusement at the goggling silence she provoked.

By the time he reached her side, normal service had resumed. A hum of conversation, the thud of darts and a whiff of chalk on the air. He swallowed hard and went in at the deep end. 'Change of plan, lovely. I've got to go away.'

Her smile widened, and she toasted him calmly. 'Bottoms up. This is a long-term assignment; there's no rush.'

He followed her lead automatically, tasting nothing but bubbles. 'It's not that simple.'

She was reading him now, he could see the sudden concern. 'Where are you going? How long will you be?'

He shook his head wearily. 'I don't know.'

She set her glass down carefully, untouched. 'You can't tell me? Or you won't?'

'Not now. Probably, not ever.'

'Something I can't write about, you mean?' She was leaning towards him again, a waft of citrusy perfume and her lovely face tense. The pub and everyone in it might've been on another planet. 'Take me with you.'

He stared at her in utter amazement. 'You don't know what you're asking, girl.'

She shook her head impatiently. 'No, you don't understand; I mean tonight.'

'Come on, Jane, you haven't seen it. A bachelor, mind, the place is a shambles.'

She sat upright, her eyes aflame, her breasts rising sharply beneath the clinging blouse. 'I heard you, Huw. You're going away and you may not come back. Take me home; now!'

So he did.

INTERLUDES

1965–76

They set Kevin Daly down like a prince, and half of the county there. Sean sat dry-eyed and dumb throughout his mother's keening. Then as he knelt in myrrh-sharp gloom between the shadowed pews, a terrible vision filled his mind. Herself on the quilt ablush with love, and his daddy's corpse beside her. To this she must wake each morn, he thought, until the end of her days.

Her prayers were falling, unheeded, 'neath sacred silver and painted saints. The sham of it disgusted him — an empty house, an absent God.

'I'll not be present at church again,' he vowed, back in her smoky parlour. ''Twas a godless act, to be sure and no use troubling *Him*!'

'Whisht, boy, guard your tongue! I'll bide no blasphemy here!'

He cocked his chin and folded his arms, proud and stubborn and twelve. 'I'll not go with you, Mother.' And saw the sorrow of ages take her, the tears she couldn't contain.

''Tis the image of himself I see, and bound for the same fierce, short span. For pity's sake, child, ye're all I have left!'

'The childhood is over, Molly,' he said. 'You'll be needing a man at your side.'

Never before had he used the given name; she watched him in anguish and wonder. 'Grown so soon, then,' she muttered, 'and dreaming of glory already. A

100

vain and foolish cause, Sean; you'll have no blessing from me.' She settled the shawl around her, rocked in her chair and frowned like an invalid at the quiet dance of blue flame.

He moved behind her, resting hands on the bowed and woolly shoulders.

'Leave me be,' she hissed, 'for I'll lay ye beside him soon enough!'

'Not yet,' he promised. 'There's work to be done, meanwhile.' But she wouldn't be comforted, then or ever; except by a hopeless, unshakeable faith he could no longer share.

He went forth next dusk, alone and unseen. There was mist down the glen, frost on the air, the smell of cattle, and a weasel of fear in his belly. Under the whispering rowans he went, through deep green dripping shade. A sense of himself was growing. He was back in that bright scarlet morning, and memories visited him one by one.

The cleaving of man to a woman; some day he would earn it himself. The abandoned rod, the comfort of treading Kevin's path; shots and a whiff of killing in the wind; trespass, triumph and terror and the first glimpse of ancestral enemies. The death of his father had fashioned fresh life of his own: he had *known* it was going to happen.

He was striding out now, surefooted as a creature of the night. He had entered that world beyond reason, whence all is foretold by the play of light and the shift of breeze and sureness, born in the blood. He'd been here before, been and seen and survived. And would again, so long as he fought the fear and clung to his truth and heeded the force of his instincts. They drew him onward through the scent of hidden wild flowers.

Drew him, at last, to the place where Kevin had fallen, and the sudden rise of the moon.

An ancient anthem surged from the soil and flowed the whole length of his body; and the shackles of doctrine parted. For *here* was the holy ground, a site of old and tragic wrong, more worthy than pious stone. His land and his home, which must never more be stained by foreign curse or native blood. He waited, blinded in silver. His power took flight, singing. And the power was a name and a deed to be done, and the cost of his daddy's dying.

He needed no moon to see by, nor a compass to point him the way. He marched to the glinting line of the fence and set his face to the North. Gripping the cold and rusted strands, he turned his eyes inward and measured the plan in his mind. Saw it clean and sharp and perfect, the where and the how and the why. And *knew*, beyond any shadow of doubt, he could make it come to pass . . .

He woke before dawn, padding the pitch-black cottage like a thief for fear of waking Molly. It took but a moment to dress and slip out, a crust of bread in one hand and his grandad's knobkerrie in the other.

Under silent stars, he shivered and munched and made for the river. There, he groped for icy, fist-sized pebbles till his pockets bulged and a grey gleam touched the sky. Even so, fording was a terrible frigid thing, to be approached with caution despite his hurry.

Up, then, in the dawn chorus to the heather slope where rabbits ran and poacher O'Dee set snares. Only the one he needed, yet it took him an hour to find. This was his last and most vital weapon, of which he had learned little skill. But he held it now and grasped its usage, and would take it into the Plan.

He found the place quite soon, a long curve of river which chewed at the hill; a high limestone cliff, and trees thick to the very lip. Here the water lay shaded and deep, giving rest for weary salmon; and new force to his waking, moonlit dream.

Fording again, quicker by daylight, but no less cold. He scrambled upward, sweating hard, hampered by the weight of the pebbles and counting the pass of minutes. He prowled the wooded glades, watching the spread from bole to bole and judging the span from the edge. And went, at last, to his squelchy knees and finished the job, where ferns stood tall and smelled green; and covered his tracks.

Nine of a blazing morning, and naught to do but mark an inward passage and cut the line of patrol; due to come before ten. He lay in the heather and spied on the wheeling larks till the sky was all at once empty and tobacco tainted the breeze. He waited yet, taut as a leveret in its form: for he had to be sure.

'Give us a break, Sarge. There's no fuckin' Micks rahnd 'ere.' A familiar whine which sliced to the quick.

The sergeant's reply squashed all doubt. 'Christ, Mills, doncha ever stop moaning?'

Worming away to a safe distance, Sean delivered a maidenly scream and paused to assess the effect. Between bronze strands of bracken, he observed the classic triangle: Mills at point, the other two quartering wide. Retreating upward, he flighted his barrage of rocks prettily, pushing the flankmen deeper and coaxing Mills to the fore. Wind in the trees was behind him, and joy possessed his soul. He rose in pride and fury and hurled the worst word in their teeth. He'd misjudged the distance sorely. Mills was upon him, red-faced with the heat of the hunt. He turned and fled for his life. Sweet Mary, he thought, what if he fires the gun?

In through a fiery clasp of brambles, and the crash of pursuit at his heels.

The lip yawned sudden and empty. He jinked and

dived to his left. Sprawling, he clawed the sweet sod and watched the full bloom of the Plan. Saw the check of khaki shins against the tight-drawn wire. Actually heard the twang of release as Mills plunged outward and down. Dark waters stretched to receive him and the spray climbed, thinning and whirling and rainbowing into the sun.

On his feet in a trice, Sean shinned down the cliff like a witless goat. He perched on a boulder where the current regrouped, and all that went under must surface. Above him, a blunder and thrash in the trees; beneath, the sheen of the river. He set his feet and hefted the club, poised and prepared for the kill.

The moment eked past, then another, and comrades bawled the hated name. The water slid on, unruffled and indifferent. 'Tis the rifle, thought Sean, and weight of the boots that hold him. Fish will be feasting soon . . .

At first in the school yard, they let him alone, a mark of respect for his troubles. But weeks passed and the seasons changed and they egged him into their games. Till the day his power stirred and cowed them.

Winter, raw and biting, and catch-as-catch-can for the warmth. Fleeing, grinning over his shoulder in the thrill of the chase, he crashed into Conor Kelly and flattened him to the gritty black asphalt.

A fearsome bully was Conor, near sixteen and built like a lusty bullock. Up he came in a lather, ham-sized fists at the ready.

'An accident, Conor, I'm sorry.'

'Aye, sorry, ye'll be, sure enough!'

The whoops declined in a scurry of boyish boots. The circle closed quickly, pale avid faces and the steam of the breath, rising.

'I'll not be fighting,' Sean said and turned away.

The eddy of air at his back gave warning. Ducking the clumsy lunge, he whirled and stood chest to chest, staring coldly up into a pink and piggy squint. 'I'll come for you, Kelly, out of the mist at dead of night, and the shade of Kevin beside me. Leave me be!'

Gasps and mutters and chapped hands sketching the sign of the cross. It was heresy to summon the dead. The bruiser Kelly retreated, laughing hollow and gobbing on the ground.

'Ah, and he's not worth the trouble, the godless whelp!'

Then and later they granted his wish. Sean Daly walked and studied alone . . .

Years hurried on, and with them the last of his boyhood. His voice cracked and steadied low and stubble mottled his chin. The lines of his body shifted and spread, and set in the shape of the man. Through it all, the strangest mystery yet; he grew not an inch taller. It took them a while to notice, before the whispers broke out.

'*What* a man was the Daly, to leave such a mark on the son!'

'Cover your face, Mrs Francis, for 'tis sinful to gaze on the cursed.'

'Hush now, baby dear, or the dwarf Sean Daly will bate ye!'

''Tis the wrath of heaven upon him for having denied the faith.'

He heard and walked on, untouched by their crude superstitions and burrowing deep in his books. He cared not a whit for stature, and welcomed the smallness which set him apart.

There were practical boons, too. For hadn't he already crossed the border a hundred times, and rambled the road past the Army camp, his notebook and pencil at hand? And had suffered a score of challenges from the haughty, hard-voiced English? At which he would raise a guileless face, and doff his school cap and speak in a pure, clear treble. ''Tis motor-car plates, mister – here, see for yourself.' So they came to give him good day, and tell him when the colonel was due, that he might add an exalted number to his list. Home he would go through the gathering dusk by the singing river and night sounds he knew so well. Mark my progress, Father. Whilst learning of battles long past, I arm for the war yet ahead.

Meetings, there were, on windswept slopes and in lonely glens, with the quiet friends of dead Kevin. Whence, while the wind tugged the pages and distant cattle lowed, he would give the real sense of his numbers. Troops observed and weapons counted, the movements of men and stores, and how often the high-ups came. The quiet ones smiled, smelling of whiskey and farmyards; and clapped his shoulder and called him their finest cadet.

In this fashion did Sean Daly prepare for the entry exams. And though his frame remained stunted, his legend continued to grow.

He read Modern Irish History at Trinity College – an endless dirge of martyrs, famine and English oppression. At first, new knowledge only stoked old rage. Then, as he studied the post-war birth of Eire, he understood a fundamental truth. Stealth and patience win the day where ill-starred bloodshed fails.

By way of celebration, he took to the singing pubs. And carried his birth certificate to confound the Garda who looked askance at his size. On one such boozy evening, he sat flushed and sweaty beside a medical student he scarcely knew and suffered an owlish, unsought diagnosis.

'Achondroplasia you have, meboy, a classic case. Came on at fourteen or thereabouts, I'd wager.'

'Twelve,' snapped Sean, sinking his snout in creamy foam and supping the fifth pint of dark, metallic stout. Or maybe it was the sixth. 'Back in Leitrim,' he boasted, 'they call it the Wrath of God.'

'*Farmers!* A random quirk of the genes is all, and naught to be bothered about. Technically, you're not a dwarf at all.' The would-be healer nudged him slyly. 'Not hereditary, mind you; breed as much as you like.'

Sean set the glass down hard, speaking cold and clean across the roar of conversation. 'And why would a man raise offspring, I wonder, to be slaughtered by British pigs?'

His companion's attention had shifted; he pawed, heedless, at the Arran-clad breasts of the girl to his left.

Not long after dawn next morning, Sean prowled O'Connell Bridge with a fierce turmoil in his guts and powerful ache in his head. The waters of the Liffey heaved frigid and grey, and November chill raked his face. Mortified, he was, for giving too much away. Alcohol's a poison, he thought, and, like any other, effective according to bodyweight. When you're built in miniature, you must tipple to match.

He never got messy again . . .

By now, poets and wordsmiths were striking sparks from his soul. While winter shrouded the library, he perched on a cushion for extra height and rested his elbows on polished oak and breathed in the scent of leather bindings. He read till the lines blurred together and their metre invaded the blood. Stay-at-home Synge and O'Casey, and the Anglos Wilde and Shaw who crossed the water to claim diverse heights of notoriety. Ringing through and above them all, the great bardic paeans of Yeats. He tried his own hand at rhyming, and usually burned the results. His purpose wavered. For the first time, he was in love; or something like it.

A noble O'Neill was she, the wildest of beauties, a spirit to rival the burn in her hair, and no thought of his deformity at all. In her alone he confided, and she damned him for a bloodthirsty fool. 'There's a priceless gift in you, Sean; why waste it on some doomed crusade?'

He hushed her with kisses and a desperate hunger, discovering at last the tumbledown joys of the bed.

She taunted him yet, glowing with fervour and passion. 'The warlords are gone, and only sad ballads to name them. The pen is mightier by far, for the written word lives on!'

She paced like a naked princess in her rich and perfumed room. Beside the wardrobe a daub of her family mansion which stood bare five miles from Molly's but belonged to a world apart.

She tempted him sorely; for a week, the whole span of his future hung poised. Then the Fenian came.

An anonymous, mudsmeared van more at home in a rural market. At the wheel, a weatherworn face, watchful blue eyes, and a hand-rolled fag-end dangling.

'In with ye,' ordered the Quiet One who had praised him so long ago. The east wind scalpelled down Dame Street, slashing the walkers to blindness and the scales from Sean's dulled sight. The cause must be nourished by action, not words, and pursued over free green land. A homeground for soldiers were cities, and this one had smothered his power. It was time to stand and be counted; and obey.

They rattled north-eastward, pausing but once for passengers as night and hoarfrost fell on Finglas. 'Keeling and Cavanaugh,' breathed the Quiet One, 'cadets like yourself. They'll not believe in ye, Sean.'

Cavanaugh was folded, knees to his chest, lumpen and

108

large in the gloom. He sounded as scornful as Conor Kelly. 'True. For what use is a dwarf in a barney?'

'No more use than the mouth of a jackass,' Sean admitted; whereafter they travelled in silence and a lingering reek of swine.

The journey ended in a lurch to the left and a scrunch of gravel; dimness, the tick of cooling metal, and a blether of rain-swollen stream. The Quiet One was away to the rear in a trice, leaving a map on the seat. Seizing it gladly, Sean squatted 'neath a glimmer of sidelights and the welcome warmth of the engine. Fear faded as he studied route and contour. The lie of the country loomed clear in his mind. From behind, a whiff of gun-oil and Cavanaugh's growl of delight. 'Automatics, by God, I'd not thought to see the day!'

A dangerous whinny from Keeling provoked the Quiet One's ire.

'Be sure and return them safe, for they've far more value than yourselves.'

They came forward together, with the mist of their breath for a shroud. Eerie and hollow in the upward glow, the Quiet One made an unusually lengthy speech.

'The border's a short step yonder, and the camp half as far again. The sentries'll stick by their braziers this night: the fence is as flimsy as cobwebs.' Here, he passed Sean bolt-cutters, icy steel to deaden the hands. 'Hit and run, mind you, and no heroics. Just so they know we were there.' The glint of his watch in the starlight. 'Ye have three hours, after which I'll be leaving. Alone!'

Sean led them in briskly, sliding like a childish ghost between gaunt and leafless trees, and the brawl of the waters to guide him. When the cover gave out, he went down on all fours in the rime-sharp grass, and wormed to the line of the fence. To his left, the glow of sentinel fires; ahead, a huddle of Quonsets. Though they freeze-burned his flesh, the wires parted no louder than gentle harpstrum. With a pang of envy, he beckoned them on to the sleeping foe, and stayed to mark the escape.

Big and bold was Cavanaugh, up to the nearest hut and his weapon held poised and gleaming. A bully, maybe, but let no man call him a coward. Whereas Keeling hung back and dithered. Even at this bone-chilled distance, Sean could sense the curdle of fright.

Pandemonium. A splintering crash of boot on wood, muzzle flash, violent and yellow, and the harsh fierce stutter of automatic fire. The night air was tainted with cordite and smoke and the cries of men in confusion; and the second gun still silent.

Lights blazed. Keeling whirled like a dazzled hare and bolted for the fence. Sean's cry of contempt merged with a single shot. The running figure checked in full stride and reared up to the pitiless stars; and crumpled and fell. The precious rifle lay unblooded and lost.

No time for thinking. He sprinted low, scooped up the weapon, and made for Cavanaugh's side. Squinting against the glare, he braced his legs and squeezed the trigger; and learned the terrible lust of the warrior. Take me now, he challenged the despised God, with the buck of the gun in my palm and the whump of my bullets on alien flesh.

He steadied, aware of the hush at his side and a fumble of heated metal.

Cavanaugh grinned, rueful and pained. 'I'm hit in the arm. Can't load the feckin' thing.'

''Tis finished, then,' snapped Sean, and dragged him away by main force.

And into the jaws of a trap. The roar of a motor-cycle, and iced white beams closing towards the gap in the fence. Above the screams of the wounded, a pound of feet on the iron-hard sod and a volley of shots from the right.

'Finished we are, to be sure,' said Cavanaugh. 'But bejaysus, *wasn't* it grand?'

Sean was standing easy, tuned to the prickle of instinct and deaf to the Babel abroad. There was something he'd seen from his post at the fence, a desperate hope in the very eye of the storm. He shoved Cavanaugh round and crept forward.

'I'll never surrender, Daly.'

'Whisht, ye great fool, I'm after saving your skin!' And hauled the big man to the heart of a stinking briar patch in a saucered hollow not ten yards from the hut. 'They'll be scouring the country *outside* the gap,' he hissed. 'This is the last place they'll look.'

Briefly, he thought Cavanaugh had broken, feeling the quake at his side. But 'twas only the ague of the wound and softly admiring laughter. 'I'll say this for ye, Daly: ye've a powerful nerve – for a dwarf!'

They lay there for an age while boots pounded before their eyes and the cold came close to killing them, anyway. Till at last the sound of dying faded and the lights blinked out, one by one.

It was a fearsome business, chivvying a weakened bruiser and two long guns free from the rustle of a bramble and across the hostile dark.

'Where are ye headed, ye loony? The gap's away over here!'

'Aye. Which they'll surely be watching.' So he quartered the fence from a distance, and saw them there, just as he'd said. And led Cavanaugh a half-mile further before cutting the wire once more and dashing and staggering over the perimeter road to the refuge of woodland beyond . . .

* * *

In the years that followed, given select company and a measure of strong waters, the Quiet One might be prompted to take up the tale. He would shake his head and roll his fierce thin smokes and laugh at the wonder of it all.

'Something told me to stay, lads. The Dear, maybe, though you'll not get *him* to believe it. Near to freezing was I, and the dawn up grey as a sickly widow. And down comes Sean through stark black trees, the Cavanaugh draped on one shoulder and rifles slung over the other. Imagine, now. Fourteen stones was Cav, and babbling as though in drink. And *him*, no larger than a stripling. 'Tis a miracle, thinks I, and out good and sprightly to shake his hand. Ye know what himself did then?' He would pause for the drama and pull at his drink and aim blue smoke at the thatch. 'He drops the whole disaster at me feet, lads, and looks me square in the eye. Ye'll be knowing that cold and tawny gaze, I'm thinking. "Ye're rid of a coward," says he. "Better soon than later. I've brought ye a brave fool to patch up, aye, and some scrap iron ye're seeming to prize. Now get me back to the college, I've an essay to hand in at one. And next time you're wanting a porter, *send for a bigger man*!"' And he would raise his glass and toast absent friends and round off his story neatly. 'It was the way of a test, ye see. He passed, as he did his learned degree, with the highest honours in the land.'

CHAPTER SIX

The Voice has a name and his name is Cav, hummed Harriet Slade to herself; a maid in waiting on a tatty bridal bed. He has almost certainly killed people before, and probably will again. He owns a wicked knife and a temper to match and the hardest, readiest, most super male body ever. At this very moment, the distant corner of the humid room glowed red with his cigarette and the smouldering violence of his presence. She stretched voluptuously, willing away squalor and the stench of overheated flesh, glorying in the nearness of his touch. And looked back in the darkness on her sunwashed day of discovery . . .

It had begun around the middle of another breathless morning, and there had been only two other reliable witnesses: Pete, the bass guitarist, and his bovine common-law wife. Peg was broad-faced and sweet-natured and enormous with child. She had forsaken smack 'for the good of our bump' and bullied Pete into sharing the sacrifice. 'Sympathetic pregnancy,' he'd grumbled, without the ghost of a smile on his long, pimply face.

With little hope and less reason, Harriet and Pete had hauled out the ghastly square which passed for a carpet and were flaying great filthy clouds over the weeds that choked the front yard. Peg squatted on the warm step, cradling her belly and giggling like the half-wit she was.

Pete saw them first, dropping his dusty lath and bawling the news to a flawless sky.

'Stone me, it's the friggin' Philharmonic!' He capered like a lanky skeleton in skintight jeans and a greasy black shirt. Peg simply stared, her silly mouth forming a large pink O.

'Hey,' protested Harriet, hammering and sneezing gamely on, 'what about the workers?' Receiving no answer, she turned and watched them come.

Irish fiddlers, Gerry had once called them, in a rare if unwitting moment of prescience. But the cases they carried looked big enough for cellos at least. Joe was the colour of Victoria plums, and sweat had darkened the whole of his pale blue T-shirt. Even the Voice's powerful body was canted at a curious angle, to offset the strain. They weigh a ton, thought Harriet at once, but we're not supposed to know. You can see by the Voice's forced smile and the effort it costs him to stride free.

They marched straight into the fetid gloom, the Voice and Joe in the van, the smackless parents-to-be at their heels and Harriet hanging back; sensing trouble already. They had laid their great black and silver burdens down, gentle and pious as a pair of funeral directors.

'Here, give us a butchers,' Pete had pleaded, reaching a grubby hand towards the clasps. 'Always fancied a touch of the old Yehudis.'

The Voice had turned on him, a jut and bristle of black beard and the snarl of a wounded bear. 'Ye so much as *breathe* on those things and the child will grow up an orphan!'

'He's powerful cautious,' Joe told them later, when the Voice had stamped upstairs. 'Ever since some eejit stove in the side one time down Kerry way.' But his baby-blue eyes looked hunted, and Harriet for one didn't believe a word.

* * *

Wait a minute, she thought, still aching for Cav, it *really* began with Gerry. She frowned in disgust at the stinking, snoring huddle beside her . . .

Gerry had gone downhill faster than a Cresta bob-sleigh. These days he smoked and drank whatever he could lay hands on, and spent his few lucid intervals gazing blankly at the wall. His hair, once the performer's crowning glory, lay like a mangy poodle round his grey and wasted face. He cared only for money; money to buy the H which took him away from the here and now. You couldn't altogether blame him for *that*, of course. This afternoon, his one remaining interest had almost got him killed.

Joe and the Voice had been upstairs again, you could hear their restless footfalls and an occasional low-voiced argument. Pete and Peg had withdrawn to a corner, huddled together like babes in the wood and watching the ceiling fearfully. Harriet was hot and bored; but uneasy. And Gerry had chosen this moment to blear into something like consciousness and enter forbidden territory.

'There's loot in these bleeding things,' he had mumbled, pointing a shaky finger at the cases. 'I can feel it in me water.' He'd blundered towards them, surprisingly strong as she tried to haul him away. 'Gerroff, woman,' he'd growled when she tugged vainly at his belt. 'Can't you think of anything else?'

Even now, she still wasn't sure of the sequence. A sudden eddy of humid air, a hiss of animal fury, and the Voice had simply *appeared*. She'd watched wide-eyed and frozen as Gerry was jerked clean off his feet and thrust, one-handed, against the wall. And propped there without effort, like a boneless, dangling rag-doll. Bare steel had blazed brightly in the gloom and she could *smell* the mortal terror from ten feet away.

'I warned ye, ye feckin' hophead!'

Once more, only Joe could placate him, hopping nervously from one foot to the other and pleading for all he was worth.

'He meant no harm, Cav, the dope has ruined his mind.' The big blade twitched and shimmered, and Joe's voice had risen another octave. 'Cav, for the Dear's sake, there's bigger fish to fry!'

A thud and a whimper, an all-at-once empty space, and Gerry had been left in a slobbering heap at the skirting.

'I'll not tell ye again,' the Voice had promised, from the shadowed midstair landing. 'Keep your thieving paws *off*!' After which, as Harriet would later have cause to recall, the entire commune had tiptoed round the cases as though they were lacquered land mines . . .

I *will* go home, she promised herself, but not just yet. It's dirty and dangerous, but I'm still having *fun*. My Voice has a name and his name is Cav. She breathed it soft into the unclean dark, hearing the stealthy rustle of his long-awaited approach. And pushed the scratchy blanket down joyfully.

The placard stood on Church Street, bold as brass and blocking half the pavement. 'Support the Provos', it bellowed, in blood red letters two feet high. While Beddoes gawped in outrage, no one else spared a second glance. It's propaganda he reckoned, like Buy British or Save the Whale. His hackles rose, though. Walk soft, my son; here beginneth badlands.

They had a point, judging by the crossing. The briny as flat as Snow's duckpond and a ferry that wallowed under sickly wafts of par-boiled diesel. Brits at play, the whole bleedin' catastrophe. Bulgy birds in too-tight shorts, hordes of screaming kids and a queue for the heads which went halfway back to Holyhead. The bars were worse; loud-mouthed drunks and the stench of wrestlers' jockstraps. By the time they hit Dun Laoghaire, he could've put a bomb to *that* lot himself. There must be better ways to land a Judas.

He shrugged and moved on, elbowing past suncreamed tourists and the Georgian face of Dublin. Classier than expected, he had to admit. What do Irish toffs do, he wondered – buy their wellies from Harrods? Forced humour; he didn't feel like smiling. 'Hoof it into the cheap side,' the Chief had ordered, his gaze fevered and malicious. '*You'll* soon be at home.'

He ought to be, really. Shades of his past here, all right: crumbling brickwork, sunless alleys and a reek of unflushed drains. But it didn't come off, quite. The shouts rang mocking and hollow and there were unfriendly eyes at his back. So what d'you expect? They're *foreign*.

Guided by Smythe's almanac and a well-thumbed street-map, he made it to the spot marked X; and total disillusion. The once-imposing façade was mouldered with age and neglect. In the downstairs bay window, a threadbare marmalade moggy dozed between yellowing nylon drapes and twin vases of plastic tulips. And second prize is *two* weeks at the Erinmore Hotel. Terrific. An invisible cloud of burnt barley billowed down and his map confirmed the worst. The home of Guinness, this, you could get half-cut just breathing.

It *was* cheap, no argument. Mine host, bevested and potbellied and already unsteady on his feet, seized the readies greedily and led him to a musty cubicle with a cracked washbasin and a monstrous Victorian wardrobe. ''Tis a charming room, Mr Meadows,' he fawned, 'and me own fair daughter to smooth the sheets of a morn.'

117

Another refusable offer, Beddoes thought, stowing his hard-man gear and taking a nasty clout from the skew-hung door.

Nursing a numbed elbow, he made his way through gloomy passages to the entertainments lounge. Geriatric ward, more like. Overstuffed chairs full of wrinkled mummies with empty eyes and hacking coughs, and the deaf-aids tuned to TV Eireann. They were showing a documentary on peat-growing; the funniest thing he'd seen all day. And why do doss-houses always pong of rancid bacon?

'Cos that's what they serve, stupid, he thought, chewing doggedly and flicking drowsy bluebottles from the soup-soiled tablecloth. It's a survival test, okay? If the Dalys don't get you, the catering will.

Uptight and edgy, he prowled his cell and waited for dusk; again, as Smythe had decreed. 'Go to Slaney's Bar at nightfall and collar a chap called Fergus.'

Not so convincing from here – bad lines for stage heavies. You had to believe in the bastard, though, else you'd end up climbing walls.

He left early, sporting the denims and a full day's growth. Roy Vicious, see, the fastest gun in the east. The bravado lasted all of two minutes. Outside was half as beery and twice as bad: unfamiliar dim streets and an ever-present sense of hidden watchers. Get a grip, sunshine, they don't even know you're here. You hope.

Slaney's was spit and sawdust, a place his dad might've fancied, years ago. But old Alf was long gone, and they didn't allow pubs like this in England any more. Thank God.

He ordered a half of bitter, which he had to explain in sounds of one syllable to the muddy-eyed teenage moron who served him; and ship derisive stares while he nursed it, as if he was wearing a dress. Asking politely after

Fergus, he won a gust of vintage halitosis, a snag-toothed sneer and the single word 'Later'.

He endured twenty minutes of fug and hostility, feigning ease at the stout-swilled counter and feeling about as natural and unobtrusive as a padded bra. Sod it, he fumed, there's got to be a limit to patriotism. But the tribal drums must've spoken. As he set down his glass and turned to go, a small swathed figure paused at his side.

'The name's Fergus,' it wheezed. 'I'll thank ye to join me in yonder nook, after me leak is repaired. And bring a man's beverage.'

In for a penny, thought Beddoes, ordering a brace of Guinness: which pleased the bar oaf not one whit more.

Fergus was short and grizzled, and seemed to wield a fair bit of local muscle. Tagging along to a corner table, Beddoes registered the easing of tension. The noise grew loud and careless; no one was watching him now.

Except Fergus. Pale as rice pudding, and hard ferrety eyes which stared over the soapy rim of a glass half-emptied.

His survey complete, he placed the drink carefully aside, smacked thin lips and demanded, 'Now, what would yerself be wanting with the likes of me?'

Remember your lessons, sunshine, Beddoes warned himself. And delivered Smythe's gospel, chapter and verse, in the tones of a cockney headbanger.

Fergus hadn't heard, apparently, for he sat stock still and absent in all but body. Then he bent forward, rigid and cold as a hanging judge. ''Tis a glib tongue ye have, for who's to say ye're not a British spy?'

This time, a Funny's foresight armed him. Preserve the moment, Snow had said, through an aura of birdshit and disillusion: hate us while you serve.

'Listen, uncle, I put me neck on the block for the great

119

unwashed more times than you've had 'ot dinners. One mistake is all, and Chummy pushin' up daisies. They stitched me up, see – call that justice? Don't talk *British* to me!'

'Indeed,' breathed Fergus, crystal clear through the babble, 'then who was it gave you the name, I'm wondering?'

'Leave it out,' snarled Beddoes. 'Your lot jerry-built 'alf the 'igh-rise in England. A copper, right, you think I don't know 'oo to ask?'

Sensing the doubt which hovered in tobacco-blue air between them, he gave the fiction a gloss of heartfelt fact. Tapping himself on the breastbone, he hissed, 'Minded royalty, I have, and done me stint at Wembley. Charity balls, world premières, you name it. Reckon I'd be 'ere in this rat hole, do yer, if I didn't want something bad?'

There was a hot red glimmer deep in the dark eyes. Watch your back, my son, he'll make you pay for that. But Fergus was supping again and, when the dead glass came down, the unhealthy bland mask was back. A serpentine flicker of pink tongue, then: 'A marksman, ye say. Would ye be having a weapon at all?'

Beddoes gazed up at the tar-pocked ceiling. 'You're unreal, mate. A busy in schtook, with a shooter?'

Fergus ignored the insult. 'Martial arts, too, by all the saints.' He aimed a silver-shot jaw at the bar. 'How would ye fancy the Flynn, there, outside in the street for a tenner a head and no holds barred?'

Your actual Irish giant, Flynn, built like Godzilla with a face someone had used for a punchbag. Beddoes risked a pull at his stout, barely controlling a shudder. Sour treacle, it was. 'Which arm d'you want me to break?'

Whereupon Fergus produced a wide and beguiling

120

grin, 'Ah now, isn't it grand? Would ye care to arm *wrestle*, then?'

''Ang about, Flynn's got four stone over me!'

''Tis meself that's asking, meanwhile.'

Fifty-five in the shade, Fergus, a weedy little runt in a potty coat which came down to his knuckles. He meant it, though, anyone could see. Calm as you please, and the pasty features untouched by the smallest doubt.

Beddoes recognized the trap at the very instant it was sprung. The room had fallen quiet; he looked up into a closed ring of gloating, expectant smiles. Then Fergus rolled up his sleeve.

Unbelievable. A forearm as thick as Beddoes' own thigh, marbled and muscled and almost completely hairless. The ridiculously small fist clenched and tendons rolled like thick white cables.

'I'll never walk among princes,' Fergus murmured, 'nor touch the hem of the mighty. A humble mason am I, and nothing to show but this trusty ould limb. Ye'd not be fearin' it, would ye? Just for the sport, mind you, and the price of Slaney's best tot?'

Though the grin stayed in place, he couldn't've made it plainer. Take me on, he was saying, or walk away for good. Away from a bunch of witless, leering Paddies, all the way back to loathsome McKay with your little English tail between your legs. *No* chance.

Beddoes had kept in training right up to yesterday morning. Nature had given him a wiry frame and a good deal more strength than his weight deserved; and judo the mechanics of leverage and counterthrust. Meantime, he'd been blackmailed by Smythe, sold short by Snow and conned by the local Godfather. He was very, very angry.

'Right,' he snapped, planting his elbow on the slick surface, hand extended, fingers splayed and ready.

Even so, Fergus caught him cold. The sheer animal ferocity of the old man's lunge had him resisting desperately. He held, just; and applied a bit of pressure in return.

The hush was total. Even the smoke seemed suspended. He read doubt in the faces above, and drew added power from the dismay which hung on thick, boozy air. He bared his teeth and drove forward with everything he had; and saw defeat in Fergus' sloe-black eyes.

His own defeat; for the old man had been toying with him. As the pressure built, he heard the creak of over-taxed wood and felt the slow unhinging of his wrist. Sweat burst from his forehead and his breath blew harsh and quick. He fought on willpower only, his arm angling impossibly and muscles in his shoulder shrieking with pain. And watched, numb, as his knuckles came to a gentle stop on the scuffed and burn-scarred table.

Amid the rejoicing, submerged by boisterous backslappers, Fergus alone showed no elation: offering a grave smile and a curiously ceremonial nod. Wordless, Beddoes trudged off to render his dues. The barman snatched his money and shoved the drinks in his face.

'Manage them unaided, can ye?'

His cheeks burning, his vision blurred with humiliation, Beddoes began the most desolate journey of his life; over five endless yards of bare and grubby floorboard. Homeward bound, bearing only the bile of defeat at the hands of a crafty pensioner. And please, Uncle Jock, can you keep me off Traffic.

Then, as he leaned through the bedlam of alcohol and stale sweat and delivered the amber spoils of victory, there was a rasp of grey beard at his earlobe; Fergus, granting solace and reprieve.

"Tis the champion of Dublin ye faced, me dear, ask

whomever ye please. Near to a minute ye lasted, which is more than a match for any man here.' He raised the small glass and quelled the hubbub and toasted 'a most gallant loser'.

Some time during the celebration, despite the barman's still-furious glare, he invited Beddoes back 'two evenings hence'; by which time he whispered meaningfully, he would be 'about ready to do business'.

Bong went the twee overhead bell; you may now smoke. As the plane levelled, Evans' ears popped and the jet-stream rose to a steady roar. A thirsty old business, with recycled air to scour the nostrils and parch the throat. A double Scotch would go down lovely, but you couldn't arrive legless at lunchtime; even in Ireland.

Before, he'd flown only in police choppers. Sound and fury, that was, chattering over the rooftops and your mind bent on whatever mayhem lay ahead. The best way to travel, see. No time for morbid reflection.

Resting his cheek against tepid perspex, he glimpsed a patchwork of greenery through looming white cloud. Up ahead, a sweep of silver wing juddered ominously. Nearer my God to Thee, he thought. A posh, disembodied voice at the helm, a foam-rubber bucket to sit in and half an inch of metal skin between here and eternity. Cheer up, bach. After touchdown it gets *really* dodgy.

He turned away from the skyscape, rejecting a pert stewardess and the bottled temptation she offered. A forty-five-minute hop, they'd said. He'd intended to use it wisely, girding for an alien isle and the brooding enigma called Daly. But the girl's perfume lingered, raising the ghost of Jane Neale and last night's long farewell . . .

* * *

He closed the door and she clutched him fiercely, the whole eager length of her alight and trembling. He half-carried her to the bedroom, through the debris of hasty packing and a whiff of lunchtime curry. For all she noticed or cared, it might have been a honeymoon suite. There, in warm but fading daylight, they kissed and touched and fumbled with zips like starved and clumsy teenagers. Their shadowed mutual urgency left him mere impressions of erotic beauty; firm creamy skin, slender limbs and a deep inner heat which took his breath away. Then they were twined on the bed, and the meeting of flesh as easy and moist as if they'd been lovers for years. She was every woman he'd known and more. She led him smoothly to the quivering brink, held him there briefly, and urged him to a blinding climax of honey and velvet. Shattered he was: so much so that he couldn't tell if it had been as good for her . . .

Dull bugger, he told himself, as the aircraft shied through a pocket of turbulence. If you need to ask, the answer's no. Not that it had mattered at the time.

Dozing, he woke to her nude silhouette and the smell of fresh-brewed coffee.

'You're right,' she murmured, and he could hear the smile in her voice. 'The place needs a woman's touch.'

'Same as the bloke who lives here.'

'I noticed. You won't recognize it when you get back.'

He took the cup, wishing he could see her face. 'What are you on about, girl?'

'Visiting, once or twice a week. Just to keep things in order. Don't worry, I'll be very discreet.'

'Oh aye? You think coppers are nosy, you want to talk to the wives!'

'Don't tell me you're worried about the neighbours?'

She had turned side-on to the streetlit window, lifting her cup and tilting her head back. Quite a sight, fair play, even in outline; but he sensed stubbornness beneath the teasing tone.

'It's not on, sorry. Police property, see.'

'You're wriggling, Huw. I'm a professional too, remember?'

'Meaning?'

'I do my homework. Long-service rights, a standing regulation. You bought this flat six years back. Shall I name the figure?'

He drank his cooling coffee. Not enough sugar, but it wasn't the time to say so. He was conscious of an essence that was hers alone, something light and spicy and untamed: and a small inner voice of disquiet. Huw Evans shacked up with the media. What's the force coming to, I wonder. Smythe had spoken, too, crisp and assured. *'You're unattached, officially and otherwise.'* And so you should be, bach, off to track bombers through Paddyland. At rock bottom, the unyielding granite of Welsh morality – it wasn't *right*, somehow, not here and now. With this thought uppermost, he spoke his mind. 'Don't rush it, girl. I mean, it's not that serious, yet.'

A flurry of disturbed air, the rattle of the saucer as she slammed it on to the bedside table. 'Not *serious*? My God, d'you think I'm joking?'

He heard the quick pad of her footfalls and winced at the flare of sodium light between suddenly backflung curtains.

'Look here, Huw Evans. Damn you, *look* at me!'

Magnificent, she was, no question. Her eyes aflame with anger, hair that coiled and tumbled, and high breasts jutting in pride and passion. She stood in naked, orange splendour like some painted, pagan goddess of love. 'Can you guess how many men have begged for this? And *dare* to say it's not serious?'

He was already scrambling from the bed, wishing the careless words unspoken.

'Stay where you are! Don't touch me!'

He reached for her anyway, stroking her cold and unsteady shoulders and mumbling inadequate amends.

'It's special,' she sobbed. 'Can't you understand? Why kill it before it's begun?' In distress, her accent thickened, an intriguing lilt he still couldn't place.

'You've never lived with a copper,' he said gently. 'Even if there's living to be done.' Which didn't help, either.

'Isn't that just like a man? You're all the same when you can't face responsibility. Off to the wars, in the name of some schoolboy *honour*!' Ancient wounds here, he could tell by the bite of the acid. 'I'm grown-up, Huw, I make my own decisions.' She had drawn away, facing him coldly, a challenge in every taut curve of her body. 'Be honest for once; you don't really *want* a woman.'

She was right, but not the way she intended. Even now, the space between them throbbed with magnetism. In spite of his doubts about who and what she was, in spite of his own clouded future, he could deny neither her nor himself. He gave her his very best grin, raising his hands in surrender. 'I *could* be persuaded, mind.'

The moment drew out; he actually saw the tension and bitterness fade.

'Why are we fighting?' she wondered sadly, 'when there's so little time?'

He brought her close, letting his hands and his lips give the unspoken answer. He tasted salt tears and felt the yield of her, and it was beginning all over again . . .

* * *

126

'We are crossing the Irish Coast,' the posh voice declared, 'and will soon begin our descent into Dublin.' More dulcet bongs, a brief scurry of activity along the aisles and the clicking of a dozen safety belts. The nose tilted downwards and Evans' stomach lurched in sympathy. Come on, bach, get your act together. But Jane hadn't finished with him; yet . . .

Second time round, and all questions resolved. There was no mistaking the force of her cry or the joyous tremors which gripped him; making his own journey's end so much the sweeter. In the musky aftermath, she curled against him like a contented cat.

'*Now* you can tell me.'

'Give over, girl. Elderly, I am, in need of rest and recuperation.'

Her elbow was gentle but pointed and persistent at his ribs. 'It's after midnight, and only the truth will do. You promised. Well, sort of.'

He sighed, warding off sleep and an insidious glow of well-being. 'What do you want to know?'

'Where you're going, of course.'

Though the darkness and his body still tingled with the print and the scent of her, a central core of caution remained unthawed.

She sensed it at once, inching away and allowing the pain to colour her voice. 'You're *still* suspicious. All right, of course I want a story. Mostly, though, I want you home safe. Is that so hard to accept?'

'Leave it there, lovely,' he mumbled, turning over and laying an arm across her waist. Staring at the ceiling, she was, he knew without opening his eyes.

'Somewhere secret and dangerous,' she mused, and the stubborn streak was plain to hear. 'For Queen and country, in the line of duty. What if things go wrong,

Huw? They'll hush it up, they always do. The unknowable soldier; is *that* what we want?'

Not by a bloody long chalk, he thought: and said nothing.

She burrowed into him, the power of her emotion overwhelming. 'We've *had* each other, Huw. I'm saying it's more than that. Whatever happens, *someone* will know and remember and care. For God's sake, think of it as bloody insurance if you must!' She'd found him at last, laying bare her most precious gift; call it vulnerability, bach, it's too early for big words. Like love. Thing is, you can't argue with her, she's right all down the line.

'Ireland,' he grunted. 'The Reapers are starting a new mainland campaign; we need information.'

'Why you?' she cried, and her anguish was frightening. 'You're not a spy!'

'Sins of the past, girl.'

'Blackmail, you're saying?'

'Not me, Jane. It'll not be written, mind; not ever.'

Her hand touched his face, soft and beseeching. 'This is *us*. Not work, not duty, just you and me. Is there somewhere or someone specific involved?'

'I don't know where yet, and that's gospel.'

She caught the implication and pressed him for a name; the tenderest of inquisitions. In the end he told her, suppressing every professional instinct and breathing 'Daly' into the darkness between. An act of faith, really, in memory of something he'd once treasured; and lost.

Though her flank caressed his hip and her breathing fanned his cheek, he was suddenly alone in the night. Distance and silence lasted for minutes: until she sighed and clung to him and made her own declaration. 'If what they say is true, he's like no man I ever knew. Thank you for trusting me, Huw; you won't regret it. And please, *please* be careful!' . . .

A shuddering bump and the howl of reversed engines brought him abruptly to earth. Another airport under the sun – green grass, black skidmarks scored into grey tarmac and a dozen national emblems on lofty, gleaming tailplanes. Ireland, mind, don't ever forget. Movement ceased and the rumble fell to a low-pitched whine. Wrestling his battered holdall from the bay above, he gazed inward on the very last image. Jane at the doorway, tousle-headed and moist-eyed, and a glimpse of soft slim thigh beneath his dark blue dressing-gown. I'll be back, he promised grimly, even though I walk the shadowed vale . . .

CHAPTER SEVEN

Customs took his time, shuffling papers and poring over the passport.

'Would you step inside, sir, and follow me.' Deadpan, he was, and ominously polite; an order, not a request. Bloody fine start, thought Evans, trailing the uniformed back through a diligent chatter of typing: blown on arrival. At which point he received a confiding over-the-shoulder grin. 'Don't be fretting, sir. 'Tis more private here for yourself and your friend.'

The 'friend' loomed large in an unlabelled sanctum. 'Michael O'Brien,' he murmured, and offered a welcoming hand. 'Thanks, Reilly. Away to the salt mines, now.'

In the flurry of salutes and withdrawal, Evans breathed easier and measured his man. Six foot two and built to match, yet compact and graceful with it. A bit of a scholar, too, if the domed receding forehead was anything to go by. The brown eyes were sharp and level, the handshake brief but firm. And why not; he was two rounds up already. Time to level the score.

'How do,' said Evans easily. 'You'd be the one who sent the telex.'

The broad, even features coloured faintly. 'A trifle terse, perhaps. Let's call it pressure of work.'

'Daft question, I expect. Clutching at straws, we were.'

'I know the feeling well.' An apology, near enough, and equal status subtly acknowledged. Leave it there, bach.

O'Brien folded himself into his chair, enquired after Evans' comfort and hauled a stack of documents from a desk drawer.

'Time's short, so I'll brief you here and now. My office is off limits, you understand.'

'Oh, sure,' Evans conceded, watching the large-scale map unfold across the polished surface.

O'Brien leaned over it, tapping a thin blue snake with his smart gold pencil. 'Daly's river. The border's *here*. You'll be fishing downstream, of course. You've bed and board just there, and a close-mouthed biddy to fill your belly and wash your socks.' He smiled ruefully. 'A shame it's only business. The place has a powerful beauty.' A wistful note which faded fast as he detailed the earlier itinerary.

Duty, mind, and fancy brochures littered about like one of those 'holidays of a lifetime'. It could have been embarrassing, especially when O'Brien tossed a healthy wadge of garish, unfamiliar currency on to the northern-most grid square of Leitrim.

'Cash payments only, please,' he ordered. 'You'd be surprised how many initiatives come unstuck on account of a thoughtless transaction.' Evans pocketed the notes uneasily, feeling cheap and furtive. Thirty pieces of silver, duw duw.

'Want me to sign do you?'

The broad shoulders rose and fell casually. 'It's London's budget. Buy Smythe a magnum if there's loose change.'

It was odd, really. You didn't meet too many coppers who could dish out a couple of grand without turning a hair. Even when claims had passed muster there was always a flicker of envy and a barbed, defensive jibe. 'Make sure she gives receipts, mate, or you'll catch hell from Fraud Squad *and* Vice!' Whereas O'Brien handled money like your genuine toff; as if it had no worth whatever. He *dresses* like a toff, Evans realized, noting too late the cut and drape of his grey lightweight suit. Bespoke tailoring, you couldn't mistake it; nor the shimmer of pure silk in the navy blue tie. Enforcers pay on weekdays, see; and time and a half for spying?

O'Brien refolded the map, deft as a cardsharp stacking a deck. 'Any questions?'

'One small point.' Evans nodded at the disreputable bag. 'Where am I kipping tonight?'

'Well now, if you're up to a priestly brother and a couple of teenage thugs, be my guest.' Seeing Evans' doubtful expression, he added, 'Even in *our* line, a man's entitled to choose his friends.'

'When was this decided, then?'

O'Brien consulted his watch. 'About twenty minutes ago.'

How does he swing it, Evans wondered, savouring essence of Brut under a piping shower. A busy, mind, same as me; where would he go for the honey?

An impressive city, Dublin, from the little O'Brien had shown him. Mellow, sunlit stone, elegant bridges and an air of bustling prosperity. 'There's a darker side, of course,' the Irishman admitted. 'Where beat men go in pairs.' There always is, mused Evans, sparing Roy Beddoes a thought. Which O'Brien caught at once. 'Don't worry, your man has contacts.' So saying, he gunned the scarlet, near-new Volvo smartly uptown to a secluded byway in Foxrock.

The house stood on a tidy patch of ground, white walls and black paintwork and a mature honeysuckle shrouding the porch. Not your actual mansion, but solid, stately and well beyond the reach of the average inspector.

Inside was more of the same. Golden parquet and a scatter of Bokhara rugs; custom-built sofas and Waterford glass; and, drifting above and between the sparkle, Evans scented lavender polish – and wealth.

O'Brien ushered him upstairs and opened a door at random. 'Rory's the younger and tidier. He'll not mind, for one night.' About thirteen, Rory, and deep into team sports and pop, judging by the posters on his walls.

Evans hesitated, beset by a feeling of intrusion. 'A bit hard on the lad; without consent, I mean.'

'The offer stands. Of course if it's too juvenile, I'll run you to the hotel. Gladly.' He didn't look glad, though; a hint of glower and professional hardness showing through.

Evans shrugged and conceded. A minor issue and much too soon to lose allies.

'Ellen's collecting the tribe,' said O'Brien, bluff and genial again. 'Bathroom that way, toilet attached. If you're wanting a nap, you'll not be disturbed. Drinks at seven thirty, dinner at eight.'

Evans smoothed the nub of sage green Courreges towel and admired the tiles it matched. Never mind the width, feel the quality; he can't be bent, surely?

Gradually, the house came to life around him; the flushing of loos, a rumble of talk and a mouth-watering smell of roast. He donned collar and tie and his decent grey slacks and went down, forearmed, to the arena. Cool head, bach. The aggro starts *after* the kick-off.

The boys were carbon copies, lanky and coltish and painfully shy, with the stamp of O'Brien all over them. Their mother, though, was mousy and plain; only bold violet eyes betrayed her. A twinkle of impish humour, and the glow of something sensual and enduring.

'She was near to noble beforehand,' her husband explained, 'and led me a desperate dance.' He pulled a

133

long face and clutched his breast, giving the Irish free rein. 'Woe to the fool who weds for money, then loses his poor heart entirely!'

''Tis true,' she agreed, clearly enacting a familiar rite, 'for today he's rich but desolate.'

Laughter broke and the social ice melted, but O'Brien's dark gaze stayed cool and shrewd and knowing. In case you were wondering, it said.

Point taken, boyo; more power to your elbow.

A crunch of gravel and the thunk of a car door stilled the chatter. Enter a 'priestly brother', you could tell by the tone of the hush.

An older, leaner, meaner brother, no doubt, his bony figure draped in black and an air of unworldly disdain. 'A fisherman, are you? Fishing for what, I wonder.' Withdrawing his chalky, pallid hand, he delivered a scathing grace. 'You'd best be starting the orgy now Julian your conscience is here.'

Against a setting of burnished mahogany, snowy linen and Royal Doulton, Ellen O'Brien served food for the Gods. Pure white pork and golden crackling, crisp roasties and sweet green peas, and a lemon soufflé you had to hold down with a fork. Between mouthfuls, the boys talked rugby – who was the greatest ever? As the vote teetered between Gareth Edwards and Willie John McBride, Evans witnessed a very private communion. Just a glance between man and mate, quickly delivered and instantly gone; a look of mutual need and tenderness more potent than any words. Evans' mind conjured Jane in naked glory. That's how it starts, see; and if you're very lucky, this is how it continues. Hang in there, girl, *I'm coming back.*

'Fall in troops,' ordered Ellen. 'Washing-up detail to the fore.'

'Aw, *Mum*!'

'That was the bargain, as well you know. Besides, the men will be wanting to talk.' She shooed them out, stern but affectionate, and they gave their good nights from the door. Whereupon Julian repaired to a hearthside armchair and Michael manned the bar.

'I've a rather fine brandy here,' he suggested, and Evans wagged his head.

'A waste, that; sorry. Cheap whiskey'll do for me.'

Above the chime of bottle and crystal, he heard a curious sound; like the twist of an eel on glasspaper. Julian was chuckling. 'As it does for us all, in the end.'

Michael leaned at the corner, easy and neat in a tan cashmere sweater and chocolate brown breeks. 'Pay him no heed,' he advised. ''Tis a stressful task, the preserving of souls; he always gets messy on wine.'

He *looked* messy, fair play, a jointless, grey-thatched scarecrow sprawled in an upmarket seat, and the tot in his glass skewed to a dangerous angle.

'You'd be some kind of lawman, I'm thinking,' he drawled. 'Where else would young Michael turn for company? What mischief are you about, then; and what would *you* know of the Troubles?'

Hold on, thought Evans, raising his eyebrows at O'Brien; *we* ask the questions. The Garda man nodded calmly.

'Julian's *witting*,' he murmured, 'and possessed of a marvellous forgettery. From hearing confession, no doubt.'

Evans raised his own tumbler pointedly. 'Drinking your booze, I am.'

'Even so.'

Thus sanctioned, Evans rounded on the elder O'Brien more roughly than he intended. 'All right, Father, a query for *you*!'

Julian cackled spitefully. 'Now there's the Polis for you — never an answer in sight!'

'You wear the cloth and the collar,' growled Evans, 'and give absolution to any young thug with British blood on his hands.'

'Not just British, mercy, no. God's house is open to *all* who repent.'

'Only thing blokes like them repent is not having time to kill more! Call that *Christian*, do you?'

'You're a churchman yourself, Mr Evans?'

'Methodist, I was; chapel. Back home, they say it's the same God.'

'Holy Mother, will you hear the man: join hands across creeds and the Border. Did they tell you *nothing*?'

'That's what I mean, see. Leaders you are, the men of culture and education. How shall we end the violence, then, when people like you condone it?'

Julian's hollow cheeks were pink, and the dark hooded eyes blazed malice. '*People*, yes. Polis? I wouldn't know.' And he downed his whiskey in a single, savage gulp. 'I'm an Irish Catholic Priest,' he said softly. 'Not necessarily in that order. In fact, when you've a day or a year to spare, you might think on the priorities involved. Resolve them you must, if you're to understand this poor benighted isle at all!'

He stood up, lank and haggard and unexpectedly dignified; and not nearly as drunk as he'd pretended. 'Miles to go,' he mumbled, 'and promises to keep.'

'Julian has a rural parish,' Michael added, 'and enough strayed sheep for three.'

Julian paused on the doorstep, peering owlishly into the soft summer night.

'You'll be planning some sort of deception, I'd say. A word of warning, then.' In the wink of stars, he looked sombre and forbidding, though his trained voice held wryness and self-mockery. 'Stick to the truth, as near as you can, for the Irish have mastered the art of illusion. And haven't we been deceiving *ourselves* for nigh on five hundred years?'

Inside, between tidying and smalltalk, Evans offered his thanks; which O'Brien brushed firmly aside. 'It's good for us all; new faces and a fresh point of view.'

A good man, O'Brien. And, if Julian was to be believed, the *only* man in Ireland whom he, Evans, could trust.

Beddoes baulked at the threshold of day, feeling distinctly ill-used. A surfeit of Guinness left foul fur on his tongue and a nauseous knot in his belly: the last two noggins of 'Slaney's Best' still pounded at his brain. Behind closed lids the light flared harsh and red and the strange setting heightened his sense of disorientation. Piss off, Tuesday, you're in the wrong room.

Someone was, anyhow. Suddenly and painfully awake, he detected a footfall, a rustle of clothes and tang of alien sweat. Christ Almighty, Fergus got leery and set up the hit! Tunnelling gingerly out of the warm, he risked a fearful peek.

Sunshine struck him like fiery needles. His bloodshot vision cleared and he breathed a quiet sigh of relief. Bess the landlord's daughter, he thought, recalling yesterday's special deal and a snatch of O-level Lit. According to the rhyme, she'd 'plaited a deep red blood knot into her midnight hair'. Or something. This one had midnight hair, all right, and a tasty line in female accessories beneath her black nylon dress. Which explained the rustles, of course.

She bent over, gathering clothes and a good deal more of his interest. A ladder gleamed in her tights, starting behind the left knee. He followed its upward progress

137

happily into the shadow of no return. A nice pair of legs and a healthy ogle; there must be worse cures for thick heads.

''Oo let *you* in, gorgeous? Come on, give us a kiss.'

She shied like a startled filly, swinging around and shattering the illusion. Brightness ill-became her, laying cruelly on suety features and a moonscape of teenage acne.

'Mercy, sorr, and ye gave me a turn; thinking ye fast asleep!' She tossed her head haughtily. 'And don't be getting fresh now, for I'm courting steady.'

What the hell, he thought, you don't look a gift horse in the mouth; even the innkeeper's nag. He sat up, letting the bedclothes slide down and gather in his lap. 'Takes care of you, does he, sees to all your needs?'

She blushed furiously, but her brown eyes lingered over his bare chest. ''Tis a fine young Catholic, mind you, who knows how to treat a lady.'

Beddoes stared frankly at the taut sweep of bodice. Tit for tat, like. 'Pity. Waste of Grade A material.'

'You're a terrible man, Mr Meadows. I think I'd best be leaving.' But she posed at the window, letting the backlight reveal her considerable charms. She was flirting with sin, waiting for his next move, and enjoying every minute. Her reluctant eagerness reminded him of someone, but he couldn't remember who. He covered his eyes and bowed his head like a clown playing Hamlet.

'I'm a lonely man in a strange town. You're breakin' me heart!'

The smile softened her plainness and lent her a fleeting appeal.

'At least have a drink with me,' he pleaded, pretending to rummage for a bottle under the pillow.

'At *this* hour? Shame on ye, Mr Meadows!'

'Roy's the name; and yeah, it *is* a bit late.'

'I'm a respectable girl, to be sure, and never touch the stuff.' She was giggling now, the straitlaced act forgotten.

'*What*? A smart city bird like you? You oughta pop in one evenin' and sample some Irish mist.'

'Me father'll not have canoodling with the guests.'

Sure. Not till he's seen the colour of their money. 'Give over! 'Ow's 'e gonna know?'

She leaned forward confidingly. 'He watches us like a hawk, Roy, and me the closest of all.'

The closer the better, he reckoned, catching a glimpse of cleavage and a stronger whiff of her personal scent. Nothing wrong with girlish sweat, so long as there's a bed handy.

She read the intention and avoided his lunge. 'Behave yourself, now, else I'll swap floors with Maria!' And flounced off without so much as a backward glance.

Brilliant, my son. A full range of patter employed and what do you get? The brush-off; from a pimply Irish scrubber, to boot. The unwelcome sun streamed in and his hangover blossomed anew. Whereupon she sidled into the doorway, a warning finger raised to moist lips.

'Father's away to Slaney's of a Wednesday eve; for dominoes and boozin'. Back at the stroke of ten, mind you, and heard from a furlong away. I'll be in for a taste of the mist, meanwhile.'

Women: what could you say? Nice to be sure of home comforts, though, at the start of a dodgy campaign.

He yawned and fingered his stubble, wondering how Evans was doing. The advance patrol, according to Smythe, sent out a few days early 'to zero in on the source'. Swanning about more likely, with rod but no gun in Darkest Eire. Cushy number, that. On the other hand . . .

On the other hand, Huw would be deep into badlands and no one to watch his back. Funny: despite twenty years of policing and the contrary evidence he'd gleaned, Evans still took folk on trust. Till he knew different, anyhow. A bloke who piled in where angels and hard-knocks feared to tread. One of these days it would land him in serious trouble.

Beddoes stretched and eased cautiously off the bed. Outside pigeons were crooning; the lino was warm underfoot. Not too bad, being upright. Once the anaesthetic wore off.

After a while, he coaxed some vaguely tepid water into the disgraceful basin and smeared cool lather on. He smirked at the steamy, fly-blown mirror, remembering another Smythe gem. 'Deep penetration,' the Chief had decreed; we'll do our best, come Wednesday. You wouldn't catch *Evans* befriending the natives, not while he had that classy redhead in tow. Then, with lime-scented foam on his face, a razor in his fist and women in mind, Beddoes made the connection.

He'd been little more than a kid at the time, raised by near-grown sisters and dying to know the score: till Rosie took him in hand. Literally. Rosie was scrawny and crippled, and even more eager than him; they'd scaled the heights together. Two years older and decades wiser, she'd found a *man* and let him down light as a feather. The pick of the bunch, actually. He'd remember her when many a fairer successor had faded from his ken. The Irish bird was a bit that way – hot stuff between plain wraps. You can't tell a book by the cover.

He rinsed his face and sluiced the clippings away, sobering by the minute. Time to be out and about, getting a feel for the place. He didn't fancy it, somehow. Local knowledge and streetcraft had always been his stock-in-trade: he was edgy and fraught without them. Thoughts of Rosie had started a trend. As he gazed over tatty and alien rooftops, his mind winged stubbornly homeward . . .

He'd be thirteen or so, the budding scholar in daylight and running with the yobbos by night. If you lived in Dockland and went to the Grammar, you had to show your bottle.

It started around eight one balmy summer's evening. The lads had got lucky somewhere up West and were offering mystery tours. From this distance in time he couldn't even recall their names.

He remembered the motor, all right. A 2·4 Jag, new and shiny and silver and sleek as a Quemo Sabe bullet. It smelled of leather and poncy cologne and the speedo went up to 150. He remembered the birds, too, a couple of high-breasted eighteen-year-old lovelies who fondled him idly and gave him dry dreams for a week.

Magic. Purring the mean streets like royalty, waving haughty at pop-eyed mates and giving the busies the finger. Crime doesn't pay, maybe, but, Christ, it was fun for an hour or so.

He stumbled home through the cooling dusk, hugging himself in sheer pleasure; and told his folks he'd been down the park.

When he got in from school next day, his dad had a face like thunder and a brass stair-rod in his gnarlcd, arthritic paw. A docker was Alf, who swore by a strong right arm and God's honest toil.

'Get to your room,' he snapped. 'We gotta bone to pick.'

Trudging guiltily up the narrow, spotless stairway, young Roy racked his brains for excuses. In vain. So when Alf read the charges, he turned Queen's Evidence.

''Ang about, Dad, *I* never nicked it! Mindin' me own business, wasn't I, and they hauled me in.'

'Yeah, yeah, screamin' and hollerin' every step of the

way, werncher? You were swannin' around in a hot roller like little Lord Muck, and slaggin' off the Ole Bill. I warned yer once, not six months back. Okay, you 'ad yer fun. Get them trousers down and take what's comin'.'

He obeyed, baring his teeth and gripping the back of the chair till his knuckles turned white. Behind him, Alf's breath wheezed and bellowed and the slim hard metal cracked against his own tight-fleshed drawers. He hardly noticed the pain; the shame of it almost killed him.

'Next time,' the old man gasped, flinging the rod aside, 'I'll hand you over to the busies myself.'

He lurched away and the harsh rasp of his wasting cough echoed down the stairwell. A sick sound, no question; sicker than either of them realized.

The weals subsided quickly, but Alf's searing contempt hung over him like smog. He had algebra homework, his favourite. It might as well have been Chinese. In the end, he went down to make peace. 'I'm sorry, Dad, honest. It won't 'appen again, I promise.'

Alf slumped in front of the telly. Reflected light played in his eyes, but they couldn't mask the pain or the heartbreak.

'Promises! 'Ow can you hold yer head up, I wonder? Smart as a whip, schoolin' at the Grammar, and friggin' around with a bunch of oiks oo'll be doin' bird before they get the vote! Carry on, my son, and you'll wind up as bent as they are.'

He cried himself to sleep that night, the last time ever. Within the month, they'd carted Alf to the infirmary; six weeks later, they laid his wasted body to rest. He left a distraught widow, a dowry for each of the girls and a dockside lad determined to go straight. Between leaving school and joining the Force, Roy kept his head down and his nose clean. Even today, the old lags gave him respect. Roy Beddoes is the Filth, and hard as bloody nails. But he's fair as they come and honest as the day. Just like his ole man . . .

The pigeons rose with a clatter, their wings flashing steely in the sun. A chug and a whiff of diesel, and the brewer's dray pulled in. Two brawny Micks got out, spitting on their hands, raising the cellar grill and rolling brown and gold casks down the ramp. A snippet of Irish song broke through above the sullen rumble, and, with it, a warp in time and place. They're not just *foreign*, Beddoes realized, they're bleedin' prehistoric.

It's the strangeness, he thought, and the deceit. Both went directly against the grain; together they reduced him to a kind of moral paralysis. While the curtain lifted and the overture played, Roy Beddoes hovered in the wings, consumed with stagefright.

It was Alf who saved him, from somewhere beyond the grave. Because if you *really* wanted to rile him, you only had to hint that Britons no longer ruled the waves, and overseas might be better.

'Cobblers!' he would roar, his broad face purple with outrage. '*Great* Britain, and doncha ever forget it! Half the nignogs in Christendom'd still be up trees if it wasn't for us, no matter what them fancy books say. Remember 'oo you are and where you come from, Roy. You ever get the chance to do your bit for England, you oughta do it with *pride*!'

Okay, Dad. It's an older, dirtier war than yours, and no one's blowing bugles. Muggins drew a short straw, though; may as well get it over. He put on his threads and found the map and set out for a preliminary reccy.

CHAPTER EIGHT

'Dear Land of My Fathers,' a younger Huw Evans had oft times sung from the heart of the Arms Park enclosure. In Welsh, mind, and all the native fervour he could muster. Magic, it was; the poignant anthem pealing and cherished scenes upon his inner eye. Sunset over the Tawe, stack smoke limned in fiery gold and the Morriston *Orpheus* in full cry; the slate grey sweep of Aber's Front on which he'd lived and loved; fern-cloaked hills where men breathed free and sheep might safely graze. When scarlet jerseys spilled from the tunnel to a roar that split the skies, his blood surged with passion, and savage tribal pride. Especially when they were playing England.

At first, sitting on a hotel balcony and watching the sun decline into Galway Bay, he put such misplaced bloodlust down to exile. But it wasn't as simple as that. The Valleys were home all right, and no fairer spot on God's green earth. Over the past few days, though, Southern Ireland had been running a pretty close second.

Setting up the first layer of cover, he was, following Snow's script to the letter. A strange old business, playacting to an empty house. Who among the many watchers and waiters was Daly's creature? Could the blue-sweatered, nimble-fingered boatgirl who'd chummed for shark and sucked a clay pipe and blarneyed so winsomely back into harbour *really* be a red-toothed Provo in drag?

He didn't know. If trouble came, it would strike when least expected; best to savour this brief busman's holiday.

He was typecast in the role, no question. The well-heeled tourist-cum-angler, mustard keen but large and a trifle awkward, a sucker for local knowledge and the tall tale. London's blood money had its uses, too. Nothing like a good fat tip to win friends and influence people.

And it worked both ways. As the sun blazed and the fish steadfastly refused to oblige and the talk and the whiskey flowed, he found himself warming to a steady procession of ghillies, gaffers and guides. The Welsh are only Irish who couldn't swim, they say. Many a true word.

Because he was picking up affinities, and hearing the echoes of home. The inbred love of music and song, and a little of what you fancy to perk up the rhythm and mellow the voice. The total lack of po-faced Anglo-Saxon *reserve*, and the sheer bloody nosiness of the gossip; and just below the surface, a glint of steely, uncompromising religion. Not Chapel, mind, but still. Change the accents, the lyrics and the hymn tunes and you could be anywhere between Pontypool and Pembroke.

A tidy country, fair play. In this most benign summer, it unfurled before the eye like a mellow tapestry wrought of green and gold. Windswept mountains with musical names – Knockmealdown, Keshcorran and Magillicuddy's Reeks; the loughs that curved in a bracelet of brightness from Sligo to County Clare; a coastline of rare splendour and startling contrasts – the enchanted haven at Dunmore East, the thundering spume on Benwee Head.

There was something in the air too; something which struck a plangent chord among the harmonies of his own Celtic heritage. A lurking aura of tragedy, of innocence lost and trust betrayed and brave blood spilt for a shining, doomed ideal. He was beginning to sense the Terrible Beauty; and why a man might hold this land so dear. No wonder his twilight thoughts had turned to patriotic fervour.

He shivered, not from the sudden chill. Someone walking over his grave, more like. Tread wary, boyo, remember whose side you're on. To know the enemy is one thing; for Christ's sake don't confuse him with your friends.

'Irish mist, ye say,' she giggled, sprawling carelessly on the faded orange quilt. 'It surely puts fog into the brain!' Not surprising, seeing as she'd drunk half a bottle in forty minutes flat. Whilst Beddoes had sipped sparingly and listened to her tale of woe. Her name was Shelagh, she said, and she slaved for a father who paid her a pittance and boozed the profits away. The boyfriend, she confided, was a fumbling lout of little brain and less ambition, but deemed a 'suitable' match. Whereas she fancied a life of *Dallas*.

'The *clothes*, Roy,' she breathed, 'and so many rich and handsome men. I'd go tomorrow, if only someone would ask.' Her brown eyes were glazed and dreamy, and her blue cotton shift had ridden a long way upward.

'Wouldn't we all,' Beddoes murmured, closing the curtains and easing alongside her with a much shorter trip in mind.

He rested his palm on her shoulder, slipping his fingertips under the strap. 'Naughty,' she muttered, without the slightest conviction. He mouthed her throat, tasting cheap scent and willing flesh. His hand slid lower and her breast nuzzled into it like a plump, hard-nosed puppy.

'You're evil, Roy. We'll both go to hell.'

'Sure. Not tonight though.'

'I'm *hot*,' she declared plaintively, fanning herself with one hand and unfastening buttons with the other.

He stripped quickly and towered over her, tugging the scrap of pink nylon down over broad pale hips.

'Tell me I'm nice,' she begged him. 'I *am* nice aren't I?'

'You're bleedin' *gorgeous*!'

But when he rose on his elbows and probed for the early connection, she wriggled and jack-knifed and lay on her side, whimpering, 'Don't do me harm!'

'Give over, girl. Assault with a friendly weapon, this.'

'You're not understanding. *Harm* will surely come of it!'

He drew back on his haunches, quivering in frustration. Warm soft light through the curtains, an eager, white body and the promised land in sight; and the gormless bird turns frigid.

'Haven't you *got* anything?' she pleaded, and the penny finally dropped. Sodding Paddyland, wasn't it, where the Pill was something they gave sick horses. How many years since you carried a rubber in your wallet, sunshine?

'Come on, Shelagh,' he coaxed, cupping a smooth taut buttock. 'I'll go careful, honest.'

She was simmering nicely, he could feel her heat; but her knees stayed tight together. Jesus, he thought, fitting himself to her clenched form and gently tracing the curve of her waist; back to square one.

The sounds came loud and shocking, an adolescent snigger and the crash of breaking glass.

'What the hell's that?'

She sat up, flushed and embarrassed. ''Tis only the local ruffians. Terrible keyholers, they are.'

'I'll give 'em bloody keyholes!' He stumbled into his trousers and heaved the door open.

The evidence was plain and damning – a shattered

147

tumbler on the threshold and mocking laughter fading in the gloom. Furious, he sprinted to the corner, skidding wide on greasy brown lino and cannoning off the opposite wall. The stairwell rang to fleeing boots and obscene jeers. He pelted down to the seedy entrance; too late. A straggle of youths in the distance and passers-by, grinning.

Still fuming, Beddoes retraced his steps. A flock of outraged, senile faces watched him from the sanctuary of the entertainments lounge.

'Ye ought to be ashamed, young feller,' whined one. 'Displaying yerself before gentlefolk, and during *EastEnders* too!'

'Sorry, Grandpa,' snarled Beddoes. 'Didn't realize it was your turn.'

The door slammed and he trudged on, not bothering to zip up his fly. Maybe she'd buy the natural method – coitus interruptus.

But when he got back, Shelagh was fully clothed and icily sober.

''Ere, what's up? 'Is Nibs isn't due for ages.'

She tossed her head and flounced past, delivering judgement from the doorway. 'You're a rat, Mr Meadows, plying the pure with liquor. I ought to be informing me father.'

Insult to injury, this, and he responded in kind. 'Oh yeah? About as pure as the driven slush!'

She had the last word, though. 'You'll get a new maid, come the morn. Two hundred pounds, six months from the pension and whiskers to rival a walrus!'

So much for home comfort, he thought, surveying the trickle which passed for a shower and leaning forward to ease the ache in his groin. So much for meeting the Provos with a clear eye and a steady hand in the wake of indoor athletics. Where are you, Pol Parrot? Our man in

Dublin wants servicing. He smiled painfully, seeing the funny side. It's Boy Scouts you need for the Irish caper – they always come prepared.

Resigned and recovered, he donned his working denims and hit the alien streets. It was muggy and dim, and stewed stout tainted the dusk like fall-out. Time to spare: he didn't fancy bumping into Shelagh's legless old man. Go the pretty way, my son, suss out the alleys and bolt-holes. Never know when you might need one.

So he prowled the meaner places, where mongrels cringed and garbage fermented and the hovels leaned together like so many crooked, rotten teeth. He was testing his inbuilt compass, discovering which of the twisted passages provided a short cut; and which were cul-de-sacs. Familiarity breeds content, he realized. Any minute now he'd be getting homesick.

He studied the map by the flickering glow of a lone, archaic streetlamp. Far enough, he reckoned: now let's escape from the maze. There was shadowy movement somewhere behind, but when he turned, the cobbles lay empty and silent. A cat yowled, near and mournful, and the jolt of it steadied his nerves. *Course* there's shadows, you berk. If it wasn't for the night hawks you'd be out of a job. Even so, he travelled briskly until he reached a corner he recognized and spotted the red neon sign. Slane s, it said: in Ireland, no one knows y.

They came in an eddy of rank dark air, from three sides at once. Jesus, he thought, in rage and disgust, another Fergus-type trial of strength. A crucial instant of hesitation which cost him dear. He managed one half-hearted throat chop, feeling the crunch and gurgle and hearing the sob of pain. Then they were all over him, reeking of armpits and Dutch courage; too many to fend off, too close for effective counterstrikes. He went down

149

under a flail of vicious punches, curling over and shielding his head with his hands. 'Okay,' he grunted, 'so I came second again.'

A boot smashed into his elbow and a pair of bony knees ground at his kidneys. 'Hold the bastard, me lads, he'll not forget this night.' A vaguely familiar subhuman growl, but the sound that followed struck cold, unbelieving horror to the depths of Beddoes' soul; the sharp metallic rasp of a handgun being cocked. They were hauling at his ankles, and his shout of denial served only to disguise the report. '*There*, me English darlin'; that'll learn ye to meddle!' A lunatic chuckle, a waft of stale booze, a release from crushing weight. Then footfalls were fading into the red-veiled night, and there was warm wet numbness somewhere below his waist.

He lay with his cheek in a scatter of grit, breathing great gouts of sour Irish dust and the sickening stench of his own blood. Pain took him like sudden fire, flaring out from his left leg, scouring his body and searing his brain. Spasms convulsed him and consciousness ebbed away. In a last instant of sanity he understood what they'd done; and plunged into blackness screaming a desolate protest. How the *fuck* did they know who I was?

Harriet Slade wrinkled her nose and sloshed her bra through half an inch of scummy grey water. Why bother, she wondered listlessly. The party's over, we're getting down to the dregs. Gerry, for instance, and a handful of his most feckless, freaked-out followers. Those with any gumption had already gathered their pots and pans and quietly stolen away. Except for Peg, who couldn't; and Pete, who wouldn't dare.

So what's a girl like *you* doing in a place like this? She slumped against the cool grimy porcelain, weak-kneed and shivery at the mere remembrance of his touch.

150

Getting withdrawal symptoms, that's what. Face it, you're hooked; denied a nightly injection, you're as twitchy as any other addict. Because Cav had gone cold. The last time — nearly a week ago — he'd taken her briefly and brutally, and left her as soon as he'd done. Since then he'd prowled the crumbling boards in silence, and you could *feel* the coil of tension in every brooding step.

Until yesterday, when his anger finally erupted.

'Look lively!' he snarled, aiming a vicious kick at Gerry's fouled and slovenly pad. 'On your feet, all of ye; take up your verminous beds and walk!' For twenty minutes he strutted and swore like some frightful, bearded stormtrooper; lurking and leering above them while they humped leaky mattresses and tatty possessions up two flights of dimly treacherous stairs.

He gave no reasons and it made no sense. The second-floor rooms were neither larger nor cleaner; the ancient whiff of tom cat was truly vile. What's more, the innards of the loo had long since rusted solid, so poor pregnant Peg had to lollup up and down whenever she wanted a pee; which was often. Now the lower levels rang hollow and deserted. The instrument cases stood in splendid isolation, clean and curved and gleaming; and somehow deadly. She shivered again, this time in real apprehension. Knowing she wouldn't leave if there was the slightest chance that he might come to her again.

She rinsed and wrung, draping the sad-looking scraps of nylon over her wrists and flicking spray from her fingers. She trudged to the top of the stairs, bearing tokens before her and leaving a damp trail behind. And paused to peer through cobwebbed glass at the surprising prospect outside.

A mature, detached residence, she mused, in several acres of ground. Well, rubble, anyway. The demolition men had done a good job, flattening the neighbourhood for half a block in at least three directions. From here you could see the length of the street, right up to the main thoroughfare. As she watched, a red double-decker trundled past, reduced to half-size by the distance. So *this* is why Cav moved us, then. He likes a room with a view. She smiled at the absurdity and groped her way creakily downward.

It was almost an action replay. Sunshine, blue sky, and a yard that smelled of summer dust. Peg lounged on the front step, arms akimbo and belly to the breeze. While Harriet wrestled the clothes-prop, Pete picked mournful, diminished chords from a battered acoustic guitar. And stopped in mid-strum to herald the new arrival.

'Hey,' he breathed, more cautious than before, 'look what the cat hauled in.'

He bloomed among their drabness like an outrageous dark-stemmed orchid; an electric blue gown, crimson jeans and the inevitable purple sunspecs. Though he had gigged with Pete for months he insisted on a formal introduction, deferring quaintly to Peg and positively drooling over Harriet herself.

'Well *ah'm* a Harry, too! Short for Harrigan, you know, but the homefolks ain't so hot on Christian names. Useter *eat* Christians, back in the good ole days.' He spread his arms and waved pink palms to outline his dilemma. 'Ah need house-room, marn. Mean old landlord done confis*cate* the skins and throw me out. All for three month back rent. Money's for spendin', right? Ah mean, what's a marn s'pose to do, die for want of rum'n'pussy? Beggin' your pardon, ladies.'

Pete cast a fearful glance at the upstairs window, but he answered boldly enough. 'You're the king of rhythm, baby. How can we refuse?'

Peg nodded vacuously, and Harriet kept her doubts to

152

herself. He *was* the only real musician around. Maybe he could salvage something from the groupwreck.

Oddly enough, his mere presence had sparked a minor miracle. As he sauntered easily up the steps and into the rancid gloom, Gerry himself stumbled forth; on his feet before midday and relatively *compos mentis*.

'Jesus, it's the spade,' he breathed, and his bloodshot eyes flared with sudden hunger. 'Got anything hard, have you?'

'Only the landlord's heart. C'mon Gerry, you know ah never use the stuff.'

'He's kippin' here a while,' Pete explained and Gerry nodded eagerly.

'Cost him, that will, at least a tenner for the kitty,' he said.

'Oh marn,' breathed Harry Two, 'you in a bad way.'

He paused in the stairwell, apparently shaking his tight black curls at Gerry. That's why he wears the shades, Harriet thought; so no one can see his eyes. Because unless she missed her guess he was actually studying the instrument cases.

Cav thought so too, looming large and sudden from the dimness in midstair. 'Have a care friend,' he warned. ''Tis sacred ground you're treading.'

A note of naked menace chilled them all. All save Harry Two, who pulled a wistful, snowy grin.

'This your gear, marn? *Im*pressive.' He broke into the old soft shoe, a snake-hipped, slick-footed blaze of blue. 'Hey, big marn,' he bellowed. 'How's about a bit of reggae rappin'?' The impromptu dance was leading him closer to the cases, and Cav's tone turned lethal. 'I'll call me own tune, thanks. Meanwhile, ye'd best walk wide of the instruments.'

Harry Two shuffled on regardless. 'Thing is,' he

drawled, 'ah never seen fiddles that big, not ever. Ah'm *curious*, marn.'

The sheer speed of it took her breath away. Four long, predatory strides and Cav had blocked the other man's advance.

'Take your evil black self away from here!'

Harriet cowered, watching the curl of Cav's fingers and waiting for the glitter of steel. And Harry Two simply stood there, loose-limbed and unafraid. 'Cool it, fella,' he advised. 'Ain't nobody *that* curious.'

He held station a little longer, just to make the point, then turned and loped upstairs. In the gloom at the top, his smile shone like a broad crescent moon. 'Listen, big marn: you show me yours and ah'll show you mine.'

He disappeared, leaving Cav to vent his rage on Peg, who'd been daft enough to giggle. 'Whisht, ye great stupid cow!'

Strange, reflected Harriet, much later. I'll lie down for Cav anytime, anywhere; but Harry Two makes me feel safe. He had something about him, an air of contained power and untapped reserves. She'd never fancied a black man before – still didn't really – but if things *did* turn nasty . . . Put it this way, us Harrys must stick together.

Now, why should the bloody alarm be going at the dead of night? Not an alarm, stupid, the phone: which made even less sense. He found it at the third fumbling attempt and hauled the receiver to his ear.

'Mr Evans in 205? 'Tis Dublin on the line.'

A whine and a click and O'Brien's voice, very terse indeed. 'Get yourself up here, now. Take this number; an all-night taxi.'

'Wait.' Still groping, Evans hit the lamp switch and

recoiled at the glare. Through slitted lids, he found a biro and scribbled on his bare thigh.

'O'Connell's statue, any driver'll know it. It'll drop you at the hospital.' A beat, and a weary, disgusted sigh. 'Your man's been shot.'

'Hold on!' Evans began, but he was already talking to himself.

He dressed and packed and called the cab, keeping his mind wilfully blank. Don't think about it, bach; do it.

In the dim empty foyer, a whey-faced clerk tallied his bill and stowed his money without surprise or comment, as though guests swanned off at three *every* morning. Outside, he paced the pavement aimlessly, conscious only of muggy air and a completely starless sky; and a first flicker of dark red rage.

The car roared up, a metallic Cortina with twin spots, a matt-black bonnet and racing spokes. Lovely, he thought, a cowboy. He chucked his bag in the back and slumped against slimy rexine upholstery. The driver twisted round, freckled and ginger and bright-eyed. In the glow of the courtesy light, he looked about fifteen.

'Where to, sorr?'

Evans told him.

'Bejaysus, that'll cost a pretty penny!'

'Pay now, shall I?'

''Tis a trusting soul I am. Full speed ahead?'

'Aye.'

'An emergency, I always know. Addition to the family?' Evans scowled and tapped his watch. 'Two minutes already, and the meter's running.'

'Right ye are!'

He slammed into gear and took off like Fittipaldi. He wasn't done though, not by a long chalk. 'How d'ye find the country, sorr?'

'Magic.'

155

The sarcasm passed unnoticed. The boy was leaning back, bawling above the engine clamour and the howl of slipstream. His ear jutted like a cup-handle. 'Would ye be here on business, then?'

'Fishing.'

A mistake, this; the questions came thick and fast. Had he tried Lough Derg, wasn't the Shannon grand, did he know the Jock Scott was death on white trout at twilight?

Evans grunted and swayed, watching the blaze of the beams. Until the weather saved him; a roll of summer thunder, and silver stair-rods arcing into the windscreen. The boy ignored it, keeping his foot on the board and probing for personal titbits.

'Are ye a married man?'

'Look,' growled Evans, 'I'm not in the mood, see. Can't you get this crate *moving*?'

After that it got quite hairy. Sheet after sheet of lightning, laying the hedgerows stark and grey; visibility down to a matter of yards; and the youthful pilot, hunched and surly, driving like the truly insane. Gripping the leather strap and bucketing wildly, Evans conducted a private post-mortem.

Less than a week from home, and the operation in ruins. Operation? Cock-up, more like. A couple of green and reluctant conscripts, an overstretched Irish double, and a hour's wisdom from a birdstruck boffin; hardly the CIA, mind, and *they* hadn't been too clever lately.

The car lurched and fishtailed viciously. ''Tis only a wayward cow, sorr. No problem at all.'

'Watch it, will you!'

The rain was easing, and the engine noise rose to a steady scream.

Was Roy screaming, he wondered? He had every right, fair play. Came up the hard way, Roy did, on native wit, professional merit and sheer hard grind. When the chips were down, he'd always face the situation square and choose right: duty. What else is there, for a cop? Tonight he lay in an alien land, bleeding for a foreign cause. Dying, maybe. Hospital, O'Brien had said; must be *some* hope, then.

If Beddoes pegs, he vowed, Jane shall have her story. The blackmail of Smythe, Snow's cynicism, Green Reapers and Uncle bloody Sean Daly and all. Hang in there, boyo, the cavalry's coming.

They entered Dublin in a dry pale glint of dawn. The boy dropped him as promised, curling his lip at the size of the tip. 'Mean beggars, the Welsh.'

And Evans rounded savagely. 'Go home, I would, before I ask for change!'

He waited while the sky lightened and O'Connell's stony eye turned pink. Come on, Mike, you're putting a hell of a strain on friendship.

The Volvo purred up on sidelights only; he was inside before it stopped moving.

'Now then,' he demanded, the anger breaking loose, '*tell* me!'

O'Brien sat bolt upright, arms straight, hands at ten-to-two. Thin light aged him and the steel was showing through. 'We're still covert,' he muttered. 'In theory, anyhow. He hasn't been named, nor will be if I can help it. Mistaken identity, right?'

'But . . .'

'Hear me out, would you mind?' A command this, a tone of unyielding authority. 'We got there as fast as we could. Deep shock, naturally, and powerful loss of blood.' He released the wheel with one hand, consulting his watch. 'They're still operating. We'll know more when they're done.'

Red sky in the morning, Evans observed distractedly, a warning for someone.

'You were travelling together, if anyone asks. A policeman rang the hotel.' O'Brien's mouth curved downward in deep distaste. 'That much at least is true. When you've seen him, come to headquarters and ask for me, official.' He swung beneath the red cross and eased into the long shade of the building. 'Away with you, now!'

'For Christ's sake,' Evans beseeched him. 'What *happened*?'

'Holy Mary, must I spell it out? The crazy young eedjit got himself kneecapped!'

CHAPTER NINE

It might have been any hospital anywhere; cool cream corridors, antiseptic air and soothing staff. 'He's in good hands, he'll be right as rain by and by.' Oh sure. Like some brave English flier with half his undercarriage shot away. They gave Evans tea and an empty waiting-room and left him to sweat it out.

The walls closed in, bearing government health warnings. 'Promiscuity – a cancer risk?' 'AIDS clinics, alternate Fridays'. 'Beware: cholesterol kills!' Same old story. Anything you fancy is immoral, illegal or fattening. He emptied his cup and checked his watch. Four whole minutes had passed.

He closed his eyes and slid into a lurid, waking dream. Roy Beddoes at the police gym, clad in yellow bathers and doing a Long John Silver. A beechwood crutch, a purple eyepatch and scarlet oozing thickly from a raw and ragged stump. '*Ah har, Huw lad, anyone for 'opscotch?'*

'Mr Evans? The surgeon will see you now.' He blinked up at a prim, bespectacled figure and a blue smock which denoted rank. A sister, probably. He dogged her squeaky stride under soft fluorescent lights and past the 'Consultants Only' sign. 'He's *Mister* O'Leary, mind you, top man in his field.'

The top man shooed her out, nodding to an upright chair. 'You're new to the custom,' he snapped. 'You'll need to grasp the *ethos*.' A dapper sort of bloke as a rule, Evans reckoned; medium height and build, jet-black hair parted dead centre and a riviera tan. Not too sunny this morning, though; the red-rimmed eyes and stubbled scowl of an undertipped Spanish waiter.

He paced the book-littered office, his muscular hands in constant motion. Beyond his window, a rain-washed sky and the rumble of distant traffic. 'He's a lucky man, Mr Evans. It used to be done head-on, the muzzle against the patella and half of the leg blown away. What with the shock and the blood loss, they killed far more than were lamed.'

'*Lucky*, is it? An innocent tourist cut down on a public street?'

O'Leary curled his lip in open disbelief. 'It's the *medical* judgement I'm giving; the lads have improved their technique. Nowadays they operate from behind.' A curious undertone of almost paternal pride. 'A cushion of flesh to take off some of the speed. Penetration through the hinge and the kneecap shattered from *inside*. Result, a frozen joint. *Stigma*, d'you see, a lasting irreparable effect.' He paused at the window, a hanging, vulpine shade against the early glare. An unguarded moment, and the Irish invaded his cultured delivery. 'Behold the fate of all who would betray. Let's see what I can show you.'

He cocked his right knee, raising the heel and keeping the ball of his foot anchored. A dip and a forward lunge, left leg leading and the other trailed behind; soft, sickening slurs across the polished floor.

'*There*,' he breathed in triumph. 'Traitor's gait!'

'Darro,' growled Evans, 'call yourself a *doctor*?'

The tone and the insult left the surgeon unmoved, provoking only a sallow, gold-capped grin. 'More of a mechanic, lately. Spare-part service, you might say. And isn't modern plastic grand?' He was performing again, enjoying every minute. He shoved his fists forward, flexing his elbows inward, fitting one set of knuckles to the other and rocking them from side to side. 'Multiplanar accommodation; as good as the real thing. Our prize replacement gets around Royal Dublin very close to par.'

There's lovely, mind. Bionic Beddoes crossing putters with a bunch of retired bank managers. 'I'll tell him; he'll be thrilled.'

O'Leary's glower was back, saturnine and resentful. 'If it's Meadows you're meaning, I've already said – more fortunate than he deserved.' He marched to his desk and sat bolt upright. Telling it straight for the first time, he was, and not liking it a bit.

'An obsolete pistol, d'you see; high calibre, low velocity, and pressure waves like an earthquake. There's massive haematoma of the sciatic nerve and the exit wound was gruesome.' Briefly, the gloating tone returned. 'He'll carry the scar to his grave.'

Exhaustion hit O'Leary suddenly; you could see the weary disgust in his hazel eyes. The words came slow and heavy, a reluctance he made no attempt to disguise. 'The bullet passed clean through. When the tissue heals and the pain eases, there'll be no impairment whatever.'

'You *bastard*!' whispered Evans. 'Why didn't you say first off?'

'You didn't ask. Go home, Mr Evans. And take your innocent tourist with you . . .'

Midday, and last night's downpour only a cooling memory. The building hummed – white coats everywhere, lifts and taps and buzzers going and the same sister setting the pace through a different, disinfected maze. 'You're to keep it brief; five minutes or less.' She herded him into a curtained room, her fobwatch poised and glinting.

161

Shades of the future here, bach; he'll be like this when he's old. A wasted grey mask on the pillow, reeking of drugs and distress. Reverent silence, an eery red seep of packeted blood through coils of transparent tubing. The bedclothes arced upwards over his knees; his breathing was shallow, and one pale hand twitched weakly. *Impairment*, duw duw: he'd do well to hang on until nightfall.

The eyes flickered open, burning dark in pain and recognition.

Evans had to crane to catch the greeting.

'Wotcha, uncle. 'Ow's it hangin'?'

'Limp,' he growled, making the standard response with giddy relief and not enough thought.

The bloodless lips stretched a parody of mirth. 'Yeah, well, a limp's better than a wheelchair.' Too sharp for his own good, Roy was, even in this state.

'You'll be okay,' Evans insisted. 'The quack says so, mind.'

'Cobblers. If it wasn't for the jabs I'd be climbin' walls.'

'It's just a bad flesh wound, nothing permanent.'

'Two minutes,' snapped the sister, and the real Roy Beddoes made a fleeting appearance.

'We were expected, Huw. Otherwise, 'ow about this lot?' He stirred weakly, pointing at the damaged leg.

'Be still, you foolish boy! D'you want to dislodge the drip?'

'Time's up, Mr Evans.'

'Someone grassed,' Beddoes whispered. 'For Chrissake, watch your back!'

'I'll find him,' Evans promised from the door. And when I do, he added silently, following starched rustles yet again, heads will surely roll . . .

O'Brien's underlings gave him the treatment – a petty inquisition and half an hour to cool his heels. Confined and overheated, his imagination ran amok. The pallid wreck in intensive care would do well to survive, let alone walk; you didn't need a doctor to tell you. O'Leary was party to the plot, anyway. Probably spent his weekends digging British bullets out of faithful Irish flesh. Meantime, Smythe and Snow were doubtless priming the next wave of gung-ho special agents. Undercover, duw duw. We'll rip the lid off, he thought. Marry Jane, sell the story to Darryl Zanuck and buy a sheepfarm in Brecon. Go home to McKay and Traffic, more likely.

Admitted at last to the presence, Evans let his anger loose. 'So what happened to the watchers? Having a pee break, were they?'

O'Brien sat pale and upright amid the clutter of enforcement. A scatter of buff files on the desk, duty rosters and mugshots covering the bulletin board, and a large-scale map with coloured pins for the trouble spots. No windows, Evans noted; like the basement, only bigger.

'Watchers? D'you think we've nothing better to do? Contacts, they said, not nursemaids for a tearaway!' The Garda man clearly had problems of his own; a bloodshot glare, an uncharacteristically dishevelled suit, and big fists clenched like ivory hammers on the dark, dull wood.

The outburst sounded genuine, and Evans' suspicions deepened. What had he asked Snow? *Not sending him in as a sacrifice, are you?* And never received an answer, come to think of it. Cool head, boyo, it's no time for an own goal. He reined himself in, an enormous effort. 'All right, it's water under the bridge. Got a suspect have we?'

O'Brien coloured and toyed with a file. 'There's no investigation. How can there be a suspect?' He glanced up defensively into Evans' appalled stare. 'What should we ask? Who shot the English spy? Holy Mother, they'd be queuing for the honour!'

'Dear God, *what* a bloody country!'

'It happens to be *my* country.'

Lunacy, it was, a heedless gallop through an historical minefield. Press on, then, the only way out is forward. 'We're soldiers, you and I,' Evans began softly. 'In no man's land, and flying the flag of truce. He's my responsibility, see. Surely you can understand *that*?'

O'Brien was up and prowling, his large figure absorbing the light and distorting the scale of the room. 'I'm allergic to shootings on my patch. They'll not go unpunished, one way or another; you have my word.' He swung round, his own frustration boiling over. 'Six hours of barter with the accursed media, and all on account of *cover*!'

'Cover?' echoed Evans, incredulous. 'For what? Going home, we are.'

'Mission continues, they're saying. Want to see the telex?'

'*Who's* saying?'

'London. Smythe, to be precise.'

They faced each other in mutual disbelief.

'He's crazy,' Evans muttered, and O'Brien's shiny dome dipped in acknowledgement.

'Even so. You've to scrap the touring and make for the border. Fish as agreed and report developments.'

You're on your own, bach, lumbered in limbo and no fall-back. And *Snow*, not Smythe, sent the message, it stood out a mile. *Funnies!* 'Listen,' he asked, in plaintive, professional appeal, 'just between you and me. Who's the *real* enemy?'

O'Brien turned away. For no good reason, the incident map had claimed his undivided attention. 'It's blindman's-buff,' he conceded. 'It's been like this for months.

London's a sieve, they say; the lads know the moves in advance.'

It rang false and speculative; an excuse, not an explanation. About to cross the lines, Evans simply couldn't afford to believe it. 'Come on, Mike. Two of a kind, remember?'

'Changed your tune, haven't you?'

It brought him back, nevertheless. Duty, see, the single common code.

O'Brien's words came slowly and against the grain; but they came. 'I'm not strong on mythology – unlike most of my countrymen. However, if I had to, I'd put my shirt on Daly. He has sources all over, I'm told; smells treachery before it's hatched.'

'Darro,' breathed Evans. 'Into the lion's den. Thanks, anyway.'

O'Brien faced him, tall and haggard under the single bare bulb. 'Two of a kind, as you said. My days are numbered, also.'

'How d'you mean?'

'If he rumbled Beddoes that fast, it's a matter of time before he settles with me.'

He came unwillingly through a soft summer morn to the glen where it all began. A trespass on time, to be sure, for the sounds and the scents were the same. The past reborn, and forgotten wounds ableeding. But the signs could no longer be doubted, and whatever befell must be faced.

A dozen winters had left their mark on the stream; a broader bend, a steeper fall, a pool which once had been shallows. Green saplings had thickened and spread, and the path took unrecalled turns. Despite larksong and the lowing of kine, a sense of unease possessed him. The crystal remembrance he'd clung to so long seemed all at once clouded and false.

Slowly, the balance shifted. Warmth at his back reassured him, and sunlight on hurrying waters. His spirit soared, his power awoke, and the mist in his mind burned away. Observe the current, Sean, see how serene it flows. Beneath is constant, a singular purpose and a solitary goal. 'Tis a perfect mirror for yourself – matured but not grown, changed yet unchanging. He went up to the fence by Kevin's Fall and considered the long, lonely journey . . .

Returning, blooded, to cloistered calm, Sean shackled the demons that drove him, and the violence that lurked in his soul. The nearness of death in the moonlight had spawned a bitter resolution.

He had to be rid of the girl.

A week ago he had faltered, lured by the blaze of her body and the vision she dared him to share, to enshrine the struggle in writing. 'You have the gift, Sean!' she would cry. 'How long shall we wait for another?'

And sometimes, drinking her untamed essence and slaking her need, he very nearly believed her.

The dream had died with Keeling, for now he knew the truth. Someday, somewhere, the spark in his nature would flare. He'd be off like his father before him, angry but unprepared, into the curve of a misty morn and a chatter of enemy guns. And *she* would be left like his mother, a barren and loveless crone. Let her go, Sean, before the bond is full-formed.

He owned little knowledge of women, and had reckoned without her guile. When he pleaded for parting and study, she thought it a marvellous joke. 'Away with you, man, you could fly the Finals tomorrow!'

Then he claimed to be weary of her, an even bigger

166

mistake. She opened her blouse and stepped from her skirt and pressed the whole vibrant length of herself against him. 'Would you care to say that again, Sean?'

He squirmed aside, that his body shouldn't betray him. 'There's somebody else,' he mumbled, hating himself and the lie. And saw the hurtful knowledge cloud her lovely eyes. '*Yes*!' she cried. 'She's fair and false and older than God. For years she's lain sighing and bleeding, and fetching the flower of Eire to a cold and early grave! She'll destroy you, Sean, like thousands before you. For the Dear's sake and mine, see sense!'

The heart of the matter at last, and not to be denied.

'I'll be leaving now,' he said.

She stormed for a while then, a beautiful naked child at odds with her man and her riches. When he stood unmoved and unmoving, she drew herself up and dried her tears and spoke like the fine Irish lady she was surely destined to be.

'You were the brightest and best, Sean. You're a fool to us both, which I can't forgive. Nor shall I ever forget. Wherever you are, whatever you want, I'll do it. For what we had, and what we might have been . . .'

The Quiet One returned in winter, and the same agricultural van. 'Action's afoot,' he confided. 'Say nothing until they ask.' He drove to the windswept hub of the town and a famous musical tavern. They breathed booze and bodyheat, threading the crush to a small, secret sanctum behind. Where, to a muffled lilt of 'Dublin in the Green', Sean scanned unit profiles and heard the cry of havoc from a youth with mad amber eyes. ''Tis powerful sure and simple. We cross on the ferry, and plastique inside of religious candles to take for our dear ould mothers. We'll be needing a week for reconnaissance; 'tis a huge old pub near the barracks, having many a shaded nook for the planting.'

167

Sean sat both listening and reading, a talent he'd learned long ago. As the speaker prattled of fuses and clocks, a fatal weakness sprang from the printed page. He was off into frigid darkness, watching the arc of Keeling rise and claw at the starry night. He closed the file and noted the name and marvelled anew at his power.

The youth was ablaze with fervour, like some beardless, unholy saint. 'We'll be in of an eve when the soldiers are there, and a harmless sports bag forgotten beneath the table. Fifty or more will be shattered and maimed, and all the headlines you're wanting!'

A lull in the singing; a waft of sloe gin stole by. The Quiet One muttered behind his hand to a ghostly man called Fergus. Three others sat hard-eyed and nameless on a bench that sealed off the door. A jury, thought Sean, hand-picked to consider *my* verdict.

'Now, *Mister* Daly,' crowed the boy, 'and what d'ye say to *that*?'

'It's your funeral.'

A flush of callow anger and a hiss of punctured pride. 'Will ye listen to this college boy, and him a puny dwarf?'

'Mind your tongue,' snapped a juror. ''Tis himself who bore the Cavanaugh half a league at dead of night.'

'Explain yourself, Sean,' Fergus grunted; more command than invitation. There was menace in the air, they were willing him to failure.

'It's four together, strange to the land and biding too long in one place.'

'Christmas, mind you,' said the Quiet One, 'when loved ones come from afar.'

The bench nodded in unison, and the boy preened like a game cock.

Sean sighed and shoved the tell-tale dossier forward.

'Your man's claustrophobic, he won't stand the wait. When he cracks, he'll betray you all.'

The room fell utterly silent. He could almost taste their collective dismay; and a kind of incredulous awe. The power stirred and he freed it, curling his lip and showing his contempt. 'You're too long away from the schoolroom. Is not one of you able to *read*?'

Alone among them, the boy fought on; a doomed and toothless challenge. 'And how would *you* do it, then?'

'Find an exile who favours the cause. Let *him* take the lie of the land. Woo him and supply him, give whatever he asks; and he'll do the job alone.' He gave the boy a pitying glance. 'And keep the hotheads at home.'

The tension simply melted away. Suddenly, stunned and unbelieving, he was staring up at a ring of grinning faces.

The youth, Sammy, clasped his hand and murmured a sheepish apology. 'Proud to know ye, Sean, 'tis an amazing gift ye have.'

Cries of agreement, heavy paws at his shoulders; until the Quiet One called them to order and took a more sober tone. 'The attempt was already made, Sean. It happened last month, and fell out precisely as you said. One dead – the betrayer, by his own hand – two jailed and one missing.' He gazed down, his creased and weatherworn features hot with shame and pleading. 'They didn't believe, Sean, I was duty-bound to show them. We *need* you, man!'

'*Charades*,' Sean said softly, 'in a sly little taproom. Did no one consider this: why should *I* need *you*?'

They left him then, hunched and tight-lipped, with hopeful, fearful glances.

Rattling homeward in icy darkness and a faint whiff of dung, the Quiet One craved forgiveness.

'Let it be,' Sean warned him. 'There's thinking and

work to be done.' And half a mile further on, in the sad certain knowledge of all their tomorrows: 'Don't ever lie to me again.'

Thus began the divided time, and trials of mind and spirit. Lectures and libraries claimed him, and midnight toil at the books. Once a month, in changing, decrepit locations, he would breathe blue fumes of tobacco and whiskey and debate the mechanics of slaughter. As the seasons wheeled and winter retreated, he began to encounter the girl; lovely as ever, distant as never before, and always with a different man. So much for oaths and endearments, he thought; she's as fickle as breeze down the glen. But sometimes, deep in the spring-scented night, he would lie alone and grind his teeth and suffer a terrible yearning.

A remedy came in the final hour of an almost-summer night. He'd read too late and too long; English and Spanish and Dutch invaders bickered and brawled in his mind, having neither sequence nor sense. He propped his aching head on his hands, watching the waver and swim of print in the bright white pool from his lamp. A skein of history tangled and lost: there wasn't enough information. Vision cleared, weariness scurried away. Four simple words to shape his campaign and he spoke them like a prayer. *'Information is the key.'*

Not yet twenty and still at the fringe of mayhem, he began to construct his web. Cosy letters to exiled family; innocent chats with those who came and went across the waters; a choice source here, a hidden contact there. He permitted neither favour nor exception. Friend or lover, woman or man, he used them all ruthlessly and never let them go – or know.

And honoured his word. War, like charity, is best advanced at home. The whispers seeped back from quiet corners of rowdy pubs. If you're needing straight gen, ask the midget; if ye want it to work, get Daly. And if ye fancy the away fixture, save your breath.

On the eve of graduation, the Quiet One brought honours from a far less public school. ''Tis getting beyond me, Sean. Baby-pink faces, new jargon, and weapons you'd never *pronounce*, much less fire. A charmed life, man and boy, and out to pasture now. It's *you* they're wanting instead.'

Where did the years go, he wondered, watching a slant of greening sun and hearing the river's song. They passed away in conflict, like too many friends and not enough foes. He went downstream, breathing crushed wild thyme from underfoot. Or perhaps it was a bitter whiff of the past. For he had fought a thousand unsung battles, not always against the English. Small clouds hid the sun, and the chill struck darker memories.

A parley with the hard men on a storm-torn day one March. Fergus, down from Dublin in a black coat to the ankles and a mood to match the weather.

'The spell is broken, Sean. Wherever we go, they're waiting; reading the intention and picking us off like flies. *What's wrong?*' Outside, the clouds sped by as grey as gunsmoke. The peatfire smouldered low and blue, and they hunched like hopeful buzzards round a plain unvarnished table; where Sean displayed coloured snapshots stolen by his secret watchers. 'Six of them, Ulstermen all, and records to curl your hair. Spies, gentlemen. What would you have me do?'

A squall of rain on thatch, a gust down the chimney which fanned the flame to pink; and Fergus, passing sentence. 'Kneecaps, Mister Daly. Send them North one-legged!'

'They've tarried a while, mind you.'

171

'It signifies naught,' snapped a Dubliner. 'Let 'em hobble and peck on the foul Orange streets; we have to make an example!'

'It would leave tongues and memories intact. Cripples can be useful, I'm saying. Hear me out. You'll have an example, all right.'

As he spoke, the gloom lifted. Soon the whole room was aglow with vengeful eyes and frankly admiring grins.

''Tis a grand wee man ye are, Daly. May the magic never desert us!' They clattered away in an elderly car, to the drum of another downpour and the strains of a rebel song.

It took him three weeks to run them to earth and orchestrate the reprisal. Then, the people of six scattered Northern towns awoke to a terrible sight in each of their well-tended squares. They formed fearful knots and drew near in the raw April dawn. A blindfold, headshot, propped-up corpse, and the slogan printed in furious red. 'Keep Eire clean — take your garbage home'. And the fame of Daly was murmured abroad, and the faithful smiled again.

And have you no regrets, Sean? He stood by a deep and silvered pool and studied his own short reflection. Remembering the times, soon and late, when he'd recovered the school clothes from mothballs and sortied across the border. And ranged the encampments unchallenged, counting heads, assessing morale and charting the next bloody ambush. We do what we can because we must, and no regrets whatever.

Under his hand, the cause had prospered, in spite of the ill-starred Brighton bomb, and the bigot Smythe's much-lauded mainland campaign. Though many who

172

ventured abroad were lost, the native soil had remained inviolate: until now.

The sky cleared, a blackbird spoke. He settled himself at the base of a tree, feeling rough bark at his back and laying his palm on cool moist earth. He closed his eyes and summoned his power and sifted rumour from fact.

For his web was aquiver with tension. From every nook and corner, the same urgent warning hummed in. The English have discovered Sean Daly and are bent on abduction and murder. They're using policemen, not soldiers, a squad of case-hardened, streetwise thugs well versed in sniping and judo. At first he refused to believe it, but the buzz and the stories persisted. In the end, he consulted the mainland and his oldest, most trusted source.

'It's true,' said the bitter, barely familiar voice from which most of the Irish had drained. 'But he's far from your average English bobby, and he's coming to *fish*, not shoot. More by luck than judgement, they've found you a worthy match.' A pause, a sigh, a note of unlikely appeal. 'Take care, Sean. If you harm him, they'll send the first team.' Still the best, after all those years in exile. Four terse sentences, and a whole new strategy revealed. They're getting wise, at last: seeking *information*.

He stood and stretched and brushed dead leaves from his seat. Moving lightly through dappled shade, he was touched by a reckless impulse. It must happen *here*, he thought, where the first fierce vow was made. A battle of wits between equals, and may the best man win.

He came to the ford in brilliance and threw back his head and laughed. The sound swelled and echoed from heather-clad slopes, and startled rooks took flight. You're only a puny dwarf, Sean, legend and lore notwithstanding. When you're playing host to enforcement, 'tis as well to be forearmed!

173

CHAPTER TEN

'It's good and stiff; now push against me.' A tasty offer, even if she did have a forbidding glare and hands like a plumber's pipewrench. But when Beddoes obliged, white-hot lances raked his thigh and sweat oozed out in buckets.

''Ere,' he gasped. 'That *hurts*!'

'We'll not be walking *this* week if we're shy of a little twinge. Come: let's be having a leg-up!'

Grasping the cool metal bedframe, he fought to raise the damaged limb despite her sinewy strength.

'*Much* better. Same time tomorrow, then. Flex those muscles, meanwhile!' She swept away in a crackle of blue nylon and a squelch of rubber-soled shoes. Physio, she reckoned: more like soddin' torture.

She wasn't the only one, either.

'You've an enviable constitution,' the quack had declared, during his crack-of-dawn round. 'In the pink already, and only twelve hours off the drip.'

'Sure. Comes from clean livin', y'know.'

At which the sallow features hardened, and the brogue turned tart and frosty. 'Is that so?' Beddoes winced and writhed as pitiless fingers probed along the dressing. 'Then what brings you here like *this*, I wonder?'

Charming people, the Irish: and all in it together.

He *was* on the mend, though. A healing itch around the wounds, and awareness of the world beyond his bed, where green gingham curtains swayed in the breeze.

Through the open window came birdsong and a distant whiff of diesel. He wrinkled his nose in perverse pleasure. Real life: makes a change from Dettol. Scores to settle out there, my son. Fergus for a start, then his Provo mockers; one of whom would be finding it hard to swallow.

He grinned bleakly at the prospect, gritting his teeth and willing the grey-blanketed lump of his knee upwards to his chest. Watch it, lovely, he cautioned his absent tormentress. By tomorrow we'll be having a leg *over*.

Settling back on starched whiteness, he rehearsed the sequence she'd taught him. Lift, bend, straighten, lower. He closed his eyes and ignored the ache, thinking of Evans instead. Walk soft, uncle, it's a bleedin' dodgy business. Stay away from the alleys and don't go talking to strange men. The rhythm of exercise drew him into a private world of effort and pain. Lift, bend, straighten . . . He never heard the turn of the latch; the voice blared sudden and loud. 'Making progress, I see. You've much to be thankful for.'

A big balding bloke in a posh lovat suit, and an air of disdain which got right up Beddoes' nose.

''Oo says?'

'O'Brien's the name: Garda.'

The joker who sent the telex, Beddoes realized. He looked the part, all right; chosen to sweet-talk the media and stay clear of the streets at night.

'Yeah, well, I think your policemen are *wonderful*!' The brown eyes narrowed. Mutual distrust stalked the room like a third presence.

'So you should. We've spent three days covering your tracks.'

'Pity you didn't start sooner.'

'Oh, but we did, Sergeant. Care to hear the official record?'

'You're gonna tell me anyhow.'

'I am indeed.'

Leaning easily near the window, O'Brien adjusted the crease in his immaculate trousers and tallied the charges on thick, splayed fingers. 'You invaded Slaney's and fell for the oldest con in Dublin.'

'*Orders*, okay?'

'Next you seduced the maid – crudely, fruitlessly and to an aroused audience.'

'Including *your* lot, no doubt!' Furious, Beddoes conjured the images. The naked squirmings, pimply lechers at the keyhole – and a bunch of sex-starved beat men drooling over the shortwave set. 'You bugged the room, you bastard!'

A casual wave of dismissal and gold cufflinks gleaming against snowy linen. 'If only the budget would stand it.' The tone sharpened, the hand stabbed forward in accusation. 'To cap it all, you exposed yourself to the entire hotel and a score of innocent bystanders. Holy Mary, you're supposed to be *undercover*!'

'I did *my* bit,' snapped Beddoes. 'A foot in the door, see. Where were *you* when the roof fell in?'

Briefly, O'Brien's composure faltered; a quick tug at the striped silk tie, a faint pink flush of embarrassment.

Hauling himself straighter in the bed, Beddoes pressed the advantage. ''Oo did you tell, then, apart from your ten best friends? You've got a rotten apple, mate. Don't talk security to *me*!'

O'Brien stiffened, formidable, and forest green in the slant of sunlight. 'You're trying my patience, Sergeant.'

'Leave it out! The Provos were waiting, how else would they know?'

'It has nothing to do with the Provos!'

'Oh? Down to the fairies, is it?'

The Garda man smiled, thin and distasteful. 'A matter

of carnal appetites, to be sure. You dipped your wick in a private well.' He made it sound thoroughly obscene. 'Erinmore maids are renowned for room service. Shelagh's boyfriend is the jealous type; he watched over her virtue.'

'Sure,' Beddoes muttered, recalling the scuffles outside, *'she's got a minder who works*!'

'Well, there you have it.' O'Brien was in control once more, righteous and aloof.

'Give over! You get kneecapped for spying, not sparking!'

'Not any more, it seems. Be grateful for bungling amateurs.' He was hiding something, you could tell by the cryptic gleam which lurked in his dark brown gaze.

Gripping the sheets and fighting a wave of nausea, Beddoes threw down the gauntlet. 'You're covering up, sunshine. Amateurs, says *who*?'

O'Brien's smile broke free, wolfish yet complacent. 'It didn't take long, given your antics and a smatter of local knowledge. I asked the boy that shot you.' He stood there in tailored assurance, casting a shadow of chill, incontestable truth.

Drained and feverish, his hold on reality slipping, Beddoes hit back out of sheer instinct. 'I wasn't followed,' he muttered. 'I'm particular about things like that. So how come they knew where to find me?'

O'Brien loomed at the bedside. His broad pale face seemed to waver and fade, leaving only a ghostly, Cheshire-cat grin. 'If you'd paused for one minute to ponder, you'd have worked it out for yourself. Shelagh's fiancé serves at Slaney's bar.'

Beddoes slumped to the pillow and closed his eyes. His mind reeled, seeing again the furious muddy glare, hearing the vicious growl at his ear; and Snow's fastidious warning: *'In Ireland, that commodity is strictly for home consumption.'*

177

O'Brien was speaking, twisting the knife. 'I've been covering up for *you*. For London's sake, I'm obliged to conceal armed assault. Away with you, I said. Check in your gun and keep your mouth shut. No charges, I told the Chief, the victim doesn't exist. *Highly* entertained, was the Chief.'

Beddoes lay still, drowning in a dull red sea of pain and humiliation. 'Does Huw know?'

'Not yet; but Smythe does. You're to go straight home as soon as you're able.' An intake of breath, a whiff of expensive aftershave, and a tone of withering contempt. 'And next time you venture abroad, get someone to padlock your flies!'

She woke to an aura of maleness, and the mattress beside her still warm. He's gone for a slash, she thought brazenly, and when he gets back I'll be ready. Again. Alleluia; Cav has returned to the fold.

It had happened without warning, less than twelve hours ago. The Irish contingent appeared, bearing odd-shaped Woolworth's parcels and an air of purpose renewed.

'Home improvements,' Joe beamed. 'Ye can watch for a dollar a head.'

An offer which Gerry's burned-out band received with glazed indifference.

The hard core accepted, Harriet to the fore, Peg and Pete as close as Siamese twins, and Harry Two guarding the rear. The yard lay baked and blinding, a fitful breeze raising miniature whirlwinds of ochre-tinted dust. A sense of open-air theatre – mild anticipation, what will they think of next?

Joe was brilliant, banging spikes into powdery mortar and scaling the dung-coloured brickwork like a pale-limbed, blue-clad chimp.

'He climbs for a hobby,' Cav grunted, paying out rope and rare confidences. 'Can ye imagine? I mean, it's feckin' *dangerous*!'

Hark who's talking, mused Harriet, recalling the flare of steel; because Pete was chancing his arm.

'Give over, he's a Paddy! Bet he learned at Wimpey's.'

Harriet cringed, hearing Peg's gasp of horror and expecting the lightning to strike. But Cav's wrath fell on Harry Two, who was tapping calypso rhythms from a rusty dustbin lid.

'Hush your racket! 'Tis like the deathwatch beetle!'

'No harm in hoping.' And Harry Two smiled innocently into the bearded glower.

Inside the hour, Joe was down, pink with exertion and too much sun. Herding them into welcome, fetid cool, Cav ransacked the ancient fusebox while Joe tacked bright grey flex along the rotted skirting. When twilight fell, they were ready; the test subdued them all.

Harriet gazed in wonder at the spotlit devastation outside; stark and rugged masonry, briar patches black and spiked as military barbed-wire. It's like *Beau Geste*, she thought; a lone, embattled fortress and concrete desert as far as the eye can see.

'Security lights,' sighed Joe, in pious satisfaction. 'Now ye'll sleep safe in your beds of an evening.' And Cav's sardonic shout of laughter chilled her to the marrow.

Later, though, he had plundered her body and turned the ice to fire; blazing hunger, pulsing need, and a joyous resurgence of frenzy. She urged him on, gnawing his shoulder and raking his back in revenge for the ache of his absence.

'You're learning, Miss Slade,' he informed her, and she basked in his glittering grin. 'Be easy a while, then we'll try for the second coming.'

Now she rose quickly and shrugged into a cotton slip.

The boards felt gritty underfoot and her breasts tingled from the rasp of his beard. Around her, the air seemed strangely wakeful: rustles and creaks and too much light. Right, let's see what's going on.

She huddled in clammy darkness at the foot of the stairs. Above and behind her, Joe's arclamps cast a diffuse inward glare. From the basement below came sounds of stealthy labour and a fainter, dustier glow. *And one of the instrument cases was missing.*

Her resolve wavered. The sinister space mocked and demeaned her. He's doing something secret, he was trying to *screw* you to sleep! The noises stopped, the darkness closed in; the whole house was poised and listening. She whirled, sensing a presence nearby. Her trailing elbow struck hollow and loud on the remaining case. Above her the stairway hung silent and densely shadowed, not a soul in sight. But there *was* movement – a savage, bearded figure rising from the basement with terrifying speed. The hand which so lately had roused her twined cruelly into her hair.

'And what have we here – a snooper!'

'Cav, please, you're hurting!' The black eyes glinted fiercely. As pain flared and her head wrenched back-wards, she glimpsed a moonlike show of teeth and heard a dark brown voice.

'Ah 'preciate the help, marn, but ah'd've caught her myself directly.'

She actually *felt* the rage flowing along the arm that held her. Through a blur of tears, she watched Harry Two stroll from the dark, wearing only mauve boxer shorts. 'A commune, right? Share'n'share alike.'

She was suddenly free. Cav's right hand swept upward in a swift and shining arc. Harry Two halted, the ebony muscles smooth and taut, the grin as white as ever. 'Easy, marn. Ain't no call for blades!'

180

'Is that so? 'Tis a powerful handy weapon for the gelding of randy black apes!' He rounded on Harriet, the knife still poised and deadly. 'Keep yerself decent, woman, you're preening about like a slut!'

Shaky with relief, she bowed her head and hugged the skimpy bodice. 'Sorry, Cav. I was only . . . I needed the loo!'

The beard twitched in disgust; Harry Two slipped her a quick, approving wink.

'Be off to your beds, the both of ye, and stay out of each other's way!'

She trudged the stairs, acutely aware of the graceful stride ahead and Cav's furious glare below. 'I don't know why,' she whispered, 'but thanks, anyway.'

A reassuring chuckle, a twitch of broad black shoulders. 'My pleasure.'

Not yet, she thought, resting uneasy in the all-at-once solitary gloom. But if this goes on, you could well be next in line . . .

He sensed it at once from the lip of the ford where the waters chattered and shone; an unseen coolness the length of the sunlit glen. The Stranger has come: as well that precautions are taken, and the power of Daly endures. He sidled upstream, keyed and soft-footed, testing the breeze like a pointer. There, through a lattice of greenery, he detected a flicker of movement and the hiss of upthrown line. And gazed down in sudden anger on a pale-eyed, sandy, bungling oaf with no art to his efforts at all. His hook had stuck fast in a branch overhead and the kerfuffle he made would alert every fish in the county. A wrench and a stumble, a glitter of spray and language to shame a navvy; then he was at it again, wielding the rod like a pickaxe and lashing the surface to foam.

181

So much for worthy opponents and the word of a trusted source. Be easy, Sean, nurse the rage and let it grow for a darker, more dangerous time. Bring the intruder downstream, meanwhile, and let Casey finish the job.

Curiosity held him, and the sly pleasure of observing unseen. As the day broadened and the Stranger toiled on, Sean was compelled to suspend judgement. Amazing what can be learned from watching a man fish.

For he had patience and purpose aplenty, and a shrewd eye for the water. Large though he was, he trod lightly; only technique let him down. Even as this thought formed, the Stranger's wrist rediscovered the knack – the subtle split second of waiting which tautens the backcast and delivers the fly straight and true. He was hunting in earnest now, at one with the pulse of the river.

Presently, in a narrow cut arched over by heavy foliage, he fashioned a delicate rollcast and reaped his just reward. Intrigued, Sean charted the private temptation. First fish on new water, and only a shade under-size. Into the creel with it and no one any the wiser. The big man shrugged wryly and followed the lore. When the victim flicked upright and arrowed away, his smile was as warm as the morning itself.

So Sean trailed him down, aware of the smell of heather and an unlikely bond already forming between them. Until, at the bend in O'Byrne's pasture, they witnessed a slow, stately rise. A choice lie, to be sure; from the depth of the swirl, this would be something special.

The Stranger checked, his freckled face tight and absorbed. He tested the leader and hunkered down and duck-walked into range. The rod came upright, glimmering, and the reel stuttered as more line was slowly drawn off. A long, tense wait; then the big figure was backing away. A flash of teeth and a glint of monofilament drifting free. He's changing the fly, thought Sean, going up a couple of sizes; just as I would myself.

But he wasn't. He retreated steadily out of sight and into the meadow behind.

Confounded yet cautious, Sean eased from the shade and beheld an astonishing sight. Alone among the cow-pats and buttercups, the sandy stranger rehearsed his casting without a hook at all. How many anglers, he wondered, could turn their backs on a marvellous rise which might cease at any moment? *Far from your average English bobby*, the sad mainland voice had said. Rightly, it seemed. Time to be finding out, then, and Casey must bide a while.

The line unfurled in a smooth orange arc. The Olive Dun settled, gossamer-light and a yard upstream of the rise. Evans watched, dry-mouthed, awaiting the speckled lunge and strike which would crown a golden morning. Purloined pleasures, in the midst of duty and danger; they couldn't last. For the moment, though, the world turned on sunlit water and a big trout, lurking.

No offers; give it another dabble. Retrieving line, he glimpsed a boyish saunter in the corner of his vision. Bad luck, watchers, his Grancher used to say: for all he cared right now, the whole of Ireland could look on. He dried the fly deftly and set it down again. In vain.

'A touch of peat to the water,' a surprisingly deep voice advised. 'He'll be taking something red.'

'Fish it regular, do you?' asked Evans, not shifting his gaze for a second.

'Not lately. You've a Coch-y-Bhundu here that'll serve. Welsh, like yourself, I'm thinking.'

Evans glared down. The kid had hunched over his open flybox, intent and unselfconscious; a mop of sunshot, chestnut hair and nimble knowing fingers. Cheeky bugger, he thought, and launched the fly once more.

'Third time lucky, we say back home.'

'Surely you're after bigger game, Mr Evans.'

A spastic twitch, a whipcrack overhead, and the cast collapsed in orange coils on the greenness at his feet. Shock, it was, not surprise. Snow had predicted something like this.

'Expected, am I?' he growled. 'So take me to your leader.'

'And who might *that* be, I wonder?' The small head tilted slowly upward. Though honed and hardened by the spread of years, there was no mistaking the face; or the haunting, tawny eyes. At last Smythe's anger made a kind of sense – '*He's fey, apparently, able to alter his form at will.*' Best to be sure, mind, hear it from the leprechaun's mouth.

'*You're* Sean Daly?'

'Himself.'

It was the sheer arrogance, probably, and the strain of the last few days. Only the two of you, see, you can break him with one hand.

It must have shown in his face. Daly skipped backwards, pointing. A far-off muffled report, and the flybox was blasted skyward in a twinkle of grey shards. Evans whirled, scanning the hillside above. Near the brow, a wisp of blue smoke eddied gently over the heather.

'The rifle is silenced,' warned Daly, 'and Casey has an eagle's eye.'

Touch and go, all the same. A flying tackle, a wrestler's lock on the slender throat, and let eagles pick friend from foe. It's not on, bach. The little bastard chose wisely; no worthwhile cover for miles. Evans cared nothing for medals; especially the posthumous kind.

184

Daly was reading him calmly, keeping a prudent distance and a soothing tone. 'Whisht, man, see sense. I could have you cut down in a trice.'

'Sure. So why don't you?'

'Let's say you have a masterly touch with the dry fly, and we both have fishing to do. Who was it sent you, meanwhile?'

'Darro,' breathed Evans. 'Might as well finish it now!'

'Your manhood is proven; the English set no great store by martyrs. Come: we're anglers both, and civilized men.'

'*Civilized?* Reapers loose on the mainland and Beddoes already lamed? You're a bloody animal, Daly!'

Something stirred in the wide-set, sun-narrowed eyes; something lean and yellow and feral. 'You are foreign polis, come to spy and murder. What did you expect: tickertape? And who, might I ask, is Beddoes?'

Cool head, boyo, too much said already.

Daly smiled, silky and knowing. 'Of course, the impetuous sergeant. A sordid affair, and sin on each side. And isn't recruitment a headache? So hard to get reliable help these days.'

Madness, really, under midday skies and a long gun, taking lip from a pint-sized Irish nutter. Just to put the tin hat on it, the bloody two-pounder was rising again.

Daly had his back to the stream. Blandly, he said, 'Use the Coch-y-Bhundu, Mr Evans. Casey will be easy when you've something to do with your hands; and besides, you've earned the chance.'

No way he could've seen. Leprechauns, duw duw.

The act of casting steadied him. The rhythm, no doubt, and the soothing swish of the line. Hopeless, mind, with the sun so high and his limbs still shaky from anger.

'Do the arithmetic, shall we? Bombs and Green Reapers, a brogue you could cut with a fork; a man called Cavanaugh, on the run from the Maze; and don't tell me Dublin muggers clobber their mark in the knee. It's evidence, mun, d'you think I'd be here on a hunch?'

'Try a bit further downstream,' counselled Daly. 'A fish that size will likely hit out behind from sheer territorial aggression.'

Evans stole a sidelong glance. Dafter by the minute — he talked like a college don, yet you could *see* the heat of the hunt on his small face. Humour him, then, there's nothing better to do.

He cast, and Daly spoke. Casual, he sounded, as if it didn't matter a damn; and the Irish more pronounced. ''Tis the stereotype which endures. Flame-eyed Paddies gone amok, one finger for the trigger and another for the self-destruct switch. Consider the history: no conspiracy there, just an ancient and almighty fuck-up.'

'Fighting each other,' drawled Evans, 'and shooting yourselves in the foot.'

'It used to be that way.' A harsher, drier note, and Evans cocked his ears, chucking the fly out at random. 'Times and the tide have turned. Now we have a common goal, a united people, and a growing respect for discipline. Which is why the Cav went across. Strong as an ox, brave as a lion — and wild as summer lightning. Bejaysus, Inspector, *ye have him*!'

The rod bucked and the pool erupted in red and gold.

'Give him the butt!' yelled Daly. 'Or he'll have you round yonder stump!'

Evans chafed his thumb on the screaming reel. Everything held, and the fish went sulky and deep.

'Up with you,' growled Daly, and tossed in a fist-sized rock.

'Jesi Mawr, whose bloody fish *is* this?'

'Nobody's, yet!' Whereupon the trout turned and

186

came straight at them. 'Get away back with ye! If he wins slack, we're done.'

He *had* won slack. The rod stood upright, gleaming but lifeless, and the line hung and swayed in the breeze. Then Daly was down on his knees in the shallows. A laugh and a lunge and the prize held aloft from hooked and dripping fingers. His jeans were soaked from ankle to crotch, and a grin as wide as the Mall. About twelve years old, he looked.

'Dear God,' Evans breathed, in an instant of bright revelation. 'So *that's* how it's done. On with the school cap and blazer and you'd pass for Wharton of Remove!'

Again the cold feline flicker; then Daly had passed him, climbing the bank and fairly crooning in pleasure. 'Will you look at this? Near to three pounds, for certain. What'll you do with him, then?' He tossed the fish at Evans' feet and stood quite still; a dark little mannikin, silhouetted against the cloudless blue. A challenge, not a question; for some obscure reason, the response would be crucial.

'What would *you* do?'

'Kill him, what else? A trophy to cherish in old age.' A minute shift in his posture, the faintest of nods at the sniper's lair.

Evans dropped the rod and strode defiantly to the water's edge. He wet his hands, flinching at the cold, then went back and cradled the fish. Spent, see, from battle and shock, the round black eye already glazing. Released in slack water, it swung belly up, the pink-lined gills fanning weakly.

Daly strolled to his side, cool and aloof, no trace of excitement whatsoever. 'An idle gesture, Evans. He's done.'

'Have a squint up the hill,' suggested Evans, very soft.

187

'Where you were looking, just now. I reckon the overhang covers half of me and all of you. Fancy a grapple, do you?'

'Don't fool yourself, man; you haven't the stomach!'

And in the end, despite bombs and Beddoes and an ache of opportunity lost, it was Evans who bowed from the clash of cold stares. And watched dully while the fish rolled over and wobbled into deep water.

Up on the bank, the heat bored in and bees droned past, burdened by pollen. Evans took down the rod and collected his gear. 'What happens now then, boyo?'

Daly selected a tump of grass and squatted there, cross-legged; like a garden gnome on a toadstool. 'Tell them I'm a reasonable man, Mr Evans. I have no truck with Reapers, or fruitless strikes on enemy soil. Remember this, though. *We join for life*, whatever the consequences.' The eyes were glacial; small as he was, he put shivers down the spine. 'I don't tolerate spies, nor waste bullets on kneecaps. Check your connections, here and at home, and beware of lecherous juniors. Mind me well; a *reasonable* man.'

'Oh sure. Kind to animals, are you, and old ladies crossing the street?'

Daly uncurled, leaning on one elbow and taking a languid, nostalgic tone. 'A most unwise assumption. Years ago the British killed my father. Unarmed, was Kevin, and not half a mile from here. The soldier responsible drowned in this very stream; the accident caused me no grief whatever.' Like a half-tame housecat, he was: sunning himself one minute, fanged and furious the next. 'This is *our land*, d'ye hear? If ye come bearing arms, you'd better be ready to die!'

He tore at the grass and scattered green fronds on the breeze. His face cleared, and rage departed his voice.

'The bargain is this: in return for honest answers, I'll

188

tell you what I can of the Reapers and point you in Cavanaugh's way.'

'*Answers*!' sneered Evans. 'That's nice.'

'We meet by the water, three days hence. Think on it, meanwhile, and consult whomever you please. Pick up the rod, Mr Evans. Slow and easy, for Casey's sake; and go back the way you came.'

'Cav and the Reapers, now, how should *I* know? 'Tis Dublin's affair; ask Fergus.' In retirement, the Quiet One had turned crusty and reclusive. But he still owned an acute brain and a marvellous poker face, and loved to display them both.

'Away with you!' snapped Sean. 'Cav's been adrift these past four years!' He closed on the rumpled, brown-sweatered form, wrinkling his nose at the essence of hard spirits, rough shag and ageing male. 'What are ye saying? Another half-baked private brigade?'

The rocking chair creaked, and the gnarled fingers fumbled with paper and baccy. The famous cigarettes, like the cottage itself, were leaner and darker these days.

'Your words, Sean, not mine. What odds, anyhow? A blow for the cause, to distract the attention and keep them guessing.' In the soft light through the single window, he was as sleepy and sly as a grizzled fox.

'It matters to *me*,' Sean warned. 'There's bargains involved, and a question of trust.'

'Trust? With the *English*?'

'He's Welsh; it's not quite the same. He wouldn't *bend*, d'you see. Alone and unarmed under Casey's gun, and he did it *his* way, whatever. We've other things in common, too.'

The abrupt yellow flare of the match threw low black rafters into relief; and the network of purple veins in the weathered cheeks. 'Ah. And what might they be?'

'Judgement of water and men, and random quirks of the mind. The schoolboy guise, for instance. He grasped it in a twinkling.' And certain mutual informants, he might have added: but didn't, even here.

''Tis trifling, Sean. You're enemies, whatever.'

'Surely. But there's potential afoot, the means to convey the message.'

The Quiet One coughed, scattering smoke and ashes. 'Hot lead and cold steel are sufficient message for Brits! Never say it, Sean, beyond these four walls. 'Tis a harder line that's wanted, and talk of a younger command. You've enemies on both sides; don't be going soft.'

Sean drew himself up, summoning the will and the power into a single savage stare. 'And where do you stand, old man? Is Daly the dwarf gone soft? I need that information, and within the next two days.'

A pale tongue flickered on tightened lips, and the fading blue eyes surrendered. 'Ye'll have it, then as always. 'Twill do us no good, though.' The rasp of his breathing quickened and his voice was a plea from the past.

'Kill him, Sean. 'Tis the only safe way.'

Sean strolled to the doorway and watched the fall of twilight over green and peaceful fields. A ring of truth, to be sure, and hazards in either course. Words from the mainland troubled his mind, and promises forged long ago.

'We'll see,' he murmured, like evensong prayer, 'when the moment is come, we'll see.'

CHAPTER ELEVEN

'Self-inflicted wounds, man, you ought to be court-martialled!' Smythe slumped in shadow behind his rose-wood desk, waxen and embittered. He'd aged years in a week, and the faultless fawn jacket looked a size too large. Off his nosh, then; the strain was telling. 'Months of planning squandered on an adolescent *fumble*!'

Beddoes didn't feel too chipper himself. It had taken a handful of Ponstan, two bus rides and an hour of wrangling to get past the Chief's gatekeepers. Any minute now, the spasms would hit him again.

''Ang about!' he protested. '*You* did the booking. A doss-house, you said, not a bleedin' knocking-shop!'

'A calculated risk. Specific warnings were given, I'm told, and noted in the record!'

Beddoes changed tack smartly. Less said about *that* the better. 'Look, I made contact, learned a few wrinkles. 'Ow about a debriefing?'

'You weren't there long enough to catch cold!'

'I caught a bleedin' packet!'

'Exactly as you deserved. You're suspended, pending medical clearance. Go away.'

'Give over, Chief, I've *had* doctors. See?' He flexed the damaged leg boldly, biting his lip and ignoring the flare of pain. Smythe watched, his eyes red-rimmed and baleful.

'Doctors? You need a bloody psychiatrist! When you're fit, report to the Pillock.'

'The *who*?'

'The Pillock of the Glen. McKay, you cretin! *If* he'll have you.'

'I don't get it, sir. 'Oo's pickin' up the pieces?' Another ill-advised question.

Smythe hunched over his purple paperweight, sounding petty and querulous. '*Funnies*, of course. Giving my people the third degree and loving every minute.' His hunted grey gaze flickered across his own curiously empty desk. 'You'll get precious little sympathy from *that* quarter!'

Beddoes cleared his throat and launched the appeal; the reason he'd come, really. 'I'm thinking of Evans, right? There's gotta be *something* I can do.'

'You've done more than enough already!'

The Chief stalked into the sunlight, brandishing crested papers. The extent of his fall was revealed; unsteady hands, a pensioner's stoop and skin the colour of putty. 'You signed the Act, remember? If I catch a single hint of private enterprise, I'll have you in the Tower! Stay off the streets and out of my hair till it's over!'

Beddoes made it home by the skin of his teeth, stumbling to the bathroom and sinking two more blue and yellow depth-charges before the rigour struck.

An hour later, drained but relatively free of pain, he began to function again. Try the personal touch, my son, it's never been known to fail.

But when Pol Parrot came to the phone, her knickers were in a right old twist. 'You're outa yer mind, callin' me on duty! If McKay gets to hear, I'll be lumbered!'

'Leave it out, girl. Got some new birthmarks to show you!'

'That's what I mean. Between you and the Inspector, it's more than me pension's worth!'

'Oh? What's Huw bin up to?'

Her tone turned warm and breathless, the way birds always are when they're telling tales. 'A live-in, down the flats. The wives are goin' spare!'

The red-head, perhaps? 'Come on round, lovely, give us all the dirt.'

'I *can't*, Roy; not for a while at least.'

'When, then?'

A tasty, suggestive giggle. 'Soon as you're off the Super's shit-list. Missin' me, are yer? Oops, someone's coming!'

He cradled the dead receiver morosely. Playtime postponed, and none the wiser; he'd have to suss McKay out himself.

When he hobbled into the nick, all chatter ceased; then started up louder than ever.

'Hey it's me, Roy.'

Sickly grins and averted eyes; nice to know who your friends are. He took the stairs one at a time, squinting into the sunshine and mopping the sweat on his shirt-sleeve. The secretary gaped in horror as he knocked once and stumped straight in.

McKay glanced up with no hint of surprise and ran exactly to form; a frigid blue gaze, the customary rasp of disdain. 'Well, now. A rat from the sinking ship.'

'Reporting for duty, sir.'

'Not tae me, ye aren't. You're Chief Superintendent Smythe's minion now, by royal and ancient decree. Very welcome he is, too!'

'Er – he sent me back, sir.'

'And damaged in transit, moreover. Nothing trivial, I hope?' He smirked at this pleasantry, a very fleeting truce. 'Since my exalted brother-in-law lured you away, he's obliged to return you intact. And since your portly

Welsh friend remains absent, there's no call for your meagre talents. I bid ye good morning, Sergeant.'

'Sir, it's about the Reapers!'

McKay sat erect, his ginger bristles gleaming hotly. 'I warned ye earlier; yon Irish scum are beyond my jurisdiction. This manor, however, is most certainly not. I'll brook no *per*sonal crusades, particularly from the likes of you! Now take yourself off. You're nobody around here till I say different.'

An unlikely pairing, Smythe and McKay, having only anger in common; but when the crunch comes, the brass close ranks. You're pissin' into the wind, my son.

Beddoes traipsed downstairs again, ignoring the shame-faced hush and the pitying glances. Outside heat and the roar of lunchtime traffic scoured his nerves. He ducked into the nearest bar for liquid consolation.

'Serve lepers, do yer?'

The landlord didn't even blink. 'Long as they drink through a straw.'

Beddoes lurched to the dimmest corner and sat there, kneading the ache from his thigh. Go on a bender, he thought, cane the grog for a day or a month and surface in time for the medal – the funeral, more likely. Tried me best, uncle, and they didn't want to know.

The cold clean bite of the beer revived him. A lot to be said for English pubs, especially after Slaney's. Funny. The last time had been with Evans, a week and a life ago; just before his fancy piece strolled in and stopped the show. Which was something he *could* check, without treading on official toes ...

She posed in the half-open doorway, *very* easy on the eye; making your actual *haute couture* out of old blue jeans and a T-shirt. A sleek red fox in the hencoop; no wonder the biddies were clucking.

194

'Yes? Can I help you?'

'Name of Beddoes, Sergeant. I'm lookin' out for Huw.'

'Good,' she said tartly. 'So am I.'

A Mexican stand-off, then. She wasn't giving an inch, and he could hardly call the cops.

Her eyes widened in recognition. 'Wait, I've seen you before. Roy, isn't it? You'd better come in.'

He stopped in the hallway, dazzled. She'd shampooed the old brown Wilton, and the pile shone thick and bronze. The loose covers had been to the cleaners and the oak table glittered in the setting sun. There were chrysanths in a vase at the window, and the whole place smelled of beeswax. Dallas it wasn't, but not for lack of elbow grease.

'Go easy,' he warned, 'he'll think it's a wrong number.'

'Promises are made to be kept, Sergeant.' She was halfway to the kitchen, looking almost as good from behind. 'Tea? Coffee? I think there's a beer in the fridge.' The air of possession grated. She should be up West, drinking shampers from a silver shoe and coaxing some landed toff towards the altar. Star quality, it shone through every move she made. So why was she risking housemaid's knee for a banished, balding busy?

'Nothing, ta. It's not a social call. Miss — ?'

'Neale. Jane, to my friends.'

'Well, Miss Neale, I'll have to ask you to move along.'

'Indeed?' She turned, nose in the air. 'Now why would I do that?' Her bodytalk was loud and provocative; muffled, he reckoned, only by thin white cotton.

'Married quarters, these.'

'So?'

'Take a quick shufty in the mirror. Temptation on wheels, for any red-blooded bloke. The wives are doing their nut!'

195

'You're unreal, Sergeant! Tell them I'm a char, not a bawd.'

'They won't be told, believe me; and Huw's gotta live here, afterwards.'

It took the wind from her sails. '*If* he gets back.' A note of foreboding which triggered alarm in his brain.

'Back from where?'

'Ireland, of course!'

'Here, 'oo told you that?' He shipped a withering, emerald glance.'

'You should have done your homework. *My* sources are protected – by law!'

'Christ,' he muttered, appalled. 'Jane Neale reveals all.'

Only the secret of the decade, and Britain's last white hope swapping pillowtalk with the media. The pain was smouldering again, he could feel the blood draining from his temples. Whereas the Neale girl seemed to be gathering force by the minute.

'You've a small, prurient mind, Sergeant. Since Huw appears to value your friendship, I'll tell you how it is. Then, perhaps, you'll leave us in peace.'

She stalked the room in the failing light, slender and auburn and feline. 'It began as a routine profile, and grew into something very special. For both of us. And *yes*, I've slept with him; and will again, the sooner the better! Would you care for the unexpurgated version?'

Contempt and fiery triumph flayed him. He stood and swayed and took it, hoping the growing shadows hid the pinkness of his cheeks.

'We're both adults, Sergeant; more than can be said of you and your prudish *married* colleagues. I'm here with Huw's knowledge and blessing, and I'll stay as long as *he* pleases. Is that quite clear?'

Not much he could say, really. He shrugged and limped to the door.

'Wait!' she cried. 'You're his partner, the one who carries a gun! What have you done to your leg?'

He turned awkwardly into a waft of subtle perfume and a blaze of accusing green eyes.

'You were together, weren't you? Has he found Daly yet?' She was clutching his arm, firing her questions with awesome fury and shaking the answers out.

'Steady on! I'm fragile, 'andle with care.'

She released him and stepped back, the T-shirt heaving brightly in the gloom. 'Tell me, damn you!'

It mattered to her, no question, he could see the small tears forming. Say nothing, sunshine, you've had enough bother from birds. She read him at once, pulling a quicksilver change of mood. The fierce hauteur softened, her hands spread in pale and abject supplication. 'Can't you see? I might be able to help!'

'Oh yeah? Spirit him home, you mean, riding pillion on the broomstick?'

'For God's sake, I'm a journalist! Don't you understand the power of the press?'

'I don't know, honest,' he mumbled. And, surprising even himself: 'Soon as I do, I'll tell you.'

He went back to a solitary pad, fantasies of Pol and another bout of the ague. Lying in darkness and rinsing capsules down with Scotch, he tried to reason it through. She cared about Huw, it stood out a mile. But birds like her weren't built to raise sprogs on a copper's pittance. A law of nature, that. She was after a story, obviously. So why all the drama, the bold declarations of worldly but undying love? He drifted into drugged and uneasy sleep, with the answer nowhere in sight.

He woke next morning, woozy but untroubled by pain. At nine, full of hope and black coffee, he settled to the phone and started in search of Jane Neale.

Soon he had collected a series of glowing references.

The editor of an upmarket gossip comic put it best. 'If it was *my* party, dahling, I'd sign her up tomorrow. She could do the scandal *and* the cover. Not a *company* animal, I'm afraid. Wildly independent and *so* secretive. I'll say this, though; she writes like an angel and she's *never* wrong. *What* I'd give for her sources!' A heavy sigh of pure envy. 'And her looks!'

Strange, that. She *was* one of the best-looking birds he'd laid eyes on; yet, despite her brazen, bra-less sensuality, old Adam had never even twitched. Hardly the most romantic of meetings, mind you; more punch-up than passion. Maybe, given soft lights and sweet music . . . Don't kid yourself, my son, it'll never happen. She was too much, somehow. The kind of intense beauty which shrivels and devours; and moves on. The sort of bird who needs a cause, a hero and a couple of randy cossacks waiting in the wings. She's down to you, uncle, and the best of British luck.

Cold comfort on another warm day; all quiet, even on the domestic front. Bored, hurting and sinking deeper into limbo, he cast about for something to do. Anything to do. Beyond the window, a single unlikely figure waited at the bus stop; regulation pinstripe and a brown briefcase. Clocking on at this hour, he had to be a toff. Harriet Slade, he remembered suddenly; wonder if she's still footloose among the freaks?

For two days, Evans had trudged the breezy slopes beset by warring loyalties. Smythe had been plain enough. Don't bargain with bombers; if you can't nick him, waste him. Eliminate, then: same difference. Whereas Snow leaned towards compromise – trade information and never mind the price. It shouldn't be hard, he thought, watching a hover of larks against the cloudless blue. We're enforcers, Smythe and me; we see things as black or white and act according. And Snow's a Funny, well beyond the pale.

But this wasn't cops and robbers, and Smythe made no secret of his Irish vendetta. He hadn't been looking well, lately; sickness and obsession cast twin shadows over his judgement. Last but not least, Daly held all the cards. If the dwarf was half as black as Smythe would paint him, he, Evans, would be wearing thumbscrews and cement-lined wellies; not strolling freely down a sunset hill.

He sat at the wheel of his rented car, gnats whining in his ears. The image came from nowhere, a gleam of gold and crimson flank through peat-tinged water. In the end, the decision hinged on the fate of a three-pound trout.

When Daly said, 'Kill it,' he'd reacted out of sheer cussedness. A sitting duck, he was, and making a pointed statement of his own. In those few moments, a fisherman's truth was enacted. The quarry would be older and wiser, and twice as hard to deceive. Knowing where to look, though, you could go back time after time. One day, given patience, cunning and a well-chosen lure, you'd persuade him to rise again. Evans started the engine, squinting into a fiery sky. That's the theory, bach; let's see if it holds for leprechauns.

First, he had to test the echoes. A series of fall-backs, Snow had said, and now Snow's word was law. So he called Dublin, and asked the crucial question.

'Your man's in quarantine,' O'Brien snapped. 'He caught a social disease. For once, our wee friend is clean.' A cryptic, disturbing message, and it boded ill for Roy. So far, though, Daly had told the truth; which meant another morning duel beneath the sniper's gun . . .

'How's old Dan'l Boone up there?' Evans enquired. 'Warm and cosy and glued to his sights?'

The early, brazen clouds were already thinning; the shadowed slope loomed much too close for comfort. Daly shrugged casually. 'Are you wanting another demonstration?'

'I'll take your word, ta. Running out of flyboxes, I am.'

'London will refund you, no doubt. Set up the rod, if you please. Let's not make Casey nervous.'

'Aye. Let's *not*!'

A taut, barbed exchange; the ground rules clearly established. Action Man, he was, in a dark brown sweater with leather patches and khaki jeans to fit a growing boy.

'Question time, then. I'll thank you to not interrupt; and answer yes, no, or not proven.' Evans selected a fly and tied it to the leader. Royal Coachman; we'll try a bit of red again.

'Smythe's involvement is public knowledge,' began Daly. 'The overt mainland element, anyhow. Lately, he's exceeded his brief – recruiting spies and seeking a foothold over here. Vainly, so far.' He rattled off a string of totally unfamiliar names and waited expectantly.

'If you say so.'

'He's also corrupted the Garda; one Michael O'Brien, I'm told.'

Evans' mouth went dry. The first cast sagged untidily into a gurgle of shallows below. Easy enough to think it through. Now he must pass sentence.

'I'll not harm him, Evans. Better to know the enemy than wonder who and where he is. So; am I right?'

'Yes!' In the distance, a cock crowed lustily. Very symbolic.

'Comfort yourself, man. Betrayal's like making love to a woman; easier the second time round.'

Listen, bach, never mind the insults. Every query tells a tale – of how much he already knows.

The mellow, mocking voice probed tender scars. 'Two city policemen, blundering into holy war. Smythe's dying throw, d'you see. He needed a coup, didn't he, to keep the Funnies off his back?'

'Aye,' Evans muttered, awed at the implications. Didn't reckon Smythe was *that* sick, no wonder it's such a bloody shambles. Deep penetration, duw duw; they've even picked up the jargon.

'Whereas *you*, Inspector, are here to escape a certain lady reporter. Be still, or Casey'll have you!'

Evans came on, seeing only blood-red haze and hefting the rod like a bludgeon. 'Better do it now, Daly!'

'Whisht, get on with your fishing; I'll not make war on women.' The sheer contempt stopped him, clearing the blindness and dousing the rage. Daly was retreating, wary but assured, holding one pale palm up to the heather; like a toy soldier directing traffic. 'Besides,' he added wryly, 'we need all the support we can get from that quarter.'

The media, he meant; no such thing as bad publicity.

'The covert wing has the foreign mandate,' Daly went on, as if nothing had happened. 'Those you call the Funnies. A tall man, cold by name and by nature.'

'Snow,' nodded Evans; and winced in self-disgust.

Daly grinned slyly. 'And what's in a name, between friends? A tougher foe, to be sure – for hasn't he tried to infiltrate these past four years?'

Evans sent the fly out absently, recovering wit and balance. 'I wouldn't know.' He glanced down, suddenly chilled, into a catlike yellow gaze which permitted no evasions.

'Indeed? Then try this one. Smythe wants my scalp; would I be right in thinking that Mister Snow would rather keep Daly alive?'

Half-hypnotized, Evans' brain conjured a livid image;

201

Casey's finger tensing on the trigger. *That's* how much it matters, bach. Get it wrong and you're dead. What the hell – there's only one answer, anyhow. 'Ten out of ten,' he said. And stood, amazed, while Daly grinned and took the rod from his unresisting hand.

'Now, isn't that grand; and your turn to ask.'

The sun inched through, putting sparkle and colour to the stream. In birdsong and the sudden scent of summer, Daly turned his back and strolled to the water's edge; not so much as a glance for the hill.

Bloody nerve, Evans thought. He's having me on, knowing he's safe; no one's up there!

Daly flexed the rod gingerly.

'A strange action, for one raised to the split cane.'

Even so, the line rolled out in a delicate orange curve. Evans moved closer and opened his own account. 'Cavanaugh went over, you said. Over to who?'

'Whom,' corrected Daly, with another gnomish grin. 'And it's not yet clear to me.' He cast again, graceful and poised, though the rod was twice his length.

'Lovely. So who and what are the Reapers? Or *whom*, should I say?'

'You should not. 'Tis part of the same. There'll be answers by noon tomorrow.'

'Bloody fine bargain that was!'

Daly fished on, apparently unruffled. Only the stony jut of his chin bespoke a hidden anger. 'We're united against the English,' he murmured, 'and divided among ourselves. More than one way to kill the cat, d'you see.' A flick of the wrist, a swish overhead, and the fly set down smooth as silk. 'I'm not party to all of the plots, or enough of the information. Nor likely to be, yet awhile.' He turned, high-browed and wide-eyed in almost comic outrage. 'You know what they're saying? The dwarf is gone soft. Can you imagine that?'

202

'It's my turn, remember?'

Perhaps there was the ghost of a smile; quickly gone as the rod bucked and the line tightened. A smaller fish, a shorter battle, and two men poles apart brought nearer by this single common pleasure. As they stood together admiring the beached and burnished beauty, Evans sensed the presence of a fleeting, fragile truce. The question slipped out, bald and clumsy. 'Why do you do it, mun?'

He seemed not to hear, bending to prise the bedraggled fly out of the trout's white gape. Then he spoke, soft above the lap of the water. 'Because of my father's dying. Because this land is forfeit to Englishmen with guns. Because of the past; bitter, black oppression, as far back as the eye can see or the heart can remember.' His hands jerked and the speckled spine snapped clean and sharp. 'It has to be stopped!'

'You'll never win,' said Evans, equally quiet. 'For each one killed, they'll send another three.'

Daly straightened, his sun-bleached mane thrown back, his shout of laughter ringing harsh and wild. 'Then 'tis only the death that matters, and taking a score of them with you!'

The fish quivered at his feet, a fading silvery reflex. He watched it, sombre once more. 'Some day the power will falter, and Daly will die as he lived. Not from English bullets; but at hands he was probably shaking, only minutes before.' He was gazing bleakly up the slope, maintaining the bluff to the last. 'Mind me well, then. There'll be news of Cav tomorrow – by which time Casey could have separate orders.'

'Licensed to kill, is it? Reckon I'll take the risk.'

'Pity.' Seeing Evans' confusion, he added, 'Being born the wrong side of the water.' He collected his catch, sliding tanned fingers between slack pink gills. 'In the end, what you believe in depends on who you are.'

He ambled into deep green pasture, the fish gleaming and dangling from his fist. The whole glen seemed mysteriously hushed and breathless; a moment to haunt the memory. He looked somehow sainted yet diminished, not much longer for this world.

His days are numbered, thought Evans, who suddenly had to know. 'Sean!' he shouted, in unabashed appeal. 'We kept faith, didn't we – and Casey's home in his bed!'

Daly swung round, erect and haloed. His jaunty whistle broke the spell and shattered the last illusion. High on the hill, the camouflaged figure rose starkly from cloven purple heather. And Irish sunlight glistened on the barrel of the gun.

'This one's for bed and board,' Mrs McBride explained, 'and these for the washing. Cash, if ye please, and ye won't be getting receipts.'

She stood in the dim hallway, shuffling scraps of paper officiously. From the kitchen came a sizzle of frying and a whiff of bubble and squeak.

'No hurry,' said Evans, 'I'm staying one more night, at least.'

She smiled grimly. 'Dublin phoned. You've to call back immediately.'

He dialled the number; O'Brien answered at the first ring.

'Match abandoned,' he said at once. 'You're booked out of Shannon at four twenty-five. Go straight home, and talk to no one. A morning's grace to prepare the report, then debriefing with Smythe at two p.m.'

'Now wait a minute! I've gone to a lot of trouble, see, and just about to pay off.'

'Orders, mind you, from the *very* top. The operation's blown sky-high. Get out while you can and be grateful.'

Oh aye; and what of those betrayed and left behind? 'Darro, Mike, I'm sorry!'

'For what? It's all in a day's work.'

Sorry I shopped you, thought Evans, in return for support and hospitality. Say nothing, bach. If Daly's straight, O'Brien has nothing to fear – no more than usual, anyhow. And if not, ignorance is bliss. 'Sorry we couldn't have a few ales together. Love to Ellen and the boys, mind.'

'Next time,' O'Brien promised, not quite able to conceal the note of relief.

So Evans packed and settled up, and took a taxi to Shannon. As traffic and the stench of molten tarmac thickened, he closed his eyes and leaned against warm leather and paid his last respects: to a violent, defiant, doomed little man and the land that he held so dear. You're all wrong, boyo – wrong size, wrong cause, wrong century. We came close, though, over a brace of trout in your haunting green glen; a pity it's done so soon.

The image lingered still; the small bright figure fading into the heat of the day. Aye, and so it should. Because there, but for a quirk of birth, go I.

CHAPTER TWELVE

Evans padded the hallway, alerted by unfamiliar brightness and a taunt of perfume. 'Hey,' he called, chancing his arm and her promise, 'who's been sleeping in *my* bed?'

She came wide-eyed and timid from the kitchen, one pale hand lifted to her throat. She looked smaller than he remembered; tousled, barefoot, swathed in a long turquoise housecoat.

'For heaven's sake,' she whispered, 'give a girl some warning!'

'Oh aye? Entertaining the Fleet, are you?'

'Officers only, and *no* uniforms.'

'Got it shipshape for them, I must say.'

'A labour of love.' She closed the distance between them, soft and swift and eager. '*God*, it's good to see you!'

It was good, fair play; to see the pleasure light her face, to drink her scent and put the Irish nightmare out of mind. At first, she seemed content merely to hold him, resting her forehead gently against his shoulder. He dropped the holdall and gathered her in, cupping her chin and tilting her mouth upwards. 'Duw,' he muttered, 'it's been a long, hot summer.'

'And not over yet.'

The kiss began chastely, in relief and celebration. Then her lips parted and her breath turned musky. She clung with velvety languor, her breasts thrusting into his chest and the fire in her loins fanning his own need.

'Dinner will be late, I'm afraid,' she admitted, coming up for air.

'No problem. There's danger money left over, we'll do the town.'

'We will *not*!' She was nudging him towards the bedroom, her eyes dark and smoky. 'Tonight, I'll not share you with anyone!'

'Only the eating I meant, mind.'

Their bodies met and merged in naked frenzy, all inhibitions paling in the blaze of mutual hunger. She matched him, thrust for thrust, a violent intensity and an explosive climax which left them both exhausted. But this time, he reckoned, drifting on the edge of sleep, they'd gone the full distance together . . .

He woke to fading twilight and a sense of physical well-being. Levering himself up on one elbow, he kissed the nape of her neck, just below the bronzed and dewy tendrils of her hair. She mumbled, stirring and stretching voluptuously; then sat bolt upright.

'My God, dinner!' She was off the bed in a tantalizing glimmer of whiteness, swaying out of his reach. 'Down boy,' she ordered, shrugging into the housecoat. 'Take a cold shower or something, I've a special treat in store.'

'*Another* one?'

'I'm talking about the meal.'

'Barged in and spoiled it, did I?'

Her throaty laughter warmed the dimness. 'Delayed, not spoiled. I try to get the priorities right.'

She slipped away. Presently, he heard a rattle of cutlery and the clunk of the oven door. A strange sensation, after all these years, and a little disconcerting; you're a marked man, bach, even the dressing-gown smells of her presence.

Candlelight, Beaujolais and very personal service – a far cry from Irish stew at Mrs McBride's. Jane gave him melon and fillet mignon, pandering to his every whim like an adoring, green-eyed houri. The act became her; satisfying one appetite, she gently fuelled another.

Afterwards, she poured coffee and curled into a big armchair. Shadow softened the planes of her cheeks and moulded the sea-blue material to her body; bare toes peeped beneath the hem. Casually, gazing through a coil of steam above the rim of her cup, she asked, 'Mission accomplished?'

'Hardly. A goosechase, really, and Beddoes retired hurt.'

'I know.'

His surprise must have shown; she detailed the hostile meeting.

'I'll be having words with young Roy, walking wounded or not!'

'Easy, Huw. Looking out for you, he said. Did you make contact with Daly?'

'Aye.'

'Just "aye"? What was he like? What did you do?'

She was leaning forward, the loveliness suddenly tense and fine-strung. Her professional instincts were showing, triggering alarm bells again. Kiss and tell, see. When you looked like Jane Neale, it had to be your stock-in-trade.

Cautiously, resenting his own suspicions, he muttered. 'We went fishing. A bit of an artist, Daly.'

The light in her face was dying. Without moving a muscle, she was retreating into herself. 'You *still* don't trust me, do you?'

He wanted to say, I'm almost there, girl, give me a bit more time. The words simply wouldn't come. A burnt child, he was, and not yet ready for her welcoming heat. Instead, he invoked an old and well-tried ally: duty.

'I'm a copper, Jane, we value our little secrets. You'll just have to get used to it.' He *was* declaring himself, but only to reflected highlights that glowed from her downcast head. 'I'll say this,' he added quietly. 'He made me wonder whose side I was on.'

'Truth and justice,' she murmured. 'On these, at least, we can agree.'

She rose abruptly, seeming somehow taller and stronger. 'Don't tell me,' she said, apparently to herself, '*show* me.' And towed him back to the rumpled bed. There, she untied the sash of his dressing-gown and pushed him firmly down. Avoiding his questing arms, she reached across and lit the bedside lamp.

Unbuttoned, the housecoat whispered from her shoulders and formed a shimmer of green at her feet. She stood, proud and abandoned; letting him see the swell and blush of her want and the moist fiery gleam between her thighs. His blood thickened and he caught his breath. An image to cherish for all time, whatever might happen later.

She knelt beside him, lifting his hand, kissing each finger lightly and pressing his palm to the scalding pulse of her breast. Her eyes closed, and she sighed in release and longing. 'Love me, Huw. Surely it's not much to ask?' Then she was around and over him, her nipples jutting, her hair flaring brightly at each delicious downward surge.

Despite the bloom of sensations which banished thought, Evans sensed the power of her purpose. Here is my last and greatest treasure, she was saying from the very depths of her soul; take it in joy, and lay your doubts to rest. Not just animal lust, then, but moments of exquisite mutual pleasure never to be repeated with some appealing stranger.

He reared and twisted, bearing her under. Her thighs

locked about his waist, silken yet steely, and the bed creaked softly. Rise and fall, stroke and counterstroke, until her cry broke clean and keening, and blended with his own deep groan of total fulfilment. The rhythm held briefly, then shuddered and faltered into slick and salty slackness. He eased on to his side, cleaving to her and smoothing the curve of her hip while thankful tears trickled along his shoulder.

'It's nothing,' she promised shakily. 'I was so afraid you wouldn't come back.'

Something inside him melted then, the icy bedrock of reserve laid down so long ago. In lamplight and the scented afterglow, he told her everything – Roy's fall, O'Brien's dilemma and the courting of Sean Daly beneath summer heather and the sniper's gunsight.

'You could have been killed,' she murmured, and he felt the chill that settled on her skin.

'We both had our chances. Which won't please Smythe one bit.'

He had to explain that, too; the bitter fruit of blackmail and the dicey debriefing yet to come.

When he'd finished she nestled into him, drowsy and wistful. 'It's nearly done. An end to deception.'

'Amen,' he said with feeling, and turned out the light.

In darkness and contentment and the warmth of her breathing, he formed one final waking thought. You're home, boyo, for the first time in your life.

Late August morning; a whiff of coffee on the air, and sunlight in and out of the kitchen between a scatter of clouds. Playing the domestic, he was, wielding a candy-striped teatowel and hearing a discourse on the shameful cost of soap flakes. Something *he* would have to get used to.

She grinned up at him, freckled and girlish. 'Finish it off, will you? I want to get ready.'

'Ready for what?'

'The reserves are low. We're doing the supermarket sortie.'

'We?'

'Of course. I like my men housetrained.' She went off, giggling and twitching her rump.

Evans had always considered shopping a necessary ordeal. With time on his hands and Jane on his arm, it didn't seem half so bad. Mostly, he chauffeured the trolley while she browsed the aisles and returned bearing highly coloured armfuls of goodies.

'Hey,' he protested, 'you're weakening my wallet.'

'Building your strength up, actually. Besides, we're going Dutch.'

'No way. Welsh women keep their place. And I like *my* women kept!'

'Oh? Are we fighting?'

'Not in public, thank you.'

She grinned again. 'Pity. Think how much fun we'd have, making up.'

He followed her progress with ill-concealed pride. Moving free yet graceful, wearing a dove-grey denim dress and high heels, she made every other female in the place look dowdy and careworn. Her hair tied back and only a hint of lipstick, she came towards him again. Try as he might, he couldn't match this self-possessed vision with the wild and wanton creature of last night. Until she smiled and leaned against him briefly, and set his pulses racing once again. A lost cause, then; better relax and enjoy it.

He left her haggling over the price of meat at the delicatessen counter; drawn, as ever, to the electronics section. There, he wandered dazedly amid rows of space-age hi-fi he would always covet and never afford. He paid scant heed to the banked TV screens. Cricket, naturally; a bunch of podgy, beleaguered Brits being routed by athletic West Indians.

'Eighty-nine for four,' said a familiar Australian voice, 'and English crickut facing another crisis. Meanwhile, back to the studio for a newsflash.'

Evans glanced up. Behind the newscaster, an outline map of Eire was overlain by a large white question mark. In the top left-hand corner, the media's pet terrorist; belligerent, balaclava'd and brandishing an M.16.

'After nearly two weeks of silence following the curry house outrage, the mysterious Green Reapers have today issued fresh demands. According to police sources, the group have threatened "devastating reprisals against selected urban centres" unless certain, "peace-loving political detainees are released".' The well-groomed talking head paused, and Evans took a quick look around the store. Bustle, chatter and unruly kids; nobody taking a blind bit of notice.

On a dozen coloured screens, the gunman had vanished. In his place, a picture of Smythe, who looked confident and soldierly in full regalia. Must've been taken a while ago, mind.

'Chief Superintendent Gerald Smythe, head of the crack anti-terrorist squad, declined to comment on the "detainees" involved, or the nationality of the Reapers. "There is no call for alarm," he said. "We have the situation closely monitored." However, he warned that holiday travellers to and from the Republic of Eire should be prepared for stringent security checks at points of entry and exit. Contacted in the House, the Prime Minister said, "We shall never surrender to the whim of mindless thugs."'

A professional smile, revealing carefully capped teeth and a hint of genuine anxiety. 'And now, back to the Oval, where things are *really* tense.'

Evans turned and shoved the trolley viciously. Why bother, he wondered, when the outcome of a footling *game* commands more air time?

She was suddenly at his side, clutching his arm and gazing upward in concern. 'What happened? You look as though you've seen a ghost!'

'No ghost, lovely. Real life, in glorious Technicolor and no one gives a damn. Back to the grindstone, see. Bloody Reapers!'

'Come on, Huw. It's not your problem any more.'

'You ought to try telling Smythe.'

Her small face set hard: another bout of unexpected determination. Red-headed, see, and stubborn with it.

'Coffee time,' she snapped. 'Get yourself upstairs and order. You and I have things to straighten out.'

'How about this lot, then?'

'I'll have it packed. Don't worry, you can pay.'

'Do that here, will they?'

'They'll do it for me!' And he believed her.

Upstairs was more of the same; self-service, thick cups and plastic trays, a reek of baked beans and the inevitable gaggle of wailing infants. He found a table by the window, mopping away the sticky brown rings with his hanky and gazing morosely at a traffic jam on the street below. Get a grip, for Christ's sake. They're people, mind, the ones you're paid to protect. Okay, so they're potty about cricket, there's still no way they should end up maimed; bomb fodder for this week's reigning nutters. Be reasonable – how would *you* fancy being hauled out of the Arms Park with Wales defending, three points up and twenty minutes to go?

Recovering he was, as she picked her way delicately

213

through the great unwashed. Her appearance literally lifted his heart. Let's hope it always will, he thought, remembering his pang of envy during O'Brien's dinner.

She sat, folding her skirt under her in a graceful, quintessentially feminine gesture.

'Before you start,' he said, 'I'll lay you a small wager. When we get back, the phone'll be ringing.'

'Precisely. When we get back.' She rummaged in her handbag, produced a small yellow box, and dropped a minute white tablet into her coffee.

'Nutrasweet,' she explained. 'One of *my* little secrets.' The smile faded quickly. She brushed an errant auburn strand aside and studied him gravely. 'All right, you're a policeman. I won't complain, I wouldn't have it any different. When we're together, though, you're plain Huw Evans, and you're *mine*!' Her mood and her eyes softened, the appeal he could never deny. 'Promise?'

'Very plain indeed,' he muttered ruefully. He reached out tentatively and covered her hand, relishing the contact and the pleasure in her face. 'Tell us your troubles, then.'

She set out to entertain, dimpled yet demure; a tale of aggro from native police wives. 'Amazing,' she concluded. 'One of them was a *real* cow. In the end, I threatened to post hourly massage rates on your door.'

'Oh, sure. Mrs Wigmore, née Pratt, no doubt: ill favoured but well named. Used to be the station bike, before poor old Wigmore got careless and put her in the club. The pot and the kettle, duw duw!'

She frowned and pushed her cup away. 'Speaking of kettles, let's repair to the house of sin and have a proper cup of tea.'

But when they got back, the phone *was* ringing. Smythe was on the line, ranting about the Irish in

214

general and the Reapers in particular. 'Where the hell *were* you, man? I've been calling since half-past nine!'

'O'Brien said two. Sir.'

'Good God, haven't you seen the newsflash?'

Evans grunted assent.

'Well, then! I expect you within the hour.'

She was watching him sadly, a Union-Jack-stamped carrier in each hand. 'Don't tell me. Duty calls.' She dropped the bags, ignoring the clank of cans and bottles. Slim warm fingers brushed his face and her jade eyes swam tenderly. 'Don't be too long, my love.'

Not bloody likely, he thought. But even then, he didn't say it.

High noon in a stifling attic; boredom, BO and Peg crying wolf again. 'It *hurts*, Pete. Oh God, I feel *awful*!' She sat splay-legged in a corner, peering greyly through lank black hair like a bloated Cabbage Patch doll. Pete knelt beside her, massaging the bump and mumbling useless advice.

'You gotta breathe deep, luv, it says in *Reader's Digest*.'

At which point, Cav's long shadow sprang from the doorway and chilled them to wary silence. 'Below with ye now. 'Tis opening time.'

'Hey,' said Gerry, emerging blearily from his habitual semi-coma, 'the man's talking *booze*!'

Harry Two squatted, relaxed and enigmatic behind his shades. Today's robe was lime green, a welcome splash of colour in the drabness. Slowly and deliberately, he slid a pair of drumsticks out of his sleeves and played a light tattoo on the dusty floor. 'If it's all the same to you, big marn, reckon ah'll take room service.'

The knife appeared from nowhere, flickering bright and cutting the sniggers dead. 'I'll not be asking again. Move!'

This time, resistance came from a wholly unexpected quarter; Pete, braving cold steel and hot dark eyes. 'Look at her, damn you, she can hardly walk!'

'Carry her, then, else I will!'

'He means it,' warned Harriet crisply. 'Here, I'll give you a hand.'

Together, they manoeuvred Peg's bulk downstairs in the wake of the chastened band. And formed a sullen audience as Joe took centre stage.

He struck a priestly pose, head bowed, hands clasped beneath his chin. The instrument case lay curved and coffin-like at his feet. The clasps, Harriet noticed, were already open.

'Holy Mary, Mother of God, bless this our celebration. Say Amen, ye heathens!'

Cáv's laughter drowned their sheepish response. 'Now's your chance, Sambo – give us a fanfare of drums.'

Harry Two contrived a defiant pause, and the sticks disappeared into lime green folds. Then, low-pitched and sarcastic, he murmured, 'Da *dum*!'

Harriet was actually bracing for battle when Joe stooped and flung back the lid.

In the awestruck hush, Pete spoke for them all. 'Christ, it's meals on wheels!'

More like Pandora's box, she thought, dazzled by the wealth revealed. Pork pies and sausage rolls, and umpteen flavours of potato crisps in multicoloured wrappers. The sultry air throbbed with greed, reminding her of illicit dorm feasts after lights-out at St Cats. Except for the booze, of course; even the lawless lower fifth steered clear of hard spirits.

Not the Irish, though. The bottles lay row upon row, some goldly and some palely gleaming. Heavy stuff: no wonder they'd had such trouble humping it in.

The inmates swooped like vultures, shouldering and

pecking and squabbling among the spoils. Gerry crabbed away, nursing a double armful of Scotch and snarling at anyone who crossed his path; two of the band were fighting over a single bottle of vodka; and Peg, miraculously restored, emerged from the mêlée with sausage rolls in both fists and greasy flakes of puff pastry plastered around her chin.

'Move along the trough, please,' shouted Pete, and went elbowing towards the crisps; and finally even Harry Two weighed in, his gorgeous raiment brightening the fray.

Harriet shivered and turned away – straight into Cav's triumphant leer.

'Ye'll not escape it, girly. Ye have only to sharpen appetites for the beast to come snuffling through.' He was leaning against the bannister, his teeth bared in a cruel smile.

Chomping sounds and a tang of cold meat taunted her own urgent hunger, and lent an acid bite to her disdain. 'They taught us self-control at school. St Catherine's girls don't *grovel* for food.'

He touched his forelock in feigned respect. 'Sure, and there's naught to beat a good Catholic education.' The smile broadened, and his dark gaze lingered over her breasts. ''Tis fine for the figure, too.'

Stronger temptation, this, and she warmed, in spite of herself. But something about him was different, almost incomplete. Watch your step, Harriet, there's a cold reason for every move he makes. She slipped quickly out of his reach, seeking a dim corner and time to think things through.

By now, Gerry and the band were into serious drinking. Pete and Harry Two shared a bag of crisps and an animated debate on Bob Marley: and Peg continued to eat for at least two. Cav mingled freely, and his heavy

217

geniality gave Harriet the creeps. He's stopped smoking, she realized, it happened when the first music case disappeared. And speaking of disappearing acts – where's Joe? In the basement, stupid. Beneath the rising roar of conversation, she could hear those curiously muffled thumps again. The early afternoon seemed unnaturally dark. It's only clouds, she told herself, the weather's breaking at last. But as the party turned rowdy and the reek of liquor sweetened the stagnant air, a sense of unease persisted. Suddenly, Joe was back, pale with plaster dust and carrying a brown cardboard box. From across the dim and babbling room, Harriet lipread the exchange.

''Tis done, Cav. We're ready.'

'About time. Keep the feckers amused, then.'

Whereupon Joe called for order and unveiled yet another wonder – a state-of-the-art radio cassette in gunmetal grey. 'A token of our esteem,' he announced, brash as a door-to-door hawker, 'for allowing us to share your home. Let there be music!'

Briefly, despite the derisive blue glint in his eyes, Harriet succumbed to the spell of hi-tech; the hypnotic wink of amber control lights, the mellow voice of Frank Sinatra. Oh to be back in civilization, she thought. And she didn't even *like* Frank Sinatra. The moment passed quickly.

Pete was spinning knobs at random, filling the air with static and a babble of foreign tongues. 'Hey,' he shouted, 'it's got short-wave send and receive! We can listen in on the fuzz!'

At which Joe's boyish face set in a mask of warning. 'The Cav has a powerful dislike of policemen. Ye'd best stick to Radio One.'

Harriet retreated further into the shadows, keeping watch on the stairs. Only one thing troubled her more than Cav's presence — not knowing where he was. Because Harry Two was approaching, large and lurid and none too steady on his feet. Dear God, not now, she pleaded silently; Cav's lurking somewhere just *dying* to make trouble. The purple sunglasses gave nothing away, but Harry Two's voice fell deep and steady and he smelled of nothing stronger than Old Spice.

'You better eat, marn.' He pressed a cellophane-wrapped pork pie into her hands. 'Ah'd 'preciate it if you'd take a look upstairs, see what the big marn's about. Ah'll keep Joe busy.'

Good news and bad, she mused bleakly. At least one sane and sober ally — and a *very* unsavoury mission. Chin up, you're a St Catherine's girl!

Pete had found a programme of Golden Oldies. Raucous and glazed, the band were singing along. Harry Two's broad green back shielded her from Joe's line of sight.

She trod the stairs cautiously, pressed to the mildewed wall; and the pie tasteless in her mouth. Instinct took her, light-footed and breathless, to the crack of the communal bedroom door. Through it, she glimpsed Cav's stark and motionless form.

He was waiting for something or somebody, you could tell by the tension in his big body. He leaned towards the grimy window, his narrowed dark eyes peering intently into the distance. There was an air of ceremony about him; the bearded black knight reaffirming allegiance to some unholy crusade while storm clouds loomed on the horizon. Come *on*, Harriet; he's just a dishy Irish thug who caught you snooping once before. This memory, and a sudden, purposeful movement inside sent her scurrying back to safety — and bedlam.

They were on to the Rolling Stones, the radio blaring

219

and Gerry stomping like a spastic Apache, bawling 'Satisfaction!' at the top of his voice. An empty vodka bottle rolled tiredly along the floor and rested eventually against the skirting.

She picked her way past the clapping mob, bent on getting the message across. As she drew near, Harry Two scowled and waved a warning pink palm; and the music died in mid-wail.

Cav had made another noiseless, unnerving entry, wearing a publican's grin and carrying a guitar in each hand. 'Enough of this canned garbage. We've musicians here, let's have a *real* hoolie!'

Gerry and Pete needed no second bidding, hunching over the instruments and making a performance out of tuning up. After a brief argument, Harry Two settled crosslegged and held his sticks at the ready. Then they were away, a pale and insipid 'Nineteenth Nervous Breakdown'.

Gradually, Harry Two's insistent drive and Pete's rhythmic bass work hauled Gerry into line; and the raw energy of the number did the rest. One by one the band joined in, howling and gyrating and glossing over the bum notes with sheer volume. Then to Harriet's horror, Peg stood up and lurched to the hub of the crowd.

Before the bump, she'd been the most faithful of groupies. Now, vast and awkward and somewhat green around the gills, she began a grotesque, slow-motion twist.

It's a genuine rave, thought Harriet, leaning weakly against the wall. Whirling, ragged figures, dust rising in great gusts from the floorboards, a pervading reek of sweat and hard spirits; and a pulsing, orgasmic crescendo of noise. In the middle of it all, a teetering Humpty-Dumpty whose disastrous fall was never more than a heartbeat away.

So overwhelmed was she that Cav's crucial move went unnoticed. By the time she sensed the flurry near the front door, he'd already brought a stranger to the feast.

Strange in more ways than one, she realized instantly. Small and neat, with dark almond eyes and glossy black hair, he was sporting a pale grey suit and rich leather shoes. A 'something in the City' man, the kind she'd sometimes met at her father's office. In this setting and company, he stood out like a prince in the poorhouse. More puzzling still, he was clearly the boss. Even from this distance, she could see him issuing orders while Joe and Cav said three bags full, sir.

As always, Harry Two fashioned a more or less simultaneous fade-out. But before anyone else could react, Gerry had launched a chorus from 'High Society'. Deprived of his backing, he looked and sounded exactly what he had become – a tuneless, burnt-out wreck. 'Cav is king' he bellowed, miles off beat. 'Cav is the thing the folks . . . dig . . . mo-o-ost!'

The sentiment, at least, won scattered applause; and gave Cav the perfect cue for an abdication speech. 'I thank ye Gerry: but Cav is not and never was the king.'

He placed a large paw on the immaculate tailoring and eased the smaller man forward. 'Best he should introduce himself.'

Sensing a subtle shift of atmosphere, Harriet tallied the impressions: Peg's ghastly sweat-streaked face and the gawping incomprehension of the band; Harry Two rising stealthily and edging towards the front door; eerie, orange light filtering between the clouds outside; and the flat, curiously lifeless gaze of the newcomer.

'I am pleased to find you all well, and in good spirits,' he began. He spoke evenly, clipped and precise and not quite English; yet his tone commanded total attention. 'I trust most of you will stay that way.' He waved a fastidious, manicured hand at the remnants of the orgy. 'This is what you may expect, as guests of the Green Reapers.'

To Harriet, the title was only vaguely familiar, but it provoked a flurry of violent action. Harry Two whirled and dived for the door, his robe billowing behind. And stopped short as two shots rang out and gouts of plaster exploded from the wall above his head. The small man stood in a coil of blue smoke, the snub-nosed pistol glinting in his hand. 'Next time,' he promised, 'I shoot to kill. I should not have said guests. You are now hostages.'

Peg collapsed, moaning like a sick cow, and Pete scuttled to her side.

Harry Two came ambling back, hands high. 'What the hell, marn, I ain't lost nothing out there.'

Pete gazed up, stricken. 'Christ,' he breathed, 'I think she's started!'

REALIGNMENTS

The Present Day

Outside, the day turned ugly and storm clouds bruised the city skyline. Within the penthouse, Smythe was a mute and bloodless ghost behind a barren desk; only an occasional flicker of quartz to show that he was there.

For fifteen minutes, Evans had browsed the Axminster, reliving the quest for Daly. 'Just this once,' he concluded, 'the talkers had it right. They'll die for him gladly: some of them have already. A legend in his own lifetime, see.'

The gloom deepened, the silence hung. Presently, a hand wavered from the shadows and set the paperweight down. Its purple glow revealed a mask of bitter pain and sarcasm. 'A legend for the damned! He's a psychopath, man, an undersized Provo butcher!'

'Know him personally, do you?'

'I don't *need* to know him! Richard the Third revisited, the deformed and ill-favoured who scrabble to power over corpses of bigger, better men.'

'Met some con artists in my time, mind. And there was me, believing him.'

'You're Welsh, and prey to the same Celtic delusions.' Smythe steadied, took a calmer tone. 'It's not important. We have to nail the Reapers.'

'Changed your tune, haven't you? Don't spook them, you said, follow their trail. And sent *us* blindfold through badlands!'

'Circumstances alter cases. We must first secure the

home front.' A curious blend of evasion and bluster, and Evans pressed the point.

'Pity. About to hear the word, I was – Cavanaugh and his new playmates – direct from the leprechaun's mouth.'

'More fables, no doubt.' But there was urgency and hope in the Super's grey glare. 'You're saying the operation was aborted too soon?'

'Oh sure. Fancied another fortnight, me, under his spell; and his mate's gunsight.'

Smythe offered a conciliatory smile. 'Don't rub it in. We're meeting the competition, we need to speak with one voice.'

He was up and on his way, a halting parody of his former military gait. Evans tracked him through overcast corridors, taking the pulse of his empire. Last time, the place had throbbed with industry. Today, shirtsleeved uniforms lounged and gossiped, computer screens stood blank and no phones rang. He was still Chief Super, though, rating a chauffeur and a fancy roller, thought Evans as they came outside to the car park.

Slumping on to plush maroon upholstery, Smythe warned, 'No talking, please; not in front of the children.' The strain of command and the gentle stroll had winded him. His chest heaved beneath sober suiting, and sweat beaded his hairline.

While the driver threaded the remnants of rush-hour traffic, Evans watched the weather and considered the symptoms of decline. The Smythe of old would have known about Jane – pedigree, profession, birthmarks and all – and played merry hell. Losing his grip, or simply beneath his notice? He'd said, 'Competition'. Meaning presumably, the Funnies with whom he'd been bosom buddies: until now. Then there was the empty desk, the reek of infirmity, and the air of *Götterdämmerung* which pervaded his realm. A dying throw, according to Daly. Talk about out of the frying pan!

If Smythe had inherited hi-tech, the Funnies clearly aspired to statelier style; an imposing façade, a doorman of bemedalled pomp. Once inside, the Super wheezed along chandeliered warrens between acres of artwork. Old Masters, they were, all cracked varnish and drab hues; designed to imbue culture and tradition. Mostly, they gave Evans the glooms. At last the two men came to a panelled door which opened mysteriously before them. Snow bade them enter, very much the lord of his domain. The same lofty detachment, the same half-spectacled, acute gaze; the same blue pinstripe, probably. But the familiar bristly silhouette at the bay window stopped Smythe in his tracks.

'What's *he* doing here?'

'Come now,' soothed Snow. 'It's his manor, they're his men.'

'Dinna fret yourself,' rasped McKay, over his immaculately uniformed shoulder. 'I'll not interfere: having no taste for cloak and dagger.'

'Except in the back!' Smythe's murmur was low but clearly audible.

Daft, it was. Two senior officers snarling like mongrels and a lanky spymaster lumbered with tribal feuding. As tempers cooled and hackles subsided, Evans took stock of the arena.

Classy, you'd have to call it. Old gold curtains gleaming against the grey beyond, a faded but obviously genuine Chinese carpet, the rich bronze of antique wood. Glass-fronted bookshelves lined the room, and every volume bound in ageing leather. Yet there was combat in the air, a whiff of genteel brutality. It's like the National Sporting Club, Evans mused; fisticuffs for toffs in dinner jackets.

Snow was calling them to order, drifting towards the

long, laquered rosewood table; and McKay had taken obstinate root by the window.

'I like the view, d'you mind?'

'It *is* pleasing,' Snow conceded. 'More so, in the sun. Nevertheless, I'd rather not address your back. Hamish?'

Evans took his appointed seat at the foot of the table. Outranked, he was, and underdressed in a shabby fawn jacket and patched elbows; he *had* to be below the salt. Smythe sat halfway along, isolated in his charcoal grey; and a complexion only a few shades lighter. And McKay, persuaded, settled brashly at Snow's right hand. Hello, thought Evans, *those* two are up to something.

'Perhaps, Inspector,' Snow began, 'you'd care to open the batting. An outline of the mission as it unfolded?'

'Abortive,' snapped Smythe at once. 'The abrupt and premature termination cost us vital insight into the Reapers. Who, I believe, are the proper subjects of this discussion.'

'The Reapers must wait, until we share your insights. Take your time, Inspector.'

There was a photograph on the deserted desk: a younger, cheerier Snow in birdwatching gear. Focusing on this and ignoring the charged atmosphere, Evans gathered fluency. A tale which improved for the telling, anyhow. By the time he'd finished, they were hanging on every word.

'Excellent!' breathed Snow; and Smythe cut in again.

'The aim was to neutralize Daly, or at least lure him to the border. *I'd* call it a golden opportunity squandered!'

There might have been a hint of pity in Snow's dark eyes. 'Your home record is exemplary, Smythe. On foreign ground, however, our people enjoy certain advantages. Longer experience, a broad overview, a more – "catholic" – range of sources. We prefer to confront the devils we know; and consider Daly something of a moderate. Would you agree, Inspector?'

Taken unawares and conscious of Smythe's discomfort, Evans trod carefully. 'A patriot, I'd say. Very strong for the Holy Ground and woe betide the invader. Not too fussed about the mainland, he reckoned, or bullets in people's knees.' He faced Snow fair and square, letting his dissent show. 'He's a killer, mind, good as told me so. Hardly Mahatma Gandhi.'

'In this business, we're seldom permitted the luxury of moral judgements. Nice to know they endure. Nevertheless, by today's standards, you have just defined a moderate – one who is selective in his slaughter. Sobering, isn't it?' Austere features softened. Snow beamed like a benevolent don. 'I congratulate you, Inspector. A perceptive portrait of opposing leadership: precisely the information we required.'

Smythe had gone very pale, eyeing Snow incredulously. 'You changed the brief! Why, for God's sake?'

'I'd rather not say. Let's get on to the Reapers.'

'You undermined the operation, overruled my orders! On whose authority? By what right?'

'Very well. Remember, you forced my hand. We've been suspicious for months – warnings from the Garda, persistent hints on the grapevine, a fistful of your agents who've simply disappeared. Your Irish network is blown, Smythe. You have at least one viper in your nest.' Rounding on Evans, Snow demanded, 'You were there, you have recent, first-hand impressions. Is mine an accurate analysis?'

A lean, Aryan face, an Oxbridge accent, a quintessentially English setting; yet Evans was suddenly back in Eire, confronting an elusive dwarf. A similar challenge, an identical target – Chief Superintendent Smythe. Funnies versus the Force, and no way to fudge it. Meeting Smythe's red-rimmed glance uneasily, he muttered, 'We were expected. O'Brien knew it, Daly implied it, even Beddoes caught the drift.'

'I would scarcely rate the Sergeant as a reliable source.'

'He was your choice, Smythe,' Snow said implacably. 'One of many misjudgements, I fear.'

Smythe was watching him with utter loathing. 'You knew all this, and sent them in anyway? What *are* you, man?'

'Just a civil servant, doing a dirty job.'

'That is precisely the point! *How* dirty?'

The best question so far. The pecking order inverted, and Funnies brought to bay.

Snow sighed and removed his spectacles. The thin features looked oddly naked, the black eyes weak and defensive. He seemed on the verge of some crucial revelation when the door opened and a frail blond boy ambled in. 'Excuse the presumption, sir,' he murmured, without a hint of apology, 'the Reapers made contact a few moments ago. I thought a synopsis might be – pertinent.' He laid a flimsy on the table, nodded in deference to McKay's badge of rank and left as languidly as he'd entered.

'Ye Gods,' growled McKay, 'you could do with a bit of discipline about the place!'

And Smythe, somewhat recovered, resorted to habitual sarcasm. 'Heaven forbid! It might stunt their intellectual talents.'

Evans, discounting the interplay, had eyes for Snow alone. He in turn sat very still, the spectacles back in place, bowed over the typeprint like a man oppressed by a friend's obituary. 'I wonder, Chief Superintendent,' he enquired, 'if you'd review the evidence – the link between Daly and the Reapers?'

'For goodness sake! It was obvious to anyone!'

'Refresh our memories, then.'

Smythe shoved his pad aside and gave the details impatiently. 'Cavanaugh planted the bomb and recorded the tape. Your explosives team and our voiceprints confirm it. He is a convicted Provo terrorist, and his preference for knives is well documented. Duffy is his known apprentice, almost certainly an accessory to the stabbing. The Inspector here has established what we had long suspected – Daly is the Provo mastermind. The link, as I said, is patently obvious.'

'Especially when you are desperate to find it.' Snow leaned back, laying long fingers across his waistcoat. 'The facts are not disputed. Daly's complicity, however, remains wishful thinking on your part. Let me finish, please! We – analysts – share a waking nightmare: a consortium of international terrorists having diverse ideologies but common targets. The tone of the Reaper message always troubled me.'

Me too, Evans thought, remembering.

'Have you ever heard an Irishman call a countryman "fella"?' continued Snow. 'Spelt with an 'h' it means Arab husbandman. And only one nation in the world flies a plain green flag.'

'Libya,' whispered McKay, his blue gaze bright with fury.

Snow nodded heavily. 'Green Reapers; suddenly, the chosen title takes an entirely new significance.' The severe mouth arced down in disgust. 'Courtesy of your Irish preoccupation, Smythe, they wrong-footed us neatly. While we sealed off the Western front, they infiltrated from the East.'

'And you accuse *me* of conjecture?' Smythe blazed. 'On the strength of a coloured flag and a dubious spelling? Cavanaugh and company are Catholic – don't

229

think I missed that clue. What would they want with Moslems?'

'Loot,' said McKay succinctly. 'They're no but common hirelings.'

Reading over Snow's shoulder, he was, and looking pretty sick. One obsession versus another, in Evans' book. But not for long.

'The Reapers have set themselves at siege,' the cultured, relentless voice explained, 'and taken British prisoners. The threat is stark and simple. Submit and obey, or they blow up the stronghold and everyone in it. Themselves included.' Snow paused, challenging the Chief Super to meet his stare above the dotty glasses. 'Grant me this; so far, self-immolation has not been a popular Provo gambit.'

'It's an Irish bluff,' Smythe insisted, 'so call it!'

Snow glanced down. The flimsy rustled in his hand. 'They have released the names of their "peace-loving detainees". Arabs, to a man, hit-squad members from Gadaffi's recent purge.' He turned to Evans. 'Daly told the truth; so much for obvious connections.'

Somewhere nearby, a telephone shrilled and was instantly silenced. Smythe's ragged breathing seemed to fill the room.

Watching the slumped grey figure dispassionately, Snow urged, 'Pull yourself together! Frailty and over-zealousness are not irredeemable. We still need your resources.'

Smythe stared, glazed and unfocused, at his own reflection in polished brown wood.

'The surveillance, he means,' Evans prompted. 'You had them cornered, remember? Darro, mun, tell him about Harrigan!'

The name woke him; a pitiful effort, an unsteady hand

to his brow, a low and laboured tone. 'Musicians. Harrigan posed as a drummer and went in after them. A derelict property somewhere in Dockland.'

'Where?' McKay was grinning, fanged and fiery. 'I'll give 'em a siege they won't forget in a hurry!'

'I don't *know* where! We lost contact, over a week ago. Doubtless, his body will turn up in some dark alley.' Smythe's precarious control finally snapped. He leaned forward, his whole frame quaking with disease and rage. 'What are you gawping at? You can't blame me for nigger foolishness and Irish mayhem! They are all murdering fanatics and hippy scum! Let them blow themselves to pieces, and good riddance!'

'Thank you, Chief Superintendent,' said Snow, deadly polite. 'We won't detain you further. I'd advise resignation, and soon. Overwork and illness, full pension and no blemish on the record.'

Smythe got up – a major triumph in itself – and moved like a sleepwalker across the rich room.

'One more thing. Don't go talking to reporters, will you?'

Wanton cruelty this, and Smythe retrieved a shred of dignity. 'Rest easy, Mr Snow. Unlike you, I don't consider subordinates expendable.'

The door closed and he was gone, an illustrious victim to a sordid, vicious war.

'Christ,' muttered McKay, in rare and heartfelt blasphemy. 'Did ye have to be so cold? He's served for half a lifetime; no man deserves an end like that!'

'You saw him, you heard him. He had become a liability; I have neither time nor temperament for charity.' Briefly, Snow's voice moderated: 'Comfort yourself, Hamish. It was none of your doing.'

In that instant, Evans saw something in Snow's black eyes. Something deep and chilling – unmistakable: the gleam of satisfaction. Smythe didn't fall, he was pushed! In this most civilized chamber, a man had been driven to professional suicide; his career shattered, his very spirit dissected. And not a single drop of blood to stain the fancy carpet. Snow had chosen a successor, the incumbent had to go. The table placings implied it, his continuing deference towards McKay confirmed it. Cold by name and nature, Daly had said; and, all unwitting, McKay echoed him. Watch your back, Hamish, it's not just the Irish who are handy with the steel! Evans forced these thoughts away, for Snow was soldiering on regardless.

'The Reapers have given us four days to release "detainees".' He consulted his watch; a glint of gold, a show of dazzling cuff. 'As from two this afternoon.'

'Where *are* they?' McKay demanded, pounding a hairy fist into his palm; and provoked a rare burst of temper.

'Think, man! In all probability, they'll tell us, if only for publicity purposes. Even if they don't, they're using short-wave radio. We'll pinpoint them within seconds of the next transmission.'

'Triangulation,' McKay mumbled, much abashed. 'Sorry.' Leaving Evans not one whit wiser.

'My assistant has already initiated contingency plans,' Snow confirmed. 'An operational and communication centre in your office, Hamish, and trained negotiators standing by.' He paused, flexing his narrow shoulders absently, new urgency invading his voice. 'We have an immediate crisis. The hostages include a pregnant woman, close to confinement. The Reapers do not wish to harm "innocent, unborn children". They're demanding an exchange.'

'Someone to go in, you mean?' asked Evans in amazement. 'They're barmy!'

'Not just someone. A policeman.'

'Like the Iranian affair.' McKay's craggy face twisted in suspicion.

'What was the laddie's name? Lock?'

'Quite.' Snow wore his professorial smile again, a short-lived concession. 'Officially, they want "an unbiased observer, to broadcast the living truth". The real motive, I suspect, is a good deal more sinister.'

Snow was all at once up and pacing, his elongated figure at odds with the scale of the room. Passing the window, blue against grey and old gold, he spoke with quite uncharacteristic apprehension. 'PC Trevor Lock took on the Iranians and won. I'm afraid the Reapers mean to go one better; a matter of Arab face. They are mounting an assault on the political and civil structure of this country. Any policeman who goes in must be primed for an attempt to break him; to coerce him into public support for their cause; so demonstrating that both the Government and the Police Force can be subverted.' He turned, trap-mouthed and stony-eyed. 'You heard the PM. *It cannot be permitted!*'

Brave words, thought Evans: how are you going to stop it?

Squinting upward, clearly dismayed, McKay had a harsher question. 'Abandon the girl and her bairn? They'll not survive, ye know.'

'Of course not! Inside information would be a priceless boon.'

'Page the lads, shall I?' Evans asked.

Snow's spectacles caught the fading light. Briefly, his face lost all expression. 'I don't want *lads* bent on vengeance and heroics. We need someone mature: quick-witted, mentally and physically resilient, having some experience of the terrorist mentality. And preferably without personal commitments.'

The kamikaze pilot again, thought Evans gloomily;

233

where are you, Yamamoto? And glanced up into two steady, enquiring gazes. 'Hold on, don't look at me!'

Hard to bear, mind. Just back from the hostile bogs, pitted against Gadaffi's nutters and a ticking time-bomb. Someone passed along the corridor, whistling. From beyond the golden curtains, a hoot and rumble of traffic. There's a world outside, bach, and life to be lived. Give them the 'personal commitment', wish them well, go home and watch it on the box. It's *got* to be a spectator sport, fair play. So tell them about Jane.

But you couldn't, when you came right down to it. Innocents at stake, see, the dross you're paid to nick when they're naughty and rescue when they're not. Evans' mind went back to an outraged Singh and a butchered tramp. And a sunbleached dwarf, laughing. *Bloody* Reapers. They'd sucked him in, set him on the hunt; he had to see it through.

The oldest, cruellest conflict of all: duty, or a kind of love. A lifetime at one, and only a promise of the other. Sorry, Jane, he told her cherished image. I don't know how to do it any other way. 'All right,' he said tiredly, regretting the words the instant they were spoken. 'You've got your volunteer.'

'Man,' said McKay softly, 'you're dafter than I thought!' But there was tribute in the tone, and open relief in the pale blue eyes.

'On three conditions,' Evans added. 'One, I want an alias. No publicity, whichever way it goes.'

'Cover,' McKay told Snow, 'that's your department.'

'Two, I want Beddoes here, at the sharp end.'

McKay pursed doubtful lips, and Snow set himself to persuade. 'Admirable loyalty, Inspector, but sadly misplaced. I've never trusted that young man; besides, as I said, we have trained staff for precisely this situation.'

'Negotiators, duw duw! Line 'em up by the dozen, for

all I care. To listen, I mean; I'll only talk to Roy. Look, you reckon it could be dodgy, getting the message across. Need someone who *knows* me, don't you, someone who's on the same wavelength.'

'Makes sense,' McKay allowed; and, to Snow, 'Where's the harm, with professionals standing by?'

He didn't like it, anyone could see; proles trespassing in Funnyland. He nodded, though. What else could he do?

'Three, I want to make a private call. Now.'

'Certainly not!'

'Suit yourself.' Evans levered himself upright and was heading for the door, hardly believing his luck.

'For Heaven's sake,' hissed McKay, 'a common criminal has *that* right!'

'Police solidarity,' muttered Snow. 'How touching. Very well, Inspector, but mind what you say. Lives could depend on it.'

'Aye. 'Specially mine.'

He called her from the pay booth in the lobby. 'Listen,' he began, 'something's come up.'

'Don't tell me. You'll be late.'

Darro, I hope not, he thought. The lilt of her voice warmed him. Picturing her, easy and graceful in his hallway, he cursed himself for the biggest fool in Christendom. Aloud, he said, 'Could be a day or two, mind.'

'Huw? What's going on? You're not going away again? Not still chasing' — her voice caught, he could feel her fear — 'the little one?'

'Not exactly.' He hated the caution, and the echo of Snow's taunt — *Don't go talking to reporters, will you.* 'It's the same only different, I can't say more. Just wanted to . . . warn you. Thing is, don't believe what the papers say.'

She chuckled, anxious yet electrifying. 'No chance. I

write that stuff, remember? Huw? Will it always be like this?'

The appeal for reassurance tempted him; he thrust it aside. 'Not always. Too often, probably.'

A soft sigh, a note of almost wifely resignation. 'I'll be waiting, love. Getting used to it, you see.'

He stood there for quite a long time afterwards, wondering about the future; then trudged off to wrestle with the present.

Momentarily, Peg's keening had unnerved them all; a blend of agony and terror which gave Harriet gooseflesh and reduced even the newcomer to indecision. Then, astonishingly, Joe took charge. With a brisk 'Cover 'em, Cav,' he shoved his machine pistol into his belt, shooed Pete away and knelt beside the writhing form. His hands explored the bulge as he crooned reassurance. Presently, the moans eased to a whimper and he looked up cheerfully.

'She's a while to wait, and the waters not yet broken. Regular contractions, still well spaced; her time might come in an hour or a day.' Eyeing Pete contemptuously, he ordered, 'C'mere, she'll not bite. Cradle her back, *this* way – and for the Dear's sake stop snivelling!'

'Hey, marn,' Harry Two challenged, darkly suspicious, 'how come *you* know?'

Joe's blue eyes twinkled, his chubby face creased in a sly smile. 'Sure, and wasn't me uncle the best vet in Kerry? Many's the calf I've helped him breech.'

Pete stared at him, white as a sheet; but Cav's belly-laugh broke the tension, and Harriet had to suppress a tremulous smile. Better than the *Reader's Digest*, anyway.

But not good enough for the newcomer. Dark and dapper and devoid of humour, he demanded, 'Are you competent to deliver her, Mr Duffy?'

236

'What, *here*?' Joe's disdainful gesture took in the whole shambles — mouldering boards, cobwebbed panes, peeling walls. 'Come on, Mr Salim, I've seen cleaner cowsheds!'

Salim, thought Harriet. Of course, he's an Arab! The knowledge brought no relief and much mystery. Since when did Arabs and Irishmen hunt together? When they're after the English, silly, which frightened her even more.

She was suddenly aware of her own isolation. Harry Two squatting by the unhappy couple, offering physical and moral support. Denied further entertainment, Gerry and the band were back at their bottles; and Salim had beckoned Cav away, leaving Joe to stand guard. Cautiously, her heart pounding, she edged closer to the unlikely pair: a bearded roughneck and a delicate dandy conspiring under a storm-dimmed window.

'How do you excuse this, Mr Cavanaugh?'

'Jaysus, she's a pain. I've tried to be rid of her for days!' Which explained the callousness, the move upstairs and the restriction on loos.

'She has to go. It is necessary.' The Arab was toying with his pistol, an intent, unfeeling look which boded ill for someone. Not someone, Harriet realized in horror; Peg!

Abruptly, the sallow features cleared. 'Y'Allah, an *exchange*! A point to prove, a score to settle!' Glancing up, he caught Harriet's eye and bared small, even teeth. 'Begone, girl! Go and comfort your sister!'

Harriet blanched and scuttled off, seeking anonymity in the shadows. A lot of them about, and the first fat spots of rain pattering on the roof. Curiosity overcame fear; from a safe distance, she watched the plot develop.

The Arab spoke, and Cav's bearded jaw sagged in sheer disbelief. Craning forward, she could just make out the

237

sibilance of Salim's voice. Whatever he said, Cav obviously rejected. Gradually, the big Irishman's posture eased and his mouth curled in a grin. Pointing upward, he made strange wiping motions, like a window-cleaner. Salim nodded, clapped him on the shoulder, pointed at the radio. Then he drew paper and a gold pencil from his inside pocket; and they huddled together, whispering and scribbling.

Harry Two's figure was a broad green beacon in the gloom. Harriet drifted towards it, breathing fumes of alcohol, needing to talk to *someone*. Before she'd gone halfway, Salim was moving to the centre of the room, demanding silence. And getting it.

'We have no quarrel with the unborn,' he began. 'If your Government agrees, we shall release the woman.' Pete was on his feet, alight with hope and relief.

'Only the woman.'

And the lanky frame sagged.

'Shortly,' Salim continued, 'Mr Cavanaugh will broadcast our mission to the world. Listen well! You will learn that triumph is ours, and resistance is useless! Now hear my first command. Henceforth, you will make bowel movements upstairs. The ablution below is reserved for the Reapers.'

'But it's blocked!' The words were out before Harriet could stop them; and she was staring into Arab eyes as black and blank as gun barrels.

'It is an *order*, girl. Disobey at your peril.'

She bowed her head, to hide defiance and avoid Cav's glittering leer. All right, then: I won't go!

A rustle of movement, a crackle of static, and Cav, intent in the yellow glow, tuning the radio. 'Do you read, me little English darlins?'

A quick response, a slightly distorted but cultured voice. 'Are you the Reapers?'

238

'That we are. And ye have four days to free our comrades, after which we'll blow this gaff sky-high!'

Harriet leaned against the wall, weak-kneed and trembling. While her mind reeled, her senses continued to absorb impressions: Harry Two rising like a swift black ghost, then freezing at Joe's harsh cry; Cav's Irish accent stumbling over a list of Arab names; Gerry, mindless as usual, raising an amber bottle and giggling insanely; and Salim, poised and motionless as a male model. He *means* it, she thought despairingly. Dear God, let me wake up soon!

But it wasn't a dream. As Cav droned on about bombs and detonators, she realized she'd blundered into a well-planned military operation. Gerry and the band had been chosen for their sheer fecklessness; the house, for its isolation. With Joe's lights installed, rescue would be suicidal, day or night. The guns and explosives had filled the missing music case, and the basement was no doubt wired for the final blast. Hence the bumps in the night and Cav's rejection of cigarettes. Even today's party had been precisely timed, to lower potential resistance and distract attention from Salim's arrival. And Joe's 'token of esteem' was now 'broadcasting to the world'.

In total dismay, Harriet encountered the ugliest suspicion of all: had Cav been detailed to bed her and keep her from rational thought? He'd done that, all right – you stupid, stupid cow!

He was still talking, giving the address and demanding full-scale media participation – 'From beyond sniper range, mind you.' What he said next amazed her, and raised a flicker of hope. 'We've a girl here with child, and about to pop.' He consulted Salim's notes, a noble-sounding phrase. Then: 'We'll swap her for one of the fuzz. An honest, unbiased observer, so ye'll know the truth of it within. Deadline, nightfall.' He grinned, assumed a passable stateside drawl. '*Their* lives in *your* hands. *Do* call back, and have a nice day!'

They can't be *all* bad, Harriet reasoned desperately, if they'll turn Peg loose. Maybe their comrades *have* been misjudged, maybe the Government *will* give in. Mostly, though, she longed for someone to trust, someone who could outwit and outface the Reapers and end the siege peacefully. And no one would do better than a sturdy, solid, impeccable English bobby.

At the second attempt, she made it to the impromptu pre-natal gathering. Though still in pain, Peg seemed calmer. Gone beyond it, probably: she had that glazed, uncaring look. Pete knelt behind her, massaging her back but finding nothing to say. And Harry Two was simply there, a massive, comforting presence.

'Sorry, girl,' he muttered, deadly serious for once. 'Ah was lookin' for trouble closer to home.'

Whereupon Peg had another noisy contraction; and as her groans subsided, the radio fizzed into life. 'Hello, Reapers. Exchange agreed, I repeat, *agreed*. Volunteer constable on his way. Please state arrangements for entry.'

Pete's whoop drowned Cav's reply, and even the band mustered a ragged cheer. It's like the end of term, Harriet thought; for one of us anyway. Joe, clearly, was as relieved as anyone, winning a special concession from the reluctant Arab. Once-only use of the downstairs toilet for a departing guest; and himself minding the door.

By the time Peg emerged, scrubbed but hollow-eyed, Salim had put an end to the celebrations. Shepherding Harry Two to the heart of the band at gunpoint, he dispatched Joe and the rifle to an upstairs window. 'Watch every step, Mr Duffy. If in doubt, shoot to kill.

Mr Cavanaugh, take the woman to the door. Give our visitor a warm welcome.'

At the last minute, Pete baulked, clinging to Peg and sobbing helplessly. Harriet hauled him off, surprised at her own strength and ferocity. 'For God's sake, don't you *want* her to go?'

'Oh, Harry, I want to go with her!'

Don't we all, she thought, feeling his tears on her neck.

'Your man's coming!' Joe announced from upstairs, and Peg had time for one quick wave before Cav nudged her out and closed the hallway door behind him. And Harriet was left to hold the baby and pray for police deliverance.

CHAPTER THIRTEEN

One thing to be said for deception – it earns you top-notch travel. Disdaining British produce, Snow drove a silver BMW. Piloted, more like; air-conditioning, contoured seats and enough dials on the dash for Concorde. The interior smelled of leather and loot, the engine purred politely. A tidy old ride; pity it might be the last.

'We've settled on Constable Jenkins,' Snow announced, his perfect diction muffled by the plush, 'in deference to your accent. Use your given name. It lessens the risk of embarrassing pauses. Truth is always the most effective cover.'

Alone in the back and the splendour, Evans squirmed uneasily. The borrowed uniform chafed at neck and crutch, yet sagged around the waist. The trousers were an inch too short, exposing fawn socks and scuffed suede boots.

'An authentic touch,' Snow had insisted. 'You were summoned at short notice.'

'Volunteered, you said.'

'Don't quibble! People *expect* small inconsistencies.'

'Oh, sure. It's the big ones that bother me.'

The afternoon pavements were emptying under a violet sky. People coming in from the wet, see. Lucky dabs.

'We *know* what they want.' Snow manoeuvred the padded wheel deftly, avoiding an errant moped. 'And we know they're not going to get it. Procrastinate. Win us a chance to act, give them cause to hesitate.'

'What if it happens the other way round?' Funnies, clearly, took no heed of awkward questions.

'They are a bizarre alliance of race and creed. Play on their differences, set one against the other.'

'Divide and rule, is it? And them holding the guns?'

Now into tighter corners and meaner streets. Still, the power-steering smoothed their way; still, the cool advice and unanswered queries.

'We need information on their strength, ordnance and dispositions. Most of all, we need *time*; to assemble their profiles, study their psychology. Time to assess defences and perfect the assault; *and bring you out.*'

'Glad you mentioned that. Convinced me, you have.' Bit of a strain, this backchat, but constables can't complain.

The big car eased into the kerb. A yellowed newspaper tumbled past, pushed by the rising breeze. Snow produced a hand mike from a cushioned recess, twiddled knobs and paged McKay. A single raindrop spattered the windscreen, and the Scottish burr sliced across the static. 'All set, hereabouts. Hustle, Jenkins, yon Reapers are getting impatient.'

Evans scrambled out, clipping his helmet on the doorframe and swearing softly. Straightening, he peered down through the half-open window at a glint of spectacles and a pale, extended hand.

'First left and keep straight on. Good luck, Inspector.' The grip was surprisingly fervent, the whisper unusually fierce. 'We're briefing the SAS.'

Cold comfort, he reckoned, as the silver saloon slid past. Shoot first and ask after, they do. Following Snow's directions, his soles squelching on cracked paving stones, he reached the corner and sighted the last staging post;

squad cars and an ambulance and blue lights spinning. Rain fell fitfully, damping the dust and unleashing a smell of drains. A lonesome trudge between drab, cramped terraces, and visions of Jane to haunt him every step of the way.

McKay's greeting was terse and tight-lipped. 'When you reach the front steps, they'll free the girl. Wait till she's clear, then get yourself inside.' His blue gaze faltered, his voice turned gruff. 'There's a sniper in the upstairs window.'

'There's nice. Casey rides again.'

McKay came stiffly to attention, freckled forefingers aligned to the seams of his trousers. 'Mind how ye go, laddie.'

Touching, all these farewells; and much too final for Evans' taste.

Dignity, he thought, marching into danger and an unrehearsed role; a simple copper, long on dignity and short on brain. You've *got* to be simple, or you wouldn't be here.

The house stood sombre and solitary against a backdrop of dark-bellied cloud. Dirty great arclights, unimpeded vision all around, and not enough cover to conceal a half-grown rat. SAS? Be better off with the Ghost Squad.

The door squealed wide on rusty hinges, revealing the wreck of a girl. Lank-haired and big-bellied, her mouth a freshly lipsticked gash, she teetered down the steps. 'It's *awful* in there! Pete'll be killed, I *know* it!'

'Go on, you,' he urged, 'the blood-wagon's waiting.'

She waddled, crabwise, clutching her middle with pale blotchy arms. 'Get him away from them, *please*!'

Very reassuring. Evans took the steps cautiously, breathing in an essence of booze and decay. As he eased the door wider, a mocking voice intoned, 'Abandon

244

hope, all ye who enter here. Don't be bashful, me dear – come in!' Cavanaugh, no question, you could tell by the brogue and the gravel.

Evans swallowed hard and lunged forward. The door slammed behind, the gloom blinded him. There was movement, close and violent, the dank air roiling. Something hard and heavy crashed against his neck, the floor reared up and hit him in the face. Briefly, perception outlived pain; gurgle and splash, cool wetness at his head, and a choking reek of gin. A snigger echoed in his jumbled brain, and welcome blackness took him down . . .

Late afternoon, and painkillers winking from the hinge of the Yellow Pages. Trapping the earpiece between shoulder and cheek, dialling one-handed and clutching his thigh with the other, Beddoes sought distraction; and word of Harry Slade. So far he'd won a nil return from her father and an implied 'good riddance' from the stepmum. Now, driven by boredom and obstinacy, he paged the 'Impresario'. One more call, my son, and it's time for the next fix.

'Gerry Jewell?' queried the unctuous voice. 'The kid's burnt out already.'

'We make the decisions. So where do I catch his act?'

'Act? You'll be lucky squire. Busking the Underground, most likely. Hooked on smack, they say.'

'So?' snarled Beddoes. 'Name me one that isn't! Just tell me where to look, okay?'

'Squatting, last I heard, down the Docks. Hey, I got a better idea – Susie Sheen! Great voice, you should *see* the body! A real goer, do anything for a break. Anything, know what I mean?'

'It's Jewell I'm after. And I'll do me own pimping,

thanks.' A false note, this. Suspicion came oozing down the line.

'*Barney* Ringwood, you said, from the Beeb?'

'Sure. So what do you want, fingerprints?'

'Read the papers, squire. Barney went over to Channel Four last week. Now get off my back or I'll call the cops!'

It was funny like the weather; sick and sad and grey. Turning his back on the drizzle-smeared panes, Beddoes palmed the capsules and poured himself a Scotch. The glass was at his lips, the fumes actually scorching his nostrils, when the phone rang and McKay pronounced reprieve.

'Report to the station forthwith. Huw Evans hath need of thee. Twenty minutes; after which I'll be finding a *real* policeman!'

So Beddoes settled for Ponstan and water, and quit his solitary pad at a smartish hobble . . .

Someone had made a disco joint out of McKay's spartan lair. Cables coiled like still black snakes across the ice-grey carpet, linking decks of hi-fi gear to a single, standing mike.

'What's up, then?' Beddoes enquired. 'Auditions?' And shipped a wrathful blue glare.

'You're here on sufferance, Sergeant. There's grave business afoot. Mind your manners and speak when ye're asked!'

McKay took station at the window, confronting a storm, explaining the siege, speaking of Evans as if of the dear departed. 'The Reapers have us by the short hairs,' he confessed, unusually earthy. 'And the Inspector has gone to preach the word of Islam.'

'Christ,' Beddoes breathed, 'you bastards get your pound of flesh! Irish ink in his passport hardly dry and you chuck him to the Arabs!'

'He volunteered, man, and raised *you* from the dead! Now will ye keep your wits about you, or moon like a big, soft girl?'

'Yeah, well, when you put it like that . . . What's the bottom line?'

McKay came towards the desk, picking his way through the clutter. 'You'll be no more than a go-between, a familiar voice to keep his spirits up. The Funnies rule, remember. Snow's minions will write the script.' Cocking his ginger head, frowning at shrill female voices outside, the Super offered a slim green plastic box. 'A bleeper, same as the medics use. Keep it by you night and day. You're on permanent standby; I trust ye'll be sleeping alone!'

Beddoes pocketed the gadget, and the office door burst open.

'Superintendent!' cried Jane Neale. 'Nice to see you again! *There*,' she added, to the hovering, flustered secretary, 'I *told* you he wouldn't mind.' The belted trench-coat and matching white heels were flecked with rain, and dark damp strands of auburn accentuated her pallor. Not at her best, then; a haunted quality Beddoes couldn't quite place.

'On the contrary,' growled McKay, 'we're rather busy just now.'

'I know. I've been at the siege house myself.'

'Have ye indeed! And how did ye hear about *that*?'

'Come, Superintendent, public transmissions and ambulances rushing around? I'm a reporter, after all. It won't take long, promise!' She turned on the charm, a smile to melt icebergs. And to Beddoes' secret amusement, the frosty Scot succumbed.

'Och, very well. Five minutes, no more.'

As the relieved secretary withdrew and McKay offered a chair, Beddoes caught a beseeching green-eyed glance. Keep it dark, she meant; but *what* a nerve! If the Super

247

got wind of the Evans connection, he'd have her in the cells.

She faced him boldly, settling herself like royalty. 'I want exclusive rights,' she said . 'Sight of every official bulletin before it's released.' Straight for the jugular, mind you, and no fooling.

'My dear young woman,' McKay retorted, quick-frozen once more, 'our previous meeting, pleasant though it was, scarcely warrants such privileges!'

'Of course not. There will be mutual benefits.'

'And what have we to gain?'

'Confidentiality. Your secrets preserved.' She leaned forward, giving off hostility and expensive French perfume. 'You sent an officer into that house. Who was he?'

'Name of Jenkins,' McKay snapped. 'A volunteer from the suburbs.'

Her hands, Beddoes noted, twisted ceaselessly around the tie-belt. Hiding inner turmoil, was she, beneath the poised façade? A professional, though; her purpose never wavered. 'Is that so? He reminded me of someone we all know better: someone of higher rank. Here's the bargain, then. First bite of the cherry to myself, and I'll not speculate about Inspector Evans.'

Media, thought Beddoes in disgust, we should've known better. The lovey-dovey bit was all a con, she'd do anything and anyone for a story. Then, in a sudden shift of light, he recognized the shadows in her face. *Pain*, same as he'd seen in his own shaving-glass every morning since Dublin. Mystified, he held his peace while McKay brought out the big guns.

The Super was on his feet, a stubby finger aimed between her eyes. 'You breathe one word of speculation and I'll have a D-notice out so fast the wind'll blow you over!'

'Really? On what grounds?'

'National security, what else?' For once, McKay used the despised phrase with relish. Funnies, clearly, had their virtues.

'And what about *his* security?' Her beauty flared, vibrant and provocative. Looking out for Huw, it seemed; and Beddoes' sympathies wavered once again. 'Send your notice, Superintendent. I'm not without support or friends. You can't muzzle them all.'

'Dinna tempt me, Miss Neale,' McKay warned, the burr thriving on his anger. 'There's such a thing as protective custody!'

'You wouldn't dare! And if you do I'll shout his name from your dungeons!' She was on the ragged edge, her lips trembling, the freckles standing out like blemishes against the parchment of her skin. Beddoes *knew* for sure what she would say – '*And everything else you've forced him to do!*' Which would cook Huw's goose good and proper.

''Ang about,' he said. 'Let's keep it civil.'

'Stay out of this, laddie!'

'Tell her the *reason*, sir. She shouldn't need telling, mind you.'

Jane Neale rounded on him fiercely. 'I thought you were his *friend*!'

'It's for his own protection, luv. From people like you.'

She flinched, flushed and momentarily nonplussed. And McKay pounced like a rufous Caledonian buzzard. 'The press made PC Lock a hero, after the Iranian siege. And what happened? Months of harassment, his bairns beaten up, his car vandalized; poor man had to move house in the end. That's what your colleagues do for heroes, lassie. It's why PC Jenkins went in, and why you'll get no favours from me!'

Glaring up at the scornful, blue-clad figure, she seemed about to retaliate out of sheer stubbornness. Catching her eye, Beddoes jerked a surreptitious thumb at the

249

door. And breathed easier as she found a way to climb down.

'Will you swear it, Superintendent? No cover-up, no disowning him if things go wrong?'

Scenting victory, not quite able to hide his own relief, McKay chose a note of undignified reproach. 'No publicity, at his own request, and nothing more sinister. Ye have my word, Miss Neale.'

'Then PC Jenkins it shall be; and may he survive to enjoy his privacy.' Her eyes were moist as she said it, and Beddoes came swiftly to her rescue. 'See her off the premises, should I?'

McKay grinned knowingly; misreading the signals, probably, and thinking Beddoes fancied her.

'We-ell – be quick about it!'

Beddoes obeyed, playing the knight errant and fostering the illusion.

Her heels rang sharp down quiet corridors. Limping, dot and carry, in his effort to keep up, he was conscious of the rustle of her coat and the tautness in her body; and of the startled hungry stares she won from a couple of loitering uniforms.

Out in the car park under livid skies and light drizzle, he warned, 'It's vital now, girl. You've *got* to get out of Huw's place.'

She glanced up in burning emerald resentment. 'Can't resist it, can you – *I told you so!*'

'Ah, leave it out! He's undercover, incognito – and having it off with a newshound? Jesus, think about Huw for a change!'

'I seldom think about anyone else!' It sounded genuine; even now, he couldn't be sure. 'Tell me Sergeant, would you say the same if we were married?'

'Course not. Different, innit.'

'My God!' she whispered. 'Do people still think that way?'

'People, I dunno. Coppers *have* to.'

She walked a few more weary paces, pushing a wet red ringlet away from her face. 'All right. The scarlet woman will leave discreetly. I suppose I should be grateful. At least you don't tell tales.'

'Don't bother. He's *my* oppo, too.'

'Even so.' Her voice and mood turned poignant. 'I saw him go in and I had to *know*. The story and the bargain were ruses – the best I could do, at short notice.'

'Sure,' he consoled her, remembering the force of her threat and *still* unconvinced.

'Please,' she said softly, 'keep me in touch. Let me know how he's doing?' The hand on his arm was soft and imploring; yet she was holding something back.

'Do what I can.'

'Bless you.'

She bent and unlocked the car door. A yellow Renault Five, he noticed distractedly; what's *yours* called? The courtesy light flared. When she turned, not all the wetness on her face was rain. 'You've known him longer. He was just back, you see, whole and safe and free. So *why* volunteer?'

The root of it at last, the exposed nerve which put so much pain in her eyes. She stood in the clammy dusk, white and ghostly and distraught; he could offer only a bald and banal truth.

'They sent him after the Reapers, he's never learnt how to quit. That's Huw, I reckon. No way he'll ever change.'

And, amazingly, she seemed to take some comfort. As she drove away, he saw a faint and hopeful smile.

* * *

251

The hallway door opened, admitting a gust of gin and a ramshackle man in blue. Blank-faced and tangle-footed, he lurched across the room and cannoned into the wall. The impact spun him backward into a corner. Briefly, slack shoulders wedged and inturned fingers scrabbled for support. Then his knees buckled and he slithered down, tearing pale gouges from the faded brown paintwork.

Pete exploded from Harriet's grasp, raging across the boards, bending over the uniformed sprawl and screaming hysterical questions. 'Where is she? What have they done to Peg? *Answer* me!'

The downturned helmet lolled sideways, revealing sodden sandy hair and one watery, unfocused eye. 'Consbull Jenkins reporting, ready for shpesh – *special* duty.'

'The officer seems confused,' Salim observed ironically. 'He needed false courage before he *volunteered*.'

'The fuzz,' sneered Gerry, brandishing his own empty bottle, 'what d'you expect?'

Leadership, thought Harriet, polished buttons and a stiff upper lip. Someone to boost morale and nurse us through the nightmare. And they send a drunken wreck. Then she realized they never would, this is Cav's work. But how on earth did he do it?

No time to think it out. As Pete's outbursts grew wilder, Cav himself sauntered in. There was a sudden ripple of brilliant green; Harry Two, forestalling Irish retaliation, shifting Pete from harm's way and issuing gentle rumbles.

'She okay, marn, she out of all this.'

As Pete subsided and Cav went into another huddle with Salim, Harriet sidled further from Joe's gun and closer to the disgusting policeman. He slumped in the corner, eyes closed and mouth drooling. Two of his tunic

252

buttons were missing. Inside the navy blue gape, his shirt was drenched and his tie hung limply askew. One leg lay flexed and flaccid. The other was cocked at the knee, exposing a gleam of hairless calf, a rumpled brown sock, and a crêpe-soled brothelcreeper. Dear Lord, he's not even properly dressed; what are they *doing* to us?

A second unanswerable question, for Salim had moved to centre stage and clapped his hands like a schoolmarm. 'Our brigade is complete,' he declared. 'It is for you to decide if we dwell in harmony; or if my officers must compel your co-operation.' A flicker of steel; Cav, leaning easy against the wall, paring his fingernails with a knife and grinning coldly through his beard. Point made and taken.

'You have heard our demands,' Salim continued. 'We are tired of Western idolaters who rob us of wealth and insult our sovereignty. Yet, unlike them, we take only what is ours – valiant comrades, jailed and tortured in a foreign land: whose only crime was to enact the will of our Government and purge the Holy Islam of unworthy blood!' His dark eyes glittered, his small, immaculate figure seemed to quiver and swell. '*We shall conquer!* I, Salim, swear this; or we shall perish gladly in the attempt!' His voice had risen sharply, an ugly, Messianic note which made Harriet's skin crawl.

He's bonkers, she thought, and shivered as his obsidian glare sought her out. Apparently reading her mind, he changed subject and tone abruptly; softer words which only fuelled her fears. 'We mean you no harm, we have already freed your ailing sister. Join our struggle, obey our rules and let us all survive and prevail.' A smile flashed in the gloom, never reaching his eyes. 'See, already you have food and drink as never before!'

'Hey, Salim,' drawled Gerry. 'How 'bout another bottle?'

Cav frowned a warning, the policeman mumbled something incomprehensible, and Salim moved smoothly on.

'We seek only the release of our kinsmen and safe passage home. You must pray it is as Allah wills.'

Fading daylight softened his outline, and a distant roll of thunder seemed to reify his god.

Gerry, emboldened by liquor, shattered the eerie spell. 'Yeah, man, let's hear it for Allah!'

Harriet cringed, expecting righteous anger; which never came.

'If in the end we ride to glory on wings of flame, it will be because your masters place no value on your lives. The same masters who have raped the land and scourged the fellahin since the dawn of time. It is *them* we oppose, not the oppressed proletariat like you!'

Cunning, as well as bonkers, Harriet realized miserably, while the band broke into spontaneous applause; and Gerry, eyeing her viciously, snarled, 'Up the workers and fuck the rich!' Already, Salim had seduced the weak and intimidated the strong; and, through Cav, he had reduced the law to a laughing-stock. Right on cue, the stricken policeman tilted forward and began to retch.

Salim's small dark features writhed in disdain, and he backed off daintily. 'Come, comrades. You must witness the arrangements downstairs. Mr Cavanaugh, assist our uniformed friend to find his senses.' These were orders, not requests; pleasing only to Cav, to judge from the gleam in his eyes.

As she followed the band, Harriet heard a sharp crack of open palm across cheek. Poor devil, she thought, he'd be better off unconscious.

The basement was bigger than she'd imagined, long and low-ceilinged, lit by a single bare bulb and painted bilious cream. In one corner, a stack of long-neglected furniture; at the far end, a jumble of packing crates; against the wall, the missing instrument case. High in each corner, an irregular grey patch of fresh cement testified to small-hour industry. Otherwise it was just a bare, grubby space.

'Mr Duffy,' Salim invited, 'explain, please.'

The baby-faced Irishman outlined his design for doom, while Gerry fidgeted and made sly comments to the band. Harry Two listened intently, his black curls almost touching the ceiling, one large paw resting firmly on Pete's shoulder.

'The charges are bedded in,' said Joe, eyeing the damp blotches fondly, 'and each has a pre-set detonator.' He glanced at his watch, a black digital job. 'In about ninety-two hours, the detonators trigger simultaneously. The walls blow out and the roof drops in. No way to stop it, unless ye can find a way through the concrete.' His blue eyes twinkled slyly. 'Now *that*, me darlins, is what I *call* a deadline!'

Harriet sensed furtive movement; Harry Two edging forward, huge and tense and menacing.

'Carefully, my African brother,' warned Salim. 'Mr Duffy hasn't finished.'

'Ah'm West Indian,' growled the black man. 'Ah don't own *no* Arab brothers!'

'Ye'd best hold still, all the same.' Joe had produced a black plastic box, the kind that operates remote-control toys; and was easing the antenna out.

'Each of the Reapers has one of these. The charges have separate detonators, and one of them's primed for a pulse from this little beauty. One more step, Sambo, and we'll be finding out if they have apartheid in heaven!'

'You're bluffing, marn!'

'Is that so? Would you care to try me?' Joe's pale face

255

was suddenly bathed in sweat. Hovering over the round push-button, his finger trembled visibly.

'Please,' Harriet murmured, tugging urgently at a loose, lime green sleeve, 'I think he means it!'

Briefly, Harry Two leaned hard against her weight; then relaxed. 'What the hell. Just testing.'

'Thank you, sister,' Salim bowed quaintly. 'My people would lose much face if the mission should fail so early.' Turning on Harry Two, he added, 'Be grateful, West Indian. We were nearly brothers in death.'

Harriet shivered, and not from fear alone. There was a chill draught around her legs coming from the packing cases, carrying a reek of ancient drains.

Pete noticed, too. 'I'm cold,' he whined, winning an uneasy glance from Joe and immediate support from Gerry. 'Yeah, man, break out the brandy!'

Salim ignored them both, lifting an elegant grey-clad arm and urging the Irishman on. 'Security, Mr Duffy.'

Retracting the antenna, keeping a wary eye on Harry Two, Joe spoke with the pride of a craftsman. 'Ye'll have seen the illuminations; now hear this. I've set infra-red beams outside; just above knee-height, and no one but me knows where. Silent and invisible, working day and night. The man or beast that strays within fifty yards will trip the alarm and trigger the bells!' He aimed a sharp blue challenge at Harry Two. 'Maybe you'll be wanting to test *them*!'

'*We'll be wanting a drink!*' This time, Gerry's protest brought a predatory gleam to black Arab eyes.

From the foot of the stairs, Salim stated the all-too-obvious. 'Our fortress is impregnable. Wait and watch with us, comrades. Lend your voice to our cause!'

'Any time, baby,' Gerry assured him, blind to the danger signals. 'Long as the booze keeps flowing.'

Harriet trudged upwards, following the swagger of

256

Gerry's filthy jeans. Behind her, Harry Two was still consoling Pete. We're hostages, she thought, finally acknowledging the implications. A word you read in the papers and associate with haggard sub-humans stumbling from some hijacked aircraft. And dark green body-bags bulging on the tarmac. Go on, Daddy, use some of that political influence you're always bragging about. It's no good, my girl: he neither knows nor cares where you are.

Momentarily, the scene upstairs offered a glimmer of hope. Cav had obviously accomplished *his* mission. Though the policeman still slumped at the corner and blood oozed from his bruised lips, the pale eyes burned with awareness. This time, he countered Pete's desperation in unslurred Welsh accents. 'Easy, boyo, she's safe enough.' He grimaced painfully. 'More than can be said for some.'

'Mind your tongue,' rasped Cav. 'There's more where that came from!'

'Carry on, you. Every dog has his day.'

'Beware, Constable,' Salim warned, gunmetal glinting in his hand. 'Resistance will cost lives.'

To Harriet's dismay, the Welshman nodded meekly. 'Only joking, mun.'

Turning to Cav, inclining his sleek head towards the radio, Salim demanded, 'Any contact, any agreement?'

'Not a feckin' word!'

'It is as we expected. We must make a demonstration. Watch, Mr Policeman. Witness the force of our purpose.'

There was something familiar about Salim's selective survey of the assembly. An out-of-town gamecock in pale grey finery, eyeing the local talent; only colder, and much more deadly. Sensing tragedy, Harriet edged towards Harry Two. The reptilian gaze flickered to rest on Gerry. The small brown hand twitched as though swatting a fly. '*That* one, Mr Cavanaugh.'

Joe moved first, the machine pistol homing on Harry Two's heart. Then Cav pounced, dark and swift and eager. Crossing the boards, seizing Gerry's wrists and wrenching his arms up and back in a vicious double Nelson; and forcing the lank-locked, unresisting figure to kneel at Salim's feet. The flash was fiery, the report strangely muffled. And Gerry toppled, face first, into an eddy of dust.

'Don't try it!'

Through a haze of tears and gunsmoke, Harriet watched the blue-uniformed figure rise on unsteady legs; and subside beneath the unwavering threat of Salim's automatic.

Blindly, she buried her face in Harry Two's sleeve; feeling the rigour of his body, smelling fresh sweat and Old Spice, swallowing acid bile.

'*You will look this way!*' The command battered her, pitiless and compelling. 'Gently, marn,' the shaken, dark brown voice at her ear advised, 'they can't do anything worse.'

She turned back into a pallid ring of faces as frozen as her own.

'We regret the sacrifice,' Salim declared, without a hint of sorrow. 'Though this poisoned creature is small loss. Now, perhaps, your government will take us seriously.' A neat, brown leather shoe stirred the body casually. 'Perhaps this act will save you.'

Harriet had never seen death before. There was no mistaking it. Purplish blood had matted the hair at the base of the skull. The nose rested, squashed, on the grimy boards, and one corner of the upper lip had been wedged open. As her stomach heaved in protest, Harriet saw a gobbet of saliva ooze across yellow teeth and plop stealthily into the dust.

A small, savage figure in advancing gloom, Salim spoke to the Reapers only. '*We are as one!* Do what you must!' And horror bloomed anew.

Cav ambled forward, resting the muzzle of the rifle at the base of the spine and squeezing the trigger. The corpse arced up in blast and blaze, numbing Harriet's ears and scoring small red after-images across her vision. Then Joe followed suit, his machine pistol seeming almost gentle in contrast.

'They're taking no chances,' murmured Harry Two, steadier now. 'In case they get nicked. *All* guilty, see.'

Harriet nodded dumbly, watching scarlet patches spread lazily across dirty denim jeans. The air reeked of blood and cordite, and her senses wavered. Dimly, she saw Cav saunter across to the radio and lean into its orange glow.

'We'll be out just now, and bring ye something to ponder. Keep your distance, don't even *think* of sniping. One wrong move and you'll be seeing the grand finale.'

Incapable of further shock or terror, clinging fast to Harry Two's rocklike presence, she watched Cav and Joe drag the body into the hallway. Saw the wide red smear in the dust, heard the awful stutter of lifeless feet down concrete steps; and, turning, gazed in contempt at their uniformed saviour, who crouched in the dimmest corner holding his head in his hands.

CHAPTER FOURTEEN

'Animals!' McKay's furry red paw crashed on to the desk. 'Murdering, heathen scum!'

Yeah, thought Beddoes, imprisoned behind the dead microphone, and Huw could be next for the chop. A prospect, apparently, which left the Funnies unmoved. An angular, L-shaped silhouette against a purple dusk, Snow lolled at the window and dispensed a scholarly rebuke.

'Don't underestimate them. Fanatics they may be; mindless thugs they most certainly are not. If the demands aren't met, they will doubtless face east and launch themselves into the hereafter. Meantime, they will continue to probe our commitment and sensibility with calculated violence.' His tone hardened. 'In which case, Smythe's solution bears re-examination. Call them out, invite them to do their worst.'

'Sacrifice the hostages? Och, you're no better than them!'

Snow stiffened and half-turned. His profile looked stark and jagged; and utterly implacable. 'We can afford no such scruples. The smallest concession leaves us forever forfeit to any lunatic with a grievance and a bomb. And what do we gain? A handful of human debris.'

'Leave it out!' Beddoes blurted. 'You're talking about my oppo!'

McKay rose and stalked the length of the room.

Leaning over the radio, his index finger an inch from Beddoes' chest, he snarled, 'Hold your tongue, we're making *policy* here!' His face crumpled and he rounded on Snow in wholly uncharacteristic appeal. 'The laddie's *right*, for heaven's sake!'

'Indeed? A solitary policeman tips the balance?'

'We sent him in; forced him, moreover. Aye, and pledged him a rescue!'

'He *volunteered* – to gather intelligence and relay information. So far, we have received neither. Face facts, man; he's probably dead!'

'Ye cannae write him off until we *know*!' The craggy Scot was pleading unashamedly, his hands out-thrust and clawed in supplication. And Snow dismissed him with a shrug.

'The brief was quite specific. No compromise, negotiate for time only. And the Reapers must be taken, dead or alive.'

'All *right*! Unleash yon soldiers!'

'To do so at this point merely seals the Inspector's fate.'

'Mebbe. But at least we'll have *tried*!'

Keep at him, Jock, urged Beddoes silently, don't let the bloodless bastard wear you down. But Snow simply adjusted the dotty half-moon specs and took a gentler tone. 'You are appeasing your own conscience, a purely emotional reaction.' His glance rested on Beddoes, inviting judgement – and support. 'It won't do, I'm afraid. We must be guided by reason.'

'Don't look at me,' Beddoes muttered, 'I'm just a radio ham, rooting for me mate.'

Snow came away from the window. Patrolling like a pinstriped sentry, he gave them the military bit. 'We are at war, Superintendent – albeit undeclared. Fate has cast us as generals; and the good general is he who suppresses emotion, endures unavoidable casualties, and drives on to ultimate victory.'

So that's what we are, Beddoes mused, touching the scar on his thigh. Unavoidable casualties. Stealthily, he reached for the 'transmit' switch. No way to get you out, uncle, but you'll know the score if it's the last thing I do.

He had reckoned without McKay; drawn to his full height, eyes as hard as agate, blocking the Funny's advance. 'I'm no General, *Mister* Snow. Just a senior policeman, bound by personal and professional trust to an officer already stretched beyond the call of duty. Disown him if you will; I'll have no part of it. And since you appear to relish resignation, ye can have mine directly!'

An ill-matched confrontation in blue: a thin, besuited English stork and a uniformed Scottish bantam. Easing down on the switch, preparing to sound the warning, Beddoes sensed a subtle shift of command. Snow nodded, a curiously courtly gesture, as the last light flickered on gold-rimmed glasses. 'That won't be necessary, Hamish. Besides, it might start a trend. You'd do well to remember this debate; who said what, and why. For future reference, I mean.' He swung on his heel and headed for the door.

'Where are ye off to now?'

'To set a time-bomb of our own. The SAS will go in, come what may, twenty-four hours *before* the Reaper deadline.' Snow checked in the doorway, silver hair brushing the lintel and a cool black stare for Beddoes. 'Let us hope, Sergeant, that your – oppo – has earned his salt by then.'

'One word,' warned McKay as loping footfalls faded and thunder grumbled outside. 'Breathe a single word of this and ye'll not be here tomorrow!'

'Pardon?' Releasing the switch, disguising heartfelt

relief with an idiot's grin, Beddoes craned forward and cupped his ear. 'I don't hear too good, at this height.' Then, soft and serious, 'You played a blinder, sir.'

'Don't be too sure, laddie. It'll have to wait on the result.'

The storm had passed, muttering darkly into the night. Moonlight pierced a veil of clouds, burnishing the window and disrupting Pete's wishful dream.

'Don't leave me, Peg,' he wimpered, burrowing deeper into Harriet's lap. 'Please don't go!'

Sitting bolt upright, enduring the essence of unflushed loo, Harriet felt a surge of maternal tenderness. 'Go to sleep,' she soothed. 'Everything's going to be all right.'

Presently, his breathing deepened. She eased his head on to the mattress and massaged the cramp from her legs. He'd held up pretty well, after the shooting. The evening had brought its share of drama – enough to keep *anyone's* mind fully stretched. Yet within minutes of lights-out, he'd come sidling through the huddle of blankets to burden her with his fears. And Harriet, thankful for someone worse off than herself, had welcomed him. Nursing his angular body, muffling his sobs in case Joe the sentry heard, she'd let him pour it out.

'She's a great kid, old Peg. *Warm*, know what I mean?'

'Course I do. She'll be fine, don't worry.'

'I must be mental! Got papers, see, a qualified electrician. Doing nicely, till Gerry came bragging about the big time! Sorry. Mustn't speak ill of the dead.'

'It can't hurt him now.'

'Proper toughie, you are. How the hell d'you manage?'

With difficulty, she thought, squeezing his damp hand and keeping her own horrors at bay.

'God, she was so *big*! You *sure* she'll be okay?'

'Come on, Pete, that's what girls are for!'

'Could be twins, eh? Wouldn't that be something?' His voice caught, his narrow shoulders quivered in her embrace. 'I could be a father already, I'll never know if it's a boy or a girl. Jesus, Harry, I don't want to die in here!'

Silent spasms wracked him; his tears seeped through the thin stuff of her nightdress. She stroked his hair, pressing his face to her thighs while grief rocked him into unquiet sleep.

Now, cautiously, she stole a corner of threadbare blanket and turned her face to the wall. Get some rest, my girl, you're surely going to need it. But the images were fresh and vivid, not to be denied . . .

A clean fawn swathe of boards where the blood had pooled, and the scent of murder hanging in the air. It had been Harry Two, inevitably, who'd swabbed away the mess; and Cav who'd bullied them to therapeutic action.

'C'mon, ye mournful morons, let's have some home comforts about the place!'

Under the lash of his tongue, they'd humped table and chairs up from the basement, scrubbing grime away with various corners of their clothing; until the pitted wood gave off a reluctant gleam. Somehow, Joe had conjured watery soup in a pink plastic bowl, and enough tarnished cutlery to go round. And Pete, deathly pale yet outwardly composed, distributed more tricoloured packets of crisps. Then, as Salim settled regally into the carving chair, Cav had loomed above them and proposed an ironic toast – 'Here's to gallant nights at the kitchen table!' – and ushered Harriet graciously to her seat.

The soup was vile, the crisps were salty ashes in her mouth. She pushed her dish aside, wrinkling her nose at the reek of gin which drifted from the dimmest corner;

where the policeman still squatted in drunken stupor. Harry Two had followed suit, she noticed, eating little and watching the uniformed figure intently. And Reapers, apparently, disdained a liquid diet.

The band had no such inhibitions, slurping eagerly, scraping at the faded yellow china and washing everything down with booze. I've never known them, she realized, gazing in surprise at five callow, dissipated faces. Gerry was little enough; without him, they are nothing. I can't even remember their names! Already they had turned to Pete for leadership – wonder how long *that'll* last. Another unanswered question.

Salim gestured briskly and Joe hastened to obey. He crossed the room, collected the radio, set it on the cluttered table. Behind him, the lead flickered and curled darkly beneath the unshaded bulb. Joe bent and twiddled. Music flared and faded and the evening news began. Beirut, Washington, Afghanistan; student unrest in Seoul, a by-election in Bradford. Gerry got an indirect mention, right at the very end – 'The victim's name is being withheld until next of kin have been informed. Now here are the main points again.' The neat brown hand flickered, the set went dead. In the abrupt hush, Salim's fury was a living force. '*How can these people ignore us?*'

Not for the first time, Joe played peacemaker. 'It's the English way, comrade. It's not done to make a *fuss*.' A touch of the Blarney, thought Harriet, as the comfortable brogue continued; and very welcome, too. 'So ye see, comrade, if World War Three broke out tomorrow, the BBC would call it "a nuclear incident".'

Salim watched him minutely, the dark eyes blazing suspicion. 'If this is true, Mr Duffy, they will have to mend their ways. Watch over our guests! I must consult

265

Mr Cavanaugh.' Rising, he shot Harriet an imperious glance. 'Repair this mess, sister. Such is the female lot.'

The sheer arrogance outraged her. About to retaliate, she caught Harry Two's urgent headshake, read the risk in his frown. Easy, marn, he was saying, this ain't no place for Women's Lib.

Clattering crockery, marching tautly between the table and the greasy sink, she became aware of flurried and fitful movement. One after another, the bandsmen turned green at the gills and tottered upstairs; returning not much steadier but evidently relieved. Serves them right, she thought, drunken pigs! Then, as the unclean scent of their labours filtered down, the implications struck. Joe put something in the soup! My God, is there *nothing* they haven't planned?

Her anger dwindled, overwhelmed by despair. While Salim and Cav whispered and Harry Two ministered to the policeman, she tidied the table and washed the dishes; alone . . .

She was alone still, in the polluted night, and far away from home. '*I don't want to die in here* . . .' The worst of images surfaced – Gerry's contorted deathmask. Like Pete, she'd followed him blindly, lured by the promise of stardom, and 'real life'. Moonlight blurred, and her tears flowed for first lost love – or a tinselled, sixteen-year-old's vision of it.

Cav had killed him without a qualm. The same Cav who had woken the wanton in her, driving her fiercely to the peak of pleasure. And again, she had let him: revelling in an adolescent blush of sexuality, mistaking savagery for strength, worshipping the very ruthlessness which allowed him to murder at a stranger's whim. Now, on the brink of maturity, with truths laid bare and lessons burned indelibly on her memory, she was about to die for a desert waste and an ancient, alien prophet.

Overcome with terror, she reached out to St Cats and the final refuge of the hopeless sinner. Clasping tear-stained hands, closing her eyes and opening her heart, she whispered a childlike prayer. 'Dear God, let me grow up! I'll do anything you ask, I'll never drink or swear again, I'll be kind to Daddy and his beastly wife. I'll be a *good* girl, I promise!'

Reality drifted back. A shadow crossed the window; Joe, moonstruck and eerie, his pistol glinting silver. Beside her, Pete whinnied and settled into a foetal curl. Then, clear-eyed and rueful, she added a womanly plea. 'Lord, why do I always end up sleeping with the wrong man?'

Autumn eve in the Quiet One's cottage. Banter and baccy smoke, and Dublin Fergus cosseted by the same ould coat and some younger, meaner faces. This time, Sean knew, the inquisition would be real. Never mind the convivial air, just take heed of the placings. Fergus, smug as a porker in silk at the head of the table, and toughs at either hand. Sean himself at the far end, the pressure lamp hissing and blazing fierce into his eyes. And the Quiet One in his faithful rocker, halfway between. Though whether as hanging judge or prisoner's friend, only time and the Dear would decide.

The peat fire smouldered sullen, the whiskey jar was near to empty, and Fergus' coal-black glare brimmed with malice.

'There's ugly rumours abroad, Sean. The Lion of Leitrim gone mushy, flirting among English polis and Garda turncoats.'

'Is that so? And what of Dublin, linking hands with an infiltrator and calling it a contest of strength?'

Fergus' pallid lips drew taut, and a henchman came headlong to his defence.

''Twas a childish deception, and swiftly nipped in the bud!'

'Aye,' said Sean, 'by a slack-thighed trull and an angry cuckold!'

'Easy, Sean,' warned the Quiet One. 'Dublin held firm, whatever. You'll gain naught by evading the charges.' So saying, he lit a thin black gasper and coughed quietly into a grubby kerchief.

'Charges?' Sean echoed. '*Rumours*, himself just said!'

Fergus drained his glass and poured another, watching the flicker of light from golden spirits. 'Let's talk of O'Brien, so long suspected. And lately, I hear, a *proven* Judas.'

Rising, squinting over the lampgleam, Sean hurled their challenge back.

'Can ye not see further than your noses? There's plunder to be had, a chance to send soldiers hotfoot to any place of our choosing!'

A new voice intervened, hostile yet vaguely familiar. 'Ye'll have to expand that, Daly, for them not blessed with the second sight.'

Craning forward, Sean made out the features. Sammy, the amber-eyed youth from that same long-ago charade. No hero-worship in him now, though, only an upstart's envy of command.

'Your man O'Brien's the perfect conduit,' Sean explained, as if to the feeble of mind. 'Feed him a while – minor, easily checked truths which do no harm and may even advance the cause. Build his credit, have London panting for more. When the time is ripe, you let slip a mighty secret – a raid at the border, say, or a bomb campaign up North. And whilst they scurry to man the defences, you strike at another target entirely. Ye'll not even need to silence him. When the facts are revealed, the enemy will do it for you. Holy Mary, 'tis the oldest ruse in the game!'

A smoky hush, within which the nightwind stirred, the rocker creaked and thoughtful Dublin fingers rasped on silvered stubble.

'Too clever,' Fergus muttered at last. 'Too risky, and too long!'

'Nevertheless,' wheezed the Quiet One, ''tis a bold idea, and O'Brien's always within reach. What of the foreign polis?'

'You had him cold,' Sammy accused, 'and let him pass unscathed. A spy or worse besides!'

'He was enforcement, not intelligence; Welsh, not English. In time we might have turned him. His sympathies, at least.' A dangerous tack, this. He could see the scorn in shadowed faces. 'What are you saying, Fergus, is *Daly* traitor to the cause? Come into the dark, aye, and all your hired muscle, and tell me I'm not fit to die for Ireland!'

'Calm yourself!' snapped the Quiet One with sudden icy authority. 'It's command at issue here, not loyalty.'

'You want a land to raise your children free?' Sean demanded. 'Before that age dawns, ye'll need to muzzle the guns and *talk*. And men of goodwill on every side of the table!'

The rocker squealed again; the Quiet One sat erect. Firelight played on the faded fawn sweater and the purpled veinwork of his cheeks. 'Speed the day,' he murmured. 'We can *all* drink to that.'

One by one, they followed his lead, glasses glinting, heads thrown back, throats working in reluctant unison.

Only a truce, though. Fergus came once more to the fray, bent on evening the score. 'Now, Sean, what's this

I'm hearing of Provo secrets pilfered and intended for the Garda?'

'You'll be following the Reapers' siege, no doubt. It has passing interest for the likes of us.'

'More power to them,' growled Sammy. 'If they prevail, think what we might attempt!'

'They won't,' said Sean. 'Ye can take my word.' And after a while, the amber glare faded and dropped. Sorely though he coveted leadership, even Sammy dared not doubt the Daly sources.

'London's desperate,' Sean went on, 'for any scraps they can gather. We have profiles on Cavanaugh and Duffy.' He faced Fergus steadily. 'Not pilfered; put together by my own hand. Released, they do *us* no harm, yet will be highly prized by the English.' He swivelled slowly, speaking to the Quiet One alone. 'Leak them to O'Brien. Let *him* take the glory. Thus shall the trap be baited. Whenever we're ready, the Garda can direct the soldiers where ye will.'

'What's this?' growled Sammy. 'Daly the dwarf, preaching betrayal of our own?'

'They're lost to us, man; have been, these past few years!'

'Not lost,' Fergus objected, taking up the cudgels again. 'On loan to allies.'

'*Allies?* Since when did heathen Arabs give a camel's fart for Ireland?'

''Tis the same enemy, Sean, and a similar cause.'

'Don't tell me *causes*, Fergus. Once bought, a man for ever after seeks the highest bidder.'

From the corner of his eye, Sean caught the Quiet One's knowing smile. The hoarse old voice came softly in a haze of pale grey smoke. 'Ye can't hide from a hired gun; even in Dublin.'

Fergus had huddled deep into the coat, sudden pallor against black serge. 'Is it threats you're issuing now?'

'Cav's a killer,' said Sean. 'If he survives the siege, he'll be loose on the mainland in search of another contract. And isn't our history stained with treachery bought by green English pounds?'

Sammy's sneer swum out of the gloom, hot-eyed and yellow-fanged. 'Listen to them, Fergus. A dwarf turned soft and a toothless has-been. And yourself the best-guarded man in all Eire!'

The rocker stopped, the fire sputtered softly. Caught in its blueish glow, the Quiet One's face seemed wrought of steel. 'Ye'd best control your whelps, Fergus. If the Cav has a mind, he'll take a dozen like this for breakfast.' His hand flicked, the spent cigarette arced redly to the fire. 'Are we agreed, meanwhile?'

Fergus was already upright, and chastened hardmen gathered at his coat-tails. 'No one has ever doubted your nerve, Daly, nor the force of your commitment. So be it, then. If ye pull it off, ye'll hear no complaints from me.' In the echo of his words, an unspoken threat rang faint but clear: *And if ye don't, beware!*

No back slapping, this time. Just a nod from the leader and sullen glower from Sammy. Then they were away into chilly darkness and a fancy foreign saloon.

As the tail-lights dwindled and exhaust fumes hung, the Quiet One spoke again. ''Tis a terrible risk, Sean. If the Cav breaks out and learns of this, it'll not be Fergus he comes for.' A wry, wistful chuckle filtered out of the rocker. 'And *you've* only a toothless has-been to guard ye!'

'He *can't* come back,' Sean mused. 'They'd be taking sides in an eyeblink, the organization split from head to foot.'

271

'True. But if worst should befall, who will dare to prevent him?'

'I will.'

Evans surfaced to a whiff of Old Spice, warm breath at his ear and a heavy black hand clamped across his mouth.

'This is your friendly toilet attendant. Nod if you read me.'

Harrigan, he thought, remembering; and inclined his aching head gingerly.

'We got a chance to talk, man. Joe drew the dogwatch, and he's dozing.'

Pushing the hand away and struggling to rise, Evans mumbled. 'Take him now, shall we?'

'Easy, sir. You ain't in no shape for a rumble. Anyways, he's carrying death in his pocket.'

While morning broadened, the West Indian whisper continued; the technology of terror, the completeness of captivity. 'Guess we could scupper the alarm – hitched to the mains, right? The remote-control bit is something else, man.' Vision faltered, blurring the sombre black features. Delayed concussion, probably.

'How about the hostages?' Evans asked. 'Anyone on our side?'

'The girl, maybe. 'Cept she's scared witless, and putting out for Cav. Forget the rest. They're hopheads.'

Harrigan leaned up on one elbow, tilting his chin at the window. 'Joe could be useful. He ain't ready to die.'

Blinking tightly, straining for focus, Evans made out the hunched silhouette against an early pink sky. And the outline of a machine pistol. 'Looks like he's ready to *kill*, though.'

'Better believe it. Recall what happened last evening?'

Foggily, thought Evans. Public execution, to prove a

point and force Snow's hand; the boom of guns and the reek of fear and a riddled corpse, bleeding.

'Reckon they got something real *bad* lined up for you,' Harrigan was saying. 'Keep your head down, man. Make out you're still hurting. Watch it; company!'

Evans hugged the lumpy mattress, peeking upward through slitted lids. Faded fawn cords, a white T-shirt, a jut of curly black beard; and Cavanaugh's voice sounding reveille.

'Rise and shine, ye happy campers! Time to break your fast.' He moved cat-footed, among the sleepers, jabbing at Harrigan's blanketed buttocks with the muzzle of his rifle. 'Come on down, Sambo, let's see have ye made the headlines!'

Lurching to his feet, fingering the lump at the top of his spine, Evans joined the grumbling, unwashed exodus. The dingy landing smelt terrible, a reek of nightsoil strong enough actually to clear his brain. By the time he reached the foot of the stairs, he was feeling almost normal.

Shaven and spruce and suited in grey, Salim presided at table like an oriental prince. 'Have a date, Constable,' he offered. 'It will cure your hangover. No?' His voice turned silky. 'Soon, you shall – how do the English say it? – *eat out of my hands*!'

Not if I can help it, Evans vowed, taking his place and keeping his thoughts to himself. Breakfast, there's lovely. Stewed tea, soggy crisps and fumes of gin still rising from his collar. Helps the healing process, mind. As watery sun crept in and Joe tuned to the early news, Evans assessed the inmates.

A motley lot, they were, just as Harrigan said; a bunch of dull-eyed, bumfluffed yobs who flinched at Salim's every move. Alone among them, the girl had clung to

273

self-respect. Dark, neatly brushed hair framed her pretty pallor; and a clean if faded shirt-waist outlined a surprisingly ripe figure. Didn't care for busies, mind, judging by the frosty glance he shipped. Exactly as Salim intended no doubt.

The newsreader droned on and Evans caught the signs of rising tension: Joe's fidgets, Cavanaugh's expectant leer, the sounds of munching silenced, and dismay on every face.

'Meanwhile,' said the plummy voice, 'the Reapers' demands are being considered, and the seige site remains calm. And that ends the news.'

Joe's finger pounced, the yellow light faded. The hush was very loud. Salim seemed to uncoil from his chair, swaying forward at the waist, fixing Evans with bright black eyes. 'What does this mean, Mr Policeman?' The pose and the hiss of a desert viper; watch your step, bach.

'Normal procedures, see. High-level decisions, papers to sign. It's hopeless, hustling the Brass.'

'Papers? *Brass?* Do you dare to joke with me?'

'Honest, mun, it can't be done overnight.'

'But, my drunken friend, *you* were brought here to convince them that it *must*!' The fury gave way to a curious note of anticipation. 'First, we will make sure you have the right frame of mind. Explain, Mr Cavanaugh!'

The bearded Irishman came easily to his feet, teeth and T-shirt gleaming. ''Tis a little trick the lads dreamed up whilst abiding English gaols. Takes me back, sure it does, for many's the fine fierce screw I've seen reduced to puking faintness.'

A couple of absent, apparently aimless paces took him behind the girl's chair. Gone off him, she had, you could tell by the curl of the lip.

'Getting our own back, some reckoned,' Cav was saying, 'like the filthy bog-trotters we are. *We* called it the Dirty Protest. Are ye catching me drift, copper?'

Evans' stomach fluttered queasily. There had been rumours – unspeakable squalor in the Maze, and warders quitting by the dozen. But only rumours, surely?

Cavanaugh grinned cruelly, jerking a thumb at the ceiling. 'You've a crock of shit prepared up there. What ye do is smear it all over the walls.'

'Using your hands,' Salim added, 'and wearing the uniform. Because it is a duty.'

Evans was conscious of furtive movement all around. Wordless and appalled, the hostages were shrinking away as from some mortal contamination. The Funnies had it right; though surely Snow could not have foreseen such depravity. In a stinking hovel under sadistic Arab eyes the bounds of duty loomed stark and final. A copper, see; no way you could defile the force and go gently into the terrorist night. Sorry, Jane, not even for what might have been.

With decision came a kind of inner calm. Which of them will do it? he wondered; noting, almost incidentally, that the Irish contingent had exchanged weapons. The butt of the machine pistol jutted from Cav's belt, and Joe nursed the rifle lovingly. What the hell. At this range, one bullet's as good as another. Leaning back, he spoke to Cavanaugh alone. 'You're the biggest arsehole. Do it yourself.'

He'd missed something, he knew it at once. As the bearded grin grew wider, Salim's sibilant whisper put him straight. 'Such foolishness, Mr Policeman! Did you really think we would make it easy, permit you the prize of martyrdom? Proceed, Mr Cavanaugh!'

In a flurry of white and blue, the big Irishman lifted the girl clean out of her chair. Joe stepped from the shadows, the rifle trained on Harrigan's lime green chest. And the band watched, pale and petrified. All according to plan, Evans realized grimly, they're still two moves ahead.

Cav's brawny bicep clenched, pinning the girl's arms and crushing her breasts. His free hand rose casually, resting dull grey gunmetal against the throb of her temple. Yet there was neither pain nor fear in her cornflower eyes; only a glaze of childish disbelief.

'Oh Cav,' she breathed. 'You *couldn't*!'

'A little tip for you, girly. Never mix bed and business.'

The mean snick of the safety catch underscored his intent; and Salim set the limits.

'She is ten seconds from the afterlife, Constable.'

Aye, and fifty years before time. Women and children first, mind. *That's* duty. 'All right,' Evans muttered. 'Let her go.'

Cav seized the surrender gleefully. 'There you are, me beauties; I *told* you it was work for the filth!'

The key rattled, the lock clicked, and Joe's footfalls faded down the landing. Disturbed by the intrusion a bloat of blowflies rose above the bowl; and with them, the stench of day-old human ordure.

A Valleys childhood saved him; faded memories dredged from yesteryear. Evening in a small, terraced house. Best Welsh anthracite under the hob, reflecting scarlet from the galvanized bath beside. Squatting within it, a naked figure black from head to toe, only a cheery, bright blue squint to tell you who it was. Uncle Bryn, up from the pit; singing tenor, lathering his hair. As clean pink flesh emerged, he grins like a half-drowned monkey and repeats the same old words. 'Here we are, then; skin will wash.'

Right, thought an older, cooler Evans. Salim says to

wear the uniform; another good reason to take it off. He hung his clothes on a rusty hook and set his boots in the corner. Small, private acts of defiance, the only kind he had left. Standing nude, breathing shallow, he surveyed the ghastly, windowless cell. Planning, see. Keeps your mind off the horror. Walk forward, bend and scoop. Step into the bath and smear *that* wall. Then it'll dribble on to enamel, which washes easier than floorboards. And think of it as brown paint.

One thing to *think*; quite another to plunge your hands through soiled yellow tissues to the vileness underneath. He managed for a while, ignoring the hideous sucking sounds, moving like a robot through clammy, poisoned fog. The paint delusion wavered; have to drum up something better.

He fashioned a portrait of Jane – classic features, a tumble of coppery hair and green eyes glowing. Mind over matter; the image took a life of its own, offering more permanent escape. Soon, he was floating in her spicy musk, reliving their last acts of love, watching his own hands wander over supple, silken flesh.

He checked in mid-smear, seeing the truth on fouled and thickened fingers. Get out, girl, his mind screamed, else I'll never be able to touch you again! He threw up then, into the bath. So little, among so much. And faltered, mentally and physically crippled by the sheer degradation. Until Joe's distant, derisive voice broke through.

'Move it, fuzz, Salim's getting restless!'

Faintly from below he heard a bearded chuckle and a girlish squeal of pain. *Bastards*, he thought furiously. No wonder the Funnies rated Daly a moderate. A killer, sure enough; but he'd give you a dignity and a soldier's death. Not this awful rape of the psyche, this endless wallow in self-disgust and someone else's shit! The rage possessed

277

and drove him. Presently, astonishingly, his brimming fingernails grated on the bared bend of the bowl.

Jesi Mawr, it's done! Grinning up in savage triumph at the unsullied blue of the uniform, he bellowed, 'The closet's empty, Joseph. Call your bloody keeper!'

The stairs creaked and light footsteps approached. Evans leaned against the sink, composed and matter-of-fact. The door burst inward, revealing a maniacal Arab, a levelled gun and a tirade of invective.

'Y'Allah, you noseless whoreson, you suppurating lump of camel turd! Remove this filth, cleanse your stinking carcase! Now, now, *now*!'

Reeling under the onslaught, feeling the patter of spittle on his chest, Evans recognized the next phase of the plan. He means to keep you guessing, bach, and rub your face right in. Cool it, then, don't give him the excuse.

'Water, you cretin!' He was screaming, 'There's water in the pipes! *Move!*'

The pistol flickered, and Evans watched it calmly. Salim's frenzy faded to a frigid whisper. 'If you and this – *sewer* – are not spotless in one hour, I'll kill her anyway!' The door slammed, the furious march retreated.

Wearily, Evans stepped back on to slippery, bespattered enamel. You had to believe him. He'd murdered once already, at random and with pleasure. Funny, he thought, as the pipes belched and cold rusty water began to gush; after a while, you learn to live with the smell.

So it began again. Cup the trickle, scatter the spray, sluice it down with hands and nails and forearms. Never mind the tepid ooze down chest and belly. Skin will wash, mind. But Uncle Bryn was long dead, and boyish remembrance yielded to the crushing, reeking force of reality. Evans was losing, slithering into an abyss of utter self-loathing. This time, a scornful Irish dwarf rekindled the spark of resistance.

'Ye haven't the stomach,' Daly had taunted. Oh Sean, you should see me now! Fan the flame, then; turn the hatred outward. Not far to look for a target, either. I'll have you, Salim, he promised; some day, somehow. Hunt you down and wipe you out like the obscene vermin you are. And, sustained by nothing more than animal bloodlust, Evans laboured on, until at last the whole wall gleamed pink and wet.

'Twenty minutes,' warned Joe from the landing.

Down on his knees, Evans groped for the plughole; clearing unseen and unimaginable obstacles, willing the yellowish semi-solid to whirl a little faster. Going through the motions, he thought. You have to smile; or break. The dreadful pun diverted him till the dregs had gurgled away. Now he had only himself to restore.

Bent double, fitting his buttock over the plughole, he squirmed backwards under the tap. More than naked now, mind; hassled and humiliated to the very edge of madness, stripped of every human grace save the need to survive – and avenge. He clung to this while the icy cascade dislodged the filth and cleared his brain. *Think*, boyo, there isn't much time.

The Reapers wanted a mouthpiece, a tame cop to broadcast their propaganda. Whereas Snow needed inside gen to inform the logistics of rescue. And Beddoes would be fielding the returns. A code, then, some private language to undermine the ideological claptrap? Cricket, he thought, Roy's a cricket nut. Not exactly your number one sport in Tripoli or Dublin. Try it; what's left to lose?

He was sitting in half an inch of scum, the mixture as before. Repeating the treatment, he plumbed new depths of cunning. They'll expect a cringing puppet, and that's what they'll get. Save the rage for Salim: later and alone.

279

At long last, clear water was eddying around the blued and sunken flesh between his thighs. Shuddering, weak with relief and chill, he scrambled out. Skin *had* washed, the place *was* spotless; and the girl would live. As he wrestled the uniform over wet goosebumps, Joe's sarcastic warning filtered in. 'Ready or not, we're coming!'

There was just time to finger-comb lank hair and take a suitably craven pose before the door swung open. And Salim confounded him again. A sallow smile, a purr of admiration. 'Why, Constable, the room sparkles! How lucky your little sister; how proud your doubting comrades! Come, greet them! Then you shall speak to your police friends.'

Briefly, despite the armour he had forged, Evans' emotions almost betrayed him. Resistance dissolved, grateful tears gathered. Only a flicker of malice in dark Arab eyes forestalled complete collapse. Stand firm, bach, he's still the desert snake. Mustering a remnant of dignity, aware of the gun at his back, he blundered downstairs; straight into Salim's final, triumphant trap. A ring of blanched, disgusted faces, a communal gasp of revulsion. Even Harrigan turned aside, retching.

It's the uniform, Evans realized, and the damp. Absorption, see; you're a walking, breathing cloud of shit. Rejected and reviled, precisely as Salim intended. And you thought you could win!

No time to recover. Cavanaugh hustled him across the room, shoved him into a chair, and set the radio to 'transmit'.

'Read the message,' Salim ordered through the silk handkerchief held to his nose, 'exactly the way it is written.' He trained his pistol on the girl's cowed blue figure.

Sunlight through the window played on unlined paper and a spidery scrawl. The words blurred and swam together. Driven by instinct, clinging to the essence of his counterplan, Evans mustered two concise sentences. 'How's the Test Match going? In for another early finish, are we?' Defiance failed him; he sagged forward against the cool grey metal. 'They're telling the truth,' he whispered. 'For Chrissake give 'em what they want and get us *out*!'

He was lifted and hurled bodily into the corner. Sprawled on gritty boards, he squinted into brightness and Cavanaugh's cold black glare.

'Ye crazy fecker, who are ye trying to fool?'

CHAPTER FIFTEEN

Beddoes had risen early, plagued by foreboding and unquiet wounds. He wasn't the only one; sparrowfart in the Super's lair, and the Brass already assembled. Suited in summery beige, Snow had smiled austerely and unveiled the latest ploy.

'Hitherto unknown and unsung, the Reapers are hungry for headlines. By understating the story, we put the ball in their court. Soon, they will protest; hopefully making Evans their spokesman. Which is precisely what *we* need – liaison with an agent in place.' So saying, he'd retired to the window while McKay pushed paper and Beddoes retuned the radio.

The Super had lasted barely forty minutes. '*Soon*, eh?' he'd demanded. 'I hope you know what you're about. Meantime, there's *police* work to be done.' He marched out, leaving Beddoes to twiddle thumbs and challenge Funny predictions. Inwardly, of course.

You have to hand it to Snow, he'd conceded; draped at the sunlit sill like a lean, cream cat stalking pigeons. Relaxed yet alert, predatory yet patient, not a single movement wasted. A birdwatcher, see. Used to long hours in remote hides, waiting for great-crested whatsits to perform.

Flexing his thigh absently, Beddoes let his thoughts focus on last night: and another anxious bystander . . .

* * *

She arrived quite late, bearing several surprises. First, the hunted, furtive air, the rush to get inside. Once there, she gushed over the decor. He'd given it a lick and a promise, in the vain hope that Pol might relent. Hardly rated this, though, the Jane Neale stamp of approval. Her appearance troubled him, too. Not unkempt – she wouldn't know how; but there were violet half-moons under her eyes, her hair tumbled carelessly over a drab grey sweater. Her jeans had bagged and faded, and he glimpsed bare ankles above the sky-blue trainers. Lastly, she shook him with her choice of booze. 'Lager, please, if you have it.'

As she perched on his sofa and nursed the misty glass, everything about her seemed calculated to appease and disarm. Her next words confirmed it. 'What's wrong with me, Roy? Whenever we're getting close, he volunteers for something! What can I do with him?'

'You told me already.'

She flushed prettily. 'I shouldn't have. I was a bit – ragged – that evening.' Sipping beer without visible pleasure, she continued, 'There was a broken marriage, I know. Is he bitter, then? Afraid to commit himself?'

Beddoes gave her a glance of open admiration. 'Dunno how he swings it. *I* have to do me own chasing.' His hand slid involuntarily to his thigh, and she was on to it in a flash. The press, mind you; observant.

'Is that how you were shot? Chasing, for Huw?'

'No such luck. The red badge of shame, this is.'

She waited, sympathetic and inviting. First chance he'd had to tell anyone, and the story poured out of its own volition.

'Lucky, really,' he admitted, 'I'm still walking about.' An odd little hush, a subtle shift of expression; almost as if he deserved it. The reversal of roles unsettled him, raising all the old suspicions. We ask the questions, okay? 'Why don't you write it up?' he snapped. 'Down-fall in Dublin, another titbit for the proles! How's the article coming, by the way?'

'Terrific. It's called "Police Paranoia"!' The anger faded, the jade eyes softened in appeal. 'We're private, Huw and me, not for publication. Look: the story of a lifetime's brewing in Dockland. And I'm *here*, like some backstreet Mata Hari, asking after the man! Trust me, Roy, *he* does!'

Hard to doubt her, harder still to resist. Grudgingly, conscious of the dereliction, he fed her the scraps he'd overheard. 'He wasn't exactly gung-ho. Told you once; they played on his sense of duty.'

She was gazing into the half-empty glass. 'Islam!' she breathed. 'Who could have guessed the Irish would fall for that? I'm scared, Roy.' She looked up, ghostly against the grey. 'Afraid I might end up writing his epitaph.'

Close to midday, and even Snow was getting twitchy; a nervous patter of fingernails on glass, a tiny frown above the gold-rimmed specs. Which, together with Jane's poignant misgivings, pushed Beddoes to breaking point. Take five, my son, a whiff of fresh air and a turn round the block to ease the stiffness. And get your mind off the waiting. He was actually framing the request when McKay blew in like a small ginger tornado.

'Breakthrough!' he crowed, brandishing sheaves of telex. 'The histories of Cavanaugh and Duffy from their earliest Provo hours!'

Unreal, Snow was. A minute lift of silver brows, a calm murmur of enquiry. 'Source?'

'Aye, and there's the glory of it! Signed O'Brien, and a grand wee rider for Evans.' McKay read it out, his blue eyes ablaze with pleasure. ' "Grade A material, straight from the leprechaun's mouth. Your living has not been in vain." '

And still Snow stood aloof. 'Corroboration?'

McKay grinned savagely. 'I called O'Brien. They raided school records and paged the graphologists. There's no doubt – it's Daly's own hand.'

'Excellent! Very well, Superintendent. What's the take?'

'Thumbnail sketches, so far, the shrinks are still at it. Duffy's the weak sister, they say. A craftsman, none too fond of the early grave and likely to fold under pressure.' McKay was suddenly sober, and Beddoes' unease returned. 'The bad news is – Cavanaugh. Ruthless, dedicated, unbreakable, a known killer who'll go all the way.' The craggy features writhed distastefully. 'They'll not confirm it, but one of the medics was wittering about a "sublimated death-wish".'

'Charming,' muttered Beddoes; and found himself at the focus of bespectacled disdain.

'However unpleasant, Sergeant, knowledge is power. I trust you will remember all this when – ' Snow broke off, stiffening, and turning as the radio crackled into life.

The familiar Welsh voice was upon them, asking utterly outlandish questions; then dropping to an animal whine. '. . . get us *out*!' The plea, so frighteningly unlike Huw, seemed to echo for seconds after the connection had been abruptly broken; and brought up the small hairs at Beddoes' nape.

'What are you waiting for?' he beseeched. 'Send the troops in!'

But the long beige figure was already arcing over the desk, writing unhurriedly on McKay's memo pad. 'Standing by,' he grunted, without looking up. 'Ready to go at ten minutes' notice.'

'Just in time to collect the stiffs! Jesus, didn't you hear him?'

'Yes. Did you?' Through a haze of fury and frustration,

Beddoes watched the gold pen flicker; and heard McKay's scornful but strangely comforting rasp. 'The Test Match finished yesterday, laddie. He's using it as a blind, hoping the Reapers don't know.'

'He was *expecting* a rough time, Sergeant. Apparently he's kept his head. If you do likewise, we may still salvage something.' Straightening, pacing pale and stork-like over coiled cables, Snow laid his handiwork beside the mike. Italic, naturally, and every letter perfectly formed. 'When he contacts us again, tell him this.'

'Not when, mate; *if*!' McKay was bristling redly, but Snow ignored the impertinence.

'As of this moment, you are the most important member of the team. Read it, please.'

Beddoes obeyed, steadying. Clever stuff, he had to admit. Two innocent sentences which would affirm the code, convey *Snow*'s early deadline, and keep the channels open. And all couched in his own cockney idiom. He nodded and glanced up; seeing, for the very first time, real alarm in Funny features.

'I assume, Sergeant, that you *do* know your cricket?'

'Wait!' Salim's voice cut like whiplash, startling Harriet and freezing bearded violence in mid-swing. 'The Constable's honest outburst has done no harm! Easy, Mr Cavanaugh. Let him explain.'

Cav backed off, sneering in disgust. ''Twill be no hardship, what with the terrible stench!'

The policeman sat up, rattled yet resentful; as if insult and assault had restored some moral fibre. Too little, and too late.

He saved my life, thought Harriet, fingering her temple unsteadily. It must have been *vile* up there. Why, then, do I despise him so? Because of his drunken arrival and the stigma he carries; because, instead of a shining blue knight, they sent us a servile ragamuffin; because I hoped he'd redeem us?

He was wheedling now, his pink, puckered hands aflutter. 'A vital match, see, something to occupy our minds. Cooped up, we are, and who knows how long? Come on, Mr Salim, sir. Give us a break?'

'*Yeah*, marn!' Harry Two chimed in, baring snowy teeth. 'Ah could die happy, knowing we whopped the honkies one more time!'

'Cheats!' The policeman's charge rang childish and petulant. 'Grooming your talent on our turf, crippling our batsmen, playing hell with the rules!'

'Don't talk rules, baby – you done *invent* them!'

Salim's serpentine gaze flickered from one to the other. 'I had heard of this strange obsession. Until now, I did not believe. What do *you* say, Mr Cavanaugh?'

Cav shrugged; a ripple of muscle beneath white cotton, a tone of total dismissal. ''Tis the witless pastime of English fops. Why bother?'

'Yet our police comrade speaks wisdom. Occupied minds do not make mischief; and the rivalry could give us amusement. Let us amend the message and show the world our mercy.'

'Sure,' drawled Cav, 'so long as you don't expect *me* to listen.'

As they bent to their writing, Harriet became conscious of movement at her side: Pete, clutching her arm and whispering brokenly. 'Peg's in labour and they're squabbling over some stupid game? 'S not fair, Harry!'

The policeman was making urgent shushing gestures. Suddenly, Harry Two was there, whisking Pete to the furthest corner and doing his nursemaid act again. It's absurd, she thought. Since when have the Welsh cared for cricket? Constable Jenkins certainly did. As he settled

287

at the speakers and scanned Salim's scrawl, his blue eyes glowed in covert satisfaction . . .

'So far, we have been treated kindly, and granted a special privilege.' A sarcastic edge to Valley cadence, but the evenness was reassuring. Not for long, though. 'This will cease, unless we secure the public attention we deserve! Henceforth, our struggle shall come first in every news broadcast. You must now respond!'

Snow was already murmuring into the phone. Cupping the mouthpiece, he ordered, 'Stall them.'

Ta very much, thought Beddoes, and launched a halting improvisation. 'Sorry, mate, it'll take a while. Gotta page the Beeb and talk terms.'

'We demand immediate agreement!'

Snow nodded tautly, and Beddoes breathed, 'You got it.'

A brief, humming pause, then: 'Can I ask about the cricket, Mr Salim?'

Nice one, uncle! Now we know who's calling the shots.

But the airways had fallen silent, and Snow was frowning in concern. 'He'll have to be a lot more subtle. If they let him on again, give him O'Brien's profiles.' He rounded on McKay. 'Contact records. Ask for Libyans called Salim.'

Jesus, thought Beddoes, *that* ought to give us a fair old list.

The speakers thumped, and propaganda issued in a flat Welsh monotone. 'Islam is mightier than any individual. For every Reaper cut down, a thousand will rise in his place until pagan capitalism is wiped from the face of the earth!'

McKay was glowering like the wrath of God; Snow merely curled a lip, having heard it all before.

'Resist, and your comrades die. Obey and we go in

peace. To show goodwill, we now invite news of your national game.'

An urgent off-white flicker and Snow had eased behind the desk, his pen poised. Evans was himself again, the tone casual and nerveless. 'What's the score, boyo?' And Beddoes read the Funny's script. 'Usual tale, over by lunch on the third day. We haven't got their number, know what I mean?' Then, with McKay's 'thumbnail sketches' in mind, 'We can't fathom their opening bats. There's no budging the big guy – the one with the best record. His partner's a technician, but vulnerable in a long innings. Sometimes, you reckon he's *trying* to get out.'

'The captain's first wicket down, mind, and he's the toughest of all. Skittled us cheap, did they?'

'Yeah,' Beddoes mumbled, playing along. 'Too fast for us.'

You could hear the suppressed excitement as Evans seized the opportunity. '*Our* opener could tell 'em – the one they ran out, early on. Faced the whole attack, see, took at least one bump from everyone.'

Phoning again, Snow made urgent signals. Close him down, don't overdo it. And McKay was leaving, compact and purposeful.

'Okay, mate. We're doing our best. God and Mr Salim willing, we'll keep you up to date.' Beddoes flicked the switch and looked up into censorious dark eyes.

'Let us not invoke the Almighty, Sergeant. It's needless provocation.' The severity gave way to donnish delight. 'Wasn't Evans superb? A most auspicious choice!'

'Sure. *He* was loving it, too.'

Water off a duck's back, was this. Snow merely sniffed and pored over his notes. 'An Arab leader – "the toughest of them all". Nice to be sure. McKay's at the path. lab, checking. One bullet from each of the Reapers, according to Evans. Which will confirm the numbers.' He leaned back, offering commendation. 'You did well, on the spur of the moment. Let's hope the message proves helpful. Next time, go for dispositions — guard posts, sentry patrols, so forth. I think you might try "field placings".'

'I might. Meantime, you better square the media.'

'Not to worry, Sergeant. I already have.'

Lunch had been worse than school dinners: weak tea and soggy pies. The mere sight had sent Salim stalking to the window, a model of grey disdain. Pork, of course, hardly his sort of thing. Harriet didn't fancy it herself; or anything else, for that matter. Cav's cruel words and deadly embrace still lingered, stifling any thought of food.

The BBC hadn't helped. The afternoon bulletins remained brief and bland; it had taken all Joe's persuasion to keep the little Arab below boiling point.

As the day faded and tension simmered, Harriet registered a fresh source of danger. Some time during his dreadful ordeal, the police worm had turned. A rumpled blue heap in the corner giving off an invisible aura of foulness, he didn't *seem* much changed. Until you looked closer and longer. Something in the eyes — a hooded, feral glare which followed Salim's every move. Something in the curl and slump of the body — a pent-up fury straining to erupt. He was like some taunted, captive beast. Enduring, surviving; awaiting a single instant of overconfidence or inattention within which he could spring and strike.

And die.

Soon, she thought, shivering. Soon he will crack and blow us all to kingdom come . . .

Six o'clock. Joe twirled dials, taut and jaundiced in the upward yellow glow, while Salim prowled impatiently.

Even the band boys forsook their bottles to blear and listen. And Harriet breathed easier as the newsreader got into stride.

'In response to Green Reaper demands, the Home Office has issued the following communiqué: "The Cabinet will meet tonight to consider ways of ending the deadlock. At four maximum security centres, procedures and formalities for the release of certain inmates have been initiated. A military aircraft and a volunteer civilian crew are standing by, and International Air Traffic Control has been requested to clear certain eastbound lanes. So far, negotiations have been cordial. It is to be hoped that, with patience and goodwill on both sides, further bloodshed can be averted."

'Meanwhile, in the Bradford by-election campaign . . .' Joe flicked the switch and looked up triumphantly.

'Bejaysus, we've won!'

The bandsmen were already celebrating, clinking bottles and pounding the table. Until Salim silenced them with a contemptuous hiss. 'What is this foolishness? They are talking, not acting! Perhaps they need more persuasion.' He was hunting again, his dark gaze seeking a victim; and coming to rest on Pete. Harriet held her breath, conscious of stealthy movement in the corner. The policeman, she thought. While Salim's distracted, he'll pounce!

But it was Harry Two who moved, dull green in the fading light. Big and baleful, and a black finger pointed at Joe. 'Hey, little marn, ah'm coming for you. You gonna press the button?'

'Sure enough, Sambo!'

'Well, here's a fine thing! Ah heard tell the Catholic faith say suicide a crime! You get near them gates, ole Peter gonna say, "Joe boy, you a sinner, you go straight to *hell*!"'

'Whisht, man, ye think I care for fairy tales?'

He *does* care, Harriet realized, you can see by the quiver of lip and the haunt in his eyes.

'Let him be,' Cav advised softly. 'Try someone your own size.' He was leaning on the wall, and steel flickered in his hand.

Harry Two gave him a stately bow. 'Ah do declare, *you're* the one gonna put us in orbit. You ain't scared of *nothing*!'

Handling the blade like an old friend, Cav cleaned his fingernails and smiled nostalgically. ''Tis a family tradition, to live and die by the sword. As did my daddy and grandaddy before.'

'Y'Allah,' breathed Salim. 'Well spoken!'

'There's a story they tell, in the Maze. Of big Cav on hunger strike and drifting easy off this mortal coil. Of how, when the screws chickened and tried to force-feed, they had to pry his teeth with a crowbar.' He straightened, hefting the knife and stroking his beard. Though his words were aimed at Harry Two, his blatant leer was for Harriet alone. 'I'll tell ye a secret, Sambo. Coming's great: but going's a whole lot better!'

'*Wow*!' gasped Harry Two, in pop-eyed mock admiration. 'We gotta man here just *dyin'* to be a martyr!' Briefly, his own joke convulsed him, a great blaze of perfect teeth. Then, abruptly, he fell to a fighter's crouch. 'Some dark night, ole Harry Two gonna *oblige* you, marn.'

They squared up in the rancid dusk, heavy and heated as rutting bulls. A subtly altered tension; the hungry hush of the arena and watchers primed for blood on the sand. In spite of everything, Harriet felt a flicker of warmth in her loins; knowing the victor would claim her as his prize. It was a sickening, sordid insight. Pull yourself together, you stupid, stupid girl!

Lights blazed. Squinting into the dazzle, she saw Joe's hand at the switch.

'Cool it, Cav, for he's not worth the bother.' And suddenly, it *did* seem ridiculous. A seedy room, a black, reflecting slab of window, and grown men trading macho like schoolyard bullies.

But Salim wouldn't let it rest. 'You — West Indian! How can a helpless prisoner taunt his captors so?'

Harry Two swivelled. A graceful green swirl, a rhythmic patter of feet. Dum-diddy-dum-dum, dum-*dum*! And came to rest, knees bent, palms outsplayed like some latter-day Al Jolson. 'Amusement, marn. I gotta bedtime tale to tell, a way to solve your problem. Amusement with a moral; you-all *ready* for this?'

For the very first time, Harriet noticed, Salim looked uneasy; the wary gaze of a man discovering a hitherto unknown and potentially lethal species.

'Don't know where you hails from,' Harry Two was saying, 'and ah ain't askin'. But ah bet you-all was part of the good ole British Raj!'

'*Y'Allah!* It is why we are here!'

'So *listen*, baby, ah got news for you.' He had their total attention. Only the policeman paid no heed, bum-shuffling deeper into the corner by Joe's fusebox. Poor man, Harriet thought, denied even this diversion by the odium of his presence.

'Ah's *Anguillian*,' Harry Two declared. 'Little ole dot in the Carib. sea. Long ago, some Brits roll up, searching for plantation. Brought slaves, too.'

'*Slaves*,' echoed Salim, his puzzlement clearing. 'We are brothers, after all!'

'Don't count on it, marn. Pretty soon a bunch of Irish done shipwreck, settle for the duration.' Harry Two rounded on Cav. 'Maybe we cousins, big marn. How d'you like that?'

'Not much!'

The violence of the rejection wrung a smile from even Pete's wan face. Well it might, thought Harriet, in a flash of enlightenment. The distraction is working – Pete's off the hook!

'Anguilla, she *dry*,' mourned Harry Two. 'Nothing grow. Pretty soon, them ole Brits say what the hell, give the *blacks* the land.' He drew himself up, produced a quivering military salute and sang in a pukka strangled soprano. 'Britons never never never shall be – slaves! Nor Anguillians, neither!' Harry Two was swaying now, a silky green flicker of shoulder and hips. 'Mother England, she old and sick, done let *all* her children go. Trouble is, she hook *us* up to some *un*friendly neighbours. We ain't free, marn; we *oppressed*!' His voice had risen, he'd sidled closer to Salim, blocking the Arab's line of sight to the corner. Where, Harriet saw in sudden alarm, the policeman was opening the fusebox.

Gnawing her knuckles, feeling the pound of blood in her head, she cowered before approaching madness.

Harry Two clowned on regardless. 'One fine day, we done block the airstrip, show them neighbours the door, and take to the bush.'

'Bravo,' murmured Salim, beaming approval. 'Guerrilla comrades.'

'The Brits send the *Army*!' said Harry Two in comic awe. 'They invade our patch of sand.' He paused dramatically, the whites of his eyes huge. And behind him, the Constable's hand inched stealthily among exposed wiring. Crunch time, my girl. He's going to kill the lights and try for Joe's gun! Harry Two's bray of laughter froze the entire tableau. '*Marn*, we had a ball! Shots in the dark, capers on the beach, *important* people running every which way! And not a single casualty. Things quiet down, the Brit. soldiers work their asses off. They putting in roads and drains and phones, and we-all snooze in the shade saying thank you very much! After a while, a whole lotta turkey gets talked. Anguilla, she a *dependency*, having her own parliament.'

'Gutless niggers!' snarled Cav. 'You sold out!'

The policeman's fingers flickered and Harriet flinched; but the light stayed on and Harry Two gave Cav the sweetest of smiles. 'You ain't *listening*, Irish. The Brit. governor, he put his little rubber stamp *exactly* where we want. He a *diplomat*, marn, a long ways from home!'

At this, the dusty blue policeman seemed to sag. The fusebox was gently closed and he eased back into his corner. Lost his nerve, thought Harriet, in a wave of giddy relief. Thank God!

With a final lime green flourish, Harry Two rounded on the Arab. 'Here's the moral, baby. You want the penny *and* the bun, do like us. Come back, Brits, all is forgiven – be a colony again, marn!'

'Cretin!' Salim's almond features twisted in contempt. 'Under *our* patch of sand there lies the wealth of oil!'

'Oil runs out, my friend. Pretty soon, you gonna end up sitting on a crock, like all the rest.'

Salim's pistol had appeared again. Curiously, it only served to lower the temperature. You could see the arrogance bloom anew, hear the condescension in his tone. 'Wealth is power, my simple black brother. Power on the fields of battle, and in the free councils of the world!'

'Politics, marn. Politics done bore me.'

'Beware! Soon it will bore you to death!'

Harry Two sat on the stained boards, a boneless, fluid swoop. Crossing his legs and turning an insolent brown face upward, he murmured, 'Know something, Mr

Salim? I got respect for that there weapon, but *you* don't faze me a bit.'

Stop it, cried Harriet inwardly, seeing the white of knuckle gleam from Salim's trigger finger. She closed her eyes and bit her lip, awaiting the flare and the thunder and another tumbled corpse. And, amazed, heard *Cav* defuse the moment. 'Hey, Sambo; *now* who's got a deathwish?'

Relaxing, peering cautiously, she watched the lethal glaze fade from black eyes.

'Thank you, Mr Cavanaugh. We must not demean the mission to silence heedless fools. Instead, they must learn from *our* heritage.' Salim glanced down at the gun, turning it this way and that, studying the play of light. 'Steel,' he breathed. 'Yes! My forefathers were as lean brown wolves in a clime that knew no mercy. Those were days when a man must fight or die.' The eyes turned briefly to Harriet, and she shuddered at the emptiness within. 'Even for something as worthless as a female to preserve his line. Victory was to the fierce and strong. So it was; so it shall be again! First, we shall recover our warriors, wherever they may be. They shall show our children the power of the Prophet and the force of cold clean steel!' His voice was rising again to a messianic pitch; a voice of implacable purpose, a face of naked hate. 'When the time is ripe, we shall gather and launch a jihad such as the world has never seen!'

Holy war, and mounted by men such as this! How can we stop them, Harriet wondered despairingly. How can we, who are raised in love, stand against such pitiless ferocity? Through a veil of hopeless tears, she saw the same plea mirrored in pallid, captive faces.

Then Salim stooped like a savage grey hawk and unleashed his final challenge. 'Test my comrades all you dare. They are soldiers in the common cause against the common enemy.' He drew the remote-control console from his pocket, rested an elegant brown finger on the button. 'Never doubt this. If need should press, I will rise to glory gladly, striking the first blow for the jihad! In this, unlike you, I am deadly serious!'

Harry Two licked his lips and made a gallant bid for the last word. '*Serious?* Marn, Ah'd call your condition *critical*!'

But this time, he didn't win a single smile . . .

Amazing what tension and the need for mental alertness will do, Beddoes thought. Haven't had so much as a twinge all day. Still limping, and not quite up to judo; but there's one kind of indoor sport we ought to manage all right. Jesus, he wondered, sipping Scotch and surveying his solitary pad; how long has it been? Too long, my son. Be blowing a valve any minute.

He *was* off the shit-list, sharing the Super's eyrie and rubbing shoulders with a Funny-in-chief. Page Pol, then; bury the hatchet and other tokens of friendship.

The amber liquid took on a sudden bitterness. It wasn't right, somehow. Nothing to do with recent experience, or O'Brien's nasty crack about padlocked flies. More a question of comparisons, really. Slap 'n' tickle seemed a bit off while Huw was stuck in an Arab nuthouse sitting on half a ton of plastique.

So presently, smothering his conscience and turning Nelson's eye to the implications, he called Jane. 'Know who's speaking?'

'Surely. It's . . .'

'No names. Listen, the boy made contact.'

'Thank God!' A long pause, the suspicion of a sniffle, then, 'Is he fit?'

'Functioning, anyhow. Got something going, we've cut the odds a bit.'

'A *bit*?'

'You know what they say. The impossible takes longer.'

'Look, it might sound ungrateful, but should you be telling *me*?' A subtle emphasis on the last word, and he pictured her sitting somewhere; anxious and lovely and quick as a fox.

'If it gets out, I'll be walking police dogs tomorrow.' He sighed, acknowledging the inevitable. 'For the moment, we have things in common. Who else would I tell?'

'Very flattering, I'm sure.' The tart tone again, the one that went with the flashing green eyes.

'I could always hang up.'

'*Please!* What else?' She caught on, even at a distance, over the phone.

The thing he'd intended to say, and now wasn't so sure. Media, you couldn't get away from it, and still the chance she was shamming. He told her anyway; might as well be hung for a sheep. 'You ought to bimble down there, lunchtime tomorrow. Could be decided then, one way or the other.'

The pause was much longer, he could hear her quick, shallow breathing. 'What are you saying? An unscheduled interruption?'

'Something like that.'

'God, I shan't sleep a wink!'

'Me neither, girl.'

CHAPTER SIXTEEN

Evans lay sleepless in squalor, beset by rats and Reapers, reflecting on mice and men. Face it, bach. If, by some miracle, you should survive to old age, it won't be down to cunning codewords. It will be because for a fleeting, irretrievable moment the ramparts collapsed, pretence became reality, and you told it like it is. *Truth*, naked and defenceless, is what conquered Arab suspicion and created just the right atmosphere of Irish contempt. Cast as the coward, you are; live it to the hilt. So that they will continue to overlook the covert search for salvation, and dismiss the cricket dialogue as a sop to the defeated. Let Harrigan take the limelight, probe for small advantages, act the courageous clown. Does it well, fair play.

He shifted cautiously on the lumpy mattress. Gerry's, it was, you could tell by the reek of dope. Dead man's blankets, there's lovely. Staring into darkness, he struggled to muster a sense of self, to recover balance and purpose. Head still sore but clearing, brain in reasonable shape. Thank *you*, Mr Cavanaugh. The vile odour still clinging, the hatred smouldering nicely. I'll *have* you, Salim. Funny predictions still holding up; how about the practice, Mr Snow? And, no matter how hard he resisted, the one presence he wanted to distance and protect. Missing you, Jane. Maybe we could've made it work.

'Here, Inspector. Compliments of your Avon lady.' The deep-toned whisper jolted him out of his reverie. A bulky shadow at his side, a glimmer of friendly smile. Harrigan, naturally; another thing he did well. Who else could have come so silently between the sleepers? Evans' fingers closed around the offering: a smooth, short cylinder.

'What's this, then?'

'Deodorant. I reckon your need is greater than mine.'

Evans swallowed hard, moved almost to tears. Get a grip, boyo. Salim's evil games have left the old emotions a bit touchy.

'Spray it on,' urged Harrigan. 'I'm near to asphyxiating!'

Old Spice enveloped him; the hiss drew unwelcome attention.

'Okay, no more noise. Knock it off, you guys!' Joe's voice, thin and nervy. He hovered near the window, his face a pale blob against the spangled sky.

'Aw, c'mon Joe, just some sporting chat. We enthusiasts, marn!'

'Away with you, Sambo, you're worse than the feckin' Brits. Cricket!'

'What's wrong, we disturbin' your nap?'

Joe's chuckle sounded false and forced. '*No* chance! 'Tis a proper owl I am, perched here with one finger on the button and me weapon in hand.'

'Hey, marn, you never hear about *girls*? I done give up your pastime soon as the short hairs grow!'

'Laugh, ye great black eedjit! Some day you're gonna *die* laughing. It's naught to me, meanwhile. Ye'll quiet soon enough, once Cav takes the watch!'

'Bless you, Joe. Ah'm gonna see you right with St Peter.'

'I'll make me own enemies, thanks!'

Free at last of the awful smell, Evans was actually smiling. A fragile truce, and one he was reluctant to

300

break. He felt a surge of affection for the black man at his side, a need to prolong the respite. 'Quite a tale,' he murmured. 'About Anguilla, I mean. Fact, is it? Or just a fable to keep Pete out of schtook?'

'Mostly true, I guess. A dry ole patch of sand.' His whisper softened, yearning. 'Stuck in this ghetto, you get to appreciate what's lost. Home, know what I mean? Ain't no place like it. Mile after mile of pure white beach, the clearest, bluest ocean you ever did see. Sunshine all day long, rum 'n' reggae through the night. Oh man, that's *living*!' He was sitting up, his profile etched on the glimmer of window. Tight curls, half-closed eyes and lips upturned in wistful reminiscence. 'Got me a lady back there, waiting. Brown and slim, laughing eyes, cooks the best salt fish in all the Carib. She *decent*, okay? But sometimes, when the moon turn gold and the breeze hang soft, we nightwalk down the beach. Warm sand, the scent of loving, skin like honey velvet; and them ole waves singing husha, husha . . . Lord, Lord.' He sighed; and took a decisive note. 'If we get loose, gonna take some leave. Catch the firstest, fastest plane and tie me a wedding knot. Ain't but one chance we get, and time's awasting. *You* ever feel like that?'

Not for a while, Evans thought, keeping Jane's image at bay. Not for two days, actually.

Reluctantly, breaking the mood, he breathed, 'Speaking of time . . . Cav'll be along, just now.' He sensed the almost physical wrench, the regrouping of far-flung West Indian concentration. A professional, Harrigan. Duty first, devotions later.

'With you, man. Let's do some figuring.'

Nearby, in the dark, the girl sobbed sharply; dreaming. Joe's silhouette started, shifted, settled once more to the lone and starlit vigil. And Evans reviewed the takings.

'According to Beddoes, they'll move in regardless; lunch-time tomorrow. SAS, I expect.'

'Check. Them boys are *fast*!'

'No one's *that* fast. The bells will go when they're still fifty yards away.'

'Check two. So we have to kill the alarm.' Evans smiled, reliving the early show. 'While you were doing the minstrel bit, I took a shufty at Joe's electrics. Two brand-new fuses, you can't miss them. Ease them out in daylight, when the radio's off, and no one'll know the difference. Remote control, though; that's something else.'

'I been studying Joe. Pushed into a corner, he'd maybe use the gun; but he ain't about to press no button. Like your man says – he *trying* to get out!'

A *smart* clown, Harrigan, reading Roy's signals nicely.

'Scratch Joe,' Evans agreed. 'One down, two to go. Both of whom would do it gladly.'

'Listen here. How about we take the battery out of Cav's gizmo?'

'He'd know in a flash, by the *weight*, mun.'

'Check three. So short the terminals and put it back.'

'Oh aye? And what's he doing in the meantime? Watching TV?'

Harrigan leaned closer, his tone at once bleak and hopeful. 'He's been screwing the girl, off and on, and no complaints from her. He'll be in soon. Suppose she makes up to him, keeps him immorally occupied for ten minutes or so. Someone slips past, doctors the battery and returns it, and *Cav's* out of the reckoning.' He paused, a moment of cool self-mockery. '*My* party, this one. Ain't nobody sees Harry Two in the dark, long as he don't smile.' A flash of fine teeth to make the point; but Evans wasn't convinced.

302

'Only a kid, mind. Manage it, would she, after what he did and said this morning?'

'She'd better, man! Turns the odds around, like you said. Two of us for Salim alone. You ready for him?'

'Try and stop me, boyo!'

It's not *just* vengeance, Evans told himself as Harrigan's big body simply merged into the darkness. It's the only hope, see. We'll force a sixteen-year-old girl to mate with the man she probably detests in the *hope* that some fairly useless lives may be preserved. Because it has to be stopped; because the Funnies say so; most of all, to save our own skins.

Strange how clearly you think when you've been stripped of human dignity, when all that's left is the single, central need for survival. Awaiting the change of guard, cocking an ear towards Harrigan's attempt to recruit the girl, he trawled his memory and set his mind to certain other possibilities . . .

Harriet woke abruptly from a vision of gunfire and gore. Her heart pounded, her body was clammy with dread. Steady, my girl. You're alive and well, and still living with the Reapers. Just. The snores of the band, the reek of overcrowding, the memory of a merciless Irish voice and a gunbarrel at her head; full awareness claimed her, every bit as fearful as the dream. And she rejected it, willing herself back to the dorm of St Cats and a form of escape which had helped her endure an earlier onslaught of stress.

Beset by puberty and the trauma of parental warfare, she would languish in fresher but equally miserable darkness and resort to maudlin fantasy. Harriet Slade had met an untimely and heroic end – saving some helpless soul from storm-tossed seas, whisking a toddler from the path of a hurtling juggernaut. She lay in cold, unearthly beauty, surrounded by springtime blooms and weeping mourners. Mummy and Daddy, reconciled in grief. 'She left us the gift of love reborn, how shall we live without her?' And in the myrrh-scented chapel at St Catherine's, a chastened deputy headmistress would bestow the valediction. 'She was a noble, selfless child, the brightest and the best. May the Lord forgive us our misjudgement. May her example inspire us, for her memory will be with us, always.' Then the living girl would revel in self-induced tears. Serves them right, they'll cry an ocean for me when it's too late!

A vain conceit; how cruelly different was the reality. If I should die – as I probably will – think only this of me: no one gave a damn! Somewhere off Sardinia, her mother would say, 'She was always a wilful, earthy little madam. Too much of her father's blood.' At St Cats, her sinful shade would be used to quell the high-spirited. 'Beware, young ladies, or you will end up like that poor, wild Slade creature.' Daddy might shed a tear, doubtless on the overheated, overexposed bosom of his new bride. Who would own him completely at last, and seize the chance gladly between avid thighs. 'There, there, don't take on. Let's have our own!'

The sheer hopelessness numbed her. She was dimly aware of whispered conversation – Harry Two, she thought, trying to stiffen police resolve with cricket gossip – and of Pete's restless sleep at her side, all knees and elbows. Against these, the only three men in her life, stood a crazed Arab, a black-hearted ex-lover, and a tight-strung dealer of destruction. Heaven protect us, she pleaded. Nothing else can.

The whispers had stopped. Framed by the stars, Joe's outline swayed and nodded. There were soft slithers at her side, a whiff of Old Spice, and Harry Two's urgent murmur in her ear. She listened, rigid with horror and disbelief.

'You're mad! He was ready to kill me this morning: why would he want me tonight?'

'Baby, you got better credentials than any of us!'

'What I've got is gooseflesh, just thinking about it.'

'C'mon, marn, you're all grown up. We're counting on you.' He sounded like the St Cats hockey coach – go, Harry, screw him blind for the honour of the school!

'You're counting on a cheap thrill,' she accused. 'You and that disgusting policeman!'

'Lawdy, girl, it ain't *never* been a spectator sport! Ah reckon you're woman enough. You saying ah'm wrong?'

'I won't rut with a – butcher – while you play silly games!'

'We're playing for *keeps*, Miss Harry.' A large hand encircled her wrist and the quiet voice turned mean. 'You owe "that disgusting policeman". He done save your pretty neck. After what he went through, ah'd say you're getting off easy!'

Joe's brogue broke the impasse, sounding a timely caution. 'Hey, Sambo, ye'd best steer clear of Cav's woman.'

The grip relaxed, a large dark shadow loomed above her. 'Ain't no *woman* hereabouts. Only a timid little girl.'

'There's Cav for you! Always liked them young and green.'

All right, she thought, as the shadow and the spicy aftershave drifted away, I'll show the whole, gutless, leering bunch of you! Grit your teeth, my girl, and think of England.

Anything *Mummy* does, you can do better . . .

In the glimmer of a horned moon rising, she watched the change of guards. Waiting didn't help, but the slant of silver would; limelight for a stripper. *Now*, Harriet. Let's see how much you've learned.

She stood up, ruffling her hair, easing the strap of her slip off one shoulder.

'Hold it, girlie; that's near enough!'

A bigger, shaggier silhouette blocked the window, and the rifle gleamed dully. Her heart raced, her breath came hard and short. So much the better, she realized, and took two more wide-hipped paces. 'I'm *cold*, Cav.'

'Indeed? 'Tis a wondrous forgiving nature, after the morning's dispute.'

'We're both alive; and I'm still cold.'

'For love or for vengeance, I'm wondering? You'd not be after seizing the gun and turning the tables?'

'Later, maybe. For the moment, I need you *warm*.'

He turned sideways on, his leer bright against the bush of beard. ''Twill keep, then, till the watch is done.'

'Not for me, it won't.' She was close now, returning the hungry heat of his gaze, running her fingers across his thigh, feeling the flex of muscle beneath coarse denim. 'Take me to bed, Cav.'

'The best offer I've had all day, to be sure; and what would Lord Salim say?'

She pouted, leaning forward, knowing the material would fall away. 'Why, Cav, you're *scared* of that crazy little man!'

His hand shot out. Claw fingers snagged the vee. Brief pressure at her back, a rending sound, and two halves of thin cotton fluttered free.

The instant of truth. Instinct bade her cover up, clasp her arms across her nakedness and retreat. Coolly, in full knowledge, she arched her back, sliding her hands up her midriff and lifting her breasts towards him.

He reacted with that same silent, stunning speed. The rifle propped behind him, pale hands unhitching his belt.

306

She was lifted and swung and pressed to the wall, where he crouched and surged against her. 'Oh *dear*,' she taunted breathlessly, 'I thought you were a *man*. And what do I get? A kneetrembler in a phone booth!'

He stepped back abruptly. Her heels jarred on the floor. The dark was thick with his musk and the wind of violent movement. A hard palm slammed her cheek; his voice grated viciously. 'Don't get smart with *me*, girly!'

Suppressing the pain, tasting her own salt blood, she hit him back as hard as she could. 'Come to bed, you bastard, let's make it one to remember!'

'Bejaysus, you're asking for a rough ride!'

'*Yes!* And to hell with bloody Salim!'

He stripped in an instant, tossing his trousers into a pool of moonlight. She actually heard the thud of weighted plastic on hollow boards. His embrace smothered her, hard hands at breast and flank. And, in spite of everything, his marble maleness thawed her. Thrust down on the springless mattress, she bit her lip and spread her thighs and took him in; one single, savage stroke of joyless conjunction. His breath scalded, the beard at her throat was at once harsh and silky.

Behind and below him, Harry Two's hand scuttled from the shadows like a huge, hairless spider. The sprawl of trousers shifted, lifted and disappeared.

'Come *on*!' she urged, her hips bunching and falling instinctively. Though whether she spoke to Cav or the unseen audience, she scarcely knew nor cared. Steely arms met across the small of her back. She was whirled and grasped and raised aloft; his grin blazed at her, upwards.

'The Mother Superior,' he grunted. 'So a man can keep sight of his rifle!'

Bracing her palms on the slick of his chest, she forced herself straighter, trying to fill his vision with her own bouncing breasts. A half-turn of the head, a stolen glance; and a terrifying glimpse of empty, moonlit floorboards. Increasing the tempo, she sensed the first faint spasm inside, saw his black brows knit in anguish. 'Hurry, girl, 'tis terrible near!'

Somehow, holding her rhythm, she found a sly, maternal note, 'Enjoy, little man. It's no good for me this way.'

A throaty growl, another awesome eruption of strength; and he was above her again, his plea sharp and urgent. 'Damn you, I'll not hold off much longer!'

She met his drive, straining to peer beyond the pale cords of his shoulders. There, plain as daylight, Harry Two crouched and fumbled the console into the gaping trouser pocket.

'*Now*, Cav!' she gasped, clenching her inner muscles around him. 'Please, please, *now*!' She felt the yield and shudder of him, was battered by his mighty pumping. Clawing the quiver of buttocks dispassionately, she echoed his grateful moan. Loud enough to flatter, but not to wake the neighbours. Rising in one last, simulated heave, she saw the trousers safely returned; and Harry Two's moonstruck fingers curled in the American high-sign.

'The best, Cav,' she sighed and lied, marvelling at herself. 'Maybe you should start worrying about the rifle.'

He sagged across her, wilfully crushing her breath away with his great weight. 'I aim to please, me little hellcat, whatever the weapon.'

Unlike him, though, she'd planted in fertile ground. She could actually feel the stir of his suspicion, the unease growing within his sweat-sleek flesh.

Soon, he rose and left her, a casual, glistening, nude stroll through the silvered silence. Tensely, she watched him shrug into his shirt, haul the trousers up, tap the hip pocket lightly. Then heft the rifle, check the chamber and swagger to the gleam of window. Where, finally, he coiled on the sill with the fluid grace of a sated tomcat. A cautious tomcat, leaving nothing to chance. Well, almost nothing.

You did it, Harriet. Took him on his own ground at his own game, and won. And, God willing, he'll never know. Yet she felt no triumph, only a kind of soiled, sick relief. So *that's* how Mummy managed, down the loveless years. So simple, so painless. How absurd these men are; how touchy and macho and easy to please. And deceive.

Not all, she discovered. Settling back wearily, she shipped a pointed elbow in the ribs and a hiss of condemnation. 'You slut, Harry, rutting with that pig after what he's done! It won't save you, he'll kill us all anyway!'

Poor Pete, what does he know? The injustice pained, just the same. Sorely stung and briefly tempted, she framed an explanation. Forget it, my girl. Might as well stand up and shout it from the rooftops. 'Go to sleep, Pete. Be thankful for what you have, with Peg.'

'*Had*, you mean. Christ, we were fools, sharing a sewer with trash like Gerry – and you!' She reached out a comforting hand and he shrank away. 'Don't touch me! I can smell that animal on you!'

So can I, she admitted silently, rolling over and turning her back. Perhaps I always will. Because, throughout the whole, squalid farrago, she'd felt not the faintest flicker of pleasure. I'll kill you, Cav, she promised, drifting into distraught sleep.

Exposed on Harrigan's broad pale palm, the workings of the remote-control device looked curiously innocent. A standard nine-volt power-pack nested in black plastic. Such simplicity; such destruction.

'What now?' queried Evans tensely. 'We've no tools, mun!' Dark fingers flickered in the moonlight. The battery flipped free, dangling from thin connecting wires.

'We got lucky, Inspector. A clip-in job, right?' A swift jerk, the broken wires deftly plaited together. '*There*. That oughta do it.' The battery was thumbed into place, the cover snapped softly down. Phase one was complete in fifteen seconds flat, and the silent bulk already melting away. Waiting, Evans shrank from the sounds of the two-backed beast; laboured breathing, muffled moans, a rhythmic creak of boards. Peeping Tom, duw duw, where's your dirty raincoat?

Even in sleep, he acknowledged bitterly, Salim has the power to corrupt. Only fanatics choose decency before death. In such extremes, us common folk will squirm and deceive and wallow in filth and fornicate lovelessly; just to postpone the evil hour.

Easy, bach, don't be too hard. What was it Snow had said? *In this business, we are seldom permitted the luxury of moral judgements.* Right, as usual. So, come down from the pulpit and *think*!

Harrigan was back, a warm and welcome murmur. 'Mission accomplished, man.'

Presently, Cavanaugh sauntered naked into the slant of moon. Lean, languid and impressively muscled, he dressed, completed a soldierly weaponcheck and took station at the window.

A taut, bearded profile, a silvered slope of rifle; no way to catch *him* napping. Evans retreated to deeper shadow and another whispered council of war.

'If . . .' began Harrigan. 'If we're reading Joe and the code right, so long as Cav's gizmo stays dead, provided the alarm don't go – we've only got Salim to worry about. Plus a blade, two pistols, and that there rifle. We ain't even close, man.'

'Cutting the odds, we are, giving the cavalry a chance. Suppose, around zero hour, we create a distraction – give Salim some more amusement.' Evans expanded the idea, concluding, 'It's mostly down to you, see. Cavanaugh's no pushover!'

'Right on. Big, fast, and Irish mean. There again, I ain't no slouch myself. Trained, and sneaky with it.'

'You'll be up against the knife, mind.'

'No sweat. Old Cav *bugs* me, know what I mean?' A beat of indrawn breath and the first hint of doubt. 'You *sure* of Salim? He'll press the tit before he cuts loose with the shooter? It don't faze me much, either way, but someone could catch lead-poisoning.'

I'm not sure of anything, Evans conceded silently. No way I'm going to admit it, though. 'If and when the SAS get close, it'll be chaos. Salim won't take us out piece-meal. Set the spark, bow to Mecca and hitch a ride to glory. And that could give us just a few more seconds. To stop him, I mean.'

This time, the hush fell deeper and lasted longer. Someone – Pete, probably – whimpered quietly, and a fitful breeze rippled over the roof.

'Know what, Inspector? That's the worstest, iffiest plan I heard in my whole life. But I'll be damned if I can think of a better one.'

Movement at the window, sway and nod and sudden start, and Cavanaugh rising to his feet. Even in outline, you could *see* his guilt and self-disgust. Dozing on duty, then. In his army, it would be a capital offence.

He was alert now, though, clearly determined to atone. For minutes on end, his shadow prowled the glistening boards, rhythmic and hypnotic. Four paces, turn, four paces.

Watching, close to exhausted sleep himself, Evans barely registered Harrigan's comment.

'Okay, marn, it's on. All stations go at one o'clock tomorrow.'

Something awry, a false note, something about the time. *What?* Evans was suddenly wide awake. 'Hold on! It's a Test Match, remember? Lunch at half-twelve.'

'I'm West Indian, marn, you trying to tell *me* about cricket?' The darkness was electric now, Cavanaugh might have been miles away. And Harrigan's certainty wavered. '*Hell*, maybe you're right!'

The ultimate absurdity. Trapped in musky darkness under Irish guard and Arab sentence of death; committed to a plan only inches short of suicide; and even the timing at issue between two policemen claiming to be cricket fanatics.

'Twelve fifty,' breathed Harrigan finally. 'Ten to one. I can *see* it, printed in the *Radio Times*, clear as daylight. I'll stake my life on it.'

'Aye, you'll bloody *have* to!' Doubt swirled like deadly fog in Evans' mind. 'Listen; what if it rains?' Astonished, he caught Harrigan's suppressed chuckle. 'Darro, mun, it's nothing to laugh at!'

'No? Lord, lord, they done finished the game two days already!'

That's how it goes, Evans realized, when hope overrules reality. You start believing your own propaganda. In which case, you'd better hope soldiers have lunch at one, like everyone else.

CHAPTER SEVENTEEN

Seven fifteen on an overcast September morning, and the nick idling quietly between shifts. Short of sleep and composure, Beddoes sought the common touch; a bit of routine gossip to relax the mind and calm the nerves.

Sussing out the new desk sergeant, actually; Watson by name and mournful by nature.

'Grapevine's humming, Roy,' he confided, leaning forward and breathing last night's garlic. 'Smythe got his cards. A sick man, they say. The Reapers broke him. Your oppo's still in baulk, too.'

'Who d'you mean?'

'Evans, who else? Incommunicado, him, locked up on the funny farm ever since his trip to darkest Bogland.'

So *that* was the story. Beddoes shook his head, playing the innocent. 'News to me, mate.'

Watson's eyebrows lifted, his lugubrious face twisted in disbelief. 'Leave it out! Hobnobbing with the mighty like you are?' A note of envy slithered into his voice. 'Untouchable, wercher, till a couple of days ago. How d'you manage it, I ask meself, the greatest comeback since Mohammed Ali?'

'Blue eyes,' Beddoes grunted, weary of deception and going off the deskman rapidly. Changing the subject, bowing to impulse, he asked, 'Seen Pol Parrot around? Need to pay me respects.'

'Came in about seven. Been down the hospital with

some little scrubber bombed out on smack. Last I heard, Pol was in the canteen having a cuppa and a sniffle.'

Had a fair line in sniffles himself, did Watson. Snout in the air, silver stripes to the fore and disapproval oozing from every open pore.

'Still at it, then, are yer? Some people *never* learn.'

'Dunno what you mean.'

'The war wound, son. Know *all* about it, I do, ain't much gets past yours truly. Give it a rest, you should. Any day now, the Brass'll get wise and drop you like a hot brick.' The deskman grinned meanly, running a bony hand through greasy brown hair. 'Back on the beat, you'll be; I'll try and see you right.'

Nosy bastard, Watson, and officious with it. Just as well to know where you stand, though. Aloud, Beddoes muttered, 'Cheers, Sarge. Do the same for you, one day.' And limped through dim corridors towards the smell of frying.

She was sitting alone near the window, toying with an empty cup and gazing mistily over the deserted car park. A comely, well-made girl, Pol, even with pink eyes and a rumpled blue tunic.

'Buck up,' he advised, sliding in beside her. 'It might never happen.'

'Oh, Roy, it *will*! Fifty-fifty, the quack says, she's lying in one of those tents like a cabbage. Why do they do it, for God's sake? It's such a waste!'

He took her hand gently. 'Boredom, maybe? Keeping in with the crowd. Look, it's not *your* fault.'

'No? What if I'd got there earlier?' Her free hand twiddled an errant lock of hair; soft, shiny hair.

He edged closer, forgetting the ache in his own thigh as it nestled against hers. 'You did your best, girl, what else is there? Reckon you're needing a bit of TLC. Like someone else I know.'

'TLC?'

'Tender loving care.'

Briefly, her brown gaze warmed, rested on their linked hands. Then she stiffened and her full red lips turned thin. 'Talk about *nerve*! Not a word for weeks, then all over me like the bleedin' measles!'

'Ah, leave off. Duty, same as always.' He gave her his best smile. 'Missed you, girl.'

'Come *on*, Roy! Can't you ever keep your mind on the job?'

He felt his own smile widen, stared pointedly at the ceiling while the double meaning echoed in the empty space. A long pause; pregnant, even.

She giggled, cleared her throat. 'Ahem. I'm sorry, I'll read that again.'

'I did what you said,' he pleaded, pressing the advantage. 'Off the shit-list, right?'

'I dunno. I haven't forgotten the last disaster.'

'That's what I mean – TLC, unfinished business.'

'We-ell, it'll cost you a Chinese nosh and a bottle of plonk.'

'Best offer I've had in months. Pick you up at eight?'

At last she was smiling, albeit moistily. 'Why not?'

'Attagirl!'

He was hobbling away smartish before she could change her mind.

Halfway to the Super's den, caution and reality returned. I'll tell you why not, my son. Because by then we could be holding Huw Evans' wake . . .

Hello, thought Beddoes minutes later as he watched Snow perform, the Funnies are human after all. Showing the strain, this morning; puffy lids behind the gold rims, a shadow of stubble and yesterday's suit looking the worse for overnight wear.

'The negotiators have earned their salt,' he declared, hovering before the window and a backdrop of thinning cloud. 'The PM has conceded an appearance of co-operation; the Opposition, with no enthusiasm whatsoever, will resist the temptation to seek political gains. We spent hours drafting the statement. Shortly you shall judge the extent of our achievement.' He glanced at his watch, inclined his long, unshaven jaw at the silent radio. '*Very* shortly. Take heed of the ambiguities; and a careful note of the timing.'

Leaving them thus suspended, he turned on McKay. 'What news from the mortuary, Hamish?'

'Name of Jewell, Gerry. Addict and erstwhile pop musician.' The Super spoke the last two words scathingly; like blasphemy. 'They recovered three bullets – from an automatic rifle, a machine pistol, and a ·38 handgun.'

'If Evans and the code can be believed,' Snow mused, 'this is the sum total of personnel and armament. Curious. These chaps usually carry a more comprehensive arsenal.'

'They've no need for guns.' McKay manned his desk, compact and fiery as ever. 'They're sitting on a volcano, protected by an alarm we cannae detect.'

Snow paced. Well, *minced*, actually; head thrust forward, chin tucked in, like a large, cream flamingo. 'I hope you're on form Sergeant. We need to be sure of numbers and dispositions. Try that on Evans again, would you?'

He made it sound absurdly simple – pass the marmalade, please. Beddoes was still wracking his brains for wordplay when the eight o'clock news broke in.

'During the early hours, nine convicted terrorists were collected from various prisons and taken to an undisclosed destination near a major airport. The all-night

316

Cabinet meeting ended a few minutes ago. A spokesman issued the following statement: "Formalities are almost complete, as are transport arrangements. At one thirty this afternoon, the Prime Minister will broadcast to the nation and end further speculation." '

McKay made a shushing gesture. Beddoes returned to Reaper frequency and Snow took centre stage once more.

'*Timing*, gentlemen. The assault is scheduled for thirteen hundred hours; a mere thirty minutes before the Reapers expect complete capitulation. By then, they will be drunk on victory, planning their celebrations, imagining what they'll do when they get home. Such is human nature – the moment of lowest alertness and resistance, the ideal psychological instant to strike.' He still sounded much too glib; what makes you think they're human, Mr Snow? It wasn't something you could say, though, so Beddoes didn't.

Time passed. The day broadened, Snow did his patient birdwatcher bit again, and McKay's blunt, hairy fingers drummed on the desktop. Hang in there, Pol, hope your freaked-out cabbage pulls through. *Christ*, uncle, you don't half put a strain on friendship.

But when Evans finally did speak, the tension in his voice galvanized them all. 'Our patience is ended! We demand unconditional agreement by noon! At nine thirty we will begin to return the hostages one by one, at hourly intervals, in the same condition as the first! Leaders of Britain, the next move is *yours*.' Then, quietly and infinitely more effective, the no-nonsense Valleys tone. 'Better pull finger, boyo. I think he means it.'

McKay was on his feet, his hair gleaming redly in sudden sunshine. '*The ideal psychological instant!* You're forgetting who's in charge, man!'

Snow was already speaking crisply into the phone. 'Get me the Home Secretary. *Now!*'

And Beddoes could only watch and wait, while sweat gathered clammily on his forehead and the pain in his leg flared anew . . .

At St Catherine's, the code of the condemned had been unwritten but rigidly observed. You stood outside the headmistress's study with your chin high and your face blank, even though your insides were a quivering mass of jelly. You took your punishment meekly and stoically, and told everyone, 'It wasn't *too* bad, really.'

But this was a far cry from St Cats – a vicious, Irish-Arab variation of musical chairs played out to the strains of 'Housewives' Choice'. When the music stopped, some-one would die. Harriet leaned against the mildewed wall, peering through fly-speckled glass to the sunlit world outside. So near, yet forever beyond reach. Denied a future, unable to bear the present, she let her mind drift back; struggling to recapture the precarious balance it had forged only an hour ago . . .

She had woken late, to an empty upstairs dormitory and a lingering sense of shame. Locking herself in the freshly scrubbed bathroom, standing naked in a couple of inches of cold, rusty water, she'd used most of a precious sliver of soap to scour her body until it glowed raw and pink. A battle for survival, not an act of love, and you won. Even if we *don't* survive, no one can say you didn't try.

Clinging to this chill comfort, wearing her least provoc-ative dress and avoiding Cav's proprietary gaze, she'd endured another soggy, cheerless breakfast. And the hope which flickered, cruel and brief, at the first item on the eight o'clock news. Pete and the band took it at face value; another noisy outburst of misguided joy. Salim's dark-faced fury had nipped it in the bud.

'*Talk*!' he raged. 'Talk is all they do. It is not enough! Watch our guests, Mr Duffy. Mr Cavanaugh, we must consult.'

Pete subsided, distraught. The band fell to low-voiced squabbles over the last bottle of vodka. Only Harry Two and the policeman stayed at the table, munching pork pie stolidly. Harriet had never seen the Welshman eat before. He did it without pleasure, almost as if he wanted to keep his strength up.

An unlikely alliance, she thought distractedly, the gorgeous extrovert black man and the craven creature in blue. She sniffed cautiously, noting the absence of foulness and the heavy waft of Old Spice. Harry Two had saved him, then, brought him in from the cold.

The respite was short-lived. Cav hustled the policeman to the radio and shoved the handwritten bulletin under his nose. 'Now, me perfumed bluebottle, let's see how your friends like *this*!'

And Harriet had listened in horror to the latest threat, delivered in a hard Welsh monotone . . .

While an ageing pop-star filled the charged air with gooey messages and yesteryear's hits, Harriet's attention came reluctantly back to Salim. The exercise of power had obviously soothed him. He sat, relaxed and immaculate, his polished tan leather shoes glistening in the sun. Even the despised smell of pork failed to dent his composure.

But his eyes were never still; dark and deadly, flickering from one hostage to the next; measuring, assessing, choosing. She turned away, suppressing a shudder of despair.

Music intruded, familiar and poignant. Lionel Ritchie, 'Stuck on You'. Foolishly, she surrendered to it, drifting

319

back over two short years to a Christmas party at home. Her father, big and assured, smelling of cologne and brandy, teaching her the basic quickstep. 'Two, three, together. *That's* it; easy, isn't it?' Warmth and comfort, her mother's face glowing with pride, and her first long dress flickering brightly. Oh, Harry, *why* did you let it all go?

Fade-out; of the creamy voice, the comforting memory and the futile dream. Salim was stirring, tapping his watch and calling time. *Dead* time. '*Now*, Mr Cavanaugh; who shall be first?'

Cav prowled the sunlit boards, counting the arguments on hard, splayed fingers. 'We'll be needing the fuzz a while longer, and Miss Harriet has her uses.' The beard split, the teeth gleamed evilly at Harry Two. 'Sambo here vexes me; 'twould be a pity to let him off so light.' He gestured scornfully at the band. '*These* hopheads wouldn't know the difference. Let's see; who's left?' He struck a pose, wrinkling his brow and cupping his chin, a vicious parody of 'The Thinker'. And Pete went to his knees, his slim guitarist's fingers clawed towards Salim in total supplication. 'No, *please*!'

'Y'Allah, where is your pride? Be a *man*, just once before you die!' The pistol had appeared like magic; cold and lethal as Salim's voice. As Harriet cowered and Pete sobbed, the disc-jockey spoke excitedly. 'We interrupt this programme to bring you a newsflash. Are you listening, Green Reapers? The Prime Minister has pledged to speak one hour earlier! Stay tuned, folks. The PM will broadcast at twelve thirty, this very same spot on the dial! Now, for Mrs Elsie Rowbotham of Macclesfield, from her loving sister, Flo . . .'

'I said *noon*!' Salim hissed, easing the safety off.

Yet again, Joe intervened. ''Tis a major concession,

comrade. Why risk a great victory for thirty short minutes? A matter of face, ye understand – we have to leave
them that.'

Briefly, Arab contempt included the anxious Irishman.
Then the safety-catch snicked again, and the brown shoe
lashed at Pete's prostrate form. 'Get up, you weeping
woman! For the moment, you shall live. We, too, attach
great value to face.' He turned to the policeman. 'Call
your people, tell them we agree. But no more delays.'

The music ceased abruptly.

The Welshman obeyed, terse and to the point, and
Harriet's body sagged in relief. Too soon. Even as reprieve
was granted, the policeman began his awful wheedling
again. 'The final day of the Test, Mr Salim, sir, we never
got the close of play last night. Ask, then, can I?'

This time, astonishingly, *Cav* spoke in support. 'Sure,
and why not? 'Tis a powerful interest I'm developing,
myself.'

Salim shrugged and spread neat hands, a very oriental
gesture. Crazy white men, he was saying wordlessly, no
wonder they are losing.

The policeman shot Cav a wary glance and busied
himself at the dials. Presently, he won a response, and
the whole boring, trivial chatter began again. At least,
Harriet would have been bored, were it not for Harry
Two's posture. He was wearing a bright blue gown today.
He sat erect and tense as a bowstring, his eyes glued to
the radio. Listen, my girl, it must be important.

'Still batting, are they?' the Constable asked, as if it
really mattered. 'Still calling the shots?'

The reply came back in cool cockney. 'They declared;
it's down to us now. It's dodgy, though. They got the
boundary all sewn up.'

'Only one thing left, then. A distraction, pull 'em in

close to the bat, hit out over the top. If they can't do that, they'll have to rebuild – from basement up.'

The distant Eastender voice sounded dubious. 'Easy, innit, on the sidelines. From where *we* sit, they've got all openings covered.'

'What's left to lose, mun? Long as they get the *timing* right.'

There was a long, crackling pause. Then, 'Last day, remember, an hour earlier to lunch. We're still bothered by field placings, know what I mean?'

Cav was prowling, bearded and intent. Eyeing him apprehensively, the policeman muttered, 'Trust the batsman, boyo, it's a funny old game. If you hurry the release, we might just be there for the finish. Over and out.' He leaned back, flushed and breathless as a man finishing a hard race.

More gobbledegook, thought Harriet bitterly, how can anyone take it seriously?

Cav supplied an answer, standing wide-legged and pointing an accusing finger. 'He's up to something, Salim. All this blather and he never asked the score!'

The policeman blanched and Harry Two chimed in. 'He don't *want* no score, marn. Honkies *losing*, right?'

'Cocky bastard,' growled the policeman. 'There's many a slip, mind.' He glowered at the negro, pale-eyed and truculent. Not much of an act, Harriet reckoned, and Cav dismissed it scornfully.

'Now here's a strange sight, these deadly rivals by the light of day. Whereas upstairs in the dark they're canoodling like a pair of moonstruck queers!' A blur of movement, and sunlight flashing from the bared blade. 'What d'you say, comrade? Should we pry the truth free, meanwhile?'

Salim lounged comfortably in his chair, his sallow features creased in amusement. 'Be easy, my Irish brother. Let me tell you why their childish games must fail, why you in the West will *never* stay the might of Islam.' He stood and strolled to the window, a small grey figure who commanded total attention.

He's *evil*, Harriet thought, why can't I take my eyes off him?

He stood in profile, hawkfaced and implacable. His arm came up in a gesture at once elegant and contemptuous. 'Out there is what you call freedom. Free trade, free speech, a free press. Every day, your secrets are revealed and your strength is sapped; and you applaud the foolish laws and the greedy men who allow it to happen.' His tone hardened, and the anger darkened his cheek. 'Some years ago, a band of bungling, backward Iranians attempted a mission like ours. After their miserable failure, your wonderful free press told all the world the details – even the strategies of your police and defence forces. Do you think we are so stupid that we cannot read and learn? Do you not see that your womanly notions of Christian charity and freedom must deliver you unto your enemies? Make no mistake. *We* are your enemies, and we have learned!' He swung to face them, the pistol glinting in his hand. 'We are neither amateurs nor women. We are not afraid to suppress our enemies by force, to purge ourselves of weakness, to kill for our beliefs. And we are not afraid to die!'

The hard edge of hatred once more, raising the small hairs at Harriet's nape; and, as before, Salim controlled it quickly. 'We *know* your leaders will accept one death in every siege, before they release the troops. The Iranians taught us this; may Allah revere their names. We *know* your leaders will bend and wriggle and finally submit, rather than allow one worthless addict to perish.' He turned to Cav, a gentle smile more terrifying than any rhetoric. 'We are safe, Mr Cavanaugh; we have killed but once. Even if they should gain courage and deploy the Army, we have alarms to warn us and a final, fiery response in the cellar below. Triumph or martyrdom, what does it matter? *We have nothing to fear.*'

How foolish you were, Harriet, to trust a comic drummer and shabby policeman; to whisper wishful plans in the dark, to rut with an Irish murderer. She bowed her head, watching her own tears shimmer and fall and make dark starbursts in the dust. *This* is why you are compelled: because he reveals his intentions in broad daylight, because he has the power and the will to make them work!

Snow moved slowly and spoke slowly, scanning the notes he'd made. 'I think Evans is saying the bomb is below ground level; it's safe to create a distraction upstairs. Which fits the classic SAS assault pattern. "Pull them in" he said. "Trust the batsman". Batsmen are people who are *in*.' He glanced up, his dark, bloodshot eyes gleaming with satisfaction; like a man who'd just solved a tricky crossword puzzle. 'He has something in mind, something to keep the Reapers away from the windows – the *boundary* – while the approach is made. Sergeant?'

'Sounds about right to me.' Beddoes muttered; but honesty prompted a reluctant rider. 'He's under pressure, mind you. Signed off a bit sharpish, at the end.'

'You're grasping at straws,' rasped McKay, 'believing what you *want* to believe! What of the alarm, and those radio-operated devices?'

Snow rose to his full height. Despite the crumpled cream suit and the daft spectacles, his posture and voice took on a soldierly caste. The General, Beddoes remembered, preparing to commit the troops and count the dead. 'It's crunch time, Hamish. We've done what we can, inside and out. Further discussion is not only futile, but detrimental to morale. The priorities remain unaltered – isolate the site, contain the violence – *and let no terrorist escape alive!* From now on, the hostages are forfeit. Anyone saved must be counted as a bonus.' Meeting McKay's anguished blue gaze, he made a small concession: 'You heard the Inspector, Hamish. He *begged* us to go in!'

Snow picked up the phone. From across the room, Beddoes heard the ringing tone, abruptly cut off. 'Major? Yes, and good morning to you. There has been a change in the timing; you go in at noon. I beg your pardon?' The silver eyebrows lifted, the bony face twisted in almost comic surprise. 'My dear chap, of course we must observe protocol. It is indeed the Superintendent's jurisdiction. Here he is now.' Snow held the receiver at arm's length.

McKay took it gingerly, as if it might explode in his hand. 'Do it, laddie,' he snapped, 'and for Chrissake do it right!'

Suddenly, Cavanaugh's rifle was much in evidence; he was never far from the window. A primitive, see, reared in a climate of suspicion and not too much faith in Islam or hi-tech. No way to escape his alertness, to compare notes with Harrigan. Just have to hope he's got the message, will adjust the plan to a noon deadline. *Plan*, there's pompous! A gamble, more like, based on cricket backchat, Irish macho and an outworn Arab custom. Don't knock it, bach, it's all we've got. As the minutes ticked past, Joe took to nervous pacing and the band polished off the last of the vodka. And Evans edged nearer the fusebox, adopting a low profile and a cowed expression.

He was perfectly placed when Harrigan made his

move. Eleven thirty on the dot — a bit bloody previous! One moment, the black man was meandering casually across the room; the next, he'd swooped on Harriet Slade.

His mouth crushed hers, one large black paw lifted her dress and crawled brazenly up her pale exposed thigh.

Her eyes almost violet in outrage, she thrust him fiercely away. 'Pig!' she hissed. 'Get your filthy hands off me!'

And Cavanaugh rose to the bait, closing in two long feline strides, the rifle aimed from the hip. 'I *warned* ye, Sambo!'

Harrigan whirled to meet him, white teeth bared in a ferocious snarl. 'Come on, Irish, try it without the gun.'

'Enough!' Salim's cold authority sliced through swirling dust motes and froze them in their tracks. His pistol covered the gap between, his scorn embraced them both. 'Control yourself, ape! You, Mr Cavanaugh, are paid to defend Holy Islam, not brawl over a harlot!'

'You sought my choice, Salim. Seems like Sambo volunteered!'

'That's right. Let's have some *real* amusement, marn.'

Pete was on his feet, eyeing the negro with a kind of savage joy. 'Let him do it, Mr Salim!' The band, waking at last to the implications, seeing temporary salvation in the clash, set up a feverish playground chant. 'Fight, fight, *fight*!' Even the girl joined in, her pretty face distorted by lustful fury. The place was a cockpit of seething emotion; distraction, duw duw.

Groping behind his back for the fuses, Evans saw pleasure flare in Salim's black eyes. Done it again, he had; reduced them all to slavering beasts. And now proceeded to deny them with cool human logic. 'Beware that Irish temper, Mr Cavanaugh. I cannot afford to risk you now.'

The girl flushed in sudden shame, turning on the band reproachfully. 'How *could* you! Oh, Pete!' The tension eased, the throb of conflict faded. Then Harrigan tried the last desperate throw, the one they'd agreed last night.

'You're all *talk*, Mr Arab. Back to the old ways, you say, when men stood toe to toe for the right to bed a woman. And what happens?' Harrigan's voice rose, an accurate, falsetto imitation of Salim's clipped speech. '*Too much of a risk!* What risk, marn? Cav got his knife, you holding a gun and you-all still *scared* of little ole Harry Two!'

'For heaven's sake,' breathed the Slade child, as Evans' fingers curled around an unseen fuse, 'I don't give a damn for either of you!'

'Be still, girl! It has become an affair of male honour.' Salim's eyes blazed icily at Harry Two. 'So be it, West Indian; you shall have your wish.' He beckoned peremptorily with the pistol.

'Clear a space, here in the sunlight. Make way for the warriors! Take the rifle, Mr Duffy. *Now*, Mr Cavanaugh; show this fool the force of cold steel!'

Cavanaugh took the classic knife-artist's stance, lightly poised on the balls of his feet, the blade gleaming in his right hand, the left hand extended close beside it. In a blur of electric blue, Harrigan whipped off his gown and flourished it like a matador's cape. Once more they were the focus of every eye. Almost.

Risking a downward glance, Evans eased the two shiny fuses out, slipped them into his pocket and leaned gently backwards to close the metal door. Eleven forty-three and the alarm silenced; could Harrigan hold out long enough? It doesn't matter, he realized sickly. The doctored gadget is still in Cavanaugh's pocket – and Salim has a live one!

He had reckoned without Harrigan's fluid body and

acute mind. The ebony muscles rippled; a feint, a sway to the left. As Cavanaugh thrust forward, he stepped inside, his fingers clawing at the Irishman's hip. *Christ, he's taking chances,* Evans thought, ignoring the opening and clinging to the plan. And the thick Arab hadn't even noticed! Breathless, he watched Harrigan repeat the sequence, barely avoiding the knife and *deliberately* missing the grab for Cavanaugh's pocket.

'*Wait!*' Again, Salim's command checked them; again, his levelled pistol held them still. 'A bold attempt, West Indian, and one you will surely live to regret. But not for long!' He was smiling, cruel and superior, like a chess-master sure of mate in two moves. 'Give me the device, Mr Cavanaugh, before it is stolen away.' Cavanaugh obeyed, and Evans felt a faint flicker of hope. The Arab raised Cav's defanged plastic box aloft, and sunlight glinted from the slowly drawn antenna. 'See, comrades; it is ready for use, and I am ready to use it! Proceed!'

Salim stepped back, and the two men circled warily. Shuffling feet on creaking boards, the sheen of sweat on bared black skin, the harsh hot breath of combat. Straightening, edging out of his dim corner, Evans kept one eye on Joe's rifle and the other on the agonizingly slow trickle of seconds.

Cavanaugh attacked, the broad blade flaring and hiss-ing in two wide, lightning strikes. Rend and flutter, and Harrigan's blue protection ribboned uselessly down. *He's done for,* thought Evans, *and still five minutes to go!*

The Irishman lunged, poised and smooth, too fast for the eye to follow; and drew back, grinning.

'There, me little tarbaby; how d'you like Cav's lovebite?'

Evans caught his breath, watching scarlet well and trickle from a thin gash the whole width of Harrigan's chest. The big man faltered. One hand rose, groped among the redness. His knees buckled and he slumped to the boards, staring up with wide white eyes at the shimmer of steel above him.

'*No*, Cav!' screamed the girl; but Cavanaugh was watching Salim.

The black gaze was pitiless, the neat grey-clad shoulders rose and fell casually. 'We need no more amusement. Finish it, comrade.'

The knife rose, steadied, plunged. And Harrigan catapulted upwards, smashing his curly head into Cavanaugh's exposed midriff. The blade spun free. Cavanaugh lurched backwards, doubling over; and Harrigan went after him, quick and lethal and bloody as a gutshot panther.

But only as far as the levelled barrel of Joe's rifle.

'Enough, ye black bastard!' Ashen with fury, Joe scooped up the knife and brandished its reddened edge. 'One more step and I'll do the job myself!'

'No need, Mr Duffy!' Salim's voice, calm and assured as ever. He stepped into the sunlight, a slender brown finger poised on the destruct button. 'We are within sight of victory; and a blink away from oblivion!' Then, as Harrigan relaxed and turned away, while Cavanaugh wheezed like a grampus and the minute hand on Evans' watch inched towards noon, mocking Arab laughter filled the room. 'Tend his wound, whore. You have won the nigger!'

The explosion erupted directly overhead; deafening, stunning in its violence, fouling the air with dust and dirty flakes of ceiling plaster. There was a huge black shadow at the window, and a muffled, metallic voice. 'Hostages, get down! Take cover!'

For Evans, crouched and prepared as he was, the succeeding events seemed to happen in slow motion.

He was watching Salim: who else? Seeing, for the first

time, a range of human emotion in the harsh, sallow face. Sheer incredulity, followed by a snarl of comprehension and the dark bloom of rage. Then, as the hand flew up and a manicured finger squeezed down on the button, a smile of serene expectation and almost sexual ecstasy.

The window shattered inward. A green, lemon-shaped object struck the floor, hissing gently, bobbling over bright shards of glass. Salim was screaming insanely now, Joe's name and gouts of Arabic abuse. Through thickening, choking fumes, Evans actually saw the baby-faced Irishman shepherding Cav's hunched form towards the stairwell. The tirade stopped. The indistinct grey figure stiffened, raising and aiming the pistol. Dimly, Evans made out the girl, standing upright, tranced and immobile; her hands covering her ears, her face blank and bloodless. *Standing in Salim's gunsight!* He thrust away from the wall, unable to breathe, moving too slowly and too late.

Closer, but not close enough, he saw the familiar viperish gleam in mad black eyes, the tightening pallor in the trigger finger; and bawled his own futile protest into the wailing chaos.

He launched himself in a desperate flying tackle at Salim's shoulders. In mid-air, he heard the shot; and in the very same instant, glimpsed a black, bloodstained figure rise from nowhere full into the blinding muzzle-flare. Impact, solid and jarring. Somewhere near by, a stricken groan and an ominous, sodden tumble. Then he was down, smelling fetid dust and hair-oil, feeling Salim's frantic yet strangely feeble resistance beneath. He jack-knifed savagely, smashing his knees into Salim's kidneys, clawing his fingers under the pointed chin and heaving upward with all his might. And sensing that the smallest extra pressure would snap the neck.

Not slow motion, now. The moment of truth, a brief vacuum in time. His vision was going, the gas chewed at his lungs. A last, fleeting scruple, the coppers' code recalled: *We catch 'em, they cook 'em.* He flexed his shoulders, remembering Gerry's murder, the awful reek of shit and that unholy, ecstatic welcome for fiery death. It's what he *wants*, bach, who are you to deny him?

Coldly, in full knowledge, Huw Evans set his grip and threw his whole weight backwards. Heard the crack, felt the convulsive shudder; and rejoiced.

He was wrenched aside, flung bodily across the boards. Twisting, he looked up at a vast black-hooded figure, heard the weird Darth Vader command. 'Jenkins? Get your head down, man!' He rolled over, blocking his ears; and felt it through the boards, a tattoo of automatic fire blasting flesh and wood.

'How many more? Quick man!'

'Two.'

'Where?'

Evans waved weakly at the stairs. More shots, the drum of boots, another explosion upstairs. The alien voice again, ringing above the confusion. 'Number off, Dragons, Mag check, Mag check!' And an echo which seemed to be everywhere at once.

Darro, he marvelled, have they emptied their magazines already?

More hard hands, hauling him up, shoving him towards the front of the house. 'Get out, get some air!'

He stumbled, blind and retching, crunching glass underfoot, out of the smoke and the blood and the dying, into brightness beyond. Another vast dark storm-trooper grabbed him, trussing his hands, easing him on to what felt like a rough blanket. 'Yer made it, Jenkins, you done real good!'

Outside, alive and free; a sense of weakness and

331

unbelief, no thought for anyone else. Warm sunshine and the smell of hospital. Beside him, someone was shouting. '*Kill* the fuckers, kill them all!' Pete, by the sound. Hard to blame him, mind. A man in a check shirt passed, peering into shell-shocked faces, making notes on a clipboard. I've killed a man, Evans thought, and I'm bloody glad.

Vision cleared slowly. Large black boots beside his head, and the weird voice again. 'All hostages accounted for, sir.'

Course it's weird, stupid – muffled by the gasmask. And *Christ*, we all got out! Gentler fingers loosened his bonds, helped him up. 'Thanks,' he mumbled inadequately. 'Ta very much.'

'All in a day's work, mate.'

Evans bent, coughing at the fire in his lungs, peering through a veil of tears. Off to one side by a tumble of masonry, McKay was snarling at a uniformed officer. 'I don't care how many you havnae found, you'll not send squaddies on a rampage through *my* manor!'

A smart salute, a respectful, cultured reply. 'Very good, sir. From now on, it's your show.'

'My compliments, Major. Tell your men the first wee dram's on me, the night.'

'Gratefully accepted, sir. Form up, Dragons. By the left, quick-march!'

They plodded away, disciplined space-invaders in mid-night black, leaving only an eddy of dust and a feeling of order, returning.

Evans took another step and coughed some more. Beside him, Pete was going bananas, whooping his news to the cloudless sky. 'It's a girl, by God, and Peg's doin' fine!' Somehow, he'd found young Harriet – dazed but intact – and was waltzing her round like a lanky dervish. 'Kiss me, Harry, I'm a dad!'

'Oh Pete, I'm so pleased!' She checked in mid-swing, her pretty face suddenly haunted and aged. 'Go ahead, Pete. Be with you in a minute.'

'Tonight at the Sombrero,' he bawled. 'Shampers and cigars all round!'

Evans saw the slump of her shoulders, the swim of her cornflower eyes. Watched in all-at-once dread as she moved fearfully towards the single stretcher that lay in the stark white dust. She crumpled, rather than knelt, easing back the bloodstained grey blanket. Her head drooped, dark hair swinging down to veil her stricken pallor. He was already moving forward as she took the limp black hand gently in her own and sobbed her grief into Harrigan's lifeless, strangely peaceful face.

'His name was Sergeant Harrigan,' he told her gruffly. 'He was an undercover policeman. Don't forget when they ask.'

'*Forget*?' she whispered. 'How could I ever forget? It should be *me* lying here.' She glanced up, blindly and moistly. 'Pete's a father, and Harry Two's dead. Why is life so unfair?'

He couldn't answer, didn't know himself. 'Go on, you,' he urged. 'I'll stay with him. A colleague, see.'

A colleague who became a friend, he thought, as an ambulanceman gentled her away. A friend in need, the only ones that matter. A brave man, Harrigan, who thought fast and moved fast and smiled when the night was darkest. And died to save a precocious kid. Somewhere in the Caribbean, there's rum he'll never drink, music he'll never hear and honey velvet skin he never *will* get to love. All because of a smooth little maniac and an overdose of bloody religion! Unfair? You don't know the half of it, girl.

Someone was nudging him on, swathing *him* in a

blanket. Course they are; you're Jenkins, no one's supposed to know. Not that it matters a damn. They've got their hero, a real one. And posthumous, as usual.

Jane, he thought. Give me a bath, a beer, a bit of peace and quiet – and Jane. Not necessarily in that order.

Stumbling, weeping inside, he glanced up and saw Roy Beddoes. Large as life, a bit of a limp and a grin to sell toothpaste. Control deserted him, he quivered on the verge of total and public breakdown; about to sag and sob in the friendliest arms he'd seen for days.

And Roy saved him; drawing back, his sharp nose wrinkling in disgust. 'Jesus, uncle, where you been? Smells like plum-duff in a cesspit!'

CHAPTER EIGHTEEN

Harriet trudged towards the outer cordon, where a small but enthusiastic crowd had already gathered. Proper policemen at last; smart blue uniforms, scrubbed faces, silver buttons winking in the sun. Beyond them, a sea of smiles, waves of warmth and sympathy to lift her troubled heart. Sorry, Sergeant Harrigan, the mourning must wait. I'm just so *happy* to be out!

Until she saw the band. Strutting about, grasping offered hands like American politicians, preening in unearned and undeserved limelight. How callow they are, she thought, how easily transformed from cowering despair to boastful triumph.

There was a woman among them, slim, with red hair, in a fawn safari suit; notebook and pencil to the fore. A reporter. Standing aloof, Harriet felt a flicker of envy and the stirrings of a sudden, hitherto unconsidered ambition.

You have a story to tell, my girl. A story of courage and love and sacrifice played out beneath the cold eyes of death and religious fanaticism. The mystery girl who became a woman overnight, and used her wiles to fashion the amazing escape. Talk to the press, Harry. Smile for the cameras, write the book, become rich and famous. And *poised*, like her. Daddy will welcome his prodigal daughter, the upper fifth will be *green* with jealousy. She waved a first-aid man away. Mine are inner wounds, the kind you can't staunch with bandages. She wandered on, immersed in the vision, proud of her newfound maturity and restraint.

'Hello, I'm Jane Neale, freelance. Could we try a few questions?' The voice was soft and beguiling. At close quarters, she was disgustingly glamorous. Conscious of her own dowdiness, Harriet resorted to status and her snootiest St Cats diction. 'Harriet Slade. Daddy's a broker.'

'Really?' The green eyes twinkled. 'And what's a girl like you doing in a place like this?'

'Oh, I was Gerry Jewell's lover — before he took to drugs.'

'The boy who was murdered? How awful!'

An image of the dead, distorted face flashed in Harriet's mind. She swallowed, managing a sophisticated drawl. 'It *was*, rather. But the survivors suffered far worse. Myself and the policeman, for instance.'

'The policeman?'

'He shot him!' Harriet blurted. 'Salim was trying to kill me, and he threw himself between us! It was the bravest thing I've ever seen!' Struggling for control, she was vaguely aware of the open notebook shuddering in unsteady hands.

'But . . . I thought I saw him come out?'

'He was a drummer,' explained Harriet. 'At least, that's what we *thought*. Actually, he was plain clothes, or something.'

'Jenkins,' whispered the reporter; beseeched, in fact. 'What happened to Constable Jenkins?'

'Oh, *he's* all right. I'm talking about Harry Two.' She pointed. In the dusty, shimmering distance, the grey-shrouded stretcher was disappearing into an ambulance. She lost the battle. Tears blurred her vision once more. 'He kissed me once, and died to set me free!'

Jane Neale's eyes looked misty, too; with heartfelt relief. She held out her arms. 'You poor child!'

'I'm *not* a child!'

But Harriet's dream was fading, as doomed and ephemeral as the one which had drawn her to Gerry in the first place. She could never, ever be like this elegant woman whose subtle fragrance and welcoming embrace reminded her of the mother she hated – and missed – so much. She surrendered, leaning against the soft body, sobbing like the frightened schoolgirl she still was.

The reporter stiffened. Harriet heard a rasping Scottish challenge. 'Well, Miss Neale. What are *you* doing here?'

Lifting her head, squinting into brightness, Harriet made out craggy features and the chequered capband of high rank.

'We have our sources, Superintendent. *We* also had a deal.'

A scuffle of highly polished black shoes, an embarrassed unfriendly growl. 'The Irish broke out. No one knows how – they just vanished. *There's* your scoop, Miss Neale, and the bargain completed. You'd best be on your way, before the rest of the ratpack arrives.'

Harriet was shivering, close to nausea. The bearded ravisher loose, and no place to hide. Terror cleared her brain, ushering her back to the bare and bilious cellar. Salim, leading Gerry to sudden death upstairs; Cav's hard, urgent hand shoving her along; and a cold, smelly draught at her ankles!

'Superintendent!' she cried. 'Check the basement – behind a pile of boxes in the far corner.'

The uniformed figure started, turned, demanded an explanation.

Haltingly, all pretensions abandoned, Harriet told him. Of the inexplicable move upstairs, of music cases and bumps in the night, of Cav's violent response to moon-light snooping.

'The sappers are in there now,' he breathed. 'As well *someone* kept their wits about them! Good for you, lassie.' His hard blue gaze flickered over her, taking in the dirt and distress. 'You'll have to come with me. Tea, a shower and a full statement, right?'

Why not, she thought hopelessly. There's nowhere else to go.

Jane Neale was gazing at the drab, derelict, *ordinary* house. The sun struck copper highlights from her hair, her expression looked sombre and haunted. 'Leads to be followed,' she murmured, 'dangers to be faced. The full story yet to be told. God, will it *never* end?' She seemed to wake, tender and sympathetic again. 'Is there any-thing I can do for you, child?'

Fresh linen, thought Harriet, a room of my own and someone who *really* cares. 'Please,' she whispered. '*Please* tell my dad to come!'

'Darro,' groaned Evans, his pale tired eyes feasting on everyday hustle beyond the windscreen. 'I'm dying for a pint!'

'Sorry,' Beddoes told him, meaning it. 'No way they'd let us in, what with the pong. Do us a favour – open the window?'

'Watch it, boyo, or I'll tell you how it happened.'

'Don't bother, been there myself. In the shit, like.' He couldn't help it, it had become a reflex. The left hand sliding off the steering-wheel and touching the scar.

Evans noticed, naturally. He wasn't that knackered. 'Missed your bit, I did, never heard the story.'

So Beddoes relived the Dublin disaster, driving slowly and playing it light, trying to raise a smile. Didn't quite come off, actually, he could *hear* his own self-disgust. 'By

338

the by,' he added softly, 'little bird told me how I got back on the team. Thanks.' A pause. Engine noise and diesel fumes swirled in, the plastic felt clammy in his hands.

'Looking out for number one, I was,' Evans confessed, 'needing a friend in court. Bit leery of Funnies, by then.'

'You gotta hand it to them, uncle. O'Brien came up with the goods on the Paddies — got it from your mate Daly, he said — Snow was as good as gold. Crosstalk came in handy, too.'

'Cricket,' Evans growled. 'Never thought I'd have to stand on cricket. Never live it down, in the Valleys. Take me home, Roy. Someone there I'm anxious to see.'

Beddoes licked dry lips, eased the accelerator floorward. Need a bit of pace for this bit, my son, or he'll hit the eject switch and go clean through the roof.

'Had to move her on, didn't I.' He shot the hunched, glowering figure a conciliatory glance. 'She's *press*, for Chrissake, and you on a "most secret". How d'you think it would go down, with Snow?' From the corner of his eye, Beddoes saw rage infuse the sandy, dust-flecked stubble.

'I've been a week under Irish artillery and three days eating Arab dung. D'you think I give a fuck what anyone thinks?' The safety belt slithered and creaked, a bunched fist cracked into a cupped and grimy palm. 'Life's too short, believe me; *my* life. Keep your nose *out* of it, okay?'

'Easy, uncle. Only watching your back.'

A longer, tighter pause, a weary sigh.

'Take me there anyway, I can always phone. Be all right, after.'

'Sorry again, you're wanted at the nick. The Paddies did a Houdini: missing, presumed alive.'

Waiting at the last set of lights, Beddoes risked another sidelong glance. Evans had slumped backwards, eyes closed, face clawed with fatigue and defeat. 'Square one,' he muttered. 'All *that*, and Reapers *still* loose.'

He'd revived somewhat by the time they got in, finding a crooked grin for nosy Watson and an obscene rebuke for a couple of lounging, goggling beat men. Mid-afternoon and quiet; at least he had the locker room to himself. Beddoes laid out the well-worn sportscoat and baggy slacks. 'And plainer clothes,' he breathed, quoting a hoary enforcers' joke, 'would be *very* hard to find.'

A spark lit, somewhere behind strained, pained eyes. 'Piss off, Roy. You gotta date, I can *smell* it on you.'

Beddoes grinned, tapped the side of his nose. 'Don't talk smell to me, mate.' And ducked out, chuckling, as the rolled-up tunic smacked against the wall beside his head.

He paced the quiet corridors with only a trace of a limp. A survivor, old Huw. Give him twenty-four hours and the redhead, he'll be ready to hunt again. Meanwhile, Beddoes was out for game himself. A Chinese Parrot, and the old six-shooter fully primed . . .

If shaving was a necessary ordeal, hot soapy water felt like sheer luxury; sluicing away grime, soothing the humiliation.

Not the grief, though, nor the enduring rage. Towelling vigorously, pulling on clothes as familiar and welcome as old mates, Evans pledged Cav a reckoning and Harrigan a vengeance. And may Salim rot in some foul, Islamic hell.

Trudging the corridors, he ignored quizzical glances and drank in the comforting aura of routine. Which faded the instant he set foot inside the big office. A fervent, wordless handshake from McKay, a nod of regal approval from Snow; and urgent advice from the Identi-kit man. 'Concentrate, please, Inspector. Every moment is vital.'

He got Joe in two minutes flat, had trouble with the shade and shape of Cavanaugh's beard. Slumping into a chair, shuffling celluloid, struggling to sharpen the image in his weary brain, he heard Snow's version of the Great Escape.

'They were either very lucky or very thorough. The main sewer runs under the basement, only a couple of feet down. According to Miss Slade, they tunnelled into it before you arrived, had their bolt-hole prepared in advance.'

'The Dirty Protest,' breathed Evans, without looking up. 'Trapped, are they, suffocating somewhere down there?'

'No chance.' McKay sounded angry, and very certain. 'It's a maze, laddie, and manholes in every street. They're out by now, for sure, and no one any the wiser. Irish, y'see. Who's going to question a couple of stinking navvies? Bloody *nerve*!'

'Oh sure. Learned it from Daly, I expect.' Satisfied, he shoved the likeness across the desk. 'That's Cav, to the life.'

The Identikit man nodded, did a quick cut'n'paste, and scurried out. Lucky dab.

Snow seemed to catch the thought. 'Bear with us. There are other issues outstanding. For instance did you detect any link between Daly and the Reapers?'

'No. Irish mercenaries, Salim called them.' Glancing up, Evans saw sudden tension in the long, cream-clad frame.

'Are you *sure*?'

Again, he had to trawl his clouded memory for the precise wording. ' "Paid to defend holy Islam," he said.'

Looking a bit second-hand, Snow, uncharacteristically rumpled and bewhiskered. As Evans watched, the dark eyes took on that predatory gleam, the one they'd worn for the Smythe hunt. 'Paid *when*, Inspector, and by whom? Don't you see, man? If you're in it for money, you have to live to collect!'

Suddenly, Snow was moving, long strides over coiled electric leads. 'The Irish *always* planned to escape. To slip away on the last night, probably. Duffy wasn't afraid to push the button. He was afraid Salim might – and discover he'd been deceived! I doubt if the radio-control system was ever fully primed!'

'Hold on,' mumbled Evans. 'What are you saying?' His brain faltered, shying away from an awful possibility. He could hear the sickness in his own voice. 'You mean – we didn't *have* to pimp for Cavanaugh, scotch the battery, work a switch on Salim? Christ, mun, you're saying Harrigan fought and died for nothing!'

'*Rubbish!*' McKay was leaning over the desk, low sunlight blazing from his bristles, his eyes bright with disgust. 'It's pure conjecture, something only the sappers might know; if they ever try! The distraction was crucial, ye *had* to defuse the alarm! You did right, Huw!' He rounded on Snow furiously. '*You* tell him, dammit!'

Funny pride at stake, mind. The thin nose lifted, the half-moons glinted meanly. Then, a tone of grudging apology. 'Of course he was right, Hamish. I was merely exploring certain . . . interesting avenues. *Intellectually*, I mean.' His honour thus appeased, Snow returned to business. And Evans. 'Tell me, Inspector; did you manage to talk to Harrigan? Any clues as to the identity of Smythe's mole?'

'There wasn't much time for chat. And it's a bit late, now.'

Again, McKay came to the rescue, the burr unusually soft. 'Get it off your chest, laddie. Slowly, from the start.'

He didn't intend to, it just sort of tumbled out. After a while he steadied, keeping it tight, sparing himself nothing. The gin-soaked knock-out, the smearing of shit, squalid, moonlit humping; fumbled fuses, the engineered confrontation, the deliberate destruction of Salim. And came, at last, to the solid, central figure. 'It's down to Harrigan, see. I thought about it, he *did* it.' He met Snow's bland stare contemptuously. 'You can forget Jenkins and cover. You've got your gentle, parfait knight: a black one. Pity he won't be around for the medal.'

And still Snow wouldn't unbend. 'You mentioned a plan, Inspector. Explain please.'

So he told them that, too. The challenge to Cavanaugh's sexual pride, the reliance on Salim's code of combat, the need to exchange control boxes and leave the dud in Arab hands.

'Madness,' he confessed, at the end. 'You don't have to say it. Acts of faith, not reason. What else did we have?'

'Aye, but it *worked*!' McKay's admiration was unconcealed and unstinted. 'One more thing, Huw. *Bullets* killed Salim, fired legitimately in the course of approved military operations. The post-mortem will say it, records will confirm it. It might even be true.'

'Oh sure. Thanks.' For nothing, Evans thought. Can post-mortems and records bring Harrigan back?

Outside, the sun was sinking, the streets had emptied. Snow took top-dog post at the window and delivered what probably passed for an accolade in Funnyland. 'You kept your head, Inspector, in difficult circumstances. No one can do more.'

Another glint of fading light on gold rims, a subtle girding of well-tailored, off-white loins. 'Much remains to be done. Gathering loose ends, tidying the stables, securing the renegades. They're doubly dangerous now, and doubly valuable. Men who held *us* to ransom, and escaped. They must be taken!' He leaned forward, put the question softly. 'Are you still capable?'

'I'll nail Cavanaugh or die trying!'

'Aye, you very well might!' growled McKay, and launched a general appeal. 'The City's cordoned off, all exit routes under blanket surveillance. We have pictures, time, and the entire force itching to lay hands on them. Give it a rest, you've *done* your bit.'

But Snow was watching Evans alone, expectant and unyielding. Coming, by degrees, to the core of it. 'For some people, work is the best panacea, but you must be wary of emotional repercussions. There is no shame in this. Should you feel the need for leave, or counselling of any kind, you should say so at once.'

'How about the BMW and a month in Benidorm?'

'Spare me the jokes, man! At times like this, we can ill-afford . . . impaired performance.'

Like Smythe's, he meant. Cold by name and nature, duw duw.

Home, at last, lurching with fatigue, to an empty flat and the lingering scent of her presence. He bore it for a while, then called her. No reply. Give it an hour, he thought, wolfing cold beans and a healthy dollop of firewater. He put the Choral Symphony on, pottered about, checked the larder. It would need restocking, before she moved in.

Music sustained him until seven, when he got an engaged tone. Wonder if they've contacted Harrigan's bird yet? Leave it there, bach, you've got enough grief of your own.

Seven twenty, third time lucky for the Welsh. Sure enough, she answered on the third ring.

'Hi,' he mumbled, abruptly and absurdly tongue-tied. 'I made it.'

He couldn't put a name to the sound; something between a cry of delight and a moan of long-suppressed pain. Enough, anyway, to restore his soul, to bring him at long, long last out of the dreadful dark. Then she was sobbing and laughing, both at once. 'Oh *Huw*, is it really you?'

'I bloody hope so, girl. Had a few doubts, lately; but *yes*, it's really me.'

'It's so good to hear you, you've been out ages. What took so long? You didn't *meet* someone in there, did you?'

The mischief warmed him, he could *see* the green-eyed glow. 'Been trying since six, couldn't get through.'

Her tone sobered, the pace of her speech slowed.

'Oh. Yes. Well, you *did* make news, a reporter has to earn her crust. Following squad cars, interviewing the hostages, calling my contacts. I'm *sorry*, Huw.' The excitement simmered again, girlish and infectious. 'Listen, I'll pack a bag, don't move a muscle till I get there!'

The offer was enough, really, just to hear her joyful eagerness. Dog-tired, he was, and horror still lurking within. He had no *reason*: only, why rush it, risk a fumbling fiasco? Better to wait and sleep it off, meet her fresh and bushy-tailed somewhere clean and bright and open. All the time in the world, now.

'No hurry, girl. The place is a shambles, nothing to eat; a bit shattered, myself, to be honest.' He took the next part warily; bloody duty again. 'Reapers at large, mind, I'll have things to do, come morning. Make it the park, shall we, lunchtime?'

'I *might* wait that long – for you. Seriously, Huw, I'm not quite free of it either. I will be, by then, promise. Really free.' A mutual decision, see, she couldn't quite disguise the relief. Make an end, she was saying, *then* we can begin anew.

'Twelve thirty suit you, by the east gate?'

'Nothing could stop me. Sleep well – my love.'

That might prove a little more difficult, he thought, cradling the phone and feeling emptiness regather. A nightcap would help, maybe some more music. Beethoven's *Emperor*, for instance, sounds of majesty and triumph. Not much of it about, lately . . .

'Waiting,' mused the Quiet One. ''Tis the bane of every war.' He leaned on wooden fencing as grey and gnarled as himself. Behind, his modest byre and thin smoke coiling above the thatch; ahead, a fair sweep of County Leitrim. 'Wait we must, Sean. And is there a finer place or time?'

'None that I know,' Sean admitted. And let grandeur ease the turmoil within.

Decline of day, and bustle yielding to evening's calm. Out in the loch, an early trout was dimpling, while swallows stooped on the self-same gnats. Scented heather, the lowing of kine, and sunslant on a dozen shades of green. Mark it well, Sean, peace and beauty amid the slaughter. For *this* we strive, a land free of bombs and bloodshed, its people forever unbound. Carry it with you when you leave, as leave you surely must.

Beside, a small sudden flare, a whiff of burnt sulphur. The Quiet One puffed baccy contentedly, the blue eyes clear and steady. Waiting's a bane, he said, and made it seem like a pleasure. Another curious thing; despite the violence that dwelt in his blood, there was tranquillity in his company. He had the rare and priceless gift of undemanding silence. Aye, and will he be so tranquil when he knows?

A quarter past two in the drowsy hamlet where Sean Daly shopped for his mother. He cherished her yet, and his vow, though she grew even harder to love. With-drawn from life to the twilight of bitter bigotry, she spent her days reviling the past and haunting the Church like a banshee. Worse, she blamed her martyred husband, instead of his foreign killers; and praised the heedless God who'd let it happen.

'Kevin was a fool, son, and sought to change the unchangeable. The Dear prevent you from doing the same!' She hunched in the gloom by the fireside, mutter-ing psalms and telling her beads. He saw to her needs and daily chores out of duty, and for the love she had lost and forsaken.

He was doing it now, with sun on his back and a smell of fresh-baked bread wafting from the wicker basket.

At the steps of O'Byrne the butcher, he sensed an unlikely excitement. A gather of wives at the corner, flashing eyes and lively blether, and furtive triumph hanging on the air.

'Haven't ye heard?' breathed O'Byrne himself. 'The siege is over, the hostages out unscathed. And two of our own at large on the mainland, creating a rare hue and cry. There now, isn't it grand? Power to them, says I.'

'Grand,' echoed Sean dutifully, while coldness clawed his guts and blood from the ox liver seeped through pied newsprint.

Away, then, to the cottage of his birth, and an hour of her incessant railing. He bore it blandly, barely listening, his mind absorbed in likely repercussions and ways they might be averted.

He escaped by four, to the isolated phonebooth at the foot of the lane. Where, observing an aerial squabble of crows and blessing STD, he inserted the coins and jabbed a sequence of numbers learned by heart.

A hollow pause, a distant mechanical chatter, the second ringing burr interrupted. The familiar voice sounded weary; he wasted no time. 'Is it true, what I'm hearing of Duffy and the Cav?'

'*You!* I might have known. Forget them, Sean. They're beyond rescue.'

'Is it true?'

'They're free, if that's what you mean. Not for long, though. A policeman was killed. A thing they'll not tolerate, over here. No stone unturned, believe me.'

'You know where to look. Check the safe houses, ring me back. *Find them!*'

'I'm tired, Sean. It's dangerous now; too few people, too many watchers.'

He'd heard this before, also, the plea of an agent stretched to the aching limit. The price you pay for deceit, when separate strands of double and triple lives begin to fray. A cry of fear and yearning; leave me alone, let me *be*! Half-forgotten emotions stirred, and he smothered them. Crucial information, this, no room for faint hearts or favours. 'Your cover is sound, you've every right to be there. Must I invoke the vow you made?'

'Invoke all you like. The boon is repaid already, and more besides.' An incontestable truth, driving him to break his own strict code and frame a *personal* appeal.

'Do it for me and Eire; for the very last time, and what might yet come to pass.'

The crows were high black parentheses, seen through grubby glass. In the crackling, breathless pause, he pictured the drawn face and the anguished eyes.

'I'll try, Sean, only because of the past. Call me at seven, whatever.'

'Bless you,' he breathed with feeling, to an already empty line.

Outside, the shadows lengthened. A matron passed, cooing to her pram-bound infant. Does *she* care? he wondered, and found no ready reply.

He dialled the airport, another long-nurtured contact. It *could* be done, he heard. Last flight out and the early return, tomorrow. So all hinged on the London connection and an ageing soldier's pride . . .

The heather was reddening now, and fish were rising freely. The Quiet One lit up afresh, gave off more blue smoke. The time is come, Sean.

'Cav and Joe Duffy are loose,' he began. 'The world and his brother in pursuit. No need to explain it. *I have to reach them first!*'

The Quiet One scowled, grim and gummy. 'And didn't I warn you of the risk?'

'What's past is done. We need to secure the future.'

'You'll need to place them, then.'

'They'll go to ground, and precious few options. There's someone enquiring, meanwhile.' Tersely, Sean revealed the logistics. No names, not even here. And suffered a withering glance.

'Dark city streets, an alien land, and every hand against you?'

'Not every hand. An escort, I'm thinking, whose bearing will win no special notice. Will you be packing a bag?'

The Quiet One's face crinkled like unpolished leather. 'Meself, you mean? Too old to *venture*, let alone to prevail!'

One more time, Sean thought. Give me the power just one more time. '*A toothless has-been!*' he sneered. 'Is this what you'll have them remember? You're a *warrior*, older than most and wiser than any, the spark still fierce in your soul! I'll say only this; no man on earth I'd sooner have at my side!'

You could see the flexing of sinew, the sudden blaze of blue in narrowed eyes. And why not? Was there ever a man to resist the chance of living his youth anew? And doing whatever it was he'd once done best of all?

'So be it, Sean,' he rumbled, 'there's little enough to pack.'

Beyond the booth, in advancing dusk, the exhaust steamed and burbled. A wrinkled profile behind the wheel, the inevitable dog-end glowing. Twenty years on, and it might have been the self-same van. Green, unobtrusive, spattered with mud, unworthy of a second glance.

Sean was phoning again. This time, he won immediate response.

'Monahan's, in the East End, it wasn't hard to guess. A stone's throw from that curry house they wrecked.' There was anger in the voice now, and disillusion, and something worse than either or both. Condemnation. Gently, he said, 'You can book the ticket now. Homeward.'

'*Home?* I don't even know where it is. I'm finished, Sean. Don't call me, ever.'

'You *can't*!' he hissed – to nobody, once more. Can't resign, he intended to say. Agents must come in from the cold; or die of it. Which meant more hunting, more Irish blood on foreign soil. And more precious *time*!

He eased the glass door open, breathed the soothing scent of pasture; and checked. Not this one, Sean, not after all these years. This one was special. Still is, and always will be. Draw the line, sever the connection, walk away. Just this once, for old time's sake – let it be. 'Shannon,' he said, into the Quiet One's shadowed, expectant gaze. 'It's on.'

But it wasn't, quite. Sitting erect, his eyes only slightly higher than the dashboard's yellow glimmer, he tallied the reasons why. The sad distant voice had opened ancient wounds. If-onlys and might-have-beens. Much, much too late; it wouldn't have worked, anyway.

Beside him, the Quiet One drove serenely, despite the fearful rattle and the agricultural smell. So he might, having much to gain and nothing to lose. What had he said? *And every hand against you.* A harsh truth there, Sean.

Failure will earn endless years in a foreign cell, and the organization rent by bloody, internecine strife. *Don't fail, Sean.* Success, too, will bring its hazards. The British screaming blue murder – accurately, for once – and mounting sly reprisals. The traditional wing would cry betrayal; they were *our* boys, Daly! And pragmatists would bewail the loss of a fearless commando and an expensively trained technician. While Fergus wielded the baton, and Sammy played *first* fiddle at last. The classic no-win situation.

He was seeking ease in himself, the peace of mind a man must know before the heat of battle. Slowly, as night fell and the headlights raced palely ahead, he found it.

Trust in the Power, Sean; it has to be done this way. Be content with what has been achieved, the Daly life and legend. Whatever they say *now*, the name will endure in minds and ballads and memory. What more can a dwarf expect?

He smiled ruefully in the jouncing dark, acknowledged a final, ironic truth. Reluctant warrior you may be, but even less of a poet. It's been said before – almost two centuries before – with a force you could never hope to match. And by an Irishman, too. I die as I lived, for this country, that she shall one day be free. Till that day dawns, let no one dare to judge me – let no man write my epitaph!

351

CHAPTER NINETEEN

Cavanaugh's laughter filled the gloom, full-throated and malevolent. Clinging to the knotted muscles of his back, the once-white T-shirt oozed bilious brown. He reeked of stale sex and sewers – and triumph. Turning slowly, gloating through his beard, he revealed the glimmering blade and his latest victim. Jane.

A brutal, befouled paw trapped her mouth. Above it, her flesh gleamed pale as parchment, her eyes were huge with horror and entreaty. *Do* something, Huw!

Evans lolled uselessly, his body crushed by fatigue, his brain befuddled by whiskey. Each time he stirred, the muzzle of Joe's machine pistol stabbed viciously at his chest. 'Sit tight, fuzz, enjoy the show!'

Steel flickered. In a whisper of severed threads, the yellow dress parted and fell away. The knife point probed cruelly at the sweet, soft underswell of her left breast. 'Now, *Constable*,' Cav snarled, 'what tricks do you have up your sleeve?'

Joe's pudgy hands blurred and shifted. In place of the pistol, a black plastic box, the antenna already extended. 'Ye forgot *this*, clever dick, and read Joe Duffy wrong. I'll burn in hell before they take us alive!'

They've got more explosive, Evans realized dully. *Where?*

Vision cleared and steadied. Brassy moonlight bathed the cobwebbed window. Beyond it, Evans saw dust and devastation; and thin haze, rippling. Hooded figures advanced, huge and black and much, much too slow. *'Wait!'* he begged them. 'Get back!'

They blundered nearer, heedless. Somewhere below, a bell pealed urgently.

'You *stupid* fecker,' breathed Cav. 'I *warned* ye!'

The hairy wrist stiffened, the knife drove up and in. Blood fountained, a scarlet arc spattering hotly into Evans' face. He lunged blindly, his hands skidding on her slick, clammy skin; seeking the gape of the terrible wound, trying vainly to close it. He saw her dimly through veils of red, a chalky figure folding inward, wrinkling and shrivelling like a deflated rubber doll. The black rescuers checked, wavering in moonmist.

Joe's finger tightened on the button. Drowning in blood, *tasting* its coppery sourness, Evans screamed his protest into the savage night. 'No, no, NO!' And Cavanaugh's laughter stilled it, rising to a maniacal howl, striking hideous discord with the insistent clamour of bells . . .

Evans woke. To a lather of sweat, a rictus of terror, and his own heart thundering. And the steady shrill of the phone. Only a dream, then. *Only,* duw duw! Weak-kneed and shuddering, he stumbled across the room, had to cradle the receiver in both hands.

'Inspector Evans? Watson, on the desk. Developments, sir, in the Reaper case.'

'Nicked 'em, have we?'

'Just the messenger, I am. They don't tell me nothing.'

Breathing unevenly, barely in control, Evans put the voice to a face; thin-lipped, long-jawed and hangdog. A chronic moaner, Watson. 'Paged Beddoes already, sir. On his way, with the motor.' A beat, a narrow chuckle. 'Spoiled his fun, I bet.'

'Good news, bad news,' snapped Evans. 'Gave *you* something to snigger about, anyhow.'

The exchange calmed him. Five forty-two in the morning, no sign of blood on the lino, and a doleful deskman working off his spite. What could be more normal? In the bathroom, harsh light and cold water assisted the revival. Walk soft, Jane, don't talk to strangers. Till we've nailed them! He towelled wetness from his chin and sleep from his eyes. Couldn't *quite* get rid of the horror, still a shade of it, peering back from the mirror. A car horn burped outside, discreet but impatient. He stumbled downstairs, shivering, not from cold alone.

In the glow of the courtesy light, Beddoes looked remarkably chipper. The cat that got the cream. Thus commended, he winked slyly. 'The long wait is ended, uncle, finally rung the bell.' Seeing Evans' expression, he added, 'What's up? What did I say?'

'Bit of a sore point.'

'Know what you mean. If they'd called a bit earlier, I'd have a hump like Quasimodo meself.' He bent forward, hoisting one shoulder, pulling a gargoyle face. 'Ah, the bells, the bells!'

'Knock it off, Roy. Tell it straight, for once!'

'Sor*ree*! Getting headaches, spots before the eyes, and that. Pressure building up, hadn't had a leg-over since before Dublin. Ought to be warnings, I reckon. Abstinence can damage your health. Anyhow, *she'd* been saving it too. Fan-bloody-tastic, believe me. You could see the sparks from here, I shouldn't wonder.'

'Sparks, is it? Thought you'd stay away from the fire, having burnt your fingers in Ireland.'

'Who's talking fingers? You want to try it some time, get it off your chest.'

'Oh aye? Touch of the deep penetrations?'

'Nothing to beat it, mate.'

Evans smiled in the dark, the first time for a week. It didn't last, though, not with Reapers on the prowl and the nightmare still vivid. 'Where are we off to, then, what's the story?'

'Search me. That prat on the desk's got verbal constipation.'

The driver seemed to know, taking them fast and smoothly along the lamplit fringe of Dockland. As he eased to the kerb beside a lone, looming uniform, Evans' sense of locality stirred. Been here before, and not too long ago.

'Action replay,' breathed Beddoes. 'Singh's curry house, innit.'

It was. The tradesman's entrance, anyway. The same sinister alley, the same whiff of spice and ordure, the same cobbled glimmer. The same nastiness, too, judging by the boyish beatman's pallor.

'Asked for you by name, sir, used the Turban's phone. Saw the Identikit, didn't I. You'd better take a shufty.'

His ironshod heels echoed hollow in the rank dimness. Evans followed, conscious of the chill in his own belly, and Beddoes' tautness at his side.

'Never seen nothing like it,' the beatman muttered.

A muffled click, a white torch beam probing tumbled refuse, a hiss of indrawn breath. The scene was etched in monochrome, stark and two-dimensional. It took several seconds to decipher – and register.

They sat erect and separate, the lower halves of their bodies concertina'd and crammed into rusty garbage cans. Two drained, dead faces, each cleft by a dull, dark, downward smear; a trail of congealed blood wept from the third black eye which gleamed between each pair of open, lifeless ones. Cavanaugh and Duffy, late and obviously unlamented.

Beddoes cursed, low-voiced and obscene. Inventive, mind.

Despite the bizarre horror, Evans was impressed. 'Easy, Roy. An end, this is, not a beginning. That's the Reapers.'

'*Knew* it,' whispered the beatman, triumph and nausea mingling in his tone. 'The beard, see, and chubby chops, over there.'

Beddoes was craning distastefully forward, his face shadowed with remembrance and recognition. 'Hang about, I've seen this one before. Down the Sombrero, wasn't he? Thought he was Harry Slade's minder.'

'He *was*,' said Evans, 'in a manner of speaking.'

'Harrigan was there that night,' Beddoes continued, and you could hear him grapple with the implications. 'Jesus, uncle, if I'd known, we could've stopped it!'

'Oh sure. And if we had an elephant, we could shoot tigers. Leave it there. It's *done*.'

The beatman cleared his throat, shuffling from one foot to the other. 'Not quite, sir. Look.' The beam slithered sideways, wavered, held. The slogan leaped from darkness, in blazing crimson paint; a savage obituary scrawled on an alley wall. '*They joined for life!*'

Suddenly, Evans was back in sunlight beside an Irish stream, watching violence flicker in cold and tawny eyes. It wasn't possible, he *couldn't* have traced them so soon; yet somehow, like some small, avenging Kilroy, Daly had been here. And wanted him, Evans, to know it.

The City skyline hardened, jagged black against the grey of dawn. Beneath it, sharp and intent, Beddoes questioned the beatman, who looked about ready to throw up. Evans ignored them, weighing the consequences of intuition and action.

Blow the whistle, sound the alert at air and sea ports. A schoolboy, we're after. Five foot nothing, slightly built,

356

looks about fourteen. Shorts and blazer, probably, and wearing cap and badge. Aye, that's right, he just wasted two red-fanged, world-class terrorists; left them for the dustcart to collect. Along with his calling card, and a salutary message to all who might defect. *The* Green Reaper, no question. Sad, sick Smythe had it right, after all.

Murder; plain, simple, and on British soil. Don't just stand there, bach, do your duty.

Thing is, it's not that simple. Daly delivered, via O'Brien and Snow. Vital gen on these two charmers, filched from Provo archives at God knows what personal risk. And allowed Huw Evans to walk Scot-free from under Casey's gun. A debt, then, owed by one fisherman to another.

Forget the law for a minute, think *justice*. A horse of a very different colour, as every copper quickly learns. Gerry Jewell and Sergeant Errol Harrigan versus Cavanaugh and Duffy, an eye for an eye. Not exactly a fair exchange; Harrigan rated any fifty Irish bombers. But a line had been drawn, a *finis* written; fittingly, where it had all started. No lingering, costly court farragoes, no clever legal claptrap – and no Provos held in British gaols, to provide excuses for mainland violence and sordid political barter. Justice, of a kind; maybe the only kind such men understand or deserve. And something in it for both sides.

The sun rose, bringing depth and pinkness to the scene. Beddoes was watching him quizzically, the anger under control. 'What's up, uncle? Put you off breakfast?'

'No chance. Do it myself, anytime, for that pair. And sleep easy, after.'

Back at the car, after the ambulance came, he fired a factual report in over the radio. All Reapers accounted for; perpetrators unknown. An internal Irish affair, probably. File and forget, if they'll let you.

The City had woken, the traffic thickened around them. The driver took it gently, talking soccer to the beatman who'd been given a lift for his pains. *Soccer*, already. Beside Evans on the back seat, Beddoes sat easy, smiling quietly to himself. A Parrot on his mind, no doubt, the wound and the lesson forgotten. One day, maybe, old Adam would lead him into *real* trouble. Till then – what the hell. *One life you get*, Harrigan had said. And had lost it, and been avenged. Rest in peace.

Go in peace, Sean Daly. Last night's dark and ugly deeds will doubtless cost you dear among your own, shorten your days. Days already numbered. We're even now, all debts paid.

It's over, he thought, idly taking the pulse of the City. Back to the nick and the basement, reports to type, low-key crimes to solve. *An end to deception.*

An end to nightmares, too. Nothing left to fear out there. For the moment.

So, at last, you can meet Jane, lunchtime in the park, with a clear conscience and a tranquil mind . . .

The taxi pulled in, the door opened. Poised at the gate under autumn sun, Evans saw the slim tanned leg emerge, the white sling-back sandal brace against the pavement. She was out, lithe and fresh in a fawn skirt and a white top with cutaway sleeves. Her hair tumbled and shimmered. From twenty yards away, he saw the driver's besotted smile as money changed hands. She straightened, hitching her bag over her shoulder. A smooth, brown shoulder, a glimpse of pale flesh under her arm. You're doomed, bach: drooling over her *arms*!

She saw him, and her face lit with joy. She came forward, striding eagerly, weaving her unique spell.

Noise and bustle faded. Two of them, alone on a crowded street.

She looked up, saying his name just once. A single syllable, charged with hope and yearning, a promise for the years ahead. Doubt and duty faded, it was like being eighteen again.

'Looking good, girl,' he murmured. 'Walk, shall we?'

Her hand nestled in the crook of his elbow. 'Don't say anything, Huw, not a word. I just want to *be* with you.'

He ambled, carefree, amid the perfume of mown grass and living woman. Out across yielding turf, savouring utter contentment and the envious glances they won. *She* won. Somewhere deep inside, the ice was shifting, thawing. Worth it, the whole squalid charade, only for the magic of her nearness.

They left it behind, the sweaty City, the rumble of traffic, the chime of ice-cream vans. Over a rise, into a shaded hollow. An ancient oak, its weathered roots exposed. Soft greenness between, birdsong above, the world a million miles away.

They were concealed and close, the moment he'd conspired and endured for. Her mouth, soft and willing, her body moulding against him. He touched her hair, her neck, the unbound fullness of her breast. She sighed, deep and pleasured. Heat smouldered in his loins. He opened his eyes, watching his own fingers cup and caress.

And froze, as lurking nightmares blasted into his brain. These same fingers thickened, the reek of vileness smothering him like fog. He stepped back, shrivelled and impotent.

'What is it?' Her voice quivered, the rosy flush drained from her cheeks.

'Shades of the past, girl. Be all right, by and by.'

'*Tell* me!'

359

'Might come easier, sitting down.'

He settled, leaning on his elbow, shredding blades of grass. She sat beside him, fluid, graceful, concerned. Unwilling and ashamed, he outlined the delights of Dirty Protest. Tried to avoid the worst bits, without much success. Disgust oozed among the pauses he left.

She sensed it, pale and distraught. 'The Irish did that?'

'Salim called the shots. But it didn't seem to bother them.'

She took his hand, pressed it to her thigh. 'I want you, Huw, just as you are, whatever they made you do. *Now!*' Her flesh burned through thin fawn cotton, her face was bright with longing.

'It's mutual, believe me. The spirit is willing. You haven't heard it all, mind.' He disengaged gently, holding up splayed fingers. 'I killed a man, with these. Seems . . . obscene . . . using them on you.'

'How can that be? The SAS shot him, I heard McKay's announcement!'

'Overkill, you might say. And police solidarity.'

'You saw it through, love, did what had to be done. Truth and justice, remember? I *admire* you!'

'Steady, Jane. Enforcement, I am, paid to preserve, not destroy. That's why I let him go. Daly, I mean.' He explained that, too, vaguely aware of her sudden tension.

She moved, crouching behind him, kneading the muscles at his nape. 'Relax, let the touch console you.'

Her flanks nudged his back, her small palms soothed him. Autumn was reborn, mild and sweet-scented and dappled through the leaves. 'You absolved the dwarf,' she murmured, 'bade him Godspeed. Because, in the end, you are two of a kind. There but for the grace . . .'

'Maybe.'

Her tone and the touch lightened. 'Someday, Ireland will be free. It will take men of like mind and common

360

experience, men steeled in battle and tempered by visions of peace. Men like you – and Sean.' He half-listened, lost in the play of sunshine and the subtle lilt of her voice. 'A distant dream, no doubt. The slaughter continues, meanwhile.'

Meanwhile. *Meanwhile*. The word and the way she spoke it dispelled one small, lingering mystery. You only had to *look* at her, mind: auburn hair, green eyes, creamy, sun-flecked skin. You only had to listen, really listen, to the music of her speech, the way she pronounced Daly's name: and said 'meanwhile'.

'Darro,' he breathed, 'you're *Irish*!'

Her hands worked smoothly. She sounded amused, laying on the accent. 'To be sure, me darlin', wouldn't you know it?'

'You didn't *say*!'

'No. Nor did you ask!'

He should have, he realized grimly, long, long ago. Because despite scent and sunlight, dark suspicions were blooming in his mind. ' "Truth and justice" ' he quoted, 'in *Ireland* you meant, all along. *That's* why the Dirty Protest shook you, why you knew so much about Daly!'

'It's no secret, Huw, just a part of the job. Develop the contacts, create access, follow the lead to its source. A reporter, remember?'

The ring of truth, welcome and reassuring. All right, so maybe she sympathized with Daly and his cause. No crime, is it, to share and regret the troubles of your homeland? The ugliness inside him faltered, began to wither and die. Live for the future, enjoy her now and always.

But he couldn't. He was leaving her and the sheltering oak, drawn irresistibly back to a gleaming river and a warlike dwarf. '*We need all the help we can get from that quarter.*' Talking of Jane, he was. Jane the reporter!

Evans recalled a Funny's remark, cultured and disdainful. *'Cover, d'you see, a series of fallbacks.'* The media, the perfect cover for access and contacts. What if it was double cover? Who did she really report to?

Coldness was upon him, her caress was a distant irrelevance. The questions were breeding, feeding. *We were expected,* said Beddoes; did Jane relay the warning? *Smythe's squad has a mole,* he remembered; did she support and run him? Daly came, saw, and murdered only hours after the Reapers' break-out; who told him where to look?

The scene shifted indoors, deeper into the recent past. Warner's farewell party, raucous cheers, rowdy singing, a crowded bar. She'd picked him out, carried him off, enslaved him. On the very night he'd been co-opted to the Anti-Terrorist Squad.

Suspicion yielded to certainty, to insight which dimmed the sun and silenced the birds. Lulled by her magical aura, he'd abandoned restraint, poured out his innermost secrets. To the enemy.

Deep within him, the ice she'd thawed was setting anew, harder and colder than ever. Chilling his mind, freezing his very soul. Ultimate betrayal, crueller by far than anything Salim could wreak. Because it was spawned by a smile, nurtured by kisses, consummated by a pliant, eager body. Even now, under suddenly shadowed skies, her hands were tender upon him.

So he, Huw Evans had dared to love her, dared to believe it was real. *Self*-deception, the most painful illusion of all. He found words, somehow, rasping them out in a voice he scarcely recognized. 'What's your name, girl?'

The massage stopped. He turned slowly, appalled by the serenity of her gaze. 'I never lied to you, Huw.'

'And you never told me the truth!'

She stood up, smoothed fine wrinkles from her skirt. Her hands were perfectly steady. Breeze and dappled sunlight shimmered in her hair. She looked girlish, innocent and very lovely.

'What would you have done, I wonder? If, on that first evening, I'd said – my name is Siobhan O'Neil, I report sordid anti-terrorist gambits to my ex-lover, Sean Daly?'

Bile scoured his throat, the foulest of images writhed in his mind. 'Slept with him, did you, to keep him sweet? Daly's mole, I mean; scuttling between my bed and his?'

'Poor Huw.' Her pity and contempt scourged him. 'Look at me! Must I bed a man, to get what I want? You haven't answered. *What would you have done?*'

Unbelievable. She actually had *him* feeling soiled and guilty.

'Nicked you,' he growled. 'Fed you to the Brass. Here, I've caught a Provo spy. Laugh like drains, they would.'

She was ablaze once more, parading her beauty like armour. 'All right. Do it *now*!'

No way, he knew it at once, if only because of what they had so nearly shared. She'd given him something, she and Daly both. An alternative to duty, a deeper knowledge of self? Something precious anyway.

For the moment, he was adrift, shorn of all virtues, beset by warring desires. *Emotional repercussions*, duw duw! Mostly, he yearned to rekindle the emerald spark which lingered yet in her eyes.

'*I never lied*,' she insisted. 'When we met, it was work, nothing more. I didn't even know about the Reapers. Sean Daly belongs to the past, he owns no part of me now! *Yes*. I told him you were coming – and begged him to do you no harm. *Yes*, I serviced the mole, though not in the sense you mean. I'll never reveal his name; I'm Irish. *Yes*, I sent Sean for the Reapers. If I hadn't, you

363

would still be in danger. All for *you*, my love.' She bent towards him, sensing his doubts, begging him to believe. 'I *owed* Sean for what he taught me, years ago. To measure the heart of a man, the inner strength which prompts him to ensure and prevail. And kill, if he must, for whatever he truly holds dear. The debt is paid. I loved such a man, and lost him. *Don't let it happen again!*'

Temptation hung on the breeze; to grant her appeal, bury suspicion, make himself whole at last. Vague dread forestalled him, shades from his past he couldn't yet name.

'You wanted the truth,' she whispered. 'You have it. I've made my last call to the Provos, confessed my sins, abandoned myself to you. Can't you understand? *I love you.*' Her need blazed, lighting her eyes, outshining the sun, gleaming from parted lips. She spoke her own private charm, dreamy yet demanding. 'Don't tell me, *show* me.' And drew him like a moth to flame.

To heat which was mutual and immediate. Her tongue darted, her nipples swelled against his palms. He gloried in her and the moment; and the firm, steady throb of his own restored manhood.

She eased her mouth away, sighing contentedly, keeping the fiery, central contact. 'Take me home, Huw. We *can* make it work — *we must!*'

Drowning in musk, dazzled by wanton beauty, his brain conjured two separate memories; and forged an inescapable restraint. The afterglow of intimacy, back at the flat. Jane, languid and naked, hearing the trials of his day. Then: Megan's teasing Welsh tones, voicing the unanswerable. *When are you going to make an honest woman of me?*'

He released her, hating himself and the heedless fire in his blood. 'I'm a copper, Jane, an ordinary sort of bloke. At the end of a day, I just need to talk.' He swallowed hard and told her straight, the only way he knew. 'How am I ever going to trust you?'

She flinched as from a blow. Her face turned gaunt and ghastly as it had been in the dream. 'Don't you see what they've done?' she cried. 'These *honest* men who rule you? Perverted your sense of duty, stripped you of all you cherish? They *used* you, both sides, for their own ends! And *still* you put trust before love?'

I do, he thought, saying it inwardly like a marriage vow. Can't see the difference, really. No altar, this, more an unbridgeable chasm of misunderstanding. On one side, her vision of love, healing and cleansing the past. On the other, a copper's rigid code – if you can't trust, don't tell.

She read him as quickly as ever, the light was dying in her eyes. 'I'm finished with them, Huw, I swear it. *What must I do?*'

'Walk on, girl. Best to do it now.'

Her voice broke, tearing at raw emotions. 'Come with me, *please*, at least as far as the gate.' She offered her hand and he took it; could deny her nothing, if only she knew.

Over the rise, trudging, her fingers slack and cold, all hope and joy relinquished. Grey, it seemed, and silent, despite blue sky and shrieking kids. No future with her, see; watching words and her eyes, lying beside her, wondering. Not much future without her, come to think.

At the gate she tried once more, a naked plea which left him bleeding, inside. 'I'll go anywhere, Huw, do anything you ask. You *can't* let it go!'

'Maybe I never had it, Jane. Not capable, me.'

The last and greatest lie, to make it easier. The final deceit in the whole tortuous, doomed affair; begun and ended in deception.

She left as she had come, his name spoken softly, once. In despair, in pain; in a kind of love he could neither return nor deny. She was crying, he could tell by the blind, arrow-straight line of her retreat. She had it still, though, that marvellous, haunting grace. A slender, auburn-haired woman, walking away. She never turned, not once. He craned upward, catching an occasional flicker of red through the throng. Two hours ago, she'd caused a crowd to dissolve. Now, in turn, it swallowed her up. She was suddenly gone: taking the best of him with her.

CHAPTER TWENTY

Huw's decline had begun, reckoned Beddoes, as dawn revealed the tints of ritual murder. Tar-black blood dissecting pallid faces, scarlet splattered on a slimy wall. Half-coffined in rotten iron, festooned with rice and eggshell, the corpses lolled like defiled, abandoned dummies. You could *feel* their killer's contempt, read it plain in slashing letters and far-flung blobs of paint. *They joined for life.* A line to mock the dead and haunt the living.

Scanning it, Evans had turned morose and introspective. He took no part in the questioning – didn't miss much, actually – mooching about, kicking beer cans, never shifting his gaze from the broad red scrawl. Almost as if it held some *personal* message.

More of the same, in the car. Overcompensating, the beatman babbled soccer. City for the Cup, he *must* be sick. Normally, Evans would have squashed it, some mordant quip about his own beloved rugby. Today, he merely slumped in silence, oblivious to conversation, traffic, and the promise of another lovely day.

Back at the nick, the air throbbed with excitement and triumph.

Recovering nerve and colour, the beatman waxed unwisely eloquent. 'The Reapers are no more; all hail the conquering hero!' Which pleased Huw even less.

'Only one hero,' he snapped. 'Name of Harrigan, don't you ever forget!'

'Course not, sir. Played a blinder, he did. Considering.'

'Considering *what*, bach?'

The beatman paled, fidgeted, glanced around like a cornered rabbit. 'Well, you know. Being a West Indian, see.'

Evans' jaw set like rock, the eyes blazed ice-blue fury. 'One day, sonny, if you get really lucky, you might be half the policeman he was. When you grow up! Meantime, get out of my sight!'

The festivities faltered, the beatman scuttled away. And Desk Sergeant Watson, lingering beyond shift to gather gossip, ventured in where angels fear to tread. 'Kind of you, Inspector, to solve our little problem. Had a nice holiday, I hope?'

Old Warner might have carried it off, just. Known Huw since the Flood, Warner; had a respectful way with the needle. Whereas Watson steamrollered on, sarky and regardless. 'Sorry, sir. Forgot you'd been *busy*, what with the Funnies and that smart new char, down the flats.'

Beddoes tensed, watching the tilt of broad Welsh shoulders, fearing your actual fisticuffs. One sandy hand knotted, relaxed. A hard finger speared Watson's tunic. 'Mind your manners,' Evans advised, murderously soft. 'Watch your tongue, keep your snotty nose out of *my* business!' Then, louder but no less frigid, 'On your bike, *Sergeant*, it's past your bedtime.'

A second hasty, resentful departure. By now they had the lobby to themselves, the day dutyman having done a prudent bunk. You couldn't blame Huw, he was in the right. Just not his style to pull rank in public. Unlike him, really.

He strode like the wrath of God through sunstruck, dust-hung passages. Barged into the basement, plonked himself down, scowled at the paper mountain. 'No place like home, is there?'

He didn't want an answer; didn't get one, either.

Beddoes settled behind his own desk and skip-read a dozen files. Muggers, peepers, dipsos and junkies, the assembled flotsam of petty crime. Steady work, mind you, the kind Huw Evans needed.

Presently, the phone rang. Evans ignored it, gazing blankly, turning unread pages rhythmically.

Sighing, making a put-upon face, Beddoes walked across and lifted the receiver.

A posh, vaguely familiar voice, a hint of condescension. 'Sergeant Beddoes? Just to inform you Harriet's at home. You can call off the search.'

Stockbroker Slade, wasn't it, announcing the return of the prodigal. *Search*, he called it; if only he knew!

'Good of you,' Beddoes grunted. 'How is she, anyway?'

'As well as can be expected. She has these – harrowing dreams. Anxious to go back to school, though. Boarding, naturally.' A pause, the sound of pride being swallowed. 'What do *you* think?'

Beddoes considered, remembering her gaucheness at the dance, her crumpled, tear-stained face as she tottered from the siege. Just a kid, then, despite the mature body and haughty chat.

'Bit of discipline wouldn't come amiss,' he suggested, 'and company of her own age. No expert, me; but since you ask, I'd send her back.'

Slade's relief was palpable; his own judgement vindicated. 'Much obliged, Sergeant. Have a good day.'

You too, he thought, cradling the phone. And next time she talks music, stick her in the Nuns' Chorus.

Evans was watching him, guarded but enquiring.

'Harriet's old man,' explained Beddoes. 'She's having nightmares, he says.'

'Know the feeling.' Pain clawed at Evans' face, quickly followed by acid disapproval. 'Gave him the benefit of

369

your wisdom, I noticed. Back to the dorm, is it? What happens when media vultures fly?'

Wearing, mind you, this constant air of doom. Hovering on the brink of retaliation, Beddoes scented an opportunity. Kill two birds, so to speak. 'Down to you, that is. Use your influence, page the redhead, call 'em to heel. You *are* seeing her, right?'

For a moment, fur seemed fit to fly. Gradually, Evans' expression relented. With a bit of imagination, you could *see* her slender, auburn outline in the softened centre of his eye.

'Course I am. Worth a try, I expect.' His meaty hand rose, rasped on sandy stubble. 'Need a scrape, I do. Got to look my best. Down to the washroom, then. Hold the fort, will you?'

He stood up, square and shabby as ever in his aged brown sports coat; and just a touch shifty. Halfway to the door he checked and turned, as if struck by a sudden thought. 'Remind me, Roy. Did that uniform say something about an old man and a boy?'

'Yeah. Nothing suspicious. They passed by about three, he reckoned, casual as you please. He never saw another soul all night.'

'Odd, mind,' mused Evans. 'A boy that age, out that late. Or early. Do us a favour. Call the airports, ask if anyone answering the description left for Ireland today?' Then he was gone. Amazing how fast and silent he could be, when he wanted.

Mystified and intrigued, Beddoes obeyed. He got lucky at the third attempt. Aer Lingus, naturally. A soft and rather lovely female Irish voice remembered them well.

'Indeed I do, sir, you could see the joy of the ould country shining in their faces. Only a slip of a boy, and the air of one much older. *McRory*, the name, all documents in order. They did nothing wrong, surely?'

He reassured her, asked the obvious question. 'The 8.05 departure, less than an hour's hop. They'll be home by now.'

Evans returned, smooth-jowled, reeking of pouf mixture. He listened, nodded once, and avoided Beddoes' beseeching glance.

'Come *on*, uncle, what's the story?'

'A long shot, anyway. What does it matter, if they're gone?' He glanced up, shrugged easily. 'Daly's a dwarf, see.'

'Daly? *Daly* wasted them? Jesus, now he tells me!'

'Walk soft, Roy. Only guesswork, nothing else to go on.'

'A *dwarf*, yet!'

'Aye. He tends to grow bigger, in the memory. Listen, whoever they were, they saved us a pile of trouble. So why give yourself grey hairs?'

And *that* was unlike Huw Evans, too, who *never* let Chummy off the hook.

He'd had a rough time, obviously: rougher than anyone would ever know. Except, perhaps, the redhead. Made him hard to live with, though, because *he* was living on his nerves. At it now, actually; staring at the peeling walls, ignoring the paperwork, starting at small, commonplace noises outside.

He cracked at half-eleven, heading for the door and making a transparent excuse. 'Getting me down, this is, I fancy a breath of air. See you: after lunch.'

At which point, Beddoes risked a gentle jibe. 'Don't talk air to me, mate. You gotta date!'

'Trying the Beddoes cure, I am.'

'Mind how you go, then. I know redheads who bite.'

'No harm in hoping, boyo.'

* * *

Alone and not regretting it, Beddoes picked up the threads. Renewed some contacts, paged a few snouts, set his sights on a mugger called Billy Stone. Nice to get the enforcer's muscles working again, nice to have peace and quiet.

But not for long. Well-known footfalls approached, ringing briskly. The door opened and McKay breezed in; full dress uniform, the red bristles unusually smooth. He was unusually affable, also.

'Nose to the grindstone? That's what I like. Where's Evans?'

Beddoes sat to attention, wary of Scottish wrath. Like summer lightning, you never knew when or where it might strike. A stickler for truth, was Jock. Better tell it, then. 'Took a breather, sir. Felt hemmed in, he said.'

'Reasonable, given the circumstances. So long as it's not a habit. Unfortunate, though. I bring glad tidings.'

'Pass 'em on,' Beddoes suggested, more in hope than expectation. 'Back soon, I reckon.'

McKay hesitated, making some kind of decision. 'It's right you should hear, having been a party to the affair.' He drew himself up, seemed to grow a couple of inches on the spot. 'It's *Chief* Super now, laddie, the papers arrived this very noon. Taking over Smythe's command, in charge of the Anti-Terror Squad.'

Beddoes rose and offered his hand; and a daring note of familiarity. 'Congratulations! Tread soft, Paddies, beware the Tartan Army!'

He took it in good part, with a rueful smile. 'I never cared for Smythe *personally*. His professional act will be hard to follow.'

'Garn, you'll walk it. Huw'll be dead chuffed.'

'To see the back of me, no doubt. Don't blether, man, I'm no such a fool as you think.' No heat in him, though, the fanged grin widened. 'As it happens, he has a bonnier reason. The natural successor, d'you see, he'll be running the manor very soon.'

'*This* manor?'

'Where else? Onward and upward, laddie, from the basement to the stars! He'll maybe find *you* a wee nook at ground level!'

He paused at the doorway, resplendent in blue and silver — and satisfaction. Sobering, he delivered a confession, a tribute, and two cautions. 'I'm seldom proved wrong; I was wrong about Evans. You're a lucky wee man, after Dublin. He restored you; he needs and deserves your best. *Don't let him down*. And mind who you sleep with, meantime.'

Superintendent Evans, thought Beddoes, as the quick march faded. How high are the lowly risen. And yours truly tugged along in the jetstream. Take some getting used to, will that.

He leaned back, neglecting routine, planning the rest of a very good day. Down to the canteen for a bite and a confab with Pol. Her place tonight, for a change. Over to the gym, give the leg a work-out. Ready for judo next week, I shouldn't wonder. The basement again at two thirty, for another crack at Billy Stone. Break the news when Huw gets back, knock off a bit early, into the boozer to wet the new Super's head. Then home, all change, and the main event in Pol Parrot's friendly little cage. Thank you and good *night*, Chief Superintendent McKay . . .

It flowed like cream for a while, Pol was warm and willing, the return bout eagerly awaited. The leg stood up fine, even managed a couple of half-strength flying kicks. Mending fast, then, and not before time. There was even a moment, in the grubby, soon-to-be vacated basement, when the Billy Stone case seemed set to crack wide open. But the mobile squad went looking, drew a blank; and sent him, Beddoes, back to the drawing board.

After that, things turned a bit sour. Three o'clock, three thirty, and Evans still AWOL. The paperchase lost shape and urgency, the minutes began to drag. Come in, Huw, your time is up. Where the hell *are* you, anyway? Screwing the redhead probably. He deserved that, too.

No need to overdo it, though. Bad for him, at his age. Give over, my son, it's great at any age!'

By half-four he was decidedly twitchy. Any minute now, the Watson prat would get wind, bell Huw at home, spoil it for everyone. Grovel, he would. Had to, didn't he, after this morning's little fiasco. Forgive me, Super, and I'll tongue-bathe your royal Welsh bottom the rest of me natural.

He quit at six, drove home like a maniac, dialled Huw's number himself. Engaged.

Showering, powdering the parts even a Parrot *could* reach, he felt the forced brightness crumble; and the onset of genuine worry.

He'd been buggered about, Huw, looking and acting decidedly odd. Snarling openly at the ranks, treating files like porn and his oppo like dirt, dismissing Public Enemy Number One with a wave and a wholly uncharacteristic blessing. As if the ordeal had diminished him, cut him afrift from the code he'd honoured the better part of his life. In which case, he needed help.

Five past seven, and still engaged. Beddoes did some mental arithmetic and geography. It would only take ten more minutes to pass by the police flats on the way to Pol's. Don't hang about, then. Do it.

Driving, he had inevitable second thoughts. Huw would be having a whiff, a good long dose of TLC to see him right. Taken the phone off the hook, most likely, wouldn't fancy social calls from *anyone.*

No problem. Knock, deliver the good news, give them something to *really* celebrate. Then leg it for Pol's and do likewise. Yeah, sure. But what if he's not there? Unseen and unbidden, Beddoes' foot eased down on the accelerator . . .

Evans loomed large and swayed gently, blocking off half the doorway. Behind him, lampglow played on amber bottles, music flared and sighed. Classical stuff, naturally, something moody and elegiac.

'Roy, is it?' he mumbled. There was whisky to strip paint on his breath, you could *taste* the desolation in his voice.

Beddoes nodded, peering past him, trying to suss things out. No sign of female presence, so far as he could see. There might have been a hint of perfume mingled with the booze. Faint, though, and fading. Not tonight, Josephine. So that's it, he thought. She stood him up, he's drowning his sorrows, hoping she might show.

The insight spawned bitterness, the rage you feel when you've sweated blood for someone, imagined the very worst. Then found them, whole, safe – and legless. Sod him, thought Beddoes, *and* his sodding promotion. Scarper, my son. Get yourself across to Pol's, let Watson win some house marks.

A familiar melody checked him, carried him way, way back. The piece the Beeb had played, on and on for hours, one night when he was a kid. The night Kennedy got shot. *Heart Wounds,* wasn't it?

In that instant, Evans teetered sideways, turning his face to the light. A ravaged face, with pale, unfocused eyes. 'Coming in, are you?'

A plea, not a question, stirring fresher remembrance.

375

A year ago, Beddoes had heard the very same tone from a girl who'd just been raped. *Listen*, someone – anyone – before I stick my head in the oven.

He glanced at his watch, his anger and resolution wavering. Twenty-five minutes to spare, can't leave him in this state. You *owe* him, my son. He took you in from the cold.

'A quickie then, uncle. On a tight schedule, me.'

'Me too. Tight, I mean.'

Not your actual chaos, inside, more a touch of the slovens. The carpet looked trampled, dustfilms dulled wooden surfaces, tan curtains sagged tiredly. Huw's faithful jacket sprawled on a chair, his navy tie coiled across grey lino. Sobbing violins didn't help, either.

'Do me a favour,' said Beddoes. 'Give ole Yehudi a rest.'

A slurred response, a couple of shambling strides, and a welcome pool of hush.

Beddoes sat at the table and admired the liquor supplies. One flat-sided bottle already empty, two with red seals unbroken, one down just below the label. Evans' tumbler brimmed darkly. Drinking it straight, then. *Bathing* in it, actually.

Evans emerged from the kitchen, dishevelled and haggard. Baggy slacks, a soiled white shirt with one cuff flapping; deep, downward-curving shadows etched into his face. Flesh gleamed taut and waxen over his cheek bones, the empty, pink-rimmed eyes burned china blue. Wordless, he offered a glass and poured like there was no tomorrow.

'Easy, mate, I'm driving!' Beddoes deflected the bottle, watched scattered blobs of spirit soak up dust. He raised the glass, preparing to toast promotion – and changed his mind. Good news will always keep. Not a lot of it about, by the looks.

He sipped, savoured the glow, and went in at the deep end. 'Not interrupting, I hope?'

Evans tried, vainly, for a brave stance and an airy tone. 'Parted company, me and Jane. For *professional* reasons.'

Caught on to her at last, thought Beddoes. She'd probably pressed too hard for the exclusive. 'Reporters,' he grunted. 'Well rid of her, I'd say.'

Evans was raising the glass in both hands, ducking his head, pushing his upper lip forward. He checked in mid slurp, his tone harsh and heavy. 'Boyo, *you don't know the half*! Made me think, she did. Bad for people, too much thinking. Specially coppers.' He downed a tot to knock a horse bowlegged; shuddered, and spoke with shocking violence. 'They *fucked* us, Roy; backwards, frontwards, down the sides and up the middle!'

'Hey, steady on! Who's they?'

'*All* of them!' Despite the starboard list and occasional slur, his gaze was sharper. Sharp with rage. 'Snow, for one, and all on account of Smythe. Trespassing in Paddyland, Smythe was – and on *Funny* preserves. Secret sorties, way beyond his brief. Interfering, see, muddying foreign pools. Losing, what's more – money, men and respect. A sick man, mind: obsessed. Rabid, even, hungry to kill, and hazards for both sides.' The anger was fading. In the dim lamplight, you could see the effort of concentration sober him. 'Snow gave him rope – and us. Pointed him at the biggest Provo prize of all. Daly.'

'A dwarf, you said.'

'Told you once. He grows on you; like cancer. Where was I?'

'Smythe's big chance.'

'Aye. So Smythe shanghais us, the Queen and Country bit. And Snow stitches up some tatty shreds of *cover*.' Evans spat the word, his mouth writhing in disgust.

377

'Stitched us up lovely! Smythe's mob had a mole, see, and Snow knew it.'

Beddoes felt a tingle of unpleasant anticipation. Talking like some fiction-pedlar, was Huw; and making it sound like fact. 'Jammiest thing you ever did, screwing Shelagh. Kept you away from Slaney's, the second night.'

'Jesus, uncle, I got shot!'

Evans made a loose, dismissive gesture. 'Kneecapped, by an amateur. Fergus doesn't care for knees. He's a Daly man – shoots Pommie agents in the head!'

The implication struck, ferrying Beddoes back to spit 'n' sawdust and the powerful reek of Guinness. And naked hostility, before Fergus came in and defused it. Despite himself, he was beginning to believe.

Evans loomed over him, gaunt and grieving; and very, very certain. *'You* said it, Roy – they were waiting. *Course* they were. *Smythe had a mole, Snow knew it, and we weren't expected back!'*

'We got back, though!'

'Down to old Adam, that was, and fisherman's luck. *Suppose we hadn't?* Missing, presumed dead, in Ireland? Coppers, mind, not agents, people to miss us and wonder. McKay, for instance; and Jane. Ask the right questions, they would. Who recruited them, who sent them, why? *Smythe*, that's who. Sent them to kill a poison dwarf. Nothing to do with the Funnies. *Who*, your honour? Couple of blokes I fed ducks with? Don't even remember their names. *Cover*, duw duw. Cover for *Snow's* back!' The bitterness was corrosive – and infectious. Not finished yet either. 'So, truth rears its ugly head. Exit Smythe, a disgrace to the force, enter a new broom. New broom, new rules and boundaries, the Anti-Terror Squad stays home. And Snow controls the Holy Ground – alone!'

Bleakness gnawed at Beddoes' guts. He felt his own face contorting, as if to a nasty smell. And Evans rubbed his nose in it.

'War games, Roy, not cops and robbers, and Funnies make the rules. Medals for the general, the rankers count their dead.'

This time, Beddoes was spirited back to McKay's lair, and Snow's remorseless voice. *The good general endures unavoidable casualties, drives on to ultimate victory.* An eerily exact echo, only the accent altered. And Evans had never heard it, being already at siege!

Evans was reading him, flashing a pale-eyed challenge over the rim of his glass. 'Go on, boyo, tell me I'm wrong.'

'You're wrong,' breathed Beddoes, pouncing thankfully on an obvious flaw. 'If Daly was keen to waste us, how come *you're* walking about?'

'Remember Smythe, the danger to both sides? *That's* why Daly turned me loose – to make a deal with Snow!'

''Ang about! *What* deal?'

Evans was actually laughing, mirthless as the rattle of old bones. 'Get your nutters off my patch, I'll keep mine at home! Should've seen Snow's face when he heard – like he'd just found a real, live dodo!'

'What are you saying?' Beddoes whispered. 'Daly and Snow are *partners*?'

'Be your age, Roy! An English beanpole and an Irish dwarf? Enemies, bred in the blood. This one time, they had a common enemy, a mad dog to destroy.' Evans dragged the back of his hand across his mouth, wiped it on his shirt. Another yellowish smear on seedy whiteness. 'Common anxieties, too. Daly was under threat; from Cavanaugh and Duffy. A trained bomber and a hardened hit-man, about to outsmart the Brits. What price a dwarf, when *they* came home to glory? So Sean nipped across and spared us the bother. *His* reasons, not ours.' There was acid triumph in Evans now, much less of the booze in his speech. '*Power* was the harvest, empire-building on either side of the water. *We* were the chaff. Daly and Snow were the Reapers. *Grim* Reapers, the pair of them.'

Lamplight flickered on gold through glass as Evans' elbow bent once more. Outside, someone was calling a dog, the voice of absolute normality. Beddoes clung to it yet; and Evans denied it again. 'The unwelcome survivor, I was, who might guess where the bodies *should've* been buried. So what did our noble Funny do? Fed me to Salim, tried to keep you out of play. Because he didn't want anyone, ever, to hear what I'm saying now. Come on, be honest. How hard did he try to get me out?'

Not very hard, Beddoes had to admit. Quite the opposite, actually. *McKay* had swung it, with bristling Scottish outrage and a threat of resignation. *And had been muzzled by promotion*, drawn into the closed circle of Top Brass; men who would dismiss the whole idea as paranoia, induced by the strain of the siege.

Beddoes leaned back, beset by disgust and fumes of whisky. The law of the jungle, the convoluted logic of deceit; delivered through modern equipment, couched in the accents of Oxbridge under an autumn sun. No wonder Evans was on the sauce, looking like death warmed over. Could use a gargle of firewater himself, to drown the taste.

Huw's always been the same, he remembered. Once he gets his teeth in, he'll shake it and worry it and hang on in, till it bursts apart and truth spills out all over. This time, though, the truth had proved too ripe for even *his* cast-iron stomach.

'Getting a bit deep, am I?' Evans taunted. 'Go back to

basics, shall we? Right then. One word says it all. *Deception*. And me the most deceived.'

He came at last to the table, folded himself into a chair, set the empty glass aside. The fire of the mental hunt had dimmed, only the pain remained. 'How richly did they shaft me?' he muttered. 'Let us count the ways.' His fingers rose and spread. Sandy hairs glinted finely. 'I was Snow's stunt man, Daly's dupe, Duffy's walking bog-brush. I soldiered for Smythe, pimped for Cavanaugh – and I murdered Salim. With malice aforethought and much pleasure.'

'Leave it out! You did the job, saved a bloodbath.'

'All for duty, then. I could live with that. *I thought*. Till she taught me to think.'

Somehow, in his anguish, he'd brought her into the room. Or maybe only into his eyes; lovely, vivid and alluring. 'I did it for Jane, see. Kept me going, Jane did, under Daly's spell, through the stink of shit, even when Harrigan bought it.' His hands opened, palms upward on the dusty brown wood. 'I *made* it, boyo, home free and everything to play for. Then the nightmares started. Couple of chopsy coppers got up my nose, *and I let Daly go*. I think I knew, even then, what it meant. They'd stripped me, all of them, somewhere along the line. Sent me off to meet her with my values uprooted and a void where my instincts used to be. Sent me with deception on my mind.'

His hand came up again, thumb and finger reaching together, a sliver of light between. 'We were *that* close, Roy, it was just about to start. Had started, really. She told me things, things I'll never tell another living soul. What they had done to me, what she was trying to do *for* me. I thought like they taught me, like a spy. Nothing's straight, no one's honest, seek the maggoty motives under rotting shrouds of cover. She told me the truth, Roy. *And I heard betrayal!*'

You could see his body slacken, see the hunger drain from his eyes until they were empty blue puddles in the dimness. 'Sent her away, I did, more or less called her a liar.' His voice caught, wavered, barely held together. 'It was hard, boyo, bloody, *bloody* hard. But even then, while she faded into the crowd, I was holding on to trust and duty.' He sighed, a sound of wrenching despair. 'Two tips, before you go. Stay away from Funnies, and never, *ever* think. That's what I did, after, back here. Thought it all through, saw past what they call duty, saw where I'd put my trust. Now do you understand? They didn't just take my woman; *they took my belief*!'

Beddoes blessed the impulse which had made him withhold McKay's news. 'You're still wrong, uncle,' he cried. 'And I can prove it! McKay's got Smythe's job, and you're the new Super! You *are* a copper again, they *do* believe, so for Chrissake get that bird off your mind. Come and collect your due!'

And Evans laughed in his face. Coldly, savagely, without a trace of humour. 'I *was* a copper, Roy, a good one. They made me a spy and a killer, in the service of the crown. Superintendent? Jesus, I'm not fit to walk a beat! Can't you see it, Roy? It's what *I* believe that counts!'

What could you possibly say to him, the man you'd admired for half your life? The hard, straight copper who'd been robbed of all he valued and turned upon himself? Who sat in this dim and dusty room, his head down, his fists bunched, his eyes squeezed shut to stem the tears? Don't let him down, said McKay. More a question of how to pick him up.

Only one hope – a last appeal to whatever remained of pride and courage. Beddoes chose a scathing tone and words to match. 'Gonna take a dive, then, lie down for an Islam freak and a couple of Irish bother boys? Crawl on your belly to the Valleys, raising runner beans and telling the boyos you could've been a Super but you didn't have the bottle? Get your head up, uncle, let's have some answers, for a change! What are you gonna *do*?'

Slowly, the big, sandy head did lift. Somewhere deep behind the glaze of booze and defeat there might have been a flicker of something harder; and someone younger. 'Drink,' he growled, 'that's what. Two full ones left – should see me right till about half-two. Might be able to sleep, then.'

He wouldn't meet Beddoes' eye, though. Still a bit shifty, nowhere near a cure. 'After, if I survive the dawn, I'll maybe think some more, make some decisions. Then again, maybe not. Thanks for listening Roy, for trying. Bugger off, I would. No call for *you* to cross the bird.'

Beddoes got up, unconvinced. 'Be all right, I hope? Not planning anything *stupid*?'

Again, the awful, empty grin. 'Done that already, haven't I?'

He didn't come to the door. Halfway downstairs, in sudden darkness and chill, Beddoes heard the Kennedy requiem start up again. What the hell, he thought, there's gotta be a limit to friendship. He's a big boy now.

Beddoes legged it to the car, jumped in. Keep it warm, Pol, I'm on my way. Fumbling with the ignition key, leaning forward, he glimpsed the small orange square of Huw's window. From nowhere, a phrase leapt to mind, one he'd heard often, in court. *While the balance of his mind was disturbed.* Leave it out, my son, not Huw Evans!

But he couldn't quite turn the key. After a while, he stopped trying. He wound the seat down until, lounging there, he could watch the window comfortably. Turned up his collar, shoved his hands deep into his pockets, sent a lame apology in Pol's direction. Sorry, girl, it's going to be a long, cold night. Miss you, wish you were here. Because here *I* stay till the light goes out; or until three a.m. whichever comes first. If it *doesn't* go out, I'll be up there putting him to bed, or paging the ambulance. The coroner, even.

He settled and shivered, keeping an eye on the high, dim glow, trying to think of nothing particular. Doing the job he'd done longest and knew best.

Watching Huw's back.